JOHN BUNYAN

The Pilgrim's Progress

From This World,
To That Which is to Come

Edited with an Introduction and Notes by
ROGER POOLEY

PENGUIN BOOKS

PENGUIN CLASSICS

Published by the Penguin Group
Penguin Books Ltd, 80 Strand, London WC2R ORL, England
Penguin Group (USA) Inc., 375 Hudson Street, New York, New York 10014, USA
Penguin Group (Canada), 90 Eglinton Avenue East, Suite 700, Toronto, Ontario, Canada M4P 2Y3
(a division of Pearson Penguin Canada Inc.)
Penguin Ireland, 25 St Stephen's Green, Dublin 2, Ireland
(a division of Penguin Books Ltd)
Penguin Group (Australia), 250 Camberwell Road, Camberwell, Victoria 3124, Australia
(a division of Pearson Australia Group Pty Ltd)
Penguin Books India Pvt Ltd, 11 Community Centre, Panchsheel Park, New Delhi – 110 017, India
Penguin Group (NZ), 67 Apollo Drive, Rosedale, North Shore 0632, New Zealand
(a division of Pearson New Zealand Ltd)
Penguin Books (South Africa) (Pty) Ltd, 24 Sturdee Avenue, Rosebank, Johannesburg 2196, South Africa

Penguin Books Ltd, Registered Offices: 80 Strand, London WC2R ORL, England

www.penguin.com

First published 1678, 1684
This edition published in Penguin Classics 2008
1

Set in 10.25/12.25pt PostScript Adobe Sabon
Typeset by Rowland Phototypesetting Ltd, Bury St Edmunds, Suffolk
Printed in England by Clays Ltd, St Ives plc

ISBN: 978-0-141-43971-6

www.greenpenguin.co.uk

Penguin Books is committed to a sustainable future
for our business, our readers and our planet. The
book in your hands is made from paper certified by
the Forest Stewardship Council.

PENGUIN CLASSICS

THE PILGRIM'S PROGRESS

JOHN BUNYAN (1628–88) was born in Elstow, a village near Bedford. He went to school in the village and became a travelling brazier or tinker, like his father. His portable anvil still survives. In 1644 he joined the Parliamentary army, and served in the garrison of Newport Pagnell, a Buckinghamshire town, until 1646. He married in 1649 and had four children, though the name of his first wife is unknown. As part of her dowry she brought two popular books of devotion; and these, along with a series of experiences, triggered a complex conversion experience, not fully resolved until 1653, whe[...]edford, whose pas[...]. Soon Bunyan be[...] other religious g[...] *Truths Opened* (1[...]*e Law and Grace*[...] work. Soon after[...] aching in the villa[ge of Lower Samsell] and, because he refused to stop preaching, remained in prison in Bedford for twelve years. His account of his trial was published posthumously in 1765.

Bunyan kept himself and his family during this period by making tagged laces. As well as books of poems, he wrote an anonymous attack on the new Prayer Book, and, most importantly, *Grace Abounding to the Chief of Sinners* (1666), a spiritual autobiography. On his release in 1672 he became pastor of the Bedford Nonconformist congregation (which continues today as Bunyan Meeting Free Church). He was imprisoned again for about six months in 1676. He continued to write, and to preach in Bedfordshire and London. In 1678 he published the first part of *The Pilgrim's Progress*. It became an immediate bestseller, running through twelve editions and being translated into Dutch, French and Welsh during Bunyan's lifetime; since then it has been translated into more than two hundred languages. Its counterpart, *The Life and Death of Mr Badman* (1680), was less successful. Bunyan's next venture into allegory, *The Holy War* (1682), is epic in scope. The second part of *The Pilgrim's Progress* came out in 1684, partly in response to a number of imitations and spurious sequels. *A Book for Boys and Girls*, one of the earliest examples of literature for children, was published in 1686.

Bunyan died in 1688 from a fever contracted while riding from Reading to London to try to effect a reconciliation between a father and son. He left a number of works in manuscript, many of them published by Charles Doe in his folio of 1692, which also contained the first (brief) biography of Bunyan.

ROGER POOLEY teaches at Keele University. His Cambridge Ph.D. thesis on Bunyan was partly supervised by the late Roger Sharrock, the editor of the previous Penguin Classics *Pilgrim's Progress*. He is the author of *English Prose of the Seventeenth Century* (1993) and a number of shorter pieces on Bunyan and other seventeenth-century figures. He has co-edited *The Lord of the Journey: A Reader in Christian Spirituality* and *The Discerning Reader: Literature and Theory in Christian Perspective*. He is an active member of the International John Bunyan Society.

Contents

Acknowledgements

I am grateful to a number of libraries where I have consulted material, particularly the John Rylands Library, the Bodleian Library, the British Library and Keele University Library.

I thank the New York Public Library and the Bodleian Library for permission to reproduce illustrations from their collections. I also thank the Research Institute for the Humanities at Keele University for assistance towards the cost of reproduction, and my colleagues at Keele for covering a period of research leave. My fellow-members of the International John Bunyan Society have been an invaluable source of stimulus and encouragement over the years. I remain indebted to the great Bunyan editors, George Offor, Roger Sharrock and Richard L. Greaves; and more recently, to the editorial work of N. H. Keeble and W. R. Owens. The late Charles Swann first taught me Bunyan and continued to encourage me as a colleague; I am sorry that he is not alive to see this. Finally, I thank my family, particularly my wife Helen, for giving me the time, space and a gentle push to finish the work.

Chronology

1628 Born in Elstow, Bedfordshire, the first child of Thomas and Margaret Bunyan.

1630s Attends local school, and then follows his father's trade, as a travelling brazier or tinker.

1644 Death of mother and sister Margaret; his father remarries. Joins the Parliamentary garrison at Newport Pagnell.

1645 Probably present at siege of Leicester.

1647 Demobilized.

1649 Marries first wife (her name is unknown) and lives with her in Elstow. Beginnings of long conversion experience. Trial and execution of Charles I.

1650 First child, Mary, born blind.

1653 Joins John Gifford's congregation in Bedford.

1655 Baptized and admitted to full membership; begins to preach locally; moves to Bedford.

1656 First printed work, *Some Gospel Truths Opened*, against the new Quaker movement which was active in Bedford.

1657 *A Vindication of Some Gospel Truths Opened*.

1658 *A Few Sighs from Hell*. First wife dies, leaving him with four children.

1659 Marries Elizabeth. *The Doctrine of the Law and Grace Unfolded*.

1660 Arrested and imprisoned for unlicensed preaching in Lower Samsell shortly after the Restoration of Charles II.

1661 Tried in Bedford; remains in Bedford jail because he will not undertake to stop preaching. His wife's appeal to assizes is turned down. *Profitable Meditations*, his first book of poems.

1662 *I will pray with the Spirit*, an attack on the new Book of Common Prayer, published anonymously.

1663 *Christian Behaviour* and *Prison Meditations*.

1663/4 *A Mapp Shewing the Order and Causes of Salvation and Damnation*.

1665 *The Holy City*, *The Resurrection of the Dead* and two poems, *Ebal and Geriazim* and *One Thing is Needful*.

1666 *Grace Abounding to the Chief of Sinners*, an account of his conversion.

1672 Elected pastor of the Bedford congregation, before being released from prison and licensed to preach. Charles II issues Declaration of Indulgence. *A Defence of the Doctrine of Justification by Faith*, an attack on the Bedfordshire Latitudinarian Edward Fowler.

1673 *Differences in Judgement about Water-Baptism*, part of a dispute with some London Baptists, and *The Barren Fig-Tree, or the Doom and Downfall of the Fruitless Professor*.

1674 *Peaceable Principles and True*.

1675 *Instruction for the Ignorant*, a catechism, and *Light for them that sit in Darkness*.

1676 Father dies. *Saved by Grace* and *The Strait Gate*.

1676–7 Imprisoned for six months during a crackdown on Nonconformists.

1678 *The Pilgrim's Progress* and *Come, and Welcome to Jesus Christ*.

1679 *Treatise of the Fear of God*. Licensing Act expires.

1680 *The Life and Death of Mr Badman*.

1682 *The Greatness of the Soul* and *The Holy War*. Thomas Sherman publishes his *Second Part of the Pilgrim's Progress*.

1684 Bunyan's own *The Pilgrim's Progress, the Second Part*.

1685 Makes a deed of property to his wife. Charles II dies and is succeeded by the openly Catholic James II. Revocation of the Edict of Nantes means influx of Huguenot refugees into London. *A Discourse upon the Pharisee and the Publican* and *Questions about the Nature and Perpetuity of the Seventh-day Sabbath*.

1686 *A Book for Boys and Girls*.

1688 Dies of a fever after getting soaked riding from Reading to

London. Buried in Bunhill Fields, London. *The Advocateship of Jesus Christ, The Jerusalem Sinner Saved, A Discourse of the Building of the House of God, The Water of Life* and *Solomon's Temple Spiritualized.*

1689 Publication of *The Acceptable Sacrifice* and *Mr. Bunyan's Last Sermon.*

1692 Charles Doe publishes a folio edition of twelve new Bunyan works.

List of Illustrations

THE FIRST PART

THE SECOND PART

Introduction

*New readers are advised that the introduction makes
explicit details of the plot.*

BUNYAN'S LIFE AND WRITINGS

On 12 November 1660 John Bunyan went to a farm in Lower
Samsell in Bedfordshire to preach to a conventicle, a group of
Christians who had gathered into a congregation outside the
usual structures of worship. Charles II had been restored to the
throne in May after eleven years in exile, and though he had
promised 'liberty to tender consciences' in his Declaration of
Breda, made before he returned, in practice the established
Church of England was reasserting its power. Bunyan's own
congregation, which had met in St John's church in Bedford
during the 1650s, was now meeting in private homes. When
Bunyan arrived he was told that the local magistrate, Francis
Wingate of Harlington, had issued a warrant for his arrest. In
his own posthumously published account, Bunyan responded to
a suggestion that they cancel in these words: 'By no means, I will
not stir, neither will I have the meeting dismissed for this. Come,
be of good cheer, let us not be daunted, our cause is good, we
need not be ashamed of it, to preach God's word, it is so good a
work, we shall be well rewarded, if we suffer for that.'[1] The tone
is characteristic: the biblical phrase 'be of good cheer' (John 16:
33), the defiance, the confidence and the tenderness towards his
fearful fellow-Christians.

Bunyan was arrested, and, after defiantly refusing to stop
preaching, remained in prison for the next twelve years. At that
stage he had published two works of religious controversy with
the Quaker Jeremiah Burroughs: *A Few Sighs from Hell*, which
detailed the torments of hell for those who did not believe;

and *The Doctrine of the Law and Grace Unfolded*, his defining theological statement. Yet it was prison that turned him from the sort of talented controversialist and preacher that the Puritan movement had often thrown up before into a writer with a compelling authority. To begin with, it was a matter of survival. He made a large number of tagged laces to keep himself and his family; but he also applied himself to poetry (*Profitable Meditations* and *Prison Meditations*, both published by the radical London bookseller Francis 'Elephant' Smith), a popular manual, *Christian Behaviour*, and a pictorial *Mapp Shewing the Order and Causes of Salvation and Damnation*. But there is something else about Bunyan's early prison writings, more of the last will and testament than the religious potboiler. He thought he would die in prison. He must have been immensely strong to survive that long in jail without succumbing to jail fever. He was also aware that the laws against Nonconformists were increasing in severity, and he might be hanged. So there is defiance, too. The anonymously published *I will pray with the Spirit* (probably 1662–3; the first edition has not survived) is an attack on the reissued Book of Common Prayer and the legal compulsion that went with it. *Grace Abounding to the Chief of Sinners* (1666), his account of his conversion and calling, is another self-defence, which is also a defence of nonconformity, addressed to his congregation in Bedford.

The first part of *The Pilgrim's Progress* was not published until 1678, when Bunyan had, apart from a brief interval from December 1676 to June 1677 when he was imprisoned again, been out of Bedford jail for six years. None the less, it is clear that it has its origins as a prison document – the 'Den' in 'the Wilderness of this World' of the very first paragraph is glossed in the margin as 'The jail' – and that is one key to its power. This is not just because Bunyan was imprisoned for his faith – or, more precisely, for refusing not to preach again because he was unlicensed. In such circumstances a refusal to compromise is bound to become a touchstone of character. Whether his hero Christian is facing the big bullies, like Giant Despair or Lord Hate-good, or the more insidious temptations of 'credit and good fashion' promised by Mr Worldly Wiseman, he has to keep on the narrow way.

The Pilgrim's Progress, then, is a nonconformist text in the widest sense, as well as in the highly specific context of Restoration Nonconformity. Bunyan is continuing the Christian radical tradition that begins in the New Testament with Jesus overturning the tables of the moneychangers in the Temple (Mark 11: 15) and the apostles imprisoned for preaching (Acts 5). Theologically, he remains within the Reformed theology of Luther and Calvin just as it was going out of favour with the intelligentsia. As Christopher Hill has pointed out, Calvinism, which was, earlier in the century, the prevailing orthodoxy among the bishops in the Church of England, was slipping down the social scale.[2] Bunyan's view of the Church was even less popular. When he was arrested for unlicensed preaching in 1660 it was under an Elizabethan law against conventicles, but the legal position was about to harden further. During the first half of the 1660s a whole sequence of punitive laws, conveniently if inaccurately called the Clarendon Code, came into being, voted in by a Parliament whose anti-Puritan zeal seems to have exceeded that of the restored Charles II. In 1662, when allegiance to the new Prayer Book was demanded of all parish clergy, a clear divide opened up between conformists and Nonconformists like Bunyan and his congregation. Nonconformity turned from a viewpoint into a legal category. Puritanism, which for the first eighty years of its life had operated largely as a movement for further reform within the Church of England, was now placed firmly outside it – and, indeed, largely drops out of use as a descriptive term. Bunyan himself regards it as a rather pejorative term used for the godly in times past.

Bunyan in the 1660s was regarded as subversive, certainly by the Bedford gentry who tried him. It was not that he incited his flock to rebel, and his service in the Parliamentary army was not held against him. It was because he did not accept their authority, any more than he accepted the authority of the Church of England. He claimed authority from God, and God's word in the Bible, which he claimed to discern as well as they. Christopher

Hill argues, 'The very claim that preaching was his vocation was subversive; his vocation was being a tinker. Mechanic preaching had been the cause of all the trouble in the 1640s and 1650s. Now was the gentry's chance at last to put the mechanics back in their place.'[3] So for twelve years Bunyan was kept in prison.

The very first paragraph of *The Pilgrim's Progress*, which identifies the gaol as the place where the author slept and dreamed, takes for granted that 'the wilderness of this world' is the condition we pass through, in prison, or in other largely hostile places. The City of Destruction has to be left for good, even if (for the duration of the first part) that is where his wife and children are. His true companions, Faithful and then Hopeful, will face death with him. There is really no prospect of returning, though Obstinate, and then Pliable, do so early on. Christian has to guard against false pilgrims, those who would distract him from the true way. Such single-mindedness was no doubt reinforced by his long years in prison. But we need to go back further to find the roots of Bunyan's courage.

Bunyan had joined the Parliamentary army in 1644, when he was 16, and he served in the garrison of Newport Pagnell, not far from Bedford. (His first book was published by a bookseller in Newport Pagnell as well as in London.) He left the army in 1645 and attempted to rejoin in 1647, possibly for financial reasons. As far as we can tell, he did not join out of ideological zeal. There is some evidence that he fought at the siege of Leicester, and he might have been summoned to Ireland, but, in the end, he did not go. The army was a formative experience for Bunyan, although he is, understandably, relatively reticent about it in *Grace Abounding*, written in prison and when he was concerned that he might be executed. The one event that he dwells on in retrospect is that a man who had volunteered to replace him during an assault at the siege of Leicester was killed by a musket-ball; the post-conversion Bunyan saw this as an example of God's providence. Only with *The Holy War* (1682) do we get explicit descriptions of a siege and armies marching which might be drawn from experience.

Sir Samuel Luke, who was in charge of the Newport Pagnell garrison, was not a radical, although the young Bunyan might well have heard radical ideas being debated, either among soldiers from the Eastern Association and the New Model Army who passed through Newport Pagnell, or in the town itself, which appears to have been more receptive to new ideas. He did not stay in the army long enough to hear Leveller ideas, for example.[4] However, we can see some of the ideas of William Erbery and Captain Paul Hobson, both of whom preached controversial sermons to the Newport Pagnell garrison, emerging later in Bunyan's work.[5] And there is a striking parallel between the trial scene in Vanity Fair, and the Leveller Richard Overton's *The Arraignment of Mr. Persecution* (1645), especially in the satirical naming of the corrupt jury.

After leaving the army Bunyan married, probably in 1649, although we do not know his first wife's name. She brought with her a dowry, not of cash or property, but two popular religious books, Lewis Bayley's *Practice of Piety* and Arthur Dent's *Plain Man's Pathway to Heaven*. Influenced partly by these books, partly by his wife's own piety and partly by his own delight in going to church, in the vestments and so on, Bunyan began to take a greater interest in religion. On his own admission, he had been a great swearer in his youth, and had been more likely to read popular chivalric romance adventures than devotional texts. But churchgoing was not enough to settle his soul. Bunyan's spiritual crisis, according to his account in *Grace Abounding*, was precipitated by a sequence of events. Bunyan had heard a sermon on sabbath-breaking, which he managed to put out of his mind; however, as he was playing a game of tipcat on the village green at Elstow that same Sunday afternoon, 'a voice did suddenly dart from Heaven into my Soul, which said, *Wilt thou leave thy sins, and go to Heaven? or have thy sins, and go to Hell?*'[6] From that moment, Bunyan was buffeted by his conscience, and began to search the Bible for some answers. Texts from the Bible started to have an almost physical weight to them. It was, very largely, an individual journey, and only later did he have much to do with Christians who might guide him through; it was not a straightforward journey to conversion, although it had some of the elements of Puritan conversion stories. But it is difficult to point to a moment of conversion, for one thing.[7]

Grace Abounding is a psychological document of great vividness – so much so that many of his psychologically aware readers, starting with William James, have tentatively attempted a diagnosis. In his summative work on Bunyan, Richard L. Greaves suggests that he was suffering from depression.[8] More recently still John Sneep (a counselling psychologist) and Arlette Zinck (a distinguished Bunyan scholar) have suggested that Bunyan's initial struggle was with obsessive-compulsive disorder rather than melancholia or depression. They go on to suggest that episodes in *The Pilgrim's Progress* are evidence that writing was one of the ways in which Bunyan was released from despair; and, perhaps even more so, reading the Scriptures and other books such as Luther on Galatians, or Foxe's *Acts and Monuments* (popularly known as Foxe's *Book of Martyrs*), helped him find a way through.[9] We might want to recognize that there was something extreme about Bunyan's experience without pathologizing it, or dismissing its challenge; and diagnosis at this distance is, inevitably, prone to error.

Like so many spiritual autobiographies by sectarian preachers in the period, *Grace Abounding* is also an attempt at self-vindication: here is the man who has not been to university, but who has a command of Scripture that is not just intellectual but comes from profound spiritual experience; here is the prisoner of conscience who speaks like a prophet to an unjust world. Here, also, is Bunyan on the cusp of modernity; though, as Galen Johnson has carefully argued, his is not an absolute, autonomous notion of personal liberty. Rather, his 'conscience remained imprisoned to the same Jesus Christ who made it free', a notion of the individual which has a much longer history.[10] Bunyan's appeal is not to his subjective rights, but to his personal grasp of the objective truth of Christ. The end of *Grace Abounding* is not triumphant, or even defiant: 'These things I continually see and feel, and am afflicted and oppressed with; yet the Wisdom of God doth order them for my good.'[11]

An important component of the development of *The Pilgrim's Progress* is Bunyan's reworking of the experience he set out in one way in *Grace Abounding*, and of his prison experience more generally. The first part contains a number of episodes that recall *Grace Abounding*. However, as Michael Davies and Milo Kaufmann have both shown, it is Hopeful's account of his conversion rather than Christian's which reads more like Bunyan's.[12] There are other episodes, like the Man in the Iron Cage and Christian's terrifying walk through the Valley of the Shadow of Death, which recall Bunyan's temptation to believe that he had committed the unforgivable sin, or when he thought that his own voice had sold Christ. The time that the pilgrims are locked up in Doubting Castle by Giant Despair before they remember the key of Promise that will let them out corresponds to Bunyan's own periods of doubt, though some of his lasted much longer. The three days the pilgrims suffer is, of course, symbolic of the time Christ was in the tomb between Good Friday and Easter; and the fact they are put there by a giant takes some of the sting out of it. Everyone knows that giants in stories are scary and might eat you; but they are also stupid and can, ultimately, be tricked by the resourceful hero. The immediate impact of the corresponding *Grace Abounding* episodes is that Bunyan was never sure if he would come out of his despair; and only occasionally did he get the spiritual advice or companionship he needed. In *The Pilgrim's Progress*, Christian has a sequence of advisers, Evangelist, the inhabitants of the Interpreter's House, and the Shepherds in the Delectable Mountains, for example. They are not with him all the time, and so he has to rely on his sometimes faulty memory (memory is a key Christian virtue in both parts). He also, eventually, has companions on his journey, first Faithful and then Hopeful. But there are a number of false advisers and false pilgrims as well, and these pose as many dangers to Christian as the opponents like Apollyon who stand in his way and openly threaten him.

GODLY FEAR AND SLAVISH FEAR

What marks Bunyan's most successful writing is his ability to convey spiritual truth with the force of felt experience. His friend and fellow-minister George Cockayne wrote in the preface to *The Acceptable Sacrifice* that Bunyan 'did experience in himself (through the Grace of God) the Nature, Excellency and Comfort of *a truly Broken,* and *Contrite Spirit*'.[13] It was his particular gift to convey that experience through a variety of genres: auto-biography, sermon, treatise and fiction. A respect for his gift can even be found in that scourge of Christianity, William Empson. His poem 'Courage means Running', which starts with Bunyan, puts it this way:

> Muchafraid went over the river singing
> Though none knew what she sang. Usual for a man
> Of Bunyan's courage to respect fear.[14]

Much of the power of *The Pilgrim's Progress* comes from its many and subtle confrontations with fear. Empson is alluding here to the final scene of the second part, where the pilgrims cross the river of death. However, it is the first part that conveys the feelings of fear more tellingly, and they are often positive. As Hopeful says to Christian, 'I do believe, as you say, that fear tends much to men's good, and to make them right at their beginning to go on pilgrimage' (p. 152). When Christian fights Apollyon, or when he crosses the Valley of the Shadow of Death, we see how intense Bunyan's account of spiritual and psychological struggle is. Elsewhere he rejects the wrong kind of fear, the 'slavish fear' that Christian and Hopeful experience when they have a vision of the Heavenly City from the Delectable Mountains. Christian is almost overcome with fear at the moment of death, 'a great darkness and horror' that causes him to doubt that he will be received at the gate of heaven. Eventually he recovers, and encouraged by Hopeful's '*Be of good cheer, Jesus Christ maketh thee whole*' (p. 159), he makes it to the farther shore.

Bunyan, then, has a pastoral theology of fear. In that last episode, he also goes against a lot of Christian thinking about dying. It is not always the case, he argues, that Christians face death serenely. You cannot tell whether a person is going to heaven by the way they die. The strongest Christian can have last-minute doubts, or simply be overcome by physical pain. Mr Badman (in *The Life and Death of Mr Badman*, Bunyan's original sequel) dies like a lamb; Wiseman comments that 'if a wicked man dies quietly . . . his quiet dying is so far off from being a sign of his being saved, that it is an uncontrollable proof of his damnation'.[15] The pilgrims at the end of the second part make a good death; but, interestingly, it is those who have suffered the most psychological and spiritual hardships who have the easiest passage.

The problem of 'slavish fear', as far as Bunyan is concerned, is that it makes people take more notice of their reputation among others than of their standing with God. As Hopeful puts it about those who are awakened but then fall back, 'they have slavish fears that do over-master them: I speak now of the fears that they have of men' (p. 154). For Bunyan's heroes, the fear of God counters any passing fear of men, even if that involves loss of reputation, imprisonment and death. It enables him to strike a note of tenderness just as authentically as the sternness, and the uncompromising either/or of judgement, that make up his theology and his journeying.

THE ROOTS OF BUNYAN'S IMAGINATION: THEOLOGY AND THE BIBLE

It is difficult to exaggerate Bunyan's debt to the Bible. It operates at every level in this text – structural, tonal and theological. The text is stuffed with biblical quotations and allusions. More than any early modern text, it marks the entry of the English Bible into English literature. It may be one reason why Bunyan's text is less appreciated now, as biblical literacy becomes rarer, at least in Britain. In this edition, as with most modern editions, I have tried to draw attention in the explanatory notes to some of the biblical references that are not glossed in the margins, but that is only part of the story. The Bible supplies the overarching idea of the text; and we need to understand something of Bunyan's particular theologically informed way of reading the Bible.

There are two main biblical sources for the idea of Christian leaving his home in the City of Destruction and setting out for the Celestial City. The first is the Epistle to the Hebrews. Brainerd Stranahan argues that 'no other book in the Bible made such a deep impression on Bunyan ... It seems to have occasioned both the most anxious and the most comforting moments of his spiritual life.'[16] In particular, there are a couple of verses in chapter 11 that seem to supply the idea for the plot:

> By faith Abraham, when he was called to go out into a place which he should after receive for an inheritance, obeyed; and he went out, not knowing whither he went ... These all died in faith, not having received the promises, but having seen them afar off, and were persuaded of them, and embraced them, and confessed that they were strangers and pilgrims on the earth. (Hebrews 11: 8, 13)

Certainly Christian leaves home without knowing exactly where he is heading, and confesses that he is a 'stranger and pilgrim'. The passage alludes to Old Testament figures; and indeed Christian's leaving is a kind of exodus, too.[17] Then there are the journeys and trials in the Book of Acts, with some quite precise parallels; as when Paul takes the place of Stephen after his stoning in Luke's narrative, so Hopeful replaces Faithful after the Vanity Fair episode results in Faithful's death.[18]

The Bible gives Bunyan something of the plot and the central images, but it goes beyond that. Fragments of verses from all over the Bible appear in the dialogue, particularly when Faithful is debating with false pilgrims like Talkative or Ignorance, or when he is being instructed by Evangelist. At some stage Bunyan is supposed to have composed a concordance to the Bible (although it has not survived) and he clearly used one, judging from the abundance of references in his non-allegorical works. One method Bunyan uses a great deal to make sense of the apparently obscure or contradictory is typology. To find the meaning of the Old Testament, a Christian has to look for the Gospel sense of it, as Bunyan does, for example, in *Solomon's Temple Spiritualized*, and in some of the pilgrims' discussions. The assumption is that the Old Testament often anticipates the New – 'typology is linked indissolubly to prophecy', as Paul

Korshin puts it.[19] It is also linked to allegory, as a reading procedure; the figures and events of the Old Testament can be turned into Gospel by reading them allegorically.

Bunyan's theology is biblical, too, though it is grounded in the biblical theology of the reformers, particularly Luther. At its simplest it is a theology of grace. It is summarized twice over towards the end of the first part, first in the account of Hopeful's conversion, which mirrors that of Bunyan himself, and secondly in the dispute with Ignorance. Ignorance has good thoughts (so he thinks), because he thinks of heaven. Christian and Hopeful (echoing Calvin, though there is no evidence that Bunyan read Calvin) argue that thoughts of heaven should first of all drive one to realize one's sin, and in particular 'a necessity of Christ's personal righteousness to justify thee before God'. This sacrificial notion of the Gospel is central to the reformed tradition, and it is at the heart of Bunyan's major theological statement, *The Doctrine of the Law and Grace Unfolded* (1659). The contrast between the condemnation offered by the Law of Moses and the release offered by grace in Christ rumbles through most of *Grace Abounding*, and is there in the image of the burden falling off at the cross and the episode of Worldly Wiseman in *The Pilgrim's Progress*.[20]

ALLEGORY, ROMANCE AND FICTION

The Pilgrim's Progress presents itself as a dream narrative, and, like many such from medieval and early modern times, it is allegorical. For the reader, this presents a special challenge. Allegory was a mode of reading before it became a mode of composition. It began as a means of recovering an acceptable meaning from apparently unpromising texts – for example, of perceiving Christian truth in pagan works like Ovid's *Metamorphoses*, and as a means of making spiritual sense of parts of the Bible, such as the Song of Songs.

Is the best way of appreciating the text always looking beyond it to another level of meaning? Or, as Carolynn Van Dyke puts it, do we have to engage 'in unremitting translation from apparent to actual meaning'?[21] For many critics in the Romantic period, this proved the inferiority of allegory, its artificial and secondary character as literature; compared to the symbol, allegory is mechanical, art in the service of a concept, and thus not truly art, or at least, not the best kind of art. Nowadays, in the wake of the post-structural accounts of language by Paul de Man in particular, allegory can be seen as no more than a special case of what all literature does: saying one thing and meaning another. For Allen Michie, if Bunyan had 'rejected the literal in favour of the imaginary, he would seem modern; but by having the literal and the imaginary depend on each other for their very definition, Bunyan is clearly postmodern'.[22]

The verse 'Author's Apology' which prefaces *The Pilgrim's Progress*, apart from its value as an account of the work's genesis, does demonstrate a certain anxiety about the acceptability of the allegory to his friends, who were clearly of two minds about it. But their anxiety has nothing to do with Romantic concerns about didacticism. First of all Bunyan appeals to the Bible:

> Am I afraid to say that Holy Writ,
> Which for its Style and Praise puts down all wit,
> Is everywhere so full of all these things,
> (Dark figures, Allegories) yet there springs
> From that same Book, that lustre, and those rays
> Of light, that turns our darkest nights to days.

Bunyan is reluctant to compromise the central Reformation assertion, that the Bible is clear as well as truthful. But there are parables and metaphors in it, used by Christ and the prophets. That these are 'dark' figures is nothing sinister, simply an early modern commonplace. Spenser famously characterized allegory as a 'dark conceit' in his Letter to Ralegh about *The Faerie Queene*; Donne remarked that 'dark texts need notes'. The act of reading allegory is no more than an act of unwrapping, or opening a box (it is interesting that Bunyan's description of reading allegory itself resorts to further imagery like opening boxes, or kernels in nuts).

Personification allegory like Bunyan's is not, in fact, so very difficult to read. It does not demand the same level of multi-lingual and multi-level decoding from its reader as *The Faerie Queene*, for example. It might help to know that Apollyon means 'destroyer' in the Bible, but Hopeful is hopeful, Talkative is talkative, and Ignorance is – well, a rather special case of ignorance, within the theological understanding of the period, but ignorance of certain matters of eternal consequence none the less. Naming is characterizing, for the most part. For the heroes (and, later, heroines), part of the key to a successful journey is keeping to the path, and that produces its own levels of allegory. After all, this is a journey from the City of Destruction through 'the wilderness of this world' to the Celestial City. It is a narrow roadway, and needs to be kept to. Leave it, and you are in trouble, as Christian and Faithful are when they stray down By-Path Meadow and end up in the dungeons of Doubting Castle. Equally, the true pilgrim has to enter in the right way, as Christian does through the wicket-gate. Formalist and Hypocrisy take a short cut, and put their trust in custom, laws and ordinances; but as soon as they hit the Hill Difficulty they take less steep roads, which end in destruction – 'he stumbled and fell, and rose no more' (p. 46). So it is not just the people on the way who need to be perceived allegorically, it is the way itself.

Bunyan felt the need to defend his approach: not, of course, against those who might doubt the artistic integrity of the book, but against those of his Christian, shall we say Puritan, friends suspicious of metaphor, anything that lacks 'solidness'. In 'The Author's Apology for his Book' Bunyan begins by saying that he did not consciously choose this approach; it just happened while he was writing something else (probably a book called *The Heavenly Foot-Man*). To put it in Romantic as well as Christian terms, he was inspired – though he, perhaps revealingly, describes it as a fall rather than an elevation:

> And thus it was: I writing of the Way
> And Race of Saints in this our Gospel-Day,
> Fell suddenly into an Allegory
> About their Journey, and the way to Glory . . .

In trying to describe the moment of composition, Bunyan seems torn between being deferential to the (Puritanical?) criticism that he has just written something for his own amusement, 'mine own self to gratify', and trying to persuade his readers that, providentially, he has stumbled onto something special. By the time he reaches the conclusion he is far more assured: 'This Book will make a Traveller of thee.' In other words, Bunyan claims that his allegory about a pilgrimage will make its readers into pilgrims.

Allegory is particularly suited to religious writing. It springs from a sense that the world is not the whole case. On the contrary, there is a reality beyond this world, and this world is best interpreted as a sign system of spiritual truth. Protestantism began with a suspicion of allegory as a technique of reading the Bible; but Spenser's *The Faerie Queene* and Bunyan's *The Pilgrim's Progress* and *The Holy War* rediscovered its potency. Thomas Luxon, who takes a sceptical view of Puritan theories of representation more generally, suggests that 'allegory is a mode peculiarly suited to finessing the issue of the real, allowing Bunyan to substitute spiritual "experience" for reality'.[23] There is a parallel to this in Gordon Teskey's more general theory of allegory as a kind of poetic violence: 'The greatest allegorical poets do not simply transform life into meaning. They exacerbate the antipathy of the living to the significant by exposing the violence entailed in transforming the other.' This leads him to observe 'the uncannily familiar characters of Bunyan, who seem to be being turned into writing by a force that bends all their actions to suit what they are called'.[24] Allegory, from this sort of position, is an expression of ideological or theological violence that is needed to make sense and order of the world. We might add that it is the violence of judgement, the other side of Bunyan's courage in the face of hostility and his own doubts; the conviction that there is a way to hell, even from the entrance to heaven, for those who do wrong or are wrong.

Allegory, then, is the principal mode of this narrative, but generically it is more complex. The journey as a whole is like a quest narrative, a heroic romance. Christian and Great-heart are often portrayed as combatants in armour. Their armour (like

that of Spenser's Red-Cross Knight) can be traced, in terms
of its allegorical significance, to the picture of the Christian's
armour that Paul gives at the end of the Epistle to the Ephesians:
'And take the helmet of salvation, and the sword of the Spirit,
which is the word of God' (6: 17) is just one example. The way
they use the armour, in combat with giants and devils, owes
more to Bunyan's pre-conversion reading in popular prose
romances like *Bevis of Hampton* and Richard Johnson's *Seven
Champions of Christendom* than to biblical combats.

However, whether Bunyan had any major sources for this
work other than the Bible is unlikely. Long ago J. B. Wharey,
one of Bunyan's best editors, suggested a comparison with
Deguileville's *Pèlerinage de l'homme*, translated into verse by
John Lydgate. There is no direct evidence that Bunyan read either
the French (or that he knew how to read French, which seems
extremely unlikely) or the English version. However, this does
point to the way in which Bunyan picks up on a more general
sense of life as pilgrimage which is as much a part of Catholic
Christianity (which encouraged pilgrimages to particular holy
places) as of Protestantism (which did not, and might be said to
have internalized the idea of pilgrimage as a result). He was
undoubtedly influenced by Foxe's *Acts and Monuments*, which
he seems to have read in prison. It gave him a view of Church
history, and a means of understanding suffering and persecution,
which pervades a number of episodes in *The Pilgrim's Progress*,
most notably in the trial and death of Faithful in Vanity Fair.[25]

Although, like most Puritans, Bunyan read the Bible through
the eyes of St Paul, he draws widely on the Bible and also
responds to the different literary qualities of the biblical books.
The Pilgrim's Progress shares with the Synoptic Gospels an infor-
mal, even laconic narrative style with a sharp satiric humour.
The targets in both cases are hypocrisy, the vice to which religious
people are most susceptible.

There have been numerous attempts to locate the sources for
people and places in the allegory. While scholarly caution is
needed, modern readers should remember that many prose fictions of the seventeenth century are undoubtedly *romans-à-clef*.
There are a few figures in the allegory who might be tentatively

linked to Bunyan's contemporaries. Mr Worldly Wiseman, who misleads Christian early on in his pilgrimage, is often linked to the Bedfordshire clergyman Edward Fowler, criticized by Bunyan in his *A Defence of the Doctrine of Justification by Faith* (1672).[26] Lord Hate-good, who condemns Christian and Faithful in Vanity Fair, has elements of Justice Keeling, or Kelyng, who examined Bunyan after his arrest. According to Bunyan's account, Keeling threatened him with exile and even hanging, though most of their exchange in *Grace Abounding* is about the Book of Common Prayer. Keeling had been imprisoned from 1642 to 1660; he was then elected MP for Bedford in the Cavalier Parliament, where he was involved in the drafting of the 1662 Act of Uniformity. After Bunyan's trial he was knighted, and became a Chief Justice of the King's Bench. He had a reputation for bullying juries, fining and imprisoning those who did not deliver the verdicts he wanted. Hate-good has no need to bully the Vanity Fair jury; they are only too willing to condemn Christian and Faithful. Hate-good is a conflation of the kind of judicial persecution Bunyan himself experienced, and had read about in Foxe's *Acts and Monuments* during his imprisonment. Evangelist occupies the same structural position in Christian's conversion as John Gifford, the pastor of the Bedford church, did in Bunyan's, but beyond that it is difficult to know, as so little about Gifford survives. In the second part, Valiant-for-truth may be an allusion to the Welsh preacher Vavasor Powell (1617–70). The evidence for a link between Bunyan and Powell is largely circumstantial. However, it is possible that Bunyan was one of those who completed Powell's biblical concordance after his death. A memorial volume, *The Life and Death of Vavasor Powell* (1671), attributed to Edward Bagshaw, concludes with some acrostic poems, one of which begins 'Valiant for Truth on Earth.' The business of establishing precise connections between characters or topographical features from seventeenth-century Bedfordshire or London and those in Bunyan's allegory is occasionally tantalizing, but by and large adds very little to our understanding of the allegory. What they might do is help us to understand that a text which has had an enormous readership across social classes, countries and times is rooted in personal acquaintance and pastoral experience, as well as in Bunyan's intense, inward spiritual struggle.

THE TWO PARTS: BUNYAN, WOMEN AND THE CHURCH

If *The Pilgrim's Progress* is a fictional reworking of some of the narrative and themes of *Grace Abounding*, the second part, published in 1684 (probably not until January, which would make it 1685 in New Style dating), is a more direct revisiting of the first part. There had been spurious sequels published before. In Bunyan's mind, the first true sequel was *The Life and Death of Mr Badman* (1680), a dialogue between Wiseman and Attentive which charts the sins and downfall of the reprobate Badman. It was nowhere near as popular; indeed, one of its successes is that it makes an evil character so unambiguously unsympathetic. Of the surviving would-be sequels, the best known is that by the Baptist writer Thomas Sherman (T.S. on the title page). Although this makes no attempt to imitate Bunyan's style, it does create some new characters in the vein of the first part. Sherman's publisher John Dunton wrote two: *The Pilgrim's Guide from the Cradle to his Death-Bed* (1684) and *An Hue and Cry after Conscience: or The Pilgrim's Progress by Candlelight* in 1685. The preface to Bunyan's second part attacks those 'That counterfeit the Pilgrim' and the condescension of those who deny Bunyan's authorship of his masterwork, with its European reputation. So, in the pilgrimage of Christiana and her sons Bunyan is vindicating his authorship; he had already confronted those who said 'The Pilgrim's Progress is not mine' in the Advertisement poem in *The Holy War*. He is also answering one of the questions Christian is asked in the first part: why did you leave your wife and children behind?

In the first part, as Neil Keeble so neatly puts it, 'To be a Pilgrim is to be a man.'[27] Not just that: 'play the man' is what the pilgrims have to do in the face of danger. There are no female pilgrims. However, not all the female figures in the first half are enemies or temptations. Indeed, it is Charity, one of the damsels of the House Beautiful, who quizzes Christian in some detail about his failure to convince his family to join him. However, she concludes that they have shown themselves 'to be implacable to good' (p. 56). Fortunately, they have second thoughts. The second part echoes the first, and they travel the same way and encounter many of the same places and figures of help and hindrance that Christian did. The differences illuminate both parts.

We have already noted the importance of the loneliness of Christian in the first part, which gradually changes with his two companions and the advice he receives from Evangelist and others. In the second part, Christiana has her four children, all boys, and Mercy, a genuine pilgrim companion from the beginning. They are conducted by Great-heart, and later by Valiant-for-truth as well. The party of pilgrims continues to expand. In other words, it is a Church pilgrimage, rather than an individual's. Once Christiana and Mercy have been given into the care of Great-heart, they never want for timely advice; there is not the same tension of remembering and forgetting that is such a feature of the first part.

The pilgrimage of Christiana and Mercy foregrounds the feminine in a way that stays fairly strictly within Bunyan's conventional views of the roles of the sexes. In *Christian Behaviour* (1663), for example, Bunyan stresses that wives should be subject to their husbands, though not their slaves.[28] At the end of the section on 'The Duty of Wives', he reminds his readers that 'the believing woman is a figure of the Church' and therefore should 'nourish and instruct her Children and Servants, as the Church'. Many commentators on the second part, especially those who take a more feminist approach, have stressed the double subordination of Christiana, to her husband and to her 'Conductor', Great-heart. That subordination is not to be denied. However, it is out of that version of what the feminine represents that the narrative springs. To begin with, perhaps it is the figure of Eve, the disobedient woman, that Christiana has to confront in herself. But from then on it is the figure of the Church that she is realizing in her journey. When Mercy catechizes Christiana's children, she commends her for having instructed them so well in Christian doctrine. In the home, the mother is the teacher. If the dominant biblical metaphor for both parts is the Exodus, in the second part it is overlaid by a whole series of references to the Song of Songs, the Old Testament love song that is, in Christian tradition, allegorized as the love of Christ for his Church.

The female figures, with the young boys, are vulnerable. Early on they encounter the ill-favoured ones, hinting that they might be raped, and are rebuked for not asking for a (male) guide to accompany them. So they are given to Great-heart, an experienced conductor of pilgrims, who acts as guide, adviser and protector – the very essence of the Puritan pastor. The gendered division of roles comes out most clearly when they visit the site of Christian's battle with Apollyon. This, it is emphasized, is where '*Christian* did here play the Man' (p. 242) and so Great-heart has to meet the fiend as the manly protector of the pilgrims as well as the champion of Christ. Seeing there is such resistance, the devil flees. The second part's exploration of the female pilgrimage inescapably brings into relief the specifically masculine role as well. There is a certain amount of macho confrontation, for example, when the men attack Doubting Castle; and Valiant-for-truth has a history of combat. However, the second part also accommodates much less muscular masculine Christianity in figures like Mr Fearing and Mr Ready-to-halt.

Why do Christiana and Mercy not have burdens on their backs? It is difficult to believe that Bunyan had gone soft on sin by 1684. It may be that Christiana's early repentance, coupled with the fact that she doesn't cry out 'What shall I do?' because she knows what she has to do from Christian's example, means she does not set out with a burden. It may be that Bunyan is dealing with a possible ambivalence in the first part, that Christian is converted as he enters the wicket-gate, which represents Christ, but that he needs a separate experience of Christ's cross. It may be that, as Margaret Olofson Thickstun asserts, Christiana's femininity is her burden;[29] but this raises more problems than it solves in analysing the development of her pilgrimage, because she is actually less error-prone than her heroic husband. She

listens to the right kind of advice more often (and there is less of
the wrong kind around).

RIGHT READING

Correct interpretation of the Bible, the material world and personal experience is essential to Bunyan's spiritual practice, as it
is to his principal characters – and indeed Puritan Christianity
more generally. Right reading of his text by us, his readers, is as
important as it is for Christian reading the book in his hand. As
modern readers, we are (relatively) experts at understanding
novelistic narrative, but that is not always the point, certainly not
the whole point, in *The Pilgrim's Progress*. Above and beyond the
episodes themselves and the pilgrims' developing understanding
of them, Bunyan gives us several additional ways into the text.

First of all, there are the marginal notes, which have a variety
of functions. Maxine Hancock helpfully summarizes them as
'referring, indexing, interpreting and applying'.[30] They point us
to the biblical references embedded in the text as quotations or
allusions and so serve to tell us where we are in the text as we
read or reread.

Then there are the poems (or songs) which burst out of the
text at emotional moments, sometimes summarizing and com-
menting on what has gone before, but more often punctuating
an episode with a personal reaction. They are not unusual in
fiction of the period, though perhaps more characteristic of
romance than religious fiction. One of the best of them, 'Who
would true valour see', has become a popular hymn, more often
sung with the revised opening of 'He who would valiant be';
ironically in a way, because Bunyan's own church did not sing
hymns as part of public worship until some time after his death.

This hybrid quality to the text brings us to the question of the
novel. The novel is, famously, not so much a genre as a meeting
of genres, often in parodied form, and *The Pilgrim's Progress* is
not so much a novel as a dream vision, one which can be read
as a late, if not final, example of that genre which provides many
of the most significant religious narratives of the medieval period,

such as *Piers Plowman* or *The Dream of the Rood*, though it is unlikely that Bunyan knew any of these. At the same time it looks forward to some of the newer forms of prose fiction emerging in Europe as a whole. One might say that the first of the English novelists proper, Daniel Defoe, drew much of his inspiration from the same Nonconformist culture as Bunyan; like him, he mixes the spiritual autobiography with popular romance forms, for example. But he is not driven by the same evangelical force as Bunyan, and the allegorical element almost disappears, partly as a result.

Read the criticism and discussion of Bunyan now, and during the last two centuries, and you will realize that Bunyan's theology is an issue. Those who write about this book may be divided between those who embrace the literary qualities of the book because they coincide with their own evangelical Christian viewpoint, and those who recognize its qualities but are uneasy about Bunyan's version of Christianity – or indeed any version of Christianity. Whatever your viewpoint, it is important to think about *The Pilgrim's Progress* as a Christian book, and one that could be, indeed should be, read as a spiritual as much as a literary classic.

'Spiritual classic' is a publisher's term, intended to group together older texts into a 'Library' or a series imprint, but it is also a useful term to describe texts that have a life and a usefulness beyond their own time. 'Spirituality' is more than a useful descriptor for texts and practices that help readers to live more godly, or less materialistic lives, who have a desire to go beyond an inherited faith or a conversion experience into something deeper. Most texts recognized as spiritual classics come from a very different wing of Christianity from Bunyan. They may be written by mystics, or monks, like Dame Julian of Norwich or St John of the Cross; often they describe a version of Christian living that demands the cloister or the hermitage to enact. But there are classics that arise from a real experience of an everyday world – Brother Lawrence practising the presence of God in his kitchen, or the young Augustine praying to God to make him chaste, but not yet.

Bunyan's first spiritual classic, *Grace Abounding to the Chief of Sinners*, was written in prison, an enforced isolation from the world in one sense; but the fear that the persecution which put him there might send him to the gallows haunts the last pages. In the preface, addressed to his 'dear children' in the Bedford congregation, he exhorts them to remember the experience they first had of God in ordinary places: 'Have you forgot the Close, the Milk-house, the Stable, the Barn, and the like, where God did visit your Soul?'[31]

For the modern literary critic, the 'classic' is a text that bears rereading. For previous generations, it meant the great works of Greek or Latin that had been the foundation of humanist education, and by association those works which had a similar authority. But if we ask, with Frank Kermode, 'what happens when modern minds engage ancient texts', or what a 'view of literature that preserves our right of immediate access to the venerable works of the past' might be, then the questions of authority and experience must rank very high. In an important discussion of the spiritual classic, David Tracy argues that our experiences of such expressions (he includes the Bible in this) can themselves be events that shape our lives; they have what he calls 'the power of disclosure'. He contrasts this kind of power with the authoritarian tendency in religion. The religious classic (he cites the writing of St Teresa) insists that it is only relatively adequate as an account of God, or at least one's experience of him. It is not the violent, over-confident approach of the religious authoritarian. Rather, Tracy argues, it 'is a nonviolent appeal to our minds, hearts and imaginations, and through them to our will'.[32]

For Bunyan, the victim of persecution at a time when wars of religion in the West were not quite over, the question of religious violence is a difficult one. He is a victim, yes; and his characters experience violent opposition – think of Apollyon, or the martyr-dom of Faithful in Vanity Fair. Bunyan's imagination was formed by his reading of Foxe's *Acts and Monuments*, where being faithful is virtually coterminous with being executed. The old cliché, that wayfaring means warfaring, is no joke. Bunyan came straight to the second part of *The Pilgrim's Progress* from having finished *The Holy War*, and his heroes, Great-heart and Valiant-for-truth, are offensive as well as defensive warriors. They resist the devil Apollyon, but they also go out of their way to defeat Giant Despair, and knock down Doubting Castle.

At the same time, Bunyan is very tender towards the psychologically weak in the second part. If he is angry with those who persecute, either psychologically or physically, he protects and even admires those pilgrims who need crutches. Mr Ready-to-halt and Mr Fearing are important to the emotional and theological balance of the sequel. For one thing, if the men were all like Mr Valiant-for-truth, then there would be an even greater division in gender among the pilgrims than there is.

Violence in the pilgrims and those who stand in their way is one thing. But what about Bunyan's God? As Paul Ricoeur so trenchantly puts it: 'The connection between accusation and consolation is perhaps the most striking characteristic of religion. God threatens and protects. He is the ultimate danger and the ultimate protection.'[33] One of the strengths of *The Pilgrim's Progress* as a spiritual narrative is that it recognizes this. The opposition is Satanic; but the decree of reprobation is God's. For Bunyan himself, the questions of authority and imagination are important for the justification of what he is doing; for those who respond to the spiritual imperatives of his book with anything other than rejection or condescension, they will also be important.

SUCCESS AND CRITICAL HISTORY

The early success of *The Pilgrim's Progress* was reflected in the regular reprinting of the text (twelve editions in Bunyan's lifetime) as well as a number of translations: a Dutch translation was published in 1682, a French translation was published in Amsterdam in 1685 and a Welsh translation in 1687. It continued to be reprinted, adapted and condensed throughout the eighteenth century. The Evangelical Revival adopted it; John Wesley made an abridged version for his Christian Library of 1753; John Newton annotated a 1789 edition with hymns as well as theological comment; and his friend William

Cowper praised the 'Ingenious dreamer, in whose well told tale/ Sweet fiction and sweet truth alike prevail' in his 1784 poem *Tirocinium*. Increasingly, too, its literary qualities began to be admired, even by those who did not share Bunyan's theology. Boswell records Samuel Johnson's admiration of its 'great merit, both for invention, imagination, and the conduct of the story' in April 1773.[34] Of the Romantic poets and critics, we might have expected the Nonconformist Blake to find his fellow working-class visionary sympathetic, and he made twenty-eight water-colour illustrations of episodes in the first part. Most significant, though, is the Poet Laureate Robert Southey's edition of *The Pilgrim's Progress*, with a 100-page introduction which, in Walter Scott's opinion, finally established Bunyan's superiority over Spenser in allegory. With Hazlitt and Coleridge as well, the Romantic Bunyan is established. The great nineteenth-century novelists – Dickens, Thackeray, George Eliot, Charlotte Brontë, Hawthorne – openly allude to him and appropriate his phrases and techniques, though increasingly the view of Bunyan becomes that of the untutored genius, in spite of his theology. One imagines that Bunyan would not have approved of the 'in spite of' move. Huck Finn encountered the book thus: 'There was some books too ... One was "Pilgrim's Progress", about a man that left his family it didn't say why. I read considerable in it now and then. The statements was interesting, but tough.'[35] Well, actually it does say why, though 'interesting, but tough' is as good a description of the book as any.

As Bunyan enters the literary, and by no means Puritan, mainstream, so, during the same period, his great text becomes a missionary instrument, often the first book to be translated into tribal languages after the New Testament. Baptist missionaries in particular ensured that extracts from *The Pilgrim's Progress* were translated into hundreds of languages, many of which were being written down for the first time. Many of these are now in the John Bunyan Museum in Bedford, whence, in a neat contemporary twist, copies were sent to asylum-seekers in detention near there recently. Nor should we assume that Bunyan was read simply as a call to conversion; the leader of the Taiping rebels in China in the 1850s and 1860s counted *The Pilgrim's Progress* as one of his favourite books.

There is more on the history of this book's illustrations and adaptations in the Note on the Text and Illustrations. It may be that Bunyan's masterpiece may be following the fate of his Bible, less popular and less culturally and critically central than it used to be, but still embedded in the culture. Just the phrases – 'the slough of despond', 'Vanity Fair', 'valiant for truth' – still echo and linger. So, supremely, does the title. It may await a decent film adaptation, with a CGI Apollyon, as I write this introduction; but its challenge, and its appeal for those who will take the imaginative journey, remains powerful.

NOTES

1. 'A Relation of My Imprisonment', in *Grace Abounding to the Chief of Sinners*, ed. John Stachniewski and Anita Pacheco (Oxford: Oxford World's Classics, 1998), p. 98.

2. Christopher Hill, *Milton and the English Revolution* (London: Faber, 1977), p. 274.

3. Christopher Hill, *A Turbulent, Seditious, and Factious People: John Bunyan and his Church* (published in the United States as *A Tinker and a Poor Man*) (Oxford: Clarendon Press, 1988), p. 107.

4. Ann Laurence, 'Bunyan and the Parliamentary Army', in Ann Laurence, W. R. Owens and Stuart Sim (eds.), *John Bunyan and his England 1628–88* (London: Hambledon Press, 1990), pp. 17–29.

5. Richard L. Greaves, *Glimpses of Glory: John Bunyan and English Dissent* (Palo Alto, Calif.: Stanford University Press, 2002), pp. 21–5.

6. *Grace Abounding*, p. 10.

7. Vincent Newey, '"With the eyes of my understanding": Bunyan, Experience, and Acts of Interpretation', in N. H. Keeble (ed.), *John Bunyan: Conventicle and Parnassus. Tercentenary Essays* (Oxford: Clarendon Press, 1988).

8. Greaves, *Glimpses*, chapter 2.

9. John Sneep and Arlette Zinck, 'Spiritual and Psychic Transformation: Understanding the Psychological Dimensions of John

Bunyan's Mental Illness and Healing', *Journal of Psychology and Christianity*, 24.2 (2005), pp. 156–64.

10. Galen K. Johnson, *Prisoner of Conscience: John Bunyan on Self, Community and Christian Faith* (Carlisle: Paternoster Press, 2003), p. 210.

11. *Grace Abounding*, p. 94.

12. For the relationship of *The Pilgrim's Progress* to *Grace Abounding*, see especially Roger Sharrock, *John Bunyan* (London: Hutchinson, 1954); but see also Michael Davies, *Graceful Reading: Theology and Narrative in the Works of John Bunyan* (Oxford: Oxford University Press, 2002), pp. 175–83, and U. Milo Kaufmann, *The Pilgrim's Progress and Traditions in Puritan Meditation* (New Haven: Yale University Press, 1966), p. 228.

13. Roger Sharrock, general editor, *The Miscellaneous Works of John Bunyan* (13 vols.; Oxford: Clarendon Press, 1976–94), vol. 12, p. 7.

14. William Empson, *Collected Poems* (London: Chatto, 1955), p. 56.

15. John Bunyan, *The Life and Death of Mr Badman*, ed. James F. Forrest and Roger Sharrock (Oxford: Clarendon Press, 1988), p. 161.

16. Brainerd Stranahan, 'Bunyan and the Epistle to the Hebrews: His Source for the Idea of Pilgrimage in *The Pilgrim's Progress*', *Studies in Philology*, 79 (1982), p. 280.

17. See John R. Knott, 'Bunyan's Gospel Day: A Reading of *The Pilgrim's Progress*', *English Literary Renaissance*, 3 (1973), pp. 443–61.

18. Dayton Haskin, 'Bunyan's Scriptural Acts', in Robert Collmer (ed.), *Bunyan in our Time* (Kent, Ohio: Kent State University Press, 1989), pp. 61–92.

19. Paul Korshin, *Typology in England 1650–1820* (Princeton: Princeton University Press, 1982), p. 35.

20. For Bunyan's theology, see Richard Greaves, *John Bunyan* (Courtenay Studies in Reformation Theology, 2; Abingdon: Sutton Courtenay, 1969), and Gordon Campbell, 'Bunyan and the Theologians', in Keeble, *John Bunyan: Conventicle and Parnassus*, pp. 137–51.

21. Carolynn Van Dyke, *The Fiction of Truth: Structure of Meaning in Narrative and Dramatic Allegory* (Ithaca, NY: Cornell University Press, 1985), p. 21.

22. Allen Michie, 'Between Calvin and Calvino: Postmodernism and Bunyan's *The Pilgrim's Progress*', *Bucknell Review*, 41.2 (1998), pp. 37–56.

23. Thomas H. Luxon, *Literal Figures: Puritan Allegory and the Reformation Crisis in Representation* (Chicago: University of Chicago Press, 1995), p. 159.

24. Gordon Teskey, *Allegory and Violence* (Ithaca, NY: Cornell University Press, 1996), pp. 24–5.

25. J. B. Wharey, *A Study of the Sources of Bunyan's Allegories* (Baltimore: J. H. Furst, 1904). For Foxe and Bunyan, see John R. Knott, *Discourses of Martyrdom in English Literature, 1563–1694* (Cambridge: Cambridge University Press, 1993).

26. For Bunyan and Fowler, see Isabel Rivers, *Reason, Grace and Sentiment: A Study of the Language of Religion and Ethics in England 1660–1780*, vol. 1: *Whichcote to Wesley* (Cambridge: Cambridge University Press, 1991), pp. 140–42; but see Greaves, *Glimpses*, pp. 258–9, where he points out that Worldly Wiseman is not a minister, and may instead represent the swiftly conforming gentry. He also points out that Bunyan may not have seen Fowler's *Design of Christianity* (1671) before he completed *The Pilgrim's Progress*. Even if one accepts this early date for the completion, Worldly Wiseman does not appear until the second edition, which may indicate a reaction to questions that Bunyan felt needed further amplification after he completed what became the first edition. Whether one accepts a particular identification or not, the episode brings together two strands in Bunyan's suspicion of Restoration conformity: its apparent willingness to submerge Christianity into mere morality, and the seductions of 'credit and good fashion'.

27. N. H. Keeble, ' "Here is her glory, even to be under him": The Feminine in the Work of John Bunyan', in Laurence, Owens and Sim (eds.), *John Bunyan and his England*, pp. 131–47.

28. Sharrock (ed.), *Miscellaneous Works*, vol. 3, pp. 32–6.

29. Margaret Olofson Thickstun, 'From Christiana to Stand-fast: Subsuming the Feminine in *The Pilgrim's Progress*', *Studies in English Literature*, 26 (1986), pp. 439–53.

30. Maxine Hancock, *The Key in the Window: Marginal Notes in Bunyan's Narratives* (Vancouver: Regent College, 2000), p. 100.

31. *Grace Abounding*, p. 5.

32. Frank Kermode, *The Classic* (London: Faber, 1977); David Tracy, *The Analogical Imagination* (London: SCM, 1981), pp. 193, 177.

33. Paul Ricoeur, *Conflict of Interpretations* (Evanston, Ill.: Northwestern University Press, 1974), p. 455.

34. *Boswell's Life of Johnson*, ed. R. W. Chapman (Oxford: Oxford University Press, 1970), p. 529.

35. Mark Twain, *The Adventures of Huckleberry Finn* (Harmondsworth: Penguin, 1980), p. 159. See also A. Richard Dutton, ' "Interesting, but tough": Reading *The Pilgrim's Progress*', *Studies in English Literature*, 18 (1978), pp. 439–56.

Note on the Text and Illustrations

What became known as the first part of *The Pilgrim's Progress* was first published in 1678. It went through a further ten editions in Bunyan's lifetime, all of them published by Nathaniel Ponder. Each of these later editions bears the note on the title page, 'with additions'. For the first three, this means substantial extra text. For example, the second edition introduces the episode with Mr Worldly Wiseman, and the third adds the long discussion between the pilgrims and By-ends. After that the additions are on a smaller scale – words and phrases are added, and in some cases subtracted, marginal notes and biblical references are added or varied, or corrected. Colloquial or dialect forms, particularly 'a' for 'have' are sometimes removed. The text of the first part, then, is in process throughout Bunyan's life. It is not an unstable text, in the sense that editors and critics have used it of other early modern texts, particularly play-texts like *Dr Faustus* or *King Lear*. It is a cumulative text, though not one that puts on much weight, in the manner of Burton's *Anatomy of Melancholy*. The second part, coming towards the end of Bunyan's life (1684), produces far fewer variants. The scholarly editing of *The Pilgrim's Progress*, at least since Roger Sharrock's 1960 revision of J. B. Wharey's Clarendon Press edition, has sought to make the first edition of 1678 the basis of the text, and to insert the additions from the editions they first appeared in. The justification for this, following the principles of the Greg–Bowers tradition of bibliography, is that it is most likely to preserve the author's original intentions. The problem with it is that it produces an edition that never appeared in Bunyan's own lifetime. Instead, I have decided to base my text on the last edition published in Bunyan's lifetime, the tenth edition of the first part, and the second edition of the second part, both published in 1688. This has the advantage of preserving all the changes in the text and marginal notes that Bunyan may have overseen in a book for which he retained a proprietorial affection. I have checked this against the first, third, seventh and ninth editions to ensure that nothing significant is left out or changed. For a full account of the textual history of the two parts, the Introduction to the Oxford English Texts edition of 1960, by Roger Sharrock, revising the earlier work of J. B. Wharey, remains authoritative. Even so, I have come to different conclusions about the right text to use for an informed general reader, although that reader will not notice enormous differences.

We cannot know for certain what level of involvement Bunyan had with the revisions of his bestseller. He was certainly very protective of it, particularly against those who said, condescendingly, that he could not have written it, or who wrote spurious continuations – evidence for that is in the verse prefaces to the second part, and in *The Holy War*.

Should an editor modernize Bunyan's text? There continue to be attempts to bring Bunyan's text up to date by various means, from conservative changes in spelling and punctuation to wholesale rewriting of Bunyan's English into a modern idiom. Warren Wiersbe and Judith Markham's *The New Pilgrim's Progress* (1989) veers between a gently modernized and reduced first paragraph to the substitution of 'mentally deranged' for 'frenzy distemper' in the second. Barry Horner's 'Accurate Revised Text' substitutes 'You' for 'Thou' and, more conservatively, changes word-order. Most of these attempts stem from an identification of the religious, evangelical nature of Bunyan's text, and the felt need of modernization to make his message accessible, if not always successfully. I am sympathetic to such ambitions (and suspect Bunyan would be, too), but they are not mine in this edition. In fact, the more I tried to modernize, the more I realized that even such things that are routinely changed in, say, Shakespeare editions – spelling, punctuation, italicization and capitalization – are sometimes part of Bunyan's expressive repertoire.

Bunyan's punctuation is not ours, but it is quite a subtle instrument. As W. R. Owens has remarked, in his Oxford World's Classics edition, it is a guide to reading, a sort of speech notation. 'Hear it in your head' would be the best advice to the reader who is troubled by the 'incorrectness' of it. Sometimes it feels a lot heavier than modern punctuation, at other times a lot lighter. We do not have any manuscripts of Bunyan's works, apart from his entries in the church minute book, so we cannot be sure what is his own practice and what is his printer's. Discussions of seventeenth-century printing often refer to Joseph Moxon's Restoration guide for printers, which suggests that much of what we would call copy editing was done at the compositing stage. Here is the relevant extract:

> ... the carelessness of some good *Authors*, and the ignorance of other *Authors*, has forc'd Printers *to introduce a Custom, which among them is look'd upon as a task and duty incumbent on the* Composer, *viz. To discern and amend the bad* Spelling *and* Pointing *of his* Copy, *if it be English* ... (p. 192)

Moxon's *Mechanick Exercises on the Whole Art of Printing* was published in Dublin in 1683/4, so there is some likelihood that Nathaniel Ponder would have followed similar rules. But how would they have been applied? Would the relatively uneducated Bunyan have been regarded as ignorant, with his copy obviously needing amending? Or would the performances of an experienced author, with more than twenty years of publication behind him, lead the compositor to defer to what he had in front of him? I have decided to stick with the original, even when Bunyan himself is inconsistent in such matters as punctuating dialogue; but I have added possessive apostrophes, which I think do help the modern reader without compromising Bunyan's effects.

The italics sometimes seem quite arbitrary, but very often they serve to mark dialogue, or emphasis. They also often operate as quotation marks for dialogue. I have kept most of them, although they make some pages look unusual and daunting to a modern reader. In a few cases, where italics were used for extensive stretches for no discernible reason, they have been silently removed in the interests of readability.

Bunyan's use of capital letters also looks odd to those who are not used to books from his period. By the mid-seventeenth century capitalizing some of the proper nouns in a sentence as well as names and initial letters of sentences (and sometimes clauses following a colon or semicolon) was general practice. In some cases the extra capital might indicate emphasis, but it seems to be arbitrary as often as deliberate. Modernizing might then be the obvious response – why put up a barrier? But this is an allegory, and capital letters are sometimes an invitation to view a particular object allegorically, a process an editor should not interfere with. What counts as part of an allegory and what is just a wall and no more, for example, should not be final for his readers.

Bunyan wrote in a period where there were few settled rules of spelling, and no authoritative dictionaries. Consequently some words are spelled in different ways, sometimes on the same page, and I have not sought to iron out the inconsistencies completely. I have conservatively modernized spelling in line with most editions of early modern texts aimed at ordinary readers as well as scholars. In the few instances where it materially affects our sense of the text, I have drawn attention to it in the notes. For example, when Bunyan writes of 'humane learning' he means 'human' in a pejorative sense; or when he puns on 'travel' and 'travail'. Where Bunyan uses an obsolete form, such as 'practick' (meaning 'practical'), I have kept the older word. I have not changed those instances where Bunyan appears to be grammatically incorrect.

Some features of the text, such as the asterisks and daggers which occasionally cue in the marginal notes, have been removed in the interests of a clear, readable text. So this is not a facsimile.

One final point of regularization. In the early editions of the second part, Christiana's son Samuel is sometimes referred to as Simon. I have kept to Samuel throughout.

ILLUSTRATIONS

The Pilgrim's Progress soon became an illustrated text. The 'sleeping portrait', engraved by Robert White, appeared as the frontispiece to the third edition, in 1679. Robert White was a distinguished book illustrator, particularly of author portraits. The pencil drawing on which the likeness of Bunyan is taken is in the British Museum. The background picture of the pilgrims and the cave with the lion establishes the iconographic tradition of the book, though there is no evidence that White had any further involvement with it, although his apprentices may have done.

From the sixth edition of the first part, and the very first edition of the second part, Ponder included a number of illustrations, with accompanying verses. A notice appears in the endpaper of the 1680 (fifth) edition:

> The *Pilgrims Progress* having found good Acceptation among the People, to the carrying off the Fourth Impression, which had many Additions, more than any preceding: And the Publisher observing that many persons desired to have it illustrated with Pictures, hath endeavoured to gratifie them therein: And besides those that are ordinarily printed to this Fifth Impression, hath provided Thirteen Copper Cutts curiously Engraven for such as desire them.

Subsequent versions of the text include some or all of these illustrations as copper cuts or wood engravings, although many of the surviving versions have none because they may have been cut out for framing or pasting onto a wall. What should the editor and publisher do with these illustrations? The Clarendon edition of *The Pilgrim's Progress* does not print them, though it gives all the information about them. The Clarendon *Miscellaneous Works* volume of the poems, edited by Graham Midgley, while printing all the other poems in *The Pilgrim's Progress*, does not even mention the poems attached to the illustrations. My contention is that they are part of the book, even if it is an initiative of the publisher's, as the advertisement indicates.

The case is even stronger for the second part, which has two woodcut illustrations in both editions published in Bunyan's lifetime, as well as a revised version of the 'sleeping portrait'.

Owens, who puts them in his edition, is right to assert that this is a part of the seventeenth-century reader's experience of the text, but it is more than that. It is part of the apparatus by which the reading of the text is mediated. Two examples indicate how this works. The depiction of the martyrdom of Faithful at Vanity Fair thematically and visually recalls the woodcut illustrations in Foxe's *Acts and Monuments*, an iconic English Protestant text that Bunyan knew well. In the second part, where the woodcuts were present from the first edition, the depiction of the death of Giant Despair significantly affects our interpretation of the episode in the text. In the text, Giant Despair is killed and his head severed by Great-heart, in an echo of David and Goliath. This leads to the demolition of Doubting Castle. In the first part, Christian has been imprisoned in the castle and escaped with the key of Promise. The text of the second part at least implies that doubting is over as far as the pilgrims are concerned. Is that permanence credible? The verse to the illustration of Despair's head on a pole warns:

> Tho doubting Castle be demolished,
> And the Gyant dispair hath lost his head,
> Sin can rebuild the Castle, make't remaine,
> And make despair the Gyant live againe.

The pastoral theology is quite different; together the incident and its illustration capture the mixture of the 'already' and the 'not yet' that is Bunyan's sense of the victory of Christ – one explored more fully in *The Holy War*, which he had composed between the two parts.

The illustrations for this edition for the first part come from the Lenox Library copy of the sixth edition, now in the New York Public Library. Apart from the woodcut of the martyrdom of Faithful, they appear to be copper cuts of Dutch origin. The illustrations for the second part come from the Bodleian Library's copy of the second edition of 1687. These are cuts that were bound in with the printing, rather than separately printed, as with the copper cuts. It is possible that they were engraved by one of Robert White's apprentices, like John Sturt, who made a number of engravings for later editions, including the famous quarto edition of 1728.

I am grateful to both libraries for permission to reprint, and for the skill of their staff in reproducing these fading and fragile treasures.

Further Reading

EDITIONS OF *THE PILGRIM'S PROGRESS* AND BUNYAN'S OTHER WORKS

The Pilgrim's Progress, ed. J. B. Wharey, 2nd edn., revised Roger Sharrock (Oxford: Clarendon Press, 1960).

The Pilgrim's Progress, ed. Roger Sharrock (Harmondsworth: Penguin, 1965).

The Pilgrim's Progress, ed. W. R. Owens (Oxford: Oxford World's Classics, 2003).

Grace Abounding to the Chief of Sinners, ed. John Stachniewski with Anita Pacheco (Oxford: Oxford World's Classics, 1998).

The Miscellaneous Works of John Bunyan, general editor Roger Sharrock, 13 vols. (Oxford: Clarendon Press, 1976–94).

CRITICAL AND BIOGRAPHICAL BOOKS ON BUNYAN

Batson, E. Beatrice, *John Bunyan: Allegory and Imagination* (London and Totowa, NJ: Croom Helm and Barnes & Noble, 1984).

Brown, John, revised Frank Mott Harrison, *John Bunyan (1628–1688): His Life, Times and Work* (London: Hulbert, 1928).

Collmer, Robert (ed.), *Bunyan in our Time* (Kent, Ohio: Kent State University Press, 1989).

Davies, Michael, *Graceful Reading: Theology and Narrative in the Works of John Bunyan* (Oxford: Oxford University Press, 2002).

Dunan-Page, Ann, *Grace Overwhelming: John Bunyan, The Pilgrim's Progress and the Extremes of the Baptist Mind* (Oxford and Berne: Peter Lang, 2006).

Gay, David, Randall, James G., Zinck, Arlette (eds.), *Awakening Words: John Bunyan and the Language of Community* (Newark and London: University of Delaware Press, 2000).

Greaves, Richard L., *Glimpses of Glory: John Bunyan and English Dissent* (Palo Alto, Calif.: Stanford University Press, 2002).

—— *John Bunyan* (Courtenay Studies in Reformation Theology, 2; Abingdon: Sutton Courtenay, 1969).

—— *John Bunyan and English Nonconformity* (London: Hambledon Press, 1992).

Hancock, Maxine, *The Key in the Window: Marginal Notes in Bunyan's Narratives* (Vancouver: Regent College, 2000).

Hill, Christopher, *A Turbulent, Seditious, and Factious People: John Bunyan and his Church* (published in the United States as *A Tinker and a Poor Man*) (Oxford: Clarendon Press, 1988).

Hofmeyr, Isabel, *The Portable Bunyan: A Transnational History of The Pilgrim's Progress* (Princeton and Oxford: Princeton University Press, 2004).

Johnson, Barbara A., *Reading Piers Plowman and The Pilgrim's Progress: Reception and the Protestant Reader* (Carbondale: University of Illinois Press, 1992).

Johnson, Galen K., *Prisoner of Conscience: John Bunyan on Self, Community and Christian Faith* (Carlisle: Paternoster Press, 2003).

Kaufmann, U. Milo, *The Pilgrim's Progress and Traditions in Puritan Meditation* (New Haven: Yale University Press, 1966).

Keeble, N. H. (ed.), *John Bunyan: Conventicle and Parnassus. Tercentenary Essays* (Oxford: Clarendon Press, 1988).

——*John Bunyan: Reading Dissenting Writing* (Berne: Peter Lang, 2002).

Laurence, Ann, Owens W. R. and Sim, Stuart (eds.), *John Bunyan and his England 1628–88* (London: Hambledon Press, 1990).

Luxon, Thomas H., *Literal Figures: Puritan Allegory and the Reformation Crisis in Representation* (Chicago: University of Chicago Press, 1995).

Lynch, Beth, *John Bunyan and the Language of Conviction* (Cambridge: D. S. Brewer, 2004).

Mullett, Michael, *John Bunyan in Context* (Keele: Keele University Press, 1996).

Newey, Vincent (ed.), *The Pilgrim's Progress: Critical and Historical Views* (Liverpool: Liverpool University Press, 1980).

Sharrock, Roger, *John Bunyan* (London: Hutchinson, 1954; reissued by Macmillan, 1968).

—— (ed.), *The Pilgrim's Progress: A Casebook* (London: Macmillan, 1976).

Sim, Stuart, *Negotiations with Paradox: Narrative Practice and Narrative Form in Bunyan and Defoe* (Savage, Md.: Barnes & Noble, 1990).

—— and Walker, David, *Bunyan and Authority* (Berne: Peter Lang, 2000).

Spargo, Tamsin, *The Writing of John Bunyan* (Aldershot: Scolar Press, 1997).

Swaim, Kathleen M., *Pilgrim's Progress, Puritan Progress: Discourses and Contexts* (Urbana and Chicago: University of Illinois Press, 1993).

Talon, Henri, *John Bunyan, the Man and his Works*, trans. Barbara Wall (London, 1951).

Wakefield, Gordon, *Bunyan the Christian* (London: HarperCollins Religious, 1992).

HISTORICAL AND CRITICAL WORKS OF RELEVANCE TO *THE PILGRIM'S PROGRESS*

Achinstein, Sharon, *Literature and Dissent in Milton's England* (Cambridge: Cambridge University Press, 2003).

Bertsch, Janet, *Storytelling in the Works of Bunyan, Grimmels-*

hausen, Defoe, and Schnabel (Rochester and Woodbridge: Camden House, 2004).

Damrosch, Leopold, Jr., *God's Plot and Man's Stories: Studies in the Fictional Imagination from Milton to Fielding* (Chicago: University of Chicago Press, 1985).

Fish, Stanley E., *Self-Consuming Artefacts: The Experience of Seventeenth-Century Literature* (Berkeley: University of California Press, 1972).

Hawkes, David, *Idols of the Marketplace: Idolatry and Commodity Fetishism in English Literature, 1580–1680* (New York and Basingstoke: Palgrave, 2001).

Iser, Wolfgang, *The Implied Reader: Patterns of Communication in Prose Fiction from Bunyan to Beckett* (Baltimore: Johns Hopkins University Press, 1974).

Keeble, N. H., *The Literary Culture of Nonconformity in Later Seventeenth-Century England* (Leicester: Leicester University Press, 1987).

Knott, John R., Jr., *The Sword of the Spirit: Puritan Responses to the Bible* (Chicago: Chicago University Press, 1980).

McKeon, Michael, *The Origins of the English Novel 1600–1740* (Baltimore: Johns Hopkins University Press, 1987).

Morris, Colin, and Roberts, Peter (eds.), *Pilgrimage: The English Experience from Becket to Bunyan* (Cambridge: Cambridge University Press, 2002).

Pooley, Roger, *English Prose of the Seventeenth Century, 1590–1700* (Harlow: Longman, 1993).

Rivers, Isabel, *Reason, Grace and Sentiment: A Study of the Language of Religion and Ethics in England 1660–1780*, vol. 1: *Whichcote to Wesley* (Cambridge: Cambridge University Press, 1991).

Salzman, Paul, *English Prose Fiction, 1550–1700* (Oxford: Oxford University Press, 1985).

Spurr, John, *England in the 1670s: 'This Masquerading Age'* (Oxford: Blackwell, 2000).

Stachniewski, John, *The Persecutory Imagination: English Puritanism and the Literature of Religious Despair* (Oxford: Clarendon Press, 1991).

Thickstun, Margaret Olofson, *Fictions of the Feminine: Puritan Doctrine and the Representation of Women* (Ithaca, NY: Cornell University Press, 1988).

Van Dyke, Carolynn, *The Fiction of Truth: Structures of Meaning in Narrative and Dramatic Allegory* (Ithaca, NY: Cornell University Press, 1985).

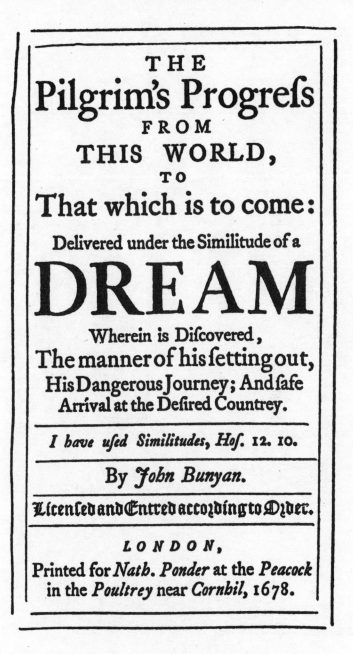

THE
Pilgrim's Progress
FROM
THIS WORLD,
TO
That which is to come:

Delivered under the Similitude of a

DREAM

Wherein is Discovered,
The manner of his setting out,
His Dangerous Journey; And safe
Arrival at the Desired Countrey.

I have used Similitudes, Hos. 12. 10.

By *John Bunyan.*

Licensed and Entred according to Order.

LONDON,
Printed for *Nath. Ponder* at the *Peacock*
in the *Poultrey* near *Cornhil,* 1678.

The Author's Apology[1] for his BOOK

When at the first I took my Pen in hand
Thus for to write; I did not understand,
That I at all should make a little Book
In such a Mode: Nay, I had undertook
To make another; which when almost done,
Before I was aware, I this begun;
*   And thus it was: I writing of the Way*
And Race of Saints in this our Gospel-Day,[2]
Fell suddenly into an Allegory
About their Journey, and the way to Glory,
In more than Twenty things, which I set down:
This done, I twenty more had in my Crown;
And they again began to multiply,
Like sparks that from the coals of fire do fly:
Nay then, thought I, if that you breed so fast,
I'll put you by your selves, lest you at last
Should prove ad infinitum, *and eat out*
The Book that I already am about.
Well, so I did; but yet I did not think
To show to all the World my Pen and Ink
In such a mode, I only thought to make
I knew not what: Nor did I undertake
Thereby to please my Neighbour; no not I,
I did it mine own self to Gratify.
*   Neither did I but vacant seasons spend*
In this my Scribble; Nor did I intend
But to divert my self in doing this,
From worser thoughts, which make me do amiss.

Thus I set Pen to Paper with delight,
And quickly had my thoughts in black and white.
For having now my Method by the end,
Still as I pull'd,[3] *it came; and so I pen'd*
It down; until it came at last to be
For length and breadth the bigness which you see.

Well, when I had thus put my ends together,
I show'd them others, that I might see whether
They would condemn them, or them justify:
And some said, let them live; some let them die:
Some said, John, *Print it; others said, not so:*
Some said it might do good; others said, no.

Now was I in a strait; and did not see
Which was the best thing to be done by me:
At last I thought, since you are thus divided,
I print it will, and so the case decided.

For, Thought I, some I see would have it done,
Though others in that Channel do not run:
To prove then who advised for the best,
Thus I thought fit to put it to the Test.

I further thought, if now I did deny
Those that would have it, thus to gratify;
I did not know, but hinder *them I might*
Of that which would to them be great delight.
For those which were not for its coming forth;
I said to them, Offend you I am loth:
Yet since your Brethren pleased with it be,
Forbear to judge, till you do further see.

If that thou wilt not read, let it *alone.*
Some love the Meat, some love to pick the Bone,
Yea that I might them better moderate
I did too with them thus Expostulate.

May I not write in such as style as this?
In such a Method *too, and yet not miss*
My end, *thy* good? *Why may it not be done?*
Dark clouds bring waters, when the bright bring
        none:[4]

Yea, dark or bright, *if they their* Silver drops
Cause to descend, the earth, by yielding Crops,
Gives praise to both, and carpeth not at either,
But treasures up the Fruit they yield together;
Yea, so commixes both, that in her Fruit
None can distinguish this from that; they suit
Her well when hungry: But if she be full,
She spews out both, and makes their blessings null.

  You see the ways the Fisherman *doth take*
To catch the Fish; what Engines doth he make?
Behold! How he engageth all his wits;
Also his snares, lines, angles, hooks, and nets:
Yet Fish there be, that neither Hook nor Line,
Nor Snare, nor Net, nor Engine can make thine:
They must be grop'd for, and be tickled too,
Or they will not be catched, what e'er you do.

  How does the Fowler *seek to catch his game*
By divers means, all which one cannot name?
His gun, his nets, his lime-twigs, light and bell:
He creeps, he goes, he stands; yea who can tell
Of all his postures?[5] *Yet there's none of these*
Will make him Master of what Fowls he please.
Yea, he must Pipe and Whistle to catch this,
Yet if he does so, that Bird he will miss.
If that a Pearl may in a Toad's-head *dwell,*[6]
And may be found too in an Oyster-shell;
If things that promise nothing, do contain
What better is than Gold; who will disdain,
That have an inkling of it, there to look,
That they may find it? Now my little Book
(Though void of all these paintings that may make
It with this or the other man to take)
Is not without those things that do excel
What do in brave, but empty Notions dwell.

  Well, yet I am not fully satisfied
That this your Book will stand, when soundly
          tried.

Why what's the matter? It is dark, *what though?*
But it is feigned: *What of that? I trow,*
Some men with feigned words, as dark as mine,
Make truth to spangle, and its Rays to shine.
But they want solidness: *speak man thy mind:*
They drown'd the weak. Metaphors make us blind.

Solidity, indeed becomes the Pen
Of him that writeth things Divine to Men:
But must I needs want solidness, because
By Metaphors *I speak? Were not God's Laws*
His Gospel-Laws, in olden times held forth
By Types, Shadows and Metaphors?[7] *Yet loth*
Will any sober Man be to find fault
With them, lest he be found for to assault
The highest Wisdom: No, he rather stoops,
And seeks to find out what by Pins and Loops,
By Calves, and Sheep, by Heifers, and by Rams;
By Birds and Herbs, and by the blood of Lambs,
God speaketh to him; and happy is he
That finds the Light and Grace that in them be.[8]

Be not too forward therefore to conclude,
That I want solidness; that I am rude:
All things solid in Show, not solid be;
All things in Parables despise not we,
Lest things most hurtful lightly we receive;
And things that good are, of our Souls bereave.

My dark and cloudy words, they do but hold
The truth, as Cabinets enclose the Gold.

The Prophets used much by Metaphors
To set forth Truth; Yea, who so considers
Christ his Apostles too, shall plainly see,
That Truths, to this day, in such Mantles be.

Am I afraid to say that Holy Writ,
Which for its Style and Praise puts down all wit,
Is everywhere so full of all these things,
(Dark figures, Allegories) yet there springs
From that same Book, that lustre, and those rays
Of light, that turns our darkest nights to days.

Come let my Carper, to his Life *now look,*
And find there darker Lines than in my Book,
He findeth any: Yea, and let him know,
That in his best things *there are* worse *lines too.*

   May we but stand before Impartial Men,
To his poor One, I dare adventure Ten,
That they will take my *meaning in these lines,*
Far better than his lies in Silver Shrines.
Some Truth, although in Swadling-clouts, I find,
Reforms the Judgement, rectifies the Mind;
Pleases the Understanding, makes the Will
Submit: The Memory too it doth fill
With what doth our Imaginations please;
Likewise, it tends our Troubles to appease.

   Sound words I know Timothy *is to use,*[9]
And old Wives' Fables he is to refuse;
But yet grave Paul *him no where did forbid*
The use of Parables: in which lay hid
That gold, those pearls, and precious stones that
        were
Worth digging for, and that with greatest care.

   Let me add one word more, O Man of God:
Art thou offended? Dost thou wish I had
Put forth my Matter in another dress,
Or that I had in things been more express?
To those that are my betters, (as is fit)
Three things let me propound, then I submit.

   1. *I find not that I am denied the use*
Of this my Method, so I none abuse.
Put on the Words, Things, Readers, or be rude
In handling Figure or Similitude,
In application; but all that I may,
Seek the advance of Truth, this or that way:
Denied, did I say? Nay, I have leave,
(Examples too, and that from them that have
God better pleased by their Words or Ways,
Than any Man that breatheth nowadays)

Thus to express my mind, thus to declare
Things unto thee that Excellentest are.

   2. I find that men (as high as Trees) will write
Dialogue-wise;[10] *yet no man doth them slight,*
For writing so: Indeed if they abuse
Truth, cursed be they, and the craft they use
To that intent; but yet let Truth be free
To make her Sallies upon Thee, and Me,
Which way it pleases God: for who knows how,
Better than he that taught us first to Plough,
To Guide our Mind and Pens for his Design?[11]
And he makes base things usher in Divine.

   3. I find that Holy Writ in many places,
Hath semblance with this method, where the cases
Do call for one thing, to set forth another;
Use it I may then, and yet nothing smother
Truth's Golden Beams: Nay, by this method may
Make it cast forth its Rays as light as day.

   And now before I do put up my Pen,
I'll show the profit of my Book, and then
Commit both thee and It unto that hand
That pulls the strong down, and makes weak ones
     stand.

   This Book it chalketh out before thine eyes
The man that seeks the everlasting Prize:
It shows you whence he comes, whither he goes;
What he leaves undone: also what he does:
It also shows you how he runs, and runs,
Till he unto the Gate of Glory comes.

   It shows too, who sets out for Life amain,
As if the lasting Crown they would attain:
Here also you may see the reason why
They lose their Labour and like fools do die.

   This Book will make a Traveller of thee;
If by its Counsel thou wilt ruled be;
It will direct thee to the Holy-Land,
If thou wilt its directions understand:

Yea, it will make the slothful active be
The blind also delightful things to see.
Art thou for something rare, and profitable?
Wouldest thou see a Truth within a Fable?
Art thou forgetful? Wouldest thou remember
From New-year's day to the last of December?
Then read my fancies, they will stick like Burrs,
And may be to the helpless Comforters.

This Book is writ in such a Dialect,
As may the minds of listless Men affect:
It seems a Novelty, and yet contains
Nothing but sound and honest Gospel strains.
Wouldst thou divert thy self from Melancholy?
Wouldst thou be pleasant, yet be far from folly?
Wouldst thou read Riddles, and their Explanation,
Or else be drowned in thy Contemplation?
Dost thou love picking-meat?[12] *Or wouldst thou see*
A Man i'th'Clouds,[13] *and hear him speak to thee?*
Wouldst thou be in a Dream, and yet not sleep?
Or wouldst thou in a moment laugh and weep?
Wouldst thou lose thy self, and catch no harm?
And find thy self again without a charm?
Wouldst read thy self, and read thou knowest not
         what,
And yet know whether thou art blest or not,
By reading the same Lines? O then come hither,
And lay my Book, thy Head, and Heart together.

JOHN BUNYAN

The
Pilgrim's Progress:
In the Similitude of a
DREAM

As I walked through the wilderness of this world, I lighted
on a certain place where was a Den: and I laid me down in *The jail*
that place to sleep:[1] and as I slept I dreamed a dream. I
dreamed, and behold, *I saw a man clothed with rags, stand-* Isa. 64.6. Luke
ing in a certain place, with his face from his own house, a 14.33. Ps. 38.4.
Hab. 2.2. Acts
book in his hand, and a great burden upon his back. I 16.31
looked, and saw him open the book, and read therein, and
as he read he wept and trembled, and not being able longer
to contain, he brake out with a lamentable cry, saying, *His outcry.* Acts
What shall I do?[2] 2.27

In this plight therefore he went home, and refrained
himself as long as he could, that his wife and children
should not perceive his distress, but he could not be silent
long, because that his trouble increased: wherefore at length
he brake his mind to his wife and children; and thus
he began to talk to them. *O my dear wife,* said he, *And*
you the children of my bowels,[3] *I your dear friend am*
in my self undone, by reason of a burden that lieth hard
upon me: moreover I am for certain informed, that this *This world*
our city will be burned with fire from heaven, in which
fearful overthrow, both my self, with thee my wife, and
you my sweet babes, shall miserably come to ruin; except
(the which yet I see not) some way of escape can be found, *He knows no*
whereby we may be delivered. At this, his relations were *way of escape*
as yet
sore amazed; not for that they believed that what he had
said to them was true, but because they thought that some

frenzy distemper[4] had got into his head: therefore, it drawing towards night, and they hoping that sleep might settle
his brains, with all haste they got him to bed; but the night
was as troublesome to him as the day; wherefore, instead
of sleeping, he spent it in sighs and tears. So when the
morning was come, they would know how he did; he told
them *worse* and *worse*; he also set to talking to them
Carnal physick again, but they began to be hardened. They also thought
for a sick soul to drive away his distemper by harsh and surly carriages to
him: sometimes they would deride, sometimes they would
chide, and sometimes they would quite neglect him: wherefore he began to retire himself to his Chamber to pray for,
and pity them; and also to condole his own misery; he
would also walk solitarily in the fields, sometimes reading,
and sometimes praying; and thus for some days he spent
his time.

Now, I saw, upon a time, when he was walking in the
fields, that he was (as he was wont) reading in this book,
and greatly distressed in his mind; and as he read he burst
Acts 16.30, 31 out, as he had done before, crying, *What shall I do to be
saved?*

I saw also that he looked this way and that way, as if he
would run; yet he stood still, because (as I perceived) he
could not tell which way to go. I looked then, and saw a
man named *Evangelist,*[5] coming to him, and asked, 'Wherefore dost thou cry?' He answered, 'Sir, I perceive by the
Heb. 9.27 book, in my hand, that I am condemned to die, and after
Job 26.21, 22. that come to judgment, and I find that I am not willing to
Exod. 22.14 do the first, nor able to do the second.'

Then said Evangelist, 'Why not willing to die; since this
life is attended by so many evils?' The man answered,
'Because I fear that this burden that is upon my back, will
Isa. 30.33 sink me lower than the grave; and I shall fall into Tophet.
And sir, if I be not fit to go to prison, I am not fit to go to
judgement, and from thence to execution; and the thoughts
of these things make me cry.'

Then said Evangelist, 'If this be thy condition, why
standest thou still?' He answered, 'Because I know not

Christian no sooner leaues this world but meets
Euangelest who loueingly him greet
with tideings of another: and doth show
him how to mount to that from this below

Conviction of
the necessity of
flying
Mat. 3.7
whither to go.' Then he gave him a *parchment roll,* and there was written within, *Fly from the wrath to come.*[6]

Mat. 7. Psal.
119.105.
2 Pet. 2.29
Christ, and the
way to him can-
not be found
without the
word
Luke 14.16
The man therefore read it, and looking upon *Evangelist* very carefully, said. 'Whither must I fly?' Then said Evangelist, pointing, with his finger over a very wide field, 'Do you see yonder *wicket-gate?*'[7] The Man said, 'No'; then said the other, 'Do you see yonder shining light?' He said, 'I think I do.' Then said *Evangelist,* 'Keep that light in your eye, and go up directly thereto, so shalt thou see the gate; at which when thou knockest, it shall be told thee what to do.'

Gen. 19.17
So I saw in my dream, that the man began to run; now he had not run far from his own door, but his wife and children perceiving it, began to cry after him to return; but the man put his fingers in his ears, and ran on crying, 'Life, life, eternal life': so he looked not behind him but fled towards the middle of the plain.

They that fly
from the wrath
to come, are a
gazing stock to
the world
Jer. 20.10
The neighbours also came out to see him run, and as he ran, some mocked, others threatened, and some cried after him to return; and among those that did so, there were two that were resolved to fetch him back by force. The name of the one was *Obstinate,* and the Name of the other was *Pliable.* Now by this time the Man was gone a good distance from them; but however they were resolved to pursue him; which they did, and in a little time *they* overtook him. Then said the Man, Neighbours, *Wherefore are you come?* They said, to persuade you to go back with us; but he said, that can by no means be. You dwell, (said he) in the City of Destruction, (the place also where I was born) I see it to be so; and dying there, sooner or later, you will sink lower then the grave, into a place that burns with fire and brimstone; be content good neighbours, and go along with me.

Obstinate *and*
Pliable *follow
him*

Obstinate
What, said *Obstinate,* and leave our Friends and our Comforts behind us!

Christian
2 Cor. 4.18
Yes, said *Christian* (for that was his name)[8] because, that *all, which you shall forsake,* is not worthy to be compared with a *little* of that that I am seeking to enjoy; and if you go along with me, *and hold it,* you shall fare as I my

self; for there where I go is enough and to spare; Come Luke 15.17
away, and prove my Words.

Obst. What are the things you seek, since you leave *all*
the world to find them?

Chr. I seek an *Inheritance, incorruptible, undefiled, and* 1 Pet. 1.4
that fadeth not away; and it is laid up in heaven, and Heb. 11.16
safe there, to be bestowed, at the time appointed, on
them that diligently seek it. Read it so, if you will, in
my book.

Obst. *Tush, said* Obstinate, *away with your book; will*
you go back with us, or no?

Chr. No, not I, said the other; because I have laid my
hand to the plough.   Luke 9.62

Obst. *Come then, Neighbour* Pliable, *let us turn again,*
and go home without him; there is a company of these
craz'd-headed coxcombs, that when they take a fancy by
the end, are wiser in their own eyes than seven men that
can render a reason.

Pli. Then said *Pliable,* don't revile; if what the good
Christian says, is true, the things he looks after are better
than ours; my heart inclines to go with my neighbour.

Obst. *What! More fools still? Be ruled by me, go back;*
who knows whither such a brain-sick fellow will lead you?
Go back, go back, and be wise.

Chr. Nay, but do thou come with thy neighbour, *Pliable,* Christian *and*
there are such things to be had which I spoke of, and many Obstinate *pull*
more glories besides; if you believe not me, read here in this *for* Pliable's *soul*
book; and for the truth of what is expressed therein, behold Heb. 9.17, 18,
all is confirmed by the blood of him that made it.   19, 20, 21

Pli. *Well neighbour* Obstinate, (saith Pliable) *I begin to* Pliable *contented*
come to a point, I intend to go along with this good man, *to go with*
and to cast in my lot with him: but my good companion, Christian
do you know the way to this desired place?

Chr. I am directed by a man whose name is *Evangelist,*
to speed me to a little gate that is before us, where we shall
receive instructions about the way.

Pli. *Come then, good neighbour, let us be going.* Then
they both went together.

Obst. And I will go back to my place, said *Obstinate:*
Obstinate *goes*
railing back
I will be no companion of such mis-led fantastical[9] fellows.

Now I saw in my Dream, that when Obstinate was gone
Talk between
Christian *and*
Pliable
back, *Christian* and *Pliable* went talking over the plain,
and thus they began their discourse.

Chr. Come neighbour *Pliable,* how do you do? I am glad
you are persuaded to go along with me; had even *Obstinate*
himself but felt what I have felt of the powers and terrors
of what is yet unseen, he would not thus lightly have given
us the back.

Pli. Come neighbour Christian; *since there is none but
us two here, tell me now further, what the things are: and
how to be enjoyed, whither we are going.*
*God's things
unspeakable*
Chr. I can better conceive of them with my mind, than
speak of them with my tongue: but yet since you are desirous to know, I will read of them in my book.

*Pli. And do you think that the words of your book are
certainly true?*
Tit. 1.2
Chr. Yes verily, for it was made by him that cannot lie.

Pli. Well said, what things are they?
Isa. 4.5, 17.
John 10.27,
28, 29
Chr. There is an endless kingdom to be inhabited, and
everlasting life to be given us; that we may inhabit that
kingdom for ever.

Pli. Well said, and what else?
2 Tim. 4.8,
Rev. 23.4,
Matt. 13
Chr. There are crowns of glory to be given us; and garments that will make us shine like the sun in the firmament
of heaven.

Pli. This is very pleasant; and what else?
Isa. 15.8, Rev. 7.
16, 17. ch. 21.4
Chr. There shall be no more crying, nor sorrow, for he
that is owner of the place will wipe all tears from our
eyes.

Pli. And what company shall we have there?
Isa. 6.2,
1 Thess. 4.16,
17. Rev. 5.11
Chr. There we shall be with *Seraphims,* and *Cherubims,*
creatures that will dazzle your eyes to look on them: there
also you shall meet with thousands, and ten thousands that
have gone before us to that place; none of them are hurtful,
but loving and holy, every one walking in the sight of God,
and standing in his presence with acceptance for ever: in a

word, there we shall see the elders with their golden crowns: Rev. 4.5
there we shall see the Holy virgins with their golden harps. Rev. 14.1, 2, 3,
There we shall see men that, by the world, were cut in 4, 5
pieces, burnt in flames, eaten of beasts, drowned in the John 12.25
seas, for the love that they bare to the Lord of the place;
all, well, and clothed with immortality, as with a garment. 2 Cor. 5.2, 3, 5

*Pli. The hearing of this is enough to ravish one's heart;
but are these things to be enjoyed? How shall we get to be
sharers thereof?*

Chr. The Lord, the Governor of the country, recorded
that in this book the substance of which is, if we be truly Isa. 55.12, John
willing to have it, he will bestow it upon us freely. 7.37, 6.37, Rev.
21.6, 22.17

*Pli. Well, my good companion, glad am I to hear of these
things, come on, let us mend our pace.*

Chr. I cannot go as fast as I would by reason of this
burden that is on my back.

Now I saw in my dream, that just as they had ended this
talk, they drew near to a very *miry slough* that was in *The Slough of*
the midst of the plain, and they being heedless, did both *Despond*
fall suddenly into the bog. The name of the slough was
Despond.[10] Here therefore they wallowed for a time,
being grievously bedaubed with dirt; and *Christian,* because
of the burden that was on his back, began to sink in the
mire.

Pli. Then said Pliable, *Ah, neighbour* Christian, *where
are you now?*

Chr. Truly, *said Christian,* I do not know.

Pli. At that *Pliable* began to be offended; and angerly
said to his fellow, *Is this the happiness you have told me
all this while of? If we have such ill speed at our first setting
out, what may we expect 'twixt this and our journey's end?
May I get out again with my life, you shall possess the It is not enough
brave country alone for me.* And with that he gave a des- to be pliable
perate struggle or two, and got out of the mire, on that side
of the slough which was next to his own house; so away he
went, and *Christian* saw him no more.

Wherefore *Christian* was left to tumble in the slough of
Despond alone; but still he endeavoured to struggle to that

Christian in trouble, seeks still to get farther from his own house side of the slough, that was from his own house, and next to the wicket gate; the which he did, but could not get out because of the burden that was upon his back: but I beheld in my dream, that a man came to him whose name was *Help,* and asked him, *what did he there?*

Chr. Sir, said *Christian,* I was bid go this way, by a man called *Evangelist,* who directed me also to yonder gate, that I might escape the wrath to come. And as I was going thither, I fell in here.

The promises   Help. *But why did you not look for the steps?*

Chr. Fear followed me so hard, that I fled the next way, and fell in.

Help lifts him out Psal. 40.2   Help. *Then,* said he, *Give me thy hand; so he gave him his hand,* and he drew him out, and set him upon sound ground, and bid him go on his way.

Then I stepped to him that plucked him out, and said, Sir, wherefore, since over this place is the way from the city of *Destruction,* to yonder *gate,* is it that *this* plat[11] is not mended, that poor travellers might go thither with more security? And he said unto me, this *miry slough,* is such a place as cannot be mended: it is the descent whither the

What makes the slough of Despond scum and filth that attends conviction for sin doth continually run, and therefore it was called the *Slough* of *Despond* for still as the sinner is awakened about his lost condition, there ariseth in his soul many fears and doubts, and discouraging apprehensions, which all of them get together, and set in this place: and this is the reason of the badness of this ground.

Isa. 35.3, 4   It is not the Pleasure of the King that this place should remain so bad; his labourers also, have by the direction of His Majesty's Surveyors, been for above this sixteen hundred years imployed about *this patch* of ground, if perhaps it might have been mended: yea, and to my knowledge, said he, *here* hath been swallowed up at least twenty thousand cart-loads; yea millions of wholesome instructions, that have at all seasons been brought from all place of the King's dominions (and they that can tell, say, they are the best materials to make good ground of the place,) if so be it might have been mended, but it is the *slough of Despond still;* and so will be, when they have done what they can.

True, there are, by the direction of the Law-giver,[12] certain good and substantial steps, placed even through the very midst of this *slough;* but at such time as this place doth much spue out its filth, as it doth against change of weather, these steps are hardly seen, or if they be, men, through the dizziness of their heads, step besides; and then they are bemired to purpose, notwithstanding the steps be there, but the ground is good when they are once got in at the gate.

The Promises of Forgiveness and Acceptance to life by Faith in Christ

1 Sam. 12.23

Now I saw in my dream, that by this time *Pliable* was got home to his house. So his Neighbours came to visit him: and some of them called him *wise man* for coming back; and some called him *Fool* for hazarding himself with *Christian;* others again did mock at his *cowardliness;* saying, *Surely since you began to venture, I would not have been so base to have given out for a few difficulties:* so *Pliable* sat sneaking among them. But at last he got more confidence, and then they all turned their tales, and began to deride poor *Christian* behind his back. And thus much concerning *Pliable.*

Pliable is gone home, and is visited by his neighbours

His entertainment by them at his return

Now as *Christian* was walking solitarily by himself, he espied one afar off come crossing over the field to meet him, and their hap was to meet *just as they were crossing the way of each other.* The gentleman's name that met him was Mr. *Worldly Wiseman,*[13] he dwelt in the town of *Carnal Policy,* a very great town, and also hard by from whence *Christian* came. This man then meeting with *Christian,* and having some inkling of him, (for *Christian's* setting forth from the City of *Destruction* was much noised abroad, not only in the town where he dwelt but also it began to be the *town talk* in some other places.) Master *Worldly Wiseman* therefore, having some guess of him, by beholding his laborious going, by observing his sighs and

Worldly Wiseman meets with Christian

groans, and the like; began thus to enter into some talk
with *Christian*.

*Talk between
Mr. Worldly
Wiseman and
Christian*

Worl. *How now, good fellow, whither away after this
burdened manner?*

Chr. A burdened manner indeed, as ever, I think, poor
creature had. And whereas you ask me, *Whither away,* I
tell you, sir, I am going to yonder wicket-gate before me;
for there, as I am informed, I shall be put in a way to be rid
of my heavy burden.

Worl. *Hast thou a wife and children?*

Chr. Yes; but I am so laden with this burden, that I
cannot take that pleasure in them as formerly; methinks,
I am *as if I had none.*

Worl. *Wilt thou hearken to me if I give thee counsel?*

Chr. If it be good I will, for I stand in need of good
counsel.

*Worldly Wise-
man's counsel to
Christian*

Worl. *I would advise thee then that thou with all speed
get thy self rid of thy burden; for thou wilt never be settled
in thy mind till then: nor canst thou enjoy the benefits of
the blessing which God hath bestowed upon thee, till then.*

Chr. That is that which I seek for, even to be rid of this
heavy burden; but get it off my self I cannot: nor is there
any man in our country that can take it off my shoulders;
therefore am I going this way, as I told you, that I may be
rid of my burden.

Worl. *Who bid you go this way to be rid of your burden?*

Chr. A man that appeared to me to be a very great and
honourable person; his name, as I remember, is Evangelist.

*Mr. Worldly
Wiseman
condemned
Evangelist's
counsel*

Worl. *I beshrew him for his counsel, there is not a more
dangerous and troublesome way in the world, than is
that unto which he hath directed thee, and that thou
shalt find, if thou wilt be ruled by his counsel; thou hast
met with something (as I perceive) already; for I see the
dirt of the* slough of Despond *is upon thee, but that* slough
*is but the beginning of the sorrows that do attend those
that go on in that way: hear me, I am older than thou,
thou art like to meet with in the way which thou goest,
wearisomeness, painfulness, hunger, perils, nakedness,*

When Christians unto carnal men give ear
out of their way they goe, and pay for't dear
for master worldly wiseman, can but shew
a saint the way to bondage and to woe.

sword, lions, dragons, darkness, and in a word death, and what not? These things are certainly true, having been confirmed by many testimonies. And should a man so carelessly cast away himself, by giving heed to a stranger!

Chr. Why, sir, this burden upon my back is more terrible to me than are all these things which you have mentioned: nay, methinks I care not what I meet with in the way, if so be I can also meet with deliverance from my burden.

The frame of the heart of a young Christian

Worl. How camest thou by the burden at first?

Chr. By reading this book in my hand.

Worldly Wiseman *does not like that man should be serious in reading the Bible*

Worl. I thought so; and it is happened unto thee as to other weak men, who meddling with things too high for them, do suddenly fall into thy distractions; which distractions do not only unman men, (as thine I perceive has done thee) but they run them upon desperate ventures, to obtain they know not what.

Chr. I know what I would obtain: it is ease for my heavy burden

Worl. But why wilt thou seek for ease this way, seeing so many dangers attend it, especially, since (hadst thou but patience to hear me) I could direct thee to the obtaining of what thou desirest, without the dangers that thou in this way wilt run thy self into: yea, and the remedy is at hand. Besides, I will add that instead of those dangers, thou shalt meet with much safety, friendship, and content.

Chr. Sir, I pray open this secret to me.

Whether Mr. Worldly prefers morality before the straight gate

Worl. Why in yonder village (the village is named Morality) *there dwells a gentleman, whose name is* Legality, *a very judicious man, (and a man of a very good name) that has skill to help men off with such burdens as thine are, from their shoulders, yea, to my knowledge, he hath done a great deal of good this way: Ay, and besides, he hath skill to cure those that are somewhat crazed in their wits with their burdens. To him, as I said, thou mayest go, and be helped presently. His house is not quite a mile from this place; and if he should not be at home himself, he hath a pretty young man to his son, whose name is* Civility *that can do it (to speak on) as well as the old gentleman himself: there, I say thou mayest be eased of thy burden, and if thou art not minded to go back to thy former habitation, as indeed I would not wish thee, thou mayest send for thy wife and children to thee to this village, where there are houses now stand empty, one of which thou mayest have at reasonable rates: provision there is also cheap and good, and that which will make thy life the more happy, is, to be sure there thou shalt live by honest neighbours, in credit and good fashion.*

Now was *Christian somewhat at a stand; but presently he concluded, if this be true which this gentleman hath said, my wisest course is to take his advice; and with that he thus farther spoke.*

Christian *snared by Mr.* Worldly Wiseman's *word*

Chr. Sir, which is my way to this honest Man's house?

Worl. *Do you see yonder high hill?*

Mount Sinai

Chr. Yes, very well.

Worl. By that hill you must go, and the first house you come at is his.

So Christian turned out of his way to go to Mr. *Legality's* house for help: but behold, when he was got now hard by the hill, it seemed so high, and also that side of it that was the next way side, did hang so much over, that *Christian* was afraid to venture further, lest the hill should fall on his head;[14] wherefore there he stood still; and wotted not what to do. Also his burden *now* seemed heavier to him than when he was in his way. There came also flashes of fire out of the hill that made *Christian* afraid that he should be burned: here therefore he sweat, and did quake for fear. And now he began to be sorry that he had taken Mr. *Worldly Wiseman's* counsel; and with that he saw *Evangelist* coming to meet him; at the sight also of whom he began to blush for shame. So *Evangelist* drew nearer and nearer, and coming up to him, he looked upon him with a severe and dreadful countenance, and thus began to reason with *Christian*.

Christian *afraid that Mount* Sinai *would fall on his head*

Exod. 19.18

Ver. 16

Heb. 12.11

Evangelist *findeth* Christian *under Mount* Sinai, *and looketh severely upon him*

Evan. What dost thou here *Christian?* said he; at which words *Christian* knew not what to answer: wherefore at present he stood speechless before him. Then said *Evangelist* farther, *Art thou not the man that I found crying without the Walls of the city of* Destruction?

How is it then that thou art so quickly turned aside, for thou art now out of the way?

Chr. I met with a Gentleman so soon as I had got over the *slough of Despond,* who persuaded me, that I might in the *village* before me, find a man that could take off my burden.

Evan. *What was he?*

Chr. He looked like a gentleman, and talked much to me, and got me at last to yield; so I came hither: but when I beheld this hill, and how it hangs over the way, I suddenly made a stand, lest it should fall on my head.

Evan. *What said that gentleman to you?*

Chr. Why, he asked me whither I was going, and I told him.

Evan. *And what said he then?*

Chr. He asked me if I had a family, and I told him: but said I, I am so loaden with the Burden that is on my back, that I cannot take pleasure in them as formerly.

Evan. *And what said he then?*

Chr. He bid me with speed get rid of my burden, and I told him 'twas ease that I sought: and, said I, I am therefore going to yonder *gate* to receive further direction how I may get to the place of deliverance. So he said that he would shew me a better way, and short, not so attended with difficulties, as the way, sir, you set me in: which way, said he, will direct you to a gentleman's house that hath skill to take off these burdens: so I believed him, and turned out of *that* way, into *this,* if haply I might soon be eased of my burden: but when I came to this place, and beheld things as they are, I stopped for fear (as I said) of danger: but now I know not what to do.

Evan. *Then* (said Evangelist) *stand still a little, that I may show thee the words of God.* So he stood trembling. *Then*

(said Evangelist) *See that ye refuse not him that speaketh;* Heb. 12.25
for if they escaped not who refused him that spake on earth, Evangelist con-
much more shall not we escape, if we turn away from him vinces Christian
that speaketh from heaven. He said moreover, *Now the* of his error
Chap. 10.38
just shall live by faith, but if any man draws back, my soul
shall have no pleasure in him. He also did thus apply them:
Thou art the man that art running into this misery, thou
hast begun to reject the counsel of the most high, and to
draw back thy foot from the way of peace, even almost to
the hazarding of thy perdition.

Then *Christian* fell down at his foot as dead, crying,
Woe is me, for I am undone: at the sight of which, *Evangelist* caught him by the right hand, saying, All manner
of sin and blasphemies shall be forgiven unto men; be
not faithless, but believing: then did *Christian* again a
little revive, and stood up trembling, as at first, before
Evangelist.

Then *Evangelist* proceeded, saying, *Give more earnest*
heed to the things that I shall tell thee of. I will now shew
thee who it was that deluded thee, and who it was also to
whom he sent thee. The man that met thee is one *Worldly* Mr. Worldly
Wiseman, and rightly is he so called; partly, because he Wiseman
described by
savoureth only the doctrine of this world (therefore he Evangelist
always goes to the town of *Morality* to church) and partly, 1 John 4.5
because he loveth that doctrine best; for it saveth him best Col. 6.12
from the cross; and because he is of this carnal temper,
therefore he seeketh to pervert my ways, though right. Now Evangelist dis-
there are three things in this man's counsel that thou must covers the deceit
of Mr. Worldly
utterly abhor. Wiseman

1. His turning thee out of the way.

2. His labouring to render the cross odious to thee.

3. And his setting thy feet in that way that leadeth unto
the administration of death.

First, thou must abhor his turning thee out of the way;
yea, and thine own consenting thereto; because this is to
reject the counsel of God for the sake of the counsel of a
Worldly Wiseman. The Lord says, strive to enter in at the Luke 13.24
strait gate, the gate to which I send thee, *for strait is the* Matthew 7.13, 14

gate that leadeth unto life, and few there be that find it. From this little wicket-gate, and from the way thereto, hath this wicked man turned thee, to the bringing of thee almost to destruction; hate therefore his turning thee out of the way, and abhor thy self for hearkening to him.

Secondly, thou must abhor his labouring to render the cross odious unto thee; for thou art to *prefer it before the treasures in Egypt:* besides, the King of Glory hath told thee, that he that will save his life shall lose it: and *he that comes after him, and hates not his father and mother, and wife, and children, and brethren, and sisters, yea, and his own life also, he cannot be my disciple.* I say therefore, for man to labour to persuade thee, that that shall be thy death, without which, the truth hath said, thou canst not have eternal life: this doctrine thou must abhor.

Thirdly, thou must hate his setting of thy feet in the way that leadeth to the ministration of death. And for this, thou must consider to whom he sent thee, and also how unable that person was to deliver thee from thy burden.

He to whom thou wast sent for ease, being by name *Legality,* is the son of the Bond-woman which now is, and is in bondage with her children, and which is in a mystery this Mount *Sinai,* which thou hast feared will fall on thy head. Now if she with her children are in bondage, how canst thou expect by them to be made free? This *Legality* therefore is not able to set thee free from thy burden. No man was as yet ever rid of his burden to him, no, nor ever is like to be: ye cannot be justified by the works of the law; for by the deeds of the law no man living can be rid of his burden: therefore Mr. *Worldly Wiseman* is an alien, and Mr. *Legality* is a cheat: and for his son *Civility,* notwithstanding his *simpering* looks, he is but an hypocrite, and can not help thee. Believe me, there is nothing in all this noise, that thou hast heard of this sottish men, but a design to beguile thee of thy salvation, by turning thee from the way in which I had set thee. After this *Evangelist* called aloud to the heavens for confirmation of what he had said; and with that there came words and fire out of the mountain

Marginal notes:

Hebrews 11.25, 26

Mark 8.34, John 13.25, Mat. 10.39
Luke 14.16

Gal. 4.21, 22, 23, 24, 25, 26, 27

The Bond-woman

under which poor Christian stood, that made the hair of his flesh stand up. The words were thus pronounced, *As many as are of the works of the law, are under the curse; for it is written, cursed is every one that continueth not in all things which are written in the book of the law to do them.* Gal. 3.10

Now Christian looked for nothing but death, and began to cry out lamentably: even cursing the time in which he met with Mr. *Worldly Wiseman;* still calling himself a thousand fools for hearkening to his counsel: he also was greatly ashamed to think that this gentleman's arguments, flowing only from the flesh, should have the prevalency with him as to cause him to forsake the right way. This done, he applied himself again to *Evangelist* in words and sense as follows.

Chr. Sir, what think you? Is there hopes? May I now go back and go up to the *wicket-gate,* shall I not be abandoned for this, and sent back from thence ashamed? I am sorry I have hearkened to this man's counsel, but may my sins be forgiven? *Christian enquired if he may yet be happy*

Evan. Then said *Evangelist* to him, Thy sin is very great, for by it thou hast committed two evils; thou hast forsaken the way that is good, to tread in forbidden paths; yet will the man at the gate receive thee, for he has *good will* for men; only, said he, take heed that thou turn not aside again, lest thou perish from the way, when his wrath is kindled but a little. Then did *Christian* address himself to go back, and *Evangelist,* and he had kist him, gave him one smile, and bid him God speed: so he went on with haste, neither spake he to any man by the way; nor if any asked him, would he vouchsafe them an answer. He went like one that was all the while treading on forbidden ground, and could by no means think himself safe, till again he was got into the way which he left to follow Mr. *Worldly Wiseman's* Counsel: so in process of time *Christian* got up to the gate. Now over the gate there was written, *Knock and it shall be opened to you.* He knocked therefore more than once or twice, saying, *Evangelist comforts him* *Psal.* 2 last *Mat.* 7.8

He that will enter in must first without
stand knocking at the gate nor need he doubt
that is a knocker but to enter in
for God can love him, and forgive his sin

> *May I now enter here? Will be within*
> *Open to sorry me, though I have been*
> *An undeserving rebel? Then shall I*
> *Not fail to sing his lasting praise on high.*

At last there came a grave person to the gate, named *Good-will,* who asked *who was there? And whence he came? And what he would have?*

Chr. Here is a poor burdened sinner, I come from the city of *destruction,* but am going to Mount *Zion,* that I may be delivered from the wrath to come; I would therefore, sir, since I am informed that by this gate is the way thither, know if you are *willing* to let me in.

Good-will. I am willing with all my heart, said he; and with that he opened the gate.[15]

So when *Christian* was stepping in, the other gave him a pull: then said *Christian,* What means that? The other told him, A little distance from this gate, there is erected a strong castle, of which *Beelzebub* is the captain; from thence both he, and them that are with him, shoot arrows at those that come up to this gate: if happily they may die before they can enter in. Then said *Christian,* I rejoice and tremble. So when he was got in, the man of the gate asked him, who directed him thither?

Chr. Evangelist bid me come hither and knock (as I did;) and he said, that you, sir, would tell me what I must do.

Good-will. An open door is set before thee, and no man can shut it.

Chr. Now I begin to reap the benefits of my hazards.

Good-will. But how is it that you came alone?

Chr. Because none of my neighbours saw their danger as I saw mine.

Good-will. Did any of them know of your coming?

Chr. Yes, my wife and children saw me at the first, and called after me to turn again: also some of my neighbours stood crying, and calling after me to return; but I put my fingers in my ears, and so came on my way.

The gate will be opened to broken hearted sinners

Satan envies those that enter the straight gate

Christian entered the gate with joy and trembling

Talk between Goodwill and Christian

Good-will. *But did none of them follow you to persuade you to go back?*

Chr. Yes, both *Obstinate* and *Pliable*: but when they saw that they could not prevail, *Obstinate* went railing back: but *Pliable* came with me a little way.

Good-will. *But why did he not come through?*

Chr. We indeed came both together, until we came at the *slough* of *Despond,* into the which we also suddenly fell. And then was my neighbour *Pliable* discouraged, and would not adventure farther. Wherefore, getting out again, on *that side* next to his own house, he told me, I should possess the brave country alone for him: so he went *his* way, and I came *mine.* He after *Obstinate,* and I to this gate.

A man may have company when he sets out for heaven, and yet go thither alone

Good-will. Then said *Good-will,* Alas poor man, is the celestial glory of so small esteem with him, that he counteth it not worth running the hazard of a few difficulties to obtain it?

Chr. Truly, said *Christian,* I have said the truth of *Pliable,* and if I should also say all the truth of my self, it will appear there is no betterment 'twixt him and my self. 'Tis true, he went back to his own house, but I also turned aside to go into the way of death, being persuaded thereto by the carnal arguments of one Mr. *Worldly-wiseman.*

Christian accuseth himself before the man at the gate

Good-will. Oh, did he light upon you? What, he would have you a sought for ease at the hands of Mr. *Legality;* they are both of them a very cheat: but did you take his counsel?

Chr. Yes, as far as I durst, I went to find out Mr. *Legality,* until I thought that the mountain that stands by the house, would have fallen on my head, wherefore there I was forced to stop.

Good-will. That mountain has been the death of many, and will be the death of many more: 'tis well you escaped being by it dash'd in pieces.

Chr. Why, truly, I do not know what had become of me there, had not *Evangelist* happily met me again as I was musing in the midst of my *dumps:* but 'twas God's mercy that he came to me again, for else I had never come hither. But now I am come, such a one as I am, more fit indeed for death, by that mountain, than thus to stand talking with my Lord: but oh! What a favour is this to me, that yet I am admitted entrance here.

Good-will. We make no objections against any, notwithstanding all that they have one before they come hither, *they in no wise are cast out;* and therefore, good *Christian,* come a little way with me, and I will teach thee about the way thou must go. Look before thee; dost thou see this narrow way? THAT is the way thou must go. It was cast up by the patriarchs, prophets, Christ, and his apostles, and it is as straight as a *rule* can make it: this is the way thou must go.

Chr. But said *Christian, is there no turnings nor windings, by which a stranger may lose his way?*

Good-will. Yes, there are many ways Butt down upon[16] this: and they are crooked and wide: but *thus* thou may'st distinguish the right from the wrong, *the* right only being straight and narrow.

Then I saw in my dream, that *Christian* asked him further, if he could not help him off with his burden that was upon his back; for as yet he had not got rid thereof, nor could he by any means get it off without help.

He told him, as to thy burden be content to bear it, until thou comest to the *place of* deliverance; for there it will fall from thy back of it self.

Then *Christian* began to gird up his loins, and to address himself to his journey. So the other told him, that by that he was got some distance from the gate, he would come at the house of the Interpreter, at whose door he should knock, and he would shew him excellent things. Then *Christian* took his leave of his friend, and he again bid him God-speed.

Then he went on, till he came at the house of the Interpreter,[17] where he *knocked* over and over; at last one came to the door, and asked, *Who was there?*

Chr. Sir, here is a traveller, who was bid by an

Christian is comforted again

John 6.37

Christian directed yet on his way

Christian afraid of losing his way

Matt. 7.14

Christian weary of his burthen

There is no deliverance from the guilt and burden of sin but by the death and blood of Christ

Christian comes to the House of the Interpreter

acquaintance of the good man of this house, to call here for my profit; I would therefore speak with the Master of the House: so he called for the master of the house; who after a little while came to *Christian,* and asked him what he would have.

Chr. Sir, said *Christian,* I am a man that am come from the city of *Destruction,* and am going to the Mount *Zion,* and I was told by the man that stands at the gate at the head of this way, that if I called you here, you would shew me excellent things, such as would be an help to me in my journey.

He is entertained *Interp.* Then said the *Interpreter,* Come in, I will shew thee that which will be profitable to thee. So he commanded
Illumination his man to light the candle, and bid *Christian* follow him, so he had him into a private room, and bid his man open a
Christian sees a brave picture door; the which when he had done, *Christian* saw the picture of a very grave person[18] hung up against the wall,
The fashion of the picture and this was the fashion of it, *It had eyes lifted up to heaven, the best of books in his hand, the law of truth was written upon its lips, the world was behind his back; it stood as if it pleaded with men, and a crown of gold did hang over its head.*

Chr. Then said Christian, *What meaneth this?*

Inter. The man whose picture this is, is one of a thousand;
1 Cor. 4.15 he can beget children, travail in birth with children, and
Gal. 4.19 nurse them himself when they are born. And whereas thou seest him with his eyes lift up to heaven, the best of books in his hand, and the law of truth writ on his lips; it is to shew thee, that his work is to know and unfold dark things
The meaning of the picture to sinners; even as also thou seest him stand as if he pleaded with men; and whereas thou see'st the world as cast behind him, and that a crown hangs over his head; that is to shew thee, that slighting and despising the things that are present, for the love that he hath to his master's service, he is sure in the world that comes next, to have glory for his reward. Now, said the *Interpreter,* I have shewed thee *this* picture
Why he shewed him the picture first first, because the man whose picture this is, is the only man, whom the Lord of the place whither thou art going, hath authorized to be thy guide in all difficult places thou mayest

meet with in the way: wherefore take good heed to what I have showed thee, and bear well in mind what thou hast seen; lest in thy journey thou meet with some that pretend to lead thee right, but their way goes down to death.

Then he took him by the hand, and led him into a very large *parlour* that was full of dust, because never swept; the which, after he had reviewed a little while, the *Interpreter* called for a man to *sweep:* now when he began to sweep, the dust began so abundantly to fly about, that *Christian* had almost therewith been choked. Then said the *Interpreter* to a *Damsel* that stood by, bring hither water, and sprinkle the room; the which when she had done, it was swept, and cleansed with Pleasure.

Chr. *Then said* Christian, *What means this?*

Int. The *Interpreter* answered, This *parlour* is the heart of a man that was never sanctified by the sweet grace of the gospel: the *dust,* is his original sin, and inward corruptions that have defiled the whole man. He that began to sweep at first is the law; but she that brought water, and did sprinkle it, is the gospel. Now, whereas thou sawest that so soon as the first began to sweep, the dust did so fly about, that the room by him could not be cleansed, but that thou wast almost choked therewith: this is to show thee, that the law, instead of cleansing the heart (by its working) from sin, doth revive, put strength into, and increase it in the soul, even as it doth discover and forbid it, for it doth not give power to subdue. Romans 7.9 / 1 Cor. 15.56 / Rom. 5.20

Again, as thou sawest the *damsel* sprinkle the room with water, upon which it was cleansed with pleasure; this is to shew thee, that when the gospel comes in the sweet and precious influences thereof to the heart, then I say, even as thou sawest the damsel lay the dust by sprinkling the floor with water, so is sin vanquished and subdued, and the soul made clean, through the faith of it, and consequently fit for the King of Glory to inhabit.[19] John 15.3, Eph. / 5.16, Acts 15.9, / Rom. 16.25, 26, / John 15.13

I saw moreover in my dream; that the *Interpreter* took him by the hand, and had him in a little room, where sat two little children, each one in his chair. The name of the *He shewed him Passion and Patience* eldest was *Passion*, and the name of the other *Patience*. *Passion* seemed to be much discontented, but *Patience* was very quiet. Then *Christian* asked, What is the reason of the discontent of *Passion*? The *Interpreter* answered, the Governor of them would have him stay for his best things, till the beginning of the next year; but he will have all now: but *Patience* is willing to wait.

Patience is for waiting
Passion hath his desire

Then I saw that one came to *Passion*, and brought him a bag of treasure, and poured it down at his feet; the which he took up and rejoyced therein, and laughed *Patience* to scorn: but I beheld but a while, and he had lavished all away, and had nothing left him but rags.

And quickly lavishes all away

Chr. *Then said* Christian *to the Interpreter, Expound this matter more fully to me.*

Inter. So, he said, these two lads are figures, *Passion*, of the men of this world; and *Patience*, of the men of that which is to come: for as here thou see'st, *Passion will have all now*, this year; that is to say, in this world; so are the men of this world: they must have all their good things now, they cannot stay till next year, that is, until the next world, for their portion of good. That proverb, *a bird in the hand is worth two in the bush*, is of more authority with them, than are all the divine testimonies of the good of the world to come. But as thou sawest, that he had quickly lavished all away, and had presently left him with nothing but rags; so will it be with all such men at the end of this world.

The worldly man for a bird in the hand

Chr. *Then said* Christian; *Now I see that* Patience *has the best wisdom, and that upon many accounts. 1. Because he stays for the best things. 2. And also because he will have the glory of his, when the other had nothing but rags.*

Patience had the best wisdom

Int. Nay, you may add another, to wit, the glory of the *next* world will never wear out; but these are suddenly gone. Therefore *Passion* had not so much reason to laugh at *Patience*, because he had good things first, as *Patience* will have to laugh at *Passion*, because he had his best things last; for *first* must give place to *last*, because *last* must have his time to come: but *last* gives place to nothing; for there is not another to succeed: he therefore that hath his portion

Things that are first must give place, but things that are last are lasting

first, must needs have a time to spend it, but he that has his portion *last,* must have it lastingly; therefore it is said of *Dives, in thy life-time thou receivest thy good things; and likewise* Lazarus *evil things, but now he is comforted, and thou art tormented.*

Luke 16. Dives had his good things first

Chr. Then I perceive, 'tis not best to covet things that are now, *but to wait for things to* come.

Int. You say truth, *for the things that are seen, are* temporal; *but the things that are not seen, are* eternal: but tho' this be so, yet since things present, and our fleshly appetite, *are such near neighbours one to another;* and again, because things to come, and carnal sense are such strangers one to another: therefore it is that the first of these do suddenly fall into *amity,* and that *distance* is so continually between the second.

2 Cor. 4.18. The first things are but temporal

Then I saw in my dream, that the *Interpreter* took *Christian* by the hand, and led him into a place where was a fire, burning against a wall, and one standing by it, always casting much water upon it to quench it, yet did the fire burn higher and hotter.

Then said Christian, *What means this?*

The *Interpreter* answered, This fire is the work of grace that is wrought in the heart; he that casts water upon it, to extinguish and put it out, is the *Devil:* but in that thou seest the fire notwithstanding burn higher and hotter, thou shalt also see the reason of that: so he had him about to the backside of the wall, where he saw a man with a vessel of oil in his hand, of the which he did also continually cast (but secretly) into the fire.

Then said Christian, *What means this?*

The *Interpreter* answered, This is *Christ,* who continually with the oil of his grace, maintains the work already begun in the heart; by the means of which, notwithstanding what the Devil can do, the souls of his people prove gracious still. And in that thou sawest, that the man stood behind the wall to maintain the fire; this is to teach thee, that it is hard for the tempted to see how this work of grace is maintained in the soul.

I saw also, that the *Interpreter* took him again by the hand, and led him into a pleasant place, where was builded a stately palace, beautiful to behold; at the sight of which, *Christian* was greatly delighted; he saw also upon the top thereof, certain persons walking, who were clothed all in gold.

Then said *Christian*, May we go in thither?

Then the *Interpreter* took him, and led him up toward the door of the palace; and behold, at the door stood a great company of men, as desirous to go in, but durst not. There also sat a man, at a little distance from the door, at a table side, with a book, and his ink-horn before him, to take the name of him that should enter therein: he saw also, that in the door-way stood many men in armour to keep it, being resolved to do to the men that would enter what hurt and mischief they could. Now was *Christian* somewhat in a maze: at last, when every man started back for fear of the armed men, *Christian* saw a man of a very stout counten-
The valiant man ance come up to the man that sat there to write, saying, *set down my name, sir:* the which when he had done, he saw the man draw his sword, and put an helmet on his head, and rush toward the door upon the armed men, who laid upon him with deadly force: but the man, not at all discour-aged, fell to cutting and hacking most fiercely, so after
Acts 14.23 he had received and given many wounds to those that attempted to keep him out, he cuts his way through them all, and pressed forward into the palace: at which there was a pleasant voice heard from those that were within, even of those that walked upon the top of the palace, saying,

> *Come in, come in;*
> *Eternal Glory thou shalt win.*

So he went in, and was clothed with such garments as they. Then *Christian* smiled, and said, I think verily I know the meaning of this.

Now, said *Christian*, let me go hence. Nay stay (said the *Interpreter*) till I have showed thee a little more, and after that thou shalt go on thy way. So he took him by the hand again, and led him into a very dark room, where there sat a man in an iron *Cage*.[20]

Despair *like an iron cage*

Now the man, to look on, seemed very sad: he sat with his eyes looking down to the ground, his hands folded together; and he sighed as if he would break his heart. Then said *Christian, What means this?* At which the *Interpreter* bid him talk with the man.

Chr. Then said *Christian* to the man, *What art thou?* The man answered, *I am what I was not once.*

Chr. *What wast thou once?*

Man. The *man* said, I was once a fair and flourishing professor, both in mine own eyes, and also in the eyes of others: I once was, as I thought, fair for the Celestial City, and had then even joy at the thoughts that I should get thither.

Luke 8.18

Chr. *Well, but what art thou now?*

Man. I am *now* a man of *despair,* and am shut up in *it,* as in *this* iron cage. I cannot get out; O *now* I cannot.

Chr. *But how camest thou in this condition?*

Man. I left off to watch, and be sober, I laid the reins upon the neck of my lusts; I sinned against the light of the Word, and the goodness of God: I have grieved the Spirit, and he is gone; I tempted the Devil, and he is come to me; I have provoked God to anger, and he has left me; I have so hardened my heart, that I *cannot* repent.

Then said *Christian* to the *Interpreter,* But is there no hopes for such a man as this? Ask him, said the *Interpreter.*

Chr. Then said *Christian, Is there no hope, but you must be kept in the iron cage of despair?*

Man. No, none at all.

Chr. *Why? The son of the blessed is very pitiful.*

Man. I have crucified him to my self afresh, I have despised his righteousness, I have counted his blood an unholy thing, I have done despite to the spirit of grace: therefore I have shut my self out of all the promises, and there now remains to me nothing but threatenings, dreadful threatenings, faithful threatenings, of certain judgement

Heb. 6.6
Luke 19.14
Heb. 10.28, 29

and fiery indignation, which shall devour me as an adversary.

Chr. *For what did you bring your self into this condition?*

Man. For the lusts, pleasures, and profits of this world; in the enjoyment of which, I did then promise my self much delight: but now every one of those things also bite me, and gnaw me like a burning worm.

Chr. *But canst thou not now repent and turn?*

Man. God hath denied me repentance; his word gives me no encouragement to believe, yea himself hath shut me up in this iron cage: nor can all the men in the world let me out. O eternity; eternity! How shall I grapple with the misery that I must meet with in eternity?

Int. Then said the *Interpreter* to *Christian*, Let this man's misery be remembered by thee, and be an everlasting caution to thee.

Chr. Well, said *Christian*, this is fearful; God help me to watch and be sober; and to pray, that I may shun the cause of this man's misery. Sir, is it not time for me to go on my way now?

Int. Tarry till I shall show thee one thing more, and then thou shalt go on thy way.

So he took *Christian* by the hand again, and led him into a chamber, where there was one rising out of bed; and as he put on his raiment he shook and trembled. Then said *Christian*, Why doth this man thus tremble? The *Interpreter* then bid him tell to *Christian* the reason of his so doing: so he began, and said, This night as I was in my sleep I dreamed, and behold the heavens grew exceeding black; also it thundered and lightened in most fearful wise, that it put me into an agony. So I looked up in my dream, and saw the clouds rack at an unusual rate, upon which I heard a great sound of a trumpet, and saw also a man sit upon a cloud with the thousands of heaven; they were all in a flaming fire, also the heavens were on a burning flame. I heard then a voice, saying, *Arise ye dead, and come to judgment;* and with that the rocks rent, the graves opened,

1 Cor. 15, 1 Thess. 4, Jude 15, John 5.28, 2 Thess. 1.8, Rev. 20.11, 12, 13, 14, Isa. 26.21, Mich. 7.16, 17, Psal. 5.1, 2, 3

and the dead that were therein came forth; some of them
were exceeding glad, and looked upward; and some sought
to hide themselves under the mountains: then I saw the
man that sate upon the cloud, open the book, and bid the
world draw near. Yet there was, by reason of a fierce flame   Malachi 3.2, 3,
that issued out and came before him, a convenient distance   Dan. 7.9, 10
betwixt him and them, as betwixt the judge and the prisoners at the bar. I heard it also proclaimed to them that
attended on the man that sat on the cloud, *gather together*   Mark 3.13,
the tares, the chaff and stubble, and cast them into the   ch. 13.30, Mal.
burning lake; and with that the bottomless pit opened, just   4.1
whereabout I stood: out of the mouth of which there came
in an abundant manner smoke, and coals of fire, with
hideous noises. It was also said to the same persons, *gather*   Luke 3.17
my wheat into the garner. And with that I saw many catch'd
up and carried away into the clouds, but I was left behind.   1 Thess. 4.16, 17
I also sought to hide my self, but I could not, for the man
that sat upon the cloud still kept his eye upon me: my sins   Rom. 2.14, 15
also came in my mind, and my conscience did accuse me
on every side. Upon this I awaked from my sleep.

Chr. *But what was it that made you so afraid of this
sight?*

Man. Why, I thought that the day of judgment was come,
and that I was not ready for it: but this frighted me most,
that the angels gathered up several, and left me behind; also
the pit of Hell opened her mouth just where I stood: my
conscience too afflicted me; and (as I thought) the judge
had always his eye upon me, shewing indignation in his
countenance.

Then said the *Interpreter* to *Christian, Hast thou considered all these things?*

Chr. Yes, and they put me in hope and fear.

Int. Well, keep all things so in thy mind, that they
may be as a *goad* in thy sides, to prick thee forward in
the way thou must go. Then *Christian* began to gird up
his loins, and to address himself to his journey. Then said
the *Interpreter,* the Comforter be always with thee,

Shall they who wrong begin yet rightly end,
Shall they at all have fast for their friend,
No no in head-strong maner they set out
And headlong will they fall at last no doubt

good *Christian,* to guide thee in the way that leads to the City.

So *Christian* went on his way, saying

> *Here I have seen things rare and profitable,*
> *Things pleasant, dreadful, things to make me stable*
> *In what I have began to take in hand:*
> *Then let me think on them, and understand*
> *Wherefore they shew'd me were, and let me be*
> *Thankful, O good Interpreter, to thee.*

Now I saw in my dream, that the highway up which *Christian* was to go, was fenced on either side with a wall, and that wall was called *Salvation.*[21] Up this way therefore did burdened *Christian* run, but not without great difficulty, because of the load on his back.

Isa. 26.1

He ran this till he came at a place somewhat ascending; and upon that place stood a *Cross,* and a little below in the bottom, a sepulchre.[22] So I saw in my dream, that just as *Christian* came up with the *Cross,* his burden loosed from off his shoulders, and fell from off his back, and began to tumble; and so continued to do, till it came to the mouth of the sepulchre, where it fell in, and I saw it no more.

Then was *Christian* glad and lightsome, and said with a merry heart, *He hath given me rest, by his sorrow; and life, by his death.* Then he stood still a while, to look and wonder; for it was very surprising to him, that the sight of the Cross should thus ease him of his burden. He looked therefore, and looked again, even till the springs that were in his head sent the waters down his cheeks. Now as he stood looking and weeping, behold three shining ones[23] came to him, and saluted him, with *Peace be to thee;* so the first said to him, *Thy sins be forgiven thee;* the second *stripped him of his Rags,* and clothed him with change of Raiment. The third also *set a mark in his forehead,* and gave him a Roll, with a seal upon it, which he bid him look on as he ran, and that he should give it in at the Celestial

When God releases us of our guilt and burden, we are as those that leap for joy

Zech. 12.10

Mark 2.2

Zech. 3.4

Eph. 1.8, 13

Who's this. the pilgrim. how: tis veri true,
Old things are past away; als becom new,
Strange: hees another man vpon mi word,
Theij be fine fethers that make a fine bird

Gate: so they went their way. Then *Christian* gave three leaps for joy, and went on singing,

> *Thus far I did come loaden with my sin,*
> *Nor could ought ease the grief that I was in,*
> *Till I came hither: what a place is this!*
> *Must here be the beginning of my bliss?*
> *Must here the burden fall from off my back?*
> *Must here the strings that bound it to me crack?*
> *Bless'd Cross! Bless'd sepulchre! Bless'd rather be*
> *The man that there was put to shame for me.*

A Christian can sing tho' alone when God doth give him the joy of his heart

I saw then in my dream that he went on *thus*, even until he came at a bottom, where he saw, a little out of the way, three men fast asleep, with fetters upon their heels. The name of the one was *Simple*, another *Sloth*, and the third *Presumption*.

Simple, Sloth, and Presumption

Christian then seeing them lie in this case, went to them, if peradventure he might awake them. And cried, You are like them that sleep on the top of a mast, for the dead sea is under you, a gulf that hath no bottom: awake therefore, and come away, *be willing also*, and I will help you off with your irons. He also told them, If he that goeth about like *a roaring lion*, comes by, you will certainly become a prey to his teeth. With that they look'd upon him, and began to reply in this sort: *Simple* said, *I see no danger*, *Sloth* said, *Every fat must stand upon his own bottom.*[24] And so they lay down to sleep again, and *Christian* went on his way.

Prov. 23.34

1 Peter 5.8

There is no persuasion will do, if God openeth not the eyes

Yet was he troubled to think, that men in that danger should so little esteem the kindness of him that so freely offered to help them, both by awakening of them, counselling of them, and proffering to help them off with their irons. And as he was troubled thereabout, he espied two men come tumbling over the wall, on the left hand of the narrow way; and they made up apace to him. The name of the one was *Formalist*, and the name of the other *Hypocrisy*.[25] So as I said, they drew up unto him, who thus entered with them into discourse.

Christian talked with them

Chr. *Gentlemen, whence came you, and whither go you?*

For. and *Hyp.* We were born in the land of *Vain-Glory,* and are going for praise to Mount *Sion.*

Chr. *Why came you not in at the gate which standeth at the beginning of this way? Know you not that it is written,*

They that come into the way, but not by the door, think that they can say something in vindication of their own practice

that he that cometh not in by the door, but climbeth up some other way, the same is a thief and a robber.

Form. and *Hyp.* They said, that to go to the gate for entrance, was by all their country-men counted too far about, and that therefore their usual way was to make a short cut of it, and to climb over the wall as they had done.

Chr. *But will it not be counted a trespass against the Lord of the City whither we are bound, thus to violate his revealed will?*

Gal. 1.16

Form. and *Hyp.* They told him, That as for that, he needed not trouble his head thereabout: for what they did they had custom for, and could produce (if need were) testimony that would witness it, for more than a thousand years.

Chr. But, *said* Christian, *will it stand a trial at law?*

Form. and *Hyp.* They told him that *custom,* it being of so long a standing as above a thousand years, would doubtless now be admitted as a thing legal, by an impartial judge. And besides, say they, if we get into the way, what's the matter which way we get in? If we are in we are in: thou art but in the way, who as we perceive, came in at the gate; and we are also in the way that came tumbling over the wall; wherein now is thy condition better than ours?

Chr. I walk by the *rule* of my master, you walk by the rude working of your fancies. You are counted thieves already, by the Lord of the way, therefore I doubt you will not be found true men at the end of the way. You come in by your selves, without his direction, and shall go out by your selves, without his mercy.

To this they made him but little answer; only they bid him look to himself. Then I saw that they went on; every man in his way, without much conference one with another;

save that these men told *Christian,* That, as to *Laws* and *Ordinances,* they doubted not but they should as conscientiously do them as he. Therefore, said they, We see not wherein thou differest from us, but by the *coat* that is on thy back, which was as we tro, given thee by some of thy neighbours, to hide the shame of thy nakedness.

Chr. By Laws and Ordinances you will not be saved, since you came not in by the door. And as for this *coat* that is on my back, it was given me by the Lord of the place whither I go; and that, as you say, to cover my nakedness with. And I take it as a token of kindness to me, for I had nothing but rags before; and besides, thus I comfort my self as I go; surely, think I, when I come to the gate of the City, the Lord thereof will know me for good, since I have his *coat* on my back! A *coat* that he gave me freely in the day that he stripped me of my rags. I have moreover a mark in my forehead, of which perhaps you have taken no notice, which one of my Lord's most intimate associates fixed there in the day that my burden fell off my shoulders. I will tell you moreover, that I had then given me a roll sealed, to comfort me by reading, as I go on the way; I was also bid to give it in at the Celestial Gate, in token of my certain going in after it; all which things I doubt you want, and want them because you came not in at the gate.

Christian *has got his Lord's coat on his back and is comforted therewith, he is comforted also with his mark and his roll*

To these things they gave him no answer, only they looked upon each other, and *laughed.* Then I saw that they went on all, save that *Christian* kept before, who had no more talk but with himself, and that sometimes sighingly, and sometimes comfortably: also he would be often reading in the roll, that one of the shining ones gave him, by which he was refreshed.

Christian *has to talk with himself*

I beheld then, that they all went on till they came to the foot of the Hill *Difficulty,* at the bottom of which was a spring. There was also in the same place two other ways, besides that which came straight from the gate; one turned to the left hand, and the other to the right, at the bottom of the hill: but the narrow way lay right up the hill (and the name of the going up the side of the hill, is called *Difficult*);

He comes to the Hill *Difficulty*

Isa. 49.10 Christian went now to the Spring, and drank thereof to
refresh himself, and then began to go up the hill, saying,

> The hill, though high, I covet to ascend,
> The difficulty will not me offend.
> For I perceive the way to life lies here;
> Come, pluck up, heart, let's neither faint nor fear.
> Better, tho' difficult, the right way to go,
> Than wrong, though easy, where the end is woe.

The other two also came to the foot of the hill; but when
they saw that the hill was steep and high, and that there
was two other ways to go; and supposing also that these
two ways might meet again with that up which *Christian*
went, on the other side of the hill: therefore they were
resolved to go in those ways, (now the name of one of those
ways was *Danger*, and the name of the other *Destruction*.)
The *Danger* of So the one took the way which is called *Danger*, which did
turning out of lead him into a great wood, and the other took him directly
the way up the way to *destruction*, which led him into a wide field,
full of dark mountains, where he stumbled and fell, and
rose no more.

I looked then after *Christian*, to see him go up the hill,
where I perceived he fell from running to going, and from
going to clambering upon his hands and knees, because of
the steepness of the place. Now about the mid-way to the
A word of grace top of the hill, was a pleasant *arbour*, made by the Lord
of the hill, for the refreshing of weary travellers. Thither
therefore *Christian* got, where also he sat down to rest him.
Then he pull'd his roll out of his bosom, and read therein
to his comfort; he also now began afresh to take a review
of the coat or garment that was given him as he stood by
the cross. Thus pleasing himself a while, he at last fell into
a slumber, and thence into a fast sleep, which detained him
He that sleeps is in that place until it was almost night; and in his sleep his
a loser roll fell out of his hand. Now as he was sleeping, there
Prov. 6.6 came one to him and awaked him, saying, *Go to the ant
thou sluggard, consider her ways, and be wise:* and with

Difficult is behinde, fear is before
Tho' liees goot on the hill the lions roer
A christian man is never long at eas
When one fright's gon another doth him siez

that *Christian* suddenly started up, and sped him on his way, and went apace till he came to the top of the hill.

Now when he was got up to the top of the hill, there came two men running to meet him amain; the name of the one was *Timorous,* and the other *Mistrust:* to whom *Christian* said, Sirs, what's the matter you run the wrong way? *Timorous* answered, That they were going to the city of *Zion,* and had got up that *Difficult* place; but, said he, the further we go, the more danger we meet with, wherefore we turned, and are going back again.

Christian *meets with* Mistrust *and* Timorous

Yes, said *Mistrust,* for just before us lies a couple of lions in the way (whether sleeping or waking we know not) and we could not think, if we came within reach but they would presently pull us in pieces.

Chr. *Then said* Christian, *you make me afraid, but whither shall I fly to be safe? If I go back to mine own country, that is prepared for fire and brimstone, and I shall certainly perish there. If I can go to the Celestial City, I am sure to be in safety there, I must venture; to go back is nothing but death, to go forward is fear of death, and life everlasting beyond it. I will yet go forward. So* Mistrust *and* Timorous *ran down the hill, and* Christian *went on his way. But thinking again of what he heard from the men, he felt in his bosom for his roll, that he might read therein and be comforted; but he felt and found it not. Then was* Christian *in great distress, and knew not what to do, for he wanted that which used to relieve him; and that which should have been his pass into the Celestial City. Here therefore he began to be much perplexed, and knew not what to do; at last he bethought himself that he had slept in the* Arbour *that is on the side of the hill; and falling down upon his knees, he asked God forgiveness for that foolish fact, and then went back to look for his roll. But all the way he went back, who can sufficiently set forth the sorrow of* Christian's *heart? Sometimes he sighed, sometimes he wept, and oftentimes he chid himself, for being so foolish to fall asleep in that place which was erected only for a little refreshment for his weariness. Thus therefore he*

Christian *missed his roll wherein he used to take comfort*

He is perplexed for his roll

went back, carefully looking on this side, and on that, all
the way as he went, if happily he might find the roll, that
had been his comfort so many times in his journey. He
went thus till he came again within sight of the Arbour
where he sat and slept; but that sight renewed his sorrow
the more, by bringing again, even afresh, his evil of sleeping
unto his mind. Thus therefore he now went on bewailing
his sinful sleep, saying, O wretched man that I am, *that I*
should sleep in the day time, that I should sleep in the midst
of difficulty! that I should so indulge the flesh as to use that
rest for ease to my flesh, which the Lord of the Hill hath
erected only for the relief of the spirits of pilgrims! How
many steps have I took in vain! (Thus it happened to Israel
for their sin, they were sent back again by the way of the
Red Sea) and I am made to tread those steps with sorrow,
which I might have trod with delight, had it not been for
this sinful sleep. How far might I have been on my way by
this time! I am made to tread those steps thrice over, which
I needed not to have trod but once: yea now also I am like
to be benighted, for the day is almost spent, o that I had
not slept! Now by this time he was come to the Arbour
again, where for a while he sat down and wept; but at last
(as Christian *would have it) looking sorrowfully down*
under the settle, there he espied his roll; the which he with
trembling and haste catch'd up and put into his bosom; but
who can tell how joyful this man was, when he had gotten
his roll again? For this roll was the assurance of his life,
and acceptance at the desired haven. Therefore he laid it
up in his bosom, gave thanks to God for directing his eye
to the place where it lay, and with joy and tears betook
himself again to his journey. But oh, how nimbly did he go
up the rest of the hill! Yet before he got up, the sun went
down upon Christian; *and this made him again recall the*
vanity of his sleeping to his remembrance; and thus he
again began to condole with himself; O thou sinful sleep!
How for thy sake am I like to be benighted in my journey!
I must walk without the sun, darkness must cover the path
of my feet, and I must hear the noise of the doleful creatures,

Christian
bewails his fool-
ish sleeping,
Rev.2.2,
2 Thess. 5. 7, 8

Christian *findeth*
his roll where he
lost it

because of my sinful sleep! *Now also he remembered the story that* Mistrust *and* Timorous *told him of, how they were frighted with the sight of the lions. Then said* Christian *to himself again, These beasts range in the night for their prey, and if they should meet with me in the dark, how should I shift them? How should I escape being by them torn in pieces? This he went on, but while he was bewailing his unhappy miscarriage, he lift up his eyes, and behold there was a very stately palace before him, the name of which was* Beautiful, *and it stood by the high-way side.*

So I saw in my dream, that he made haste and went forward, that if possible he might get lodging there; now before he had gone far, he entered into a very narrow passage, which was about a furlong off the porter's lodge, and looking very narrowly before him as he went, he espied two lions[26] in the way. Now thought he, I see the dangers that *Mistrust* and *Timorous* were driven back by. (The lions were chained, but he saw not the chains.) Then he was afraid and thought also himself to go back after them, for he thought nothing but death was before him: but Mark 13.14 the *Porter* at the lodge, whose name is *Watchful* perceiving that *Christian* made a halt, as if he would go back, cried unto him, saying, Is thy faith so small? Fear not the lions, for they are chained, and placed there for a trial of faith, where it is; and for discovery of those that have none: keep in the midst of the path, and no hurt shall come unto thee.

Then I saw that he went on, trembling for fear of the lions; but taking good heed to the directions of the *Porter,* he heard them roar, but they did him no harm. Then he clapped his hands, and went on till he came and stood before the gate where the *Porter* was. Then said *Christian* to the *Porter,* Sir, what house is this,[27] and may I stay here to night? The *Porter* answered, This house was built by the Lord of the Hill, and he built it for the relief and security of pilgrims. The *Porter* also asked whence he was, and whither he was going?

Chr. I am come from the City of *Destruction,* and I am

going to Mount *Zion,* but because the sun is now set, I desire, if I may to lodge here tonight.

Por. What is your name?

Chr. My name is now *Christian,* but my name at the first was *Graceless:* I came of the race of *Japhet,* whom God Gen. 9.27 will persuade to dwell in the tents of *Shem.*

Por. But how doth it happen you come so late, the sun is set?

Chr. I had been here sooner, but that, wretched man that I am! I slept in the *Arbour* that stands on the hill-side; nay, I had notwithstanding that, been here much sooner, but that in my sleep I lost my evidence, and came without it to the brow of the hill, and then feeling for it, and finding it not, I was forced, with sorrow of heart, to go back to the place where I slept my sleep, where I found it, and now I am come.

Por. Well, I will call out one of the virgins of this place, who will (if she like your talk) bring you in to the rest of the family, according to the rules of the house. So *Watchful* the *Porter* rang a bell, at the sound of which came out at the door of the house a grave and beautiful damsel named *Discretion,* and asked why she was called?

The *Porter* answered, This man is in a journey from the City of *Destruction* to Mount *Zion,* but being weary and benighted, he asked me if he might lodge here tonight? So I told him I would call for thee, who, after discourse had with him, mayest do as seemeth thee good, even according to the law of the house.

Then she asked him whence he was, and whither he was going? And he told her. Then she asked him, What he has seen and met with in the way? And he told her. And last, she asked his name? So he said, It is *Christian,* and I have so much the more a desire to lodge here to night, because, by what I perceive, this place was built by the Lord of the Hill, for the relief and security of pilgrims: so she smiled, but the water stood in her eyes: and, after a little pause, she said, I will call forth two or three more of the family. So she ran to the door and called out *Prudence, Piety,* and

Charity, who after a little more discourse with him, had him in to the family; and many of them meeting him at the threshold of the house said, Come in, thou blessed of the Lord; this house was built by the Lord of the Hill, on purpose to entertain such pilgrims in. Then he bowed his head and followed them into the house: so when he was come in, and sat down, they gave him something to drink; and consented together that until supper was ready, some of them should have some particular discourse with *Christian,* for the best improvement of time, and they appointed *Piety* and *Prudence,* and *Charity* to discourse with him: and thus they began.

Piety *discourses him*

Piety. *Come, good* Christian, *since we have been so loving to you, to receive you into our house this night; let us, if perhaps we may better our selves thereby, talk with you of all things that have happened to you in your pilgrimage?*

Chr. With a very good will, and I am glad that you are so well disposed.

Piety. *What moved you at first to betake your self to a pilgrim's life?*

How Christian *was driven out of his own country*

Chr. I was driven out of my native country by a dreadful sound that was in mine ears, *to wit,* that unavoidable destruction did attend me, if I abode in that place where I was.

Piety. *But how did it happen that you came out of your country this way?*

Chr. It was as God would have it; for when I was under the fears of destruction, I did not know whither to go; but by chance there came a man, even to me, (as I was trembling and weeping) whose name is *Evangelist,* and he directed me to the wicket gate, which else I should never have found, and so set me in to the way that hath led me directly to this house.

How he goes into the way to Zion

Piety. *But did you not come by the House of the Interpreter?*

Chr. Yes, and did see such things there, the remembrance of which will stick by me as long as I live: especially three

things, to wit, how Christ, in despite of Satan, maintains *A rehearsal of what he saw in the way*
his work of grace in the heart: how the man had sinned
himself quite out of God's mercy, and also the dream of
him that thought in his sleep the day of judgment was come.

Piety. *Why? Did you hear him tell his dream?*

Chr. No, he took me and had me where he shewed me a
stately palace, and how the people were clad in gold that
were in it; and how there came a venturous man, and cut
his way through the armed men that stood in the door to
keep him out; and how he was bid to come in, and win
eternal glory; me thought those things did ravish my heart;
I would have stayed at that good man's house a twelve
month, but that I knew I had further to go.

Piety. *And what saw ye else in the way?*

Chr. Saw! Why, I went but a little further, and I saw one,
as I thought in my mind, hang bleeding upon the tree; and
the very sight of him made my burden fall off my back (for
I groaned under a very heavy burden) but then it fell down
from off me. 'Twas a strange thing to me, for I never saw
such a thing before; yea, and while I stood looking up (for
then I could not forbear looking) three shining ones came
to me: one of them testified that my sins were forgiven me;
another stript me of my rags, and gave me this broidered
coat which you see; and the third set the mark which you
see in my fore-head, and gave me this sealed roll (and with
that he plucked it out of his bosom.)

Piety. *But you saw more than this, did you not?*

Chr. The things that I have told you were the best, yet
some other matter I saw, as namely, I saw three men,
Simple, Sloth, and *Presumption,* lie asleep a little out of the
way as I came, with irons upon their heels; but do you
think I could awake them? I also saw *Formality* and *Hypocrisy* come tumbling over the wall to go (as they pretended)
to *Zion,* but they were quickly lost; even as my self did tell
them, but they would not believe: but above all, I found it
hard work to get up this hill, and as hard to come by the
Lions' Mouth; and truly if it had not been for that good
man, the Porter that stands at the gate, I do not know, but

that after all, I might have gone back again: but I thank God I am here, and I thank you for receiving of me.

Then *Prudence* thought good to ask him a few questions, and desired his answer to them.

Prudence *discourses him*

Pru. Do you not think sometimes of the country from whence you came?

Christian's *thoughts of his native country.* Heb. 11.15, 16

Chr. Yes, but with much shame and detestation; *truly, if I had been mindful of that country from whence I came out, I might have had opportunity to have returned; but now I desire a better country, that is an heavenly.*

Pru. Do you not yet bear away with you some of the things that then you were conversant withall?

Christian *distasted with carnal cogitations*
Christian's *choice* Rom. 7

Chr. Yes, but greatly against my will, especially my inward and carnal cogitations; with which all my countrymen, as well as my self, were delighted; but now all those things are to my grief, and might I but choose mine own things, I would choose never to think of those things more: but when I would be a doing of that which is best, that which is worst is with me.

Pru. Do you not find sometimes, as if those things were vanquished, which at other times are your perplexity?

Christian's *golden hours*

Chr. Yes, but that is but seldom; but they are to me golden hours, in which such things happen to me.

Pru. Can you remember by what means you find your annoyances at times, as if they were vanquished?

How Christian *gets power against his corruptions*

Chr. Yes, when I think what I saw at the cross, that will do it; and when I look upon my broidered coat, that will do it; and when I look into the roll that I carry in my bosom, that will do it; and when my thoughts wax warm about whither I am going, that will do it.

Pru. And what is it that makes you so desirous to go to Mount Zion?

Why Christian would be at Mount *Zion*
Isa. 25.8. Rev. 21.4

Chr. Why, there I hope to see him *alive,* that did hang *dead* on the cross; and there I hope to be rid of all those things, that to this day are in me an annoyance to me; there, they say, there is no death, and there I shall dwell with such company as I like best. For to tell you truth, I love him, because I was by him eased of my burden, and I am weary of my inward sickness: I would fain be where I shall die no more, and with the company that shall continually cry, *Holy, Holy, Holy.*

Then said *Charity* to *Christian, Have you a family? Are you a married man?*

Chr. I have a wife and four small children.[28]

Cha. *And why did you not bring them along with you?*

Chr. Then *Christian* wept, and said, Oh, how willingly would I have done it, but they were all of them utterly averse to my going on pilgrimage.

Cha. *But you should have talked to them, and have endeavoured to have shown them the danger of being behind.*

Chr. So I did, and told them also what God had shewed to me of the destruction of our city; but I seemed to them as one that mocked; and they believed me not.

Cha. *And did you pray to God that he would bless your counsel to them?*

Chr. Yes, and that with much affection; for you must think that my wife and poor children were very dear unto me,

Cha. *But did you tell them of your own sorrow, and fear of destruction? For I suppose that destruction was visible enough to you?*

Chr. Yes, over, and over, and over. They might also see my fears in my countenance, in my tears, and also in my trembling under the apprehension of the judgment that did hang over our heads; but all was not sufficient to prevail with them to come with me.

Cha. *But what could they say for themselves, why they came not?*

Chr. Why, my wife was afraid of losing this world; and my children were given to the foolish delights of youth: so what by one thing and what by another, they left me to wander in this manner alone.

Cha. *But did you not with your vain life damp all that you by words used by way of persuasion to bring them away with you?*

Charity discourses him

Christian's *love to his wife and children*

Gen. 19.14

Christian's *fear of perishing might be read in his very countenance*

The cause why his wife and children did not go with him

Chr. Indeed I cannot commend my life, for I am conscious to my self of many failings therein: I know also that a man by his conversation[29] may soon overthrow what by argument or persuasion he doth labour to fasten upon others for their good. Yet, this I can say, I was very wary of giving them occasions, by any unseemly action, to make them averse to going on pilgrimages. Yea, for this very thing, they would tell me I was too precise,[30] and that I denied my self of things (for their sakes) in which they saw no evil. Nay, I think I may say, that if what they saw in me did hinder them, it was my great tenderness in sinning against God, or of doing any wrong to my neighbour.

Cha. *Indeed* Cain *hated his brother, because his own works were evil, and his brother's righteous; and if thy wife and children have been offended with thee for this, they thereby show themselves to be implacable to good, and thou hast delivered thy soul from their blood.*

Now I saw in my dream, that thus they sat talking together until supper was ready. So when they had made ready, they sat down to meat: now the table was furnished with fat things, and with wine that was well refined, and all their talk at the table was about the LORD of the Hill; as namely, about that HE had done, and whereof HE did what HE did, and why he had builded that house: and by what they said I perceived that HE had been a great *warrior*, and had fought with, and slain him that had the power of death, but not without great danger to himself: which made me love him the more.

For, as they said, and as I believe (said *Christian*) he did it with the loss of much blood: but that which put glory of grace into all he did, was, that he did it out of pure love to this country. And beside, there were some of them of the household that said, they had been and spoke with him since he did die on the cross; and they have attested, that they had it from his own lips, that he is such a lover of poor pilgrims, that the like is not to be found from the east to the west.

They moreover gave an instance of what they affirm'd,

Christian's *good
conversation
before his wife
and children*

Christian *clear
of their blood, if
they perish*

Ezek. 4.19

What Christian
*had to his
supper*
*Their talk at
supper time*

and that was, he had stript himself of his glory, that he might do this for the poor; and that they heard him say and affirm, *That he would not dwell in the mountain of* Zion *alone.* They said moreover, that he had made many pilgrims though by nature they were beggars born, and their original had been the dunghill.

Christ makes princes of beggars. 1 Sam. 2.8. Psal. 113.7

Thus they discoursed together till late at night, and after they had committed themselves to their Lord for protection, they betook themselves to rest: the pilgrims they laid in a large upper chamber, whose window opened towards the sun-rising: the name of the chamber was *Peace,* where he slept till break of day, and then he awoke, and sung,

Christian's bed-chamber

> *Where am I now! Is this the love and care*
> *Of Jesus, for the men that pilgrims are*
> *Thus to provide! That I should be forgiven!*
> *And dwell already the next door to Heaven.*

So in the morning they all got up, and after some more discourse, they told him that he should not depart till they had shown him the *rarities* of the place. And first they had him into the Study, where they showed records of the greatest antiquity; in which, as I remember my dream, they showed him the first *Pedigree* of the Lord of the Hill, that he was the son of the Ancient of Days, and came by that eternal generation. Here also was more fully recorded the acts that he had done, and the names of many hundreds that he had taken into his service; and how he had placed them in such habitations that could neither by length of days, nor decays of nature be dissolved.

Christian had into the study, and what he saw there

Then they read to him some of the worthy acts that some of his servants had done. As how they had subdued kingdoms, wrought righteousness, obtained promises, stopped the mouths of lions, quenched the violence of fire, escaped the edge of the sword, out of weakness were made strong, waxed valiant in fight, and turned to fight the armies of the *Aliens.*

Heb. 11.33, 34

Then they read again in another part of the records of

the house, where it was showed how willing their Lord was to receive into his favour, any, even any, though they in time past had offered great affronts to his person and proceedings. Here also were several other histories of many other famous things, of all which *Christian* had a view: as of things both ancient and modern, together with prophecies and predictions of things that have their certain accomplishment, both to the dread and amazement of enemies, and the comfort and solace of pilgrims.

Christian had into the Armoury

The next day they took him, and had him into the Armoury, where they showed him all manner of furniture, which their Lord had provided for pilgrims, as sword, shield, helmet, breast-plate, *All Prayer,* and shoes that would not wear out.[31] And there was here enough of this to harness out as many men for the service of their Lord, as there be stars in the heaven for multitude.

Christian is made to see ancient things

They also showed him some of the engines with which some of his servants had done wonderful things. They showed him *Moses's* rod, the hammer and nail with which *Jael* slew *Sisera,* the pitchers, trumpets, and lamps too, with which *Gideon* put to flight the armies of *Midian.* Then they showed him the ox's goad wherewith *Shamgar* slew six hundred men. They showed him moreover the sling and stone with which *David* slew *Goliath* of *Gath:* and the sword also with which their Lord will kill the man of sin in the day that he shall rise up to the prey.[32] They showed him besides, many excellent things, with which *Christian* was much delighted. This done, they went to their rest again.

Christian shewed the delectable mountains

Then I saw in my dream, that on the morrow he got up to go forwards, but they desired him to stay till the next day also; and then said they, we will (if the day be clear) shew you the delectable mountains, which they said, would yet further add to his comfort, because they were nearer the desired heaven, than the place where at present he was. So he consented and stayed. When the morning was up,

Isa. 33.16, 17

they had him to the top of the house, and bid him look south, so he did: and behold at a great distance he saw a most pleasant mountainous country, beautified with woods, vine-yards, fruits of all sorts; flowers also, with springs and fountains, very delectable to behold. Then he asked the name of the country; they said it was *Immanuel's Land*:[33] and it is as common, say they, as this hill is, to and for all the pilgrims. And when thou comest there, from thence thou mayest see to the gate of the Celestial City; as the shepherds that live there will make appear.

Now he bethought himself of setting forward, and they were willing he should: but first, said they, let us go again into the Armoury; so they did, and when he came there, they harnessed him from head to foot, with what was of proof, lest perhaps he should meet with assaults in the way. He being therefore thus accoutred, walketh out with his friends to the gate, and there he asked the Porter if he saw any pilgrims pass by; then the Porter answered, Yes. *Christian set forward*

Christian sent away armed

Chr. *Pray did you know him? said he.*

Por. I asked his name, and he told me it was *Faithful*.

Chr. *O said Christian, I know him, he is my towns-man, my near neighbour, he comes from the place where I was born; how far do you think he may be before?*

Por. He is got by this time below the hill.

Chr. *Well*, said Christian, *good Porter, the Lord be with thee, and add to all thy blessings much increase of the kindness that thou hast showed to me.* *How Christian and the Porter greet at parting*

Then he began to go forward, but *Discretion, Piety, Charity*, and *Prudence* would accompany him down to the foot of the hill. So they went on together, reiterating their former discourses till they came to go down the hill. Then said *Christian*, as it was *difficult* coming up, so (so far as I can see) it is *dangerous* going down. Yes, said *Prudence*, so it is: for it is an hard matter for a man to go down into the Valley of *Humiliation*, as thou art now, and to catch no slip by the way: therefore, said they, are we come out to accompany thee down the hill. So he began to go down; but very warily, yet he caught a slip or two. *The Valley of Humiliation*

Then I saw in my dream, that these good companions

Whilst christian is among his godly friends
Their golden mouths make him sufficient mends
For all his griefs and when they let him goe
Hes clod with northen steel from top to toe

(when *Christian* was gone down to the bottom of the hill) gave him a loaf of bread, a bottle of wine and a cluster of raisins,[34] and then he went on his way.

But now in this Valley of *Humiliation* poor *Christian* was hard put to it, for he had gone but a little way before he espied a foul *fiend* coming over the field to meet him; his name is *Apollyon*.[35] Then did *Christian* begin to be afraid, and cast in his mind whether to go back or to stand his ground. But he considered again, that he had no armour for his back, and therefore thought that to turn the back to him might give him greater advantage with ease to pierce him with his darts; therefore he resolved to venture, and stand his ground. For, thought he, had I no more in mine eye than the saving of my life, 'twould be the best way to stand. *Christian no armour for his back* *Christian's resolution in the approach of Apollyon*

So he went on, and *Apollyon* met him: now the monster was hideous to behold, he was clothed with scales like a fish; (and they are his pride) he had wings like a dragon, feet like a bear, and out of his belly came fire and smoke, and his mouth was as the mouth of a lion. When he was come up to *Christian,* he beheld him with a disdainful countenance, and thus began to question with him.

Apol. *Whence came you, and whither are you bound?*

Chr. I am come from the City of *Destruction* which is the place of all evil, and I am going to the City of *Zion.* *Discourse between* Christian *and* Apollyon

Apol. *By this I perceive thou art one of my subjects, for all that country is mine, and I am the Prince and God of it. How is it then that thou hast run away from thy King? Were it not that I hope thou mayest do me more service, I would strike thee now at one blow to the ground.*

Chr. I was born indeed in your dominions, but your service was hard, and your wages such as a man could not live on, *for the wages of sin is death;* therefore when I was come to years, I did as other considerate persons do, look out, if perhaps I might mend my self. Rom. 6.23

Apol. *There is no prince that will thus lightly lose his subjects, neither will I as yet lose thee; but since thou complainest of thy service and wages, be content to go* *Apollyon's flattery*

back, what our country will afford, I do here promise to give thee.

Chr. But I have left my self to another, even to the King of Princes, and how can I in fairness go back with thee?

Apol. Thou hast done in this according to the proverb, change a bad for a worse: *but it is ordinary for those that have professed themselves his servants, after a while to give him the slip, and return again to me: do thou so too, and all shall be well.*

Chr. I have given him my faith, and sworn my allegiance to him, how then can I go back from this, and not be hanged as a traitor?

Apol. Thou didst the same by me, and yet I am willing to pass by all, if now thou wilt yet turn again, and go back.

Chr. What I promised thee was in my non-age,[36] and besides, I count that the prince under whose banner now I stand, is able to absolve me, yea, and to pardon also what I did as to my compliance with thee: and besides (O thou destroying *Apollyon*) to speak truth, I like his servants, his government, his company, and country, better than thine: and therefore leave off to persuade me further, I am his servant, and I will follow him.

Apol. Consider again, when thou art in cool blood, what thou art like to meet with in the way that thou goest. Thou knowest, that for the most part, his servants come to an ill end, because they are transgressors against me and my way; how many of them have been put to shameful death? And besides, thou countest his service better than mine; whereas he never came yet from the place where he is, to deliver any that saved him out of their hands: but as for me, how many times, as all the world very well knows, have I delivered, either by power or fraud, those that have faithfully served me, from him and his; thought taken by them; and so I will deliver thee.

Chr. His forbearing at present to deliver them, is on purpose to try their love, whether they will cleave to him to the end: and as for the ill end thou sayest they come to, that is most glorious in their account: for, for present

Apollyon under-values Christ's service

Apollyon pleads the grievous end of Christians, to dissuade Christian from persisting in his way

deliverance, they do not much expect it; for they stay for their glory, and then they shall have it, when their prince comes in his, and the glory of the angels.

Apol. *Thou hast already been unfaithful in thy service to him, and how dost thou think to receive wages of him?*

Chr. Wherein, O *Apollyon,* have I been unfaithful to him?

Apol. *Thou didst faint at first setting out, when thou wast almost choked in the Gulf of* Despond, *thou diddest attempt wrong ways to be rid of thy Burden, whereas thou shouldest have stayed till thy prince had taken it off. Thou didst sinfully sleep and lose thy choice things: thou wast also almost persuaded to go back at the sight of the lions: and when thou talkest of thy journey and of what thou hast heard, and seen, thou art inwardly desirous of vain glory in all thou sayest and doest.*[37]

Chr. All this is true, and much more, which thou hast left out; but the prince whom I serve and honour, is merciful, and ready to forgive: but besides, these infirmities possessed me in thy country, for there I suck'd them in, and I have groaned under them, being sorry for them, and have obtained pardon of my prince.

Apol. Then *Apollyon* broke out into a grievous rage, saying, *I am an enemy to this prince; I hate his person, his laws, and people; I am come out on purpose to withstand thee.*

Chr. *Apollyon,* beware what you do, for I am in the King's High-way, the way of holiness, therefore take heed to your self.

Apol. Then *Apollyon* straddled quite over the whole breadth of the way, and said, I am void of fear in this matter, prepare thy self to die, for I swear by my infernal den that thou shalt go no further, here will I spill thy soul; and with that he threw a flaming dart at his breast, but *Christian* had a shield in his hand, with which he caught it, and so prevented the danger of that. Then did *Christian* draw, for he saw 'twas time to bestir him, and *Apollyon* as fast made at him, throwing darts as thick as hail; by the

Apollyon *pleads* Christian's *infirmities against him*

which, notwithstanding all that Christian could do to avoid

it, *Apollyon* wounded him in his *head,* his *hand* and *foot,* this made *Christian* give a little back; *Apollyon* therefore followed his work amain, and *Christian* again took courage, and resisted as manfully as he could. This sore combat lasted for about half a day, even till *Christian* was almost quite spent. For you must know that *Christian,* by reason of his wounds, must needs grow weaker and weaker.

Then *Apollyon* espying his opportunity began to gather up close to *Christian,* and wrestling with him, gave him a dreadful fall, and with that *Christian's* sword flew out of

his hand. Then said *Apollyon, I am sure of thee now;* and with that he had almost pressed him to death; so that *Christian* began to despair of life. But as God would have it, while *Apollyon* was fetching his last blow, thereby to make a full end of this good man, *Christian* nimbly stretched out his hand for his sword, and caught it, saying,

Rejoice not against me, O mine enemy, when I fall I shall arise, and with that gave him a deadly thrust, which made him give back, as one that had received his mortal wound.

Christian perceiving that, made at him again, saying, *Nay in all these things we are more than conquerors, through him that loved us.*[38] And with that *Apollyon* spread forth his dragon wings, and sped him away, that *Christian* saw

him no more.

In this combat no man can imagine, unless he had seen and heard, as I did, what yelling and hideous roaring *Apollyon* made all the time of the fight: he spake like a dragon: and on the other side, what sighs and groans burst from *Christian's*

A *brief relation
of the combat by
the spectator*

heart. I never saw him all the while give so much as one pleasant look, till he perceived he had wounded *Apollyon* with his two edg'd sword, then indeed he did smile, and look upward; but 'twas the dreadfullest sight that ever I saw.

So when the Battle was over, *Christian* said, I will here give thanks to him that hath delivered me out of the mouth

of the Lion; to him that did help me against *Apollyon:* and so he did, saying,

Great Beelzebub, *the captain of this fiend,*
Design'd my ruin, therefore to this end
He sent him harnessed out; and he with rage,
That hellish was, did fiercely me engage:
But blessed Michael *helped me, and I*
By dint of sword did quickly make him fly:
Therefore to him let me give lasting praise,
And thanks, and bless his holy name always.

Then there came to him an hand with some of the Leaves
of the Tree of Life, the which *Christian* took and applied
to the wounds *that* he had received in the battle, and was
healed immediately. He also sat down in *that* place to eat
bread, and to drink of the *bottle that* was given him a *little*
before; so being refreshed, he addressed himself to his journey, with his sword drawn in his hand, for he said, I know
not but some other enemy may be at hand, but he met with
no other affront from *Apollyon,* quite *thorough*[39] this valley. Christian *goes on his journey with his sword drawn in his hand*

Now at the *end* of *this valley* was another, call'd *the*
Valley of the shadow of Death, and Christian must needs
go *through* it, because the *way* to the Celestial *City* lies
thorough the midst of it: now *this valley* is a very solitary
place.[40] The prophet *Jeremiah* thus describes it; *A wilder-* *The Valley of the shadow of Death*
ness, a land of deserts, and of pits, a land of drought, and Jer. 2.6
of the shadow of death, a land that no man (but a Christian)
passeth through, and where no man dwelt.

Now here Christian was worse put than in his fight with
Apollyon, as by the sequel you shall see.

I saw then in my dream, *that when* Christian *was got on*
the borders of the shadow of Death, there met him *two*
men, children of them that brought up an evil report *of the* *The children of the spies go back* Num. 13
good land, making haste to go back, to whom *Christian*
spake as follows.

Chr. *Whither are you going?*

Men. They said, Back, back, and we would have you do
so too, if either life or peace is prized by you.

Chr. *Why? What's the matter? said* Christian.

Men. Matter, said they, we were going that way as you

Poor man where art thou now, thy day is night
Good man be not cast down, thou yet art right
Thy way to heav'n, lies by the gates of hell,
Chear up, hold out, with thee it shall goe well,

are going, and went as far as we durst, and indeed we were almost past coming back, for had we gone a little further, we had not been here to bring the news to thee.

Chr. But what have you met with, said Christian.

Men. Why! we were almost in the Valley of the shadow of Death, but that by good hap we looked before us, and saw the danger before we came to it.

Psal. 4.19, Psal. 117.19

Chr. But what have you seen? said Christian.

Men. Seen! Why, the valley it self, which is as dark as pitch; we also saw here the hobgoblins, satyrs, and dragons of the pit: we heard also in that valley a continual howling and yelling, as of a people under unutterable misery, who were sat down in affliction and irons: and over that valley hangs the discouraging clouds of confusion, Death also doth always spread his wings over it. In a word, it is every whit dreadful; being utterly without order.

Job 3.5, chap. 10.2

Chr. Then said Christian, *I perceive not yet, by what you have said, but that this is my way to the desired heaven.*

Jer. 2.6

Men. Be it thy way, we will not choose it for ours: so they parted, and *Christian* went on his way but still with his sword drawn in his hand for fear lest he should be assaulted.

I saw then in my Dream as far as the Valley reached, there was on the right hand a very deep Ditch, that Ditch into which the blind hath led the blind in all ages, and have both there miserably perished. Again, behold on the left hand there was a very dangerous Quag[41] into which, if even a good man falls, he finds no bottom for his foot to stand on. Into this Quag King *David* once did *fall,* and had no doubt there been smothered, had not he that is able plucked him out.

Psal. 69.14

The pathway was here also exceeding narrow, and therefore good *Christian* was the more put to it; for when he sought in the dark to shun the ditch on the one hand, he was ready to tip over into the mire on the other; also when he sought to escape the mire, without great carefulness, he would be ready to fall into the ditch, thus he went on, and I heard him here sigh bitterly; for beside the danger mentioned above, the pathway was here so dark, that oft-times when he lift up his foot to go forward, he knew not where, nor upon what he should set it next.

About the midst of this valley, I perceived the mouth of Hell to be, and it stood also hard by the way-side: Now, thought *Christian*, what shall I do? And ever and anon the flame and smoke would come out in such abundance with sparks and hideous noises (things that cared not for *Christian's* sword, as did *Apollyon* before) that he was forced to put up his sword, and betake himself to another weapon called *All prayer*; so he cried in my hearing *O Lord I beseech thee deliver my soul.* Thus he went on a great while, yet still the flames would be reaching towards him: also he heard doleful voices, and rushings to and fro, so that sometimes he thought he would be torn in pieces, or trodden down like mire in the streets. This frightful sight was seen, and these dreadful noises were heard by him for several miles together, and coming to a place, where he thought he heard a company of *fiends* coming forward to meet him, he stopped, and began to muse what he had best to do. Sometimes he had half a thought to go back. Then again he thought he might be half way through the valley: he remembered also how he had already vanquished many a danger: and that the danger of going back might be much more than for to go forward; so he resolved to go on; yet the *fiends* seemed to come nearer and nearer; but when they were come even almost at him, he cried out with a most vehement voice, *I will walk in the strength of the Lord God;* so they gave back, and came no further.

One thing I would not let slip, I took notice that now poor Christian *was so confounded, that he did not know his own voice; and thus I perceived it; just when he was come over against the mouth of the burning Pit, one of the wicked ones got behind him, and stepped up softly to him, and whisperingly suggested many grievous blasphemies to him, which he verily thought proceeded from his own mind. This put* Christian *more to it than any thing that he met with before, even to think that he should now blaspheme him, that he loved so much before; yet, if he could have helped it, he*

Marginal notes:

Eph. 6.18
Psal. 116.3

Christian *put to a stand but for a while*

Christian made believe that he spake blasphemies, when 'twas Satan that suggested them into his mind

*would not have done it; but he had not the discretion to
stop his ears, nor to know from whence those blasphemies
came.*

When *Christian* had travelled in this disconsolate condition some considerable time, he thought he heard the
voice of a man, going before him, saying, *Though I walk
through the Valley of the shadow of Death, I will fear none
ill, for thou art with me.* Then was he glad: and that for   Psal. 23.4
these reasons:

First, because he gathered from them that some who
feared God, were in the Valley as well as himself.

Secondly, for that he perceived God was with them,
though in that dark and dismal state, and why not, thought
he, with me, though by reason of the impediment that
attends this place I cannot perceive.   Job 9.11

Thirdly, for that he hoped (could he overtake them) to
have company by and by, so he went on, and called to him
that was before, but he knew not what to answer: for that
he also thought himself to be alone. And by and by the day
broke: then said Christian, *He hath turned the shadow of*   Amos 5.8
death into the morning.

Now morning being come, he looked back, not of desire
to return, but to see by the light of day, what hazards he
had gone through in the dark. So he saw more perfectly the   *Christian* glad at
ditch that was on the one hand, and the quag that was on   break of day
the other; also how narrow the way was which led betwixt
them both; also now he saw the hobgoblins, and satyrs, and
dragons of the pit, but all afar off; for after break of day they
came not nigh, yet they were discovered to him, according
to that which is written, *he discovereth deep things out of*
darkness, and bringeth out to light the shadow of death.   Job 12.22

Now was *Christian* much affected with his deliverance
from all the dangers of his solitary way, which dangers,
though he feared them more before, yet he saw them more
clearly now, because the light of the day made them con-
spicuous to him; and about this time the sun was rising,
and this was another mercy to *Christian,* for you must note,
that though the first part of the valley of the shadow of

The second part death was dangerous, yet this second part which he was yet
of this Valley to go, was (if possible) far more dangerous: for, from the
very dangerous place where he now stood, even to the end of the valley,
the way was all along set so full of snares, traps, gins, and
nets here, and so full of pits, pitfalls, deep holes and shelv-
ings down there, that had it now been dark, as it was when
he came the first part of the way, had he had a thousand
souls, they had in reason been cast away; but as I said just
Job 29.3 now the sun was rising. Then said he, *his candle shineth on
my head, and by his light, I go through darkness*.

In this light therefore he came to the end of the Valley.
Now I saw in my dream, that at the end of this Valley lay
blood, bones, ashes and mingled bodies of men, even of pilgrims, that had gone this way formerly: and while I was musing what should be the reason, I espied a little before me a
cave, where two giants, *Pope*[42] and *Pagan*, dwelt in old time,
by whose Power and Tyranny the Men whose bones, blood,
Ashes, &c. lay there, were cruelly put to death: But by this
place *Christian* went without much danger, whereat I somewhat wondered, but I have learnt since, that *Pagan* has been
dead many a day, and as for the other, though he be yet alive,
he is by reason of age, and also of the many shrewd brushes
that he met with in his younger days, grown so crazy and stiff
in his joints, that he can now do little more than sit in his
Cave's mouth, grinning at Pilgrims as they go by, and biting
his nails, because he cannot come at them.

So I saw that *Christian went on his way, yet at the sight
of the* old Man that sat at the Mouth of the Cave, he could
not tell what to think, especially because he spake to him,
though he could never go after him, saying, *You will never
mend, till more of you be burned*: but he held his peace,
and set a good face on't, and so went by: and catched no
hurt. Then sang *Christian*,

> *O world of wonders! (I can say no less)*
> *That I should be preserv'd in that distress*
> *That I have met with here! O blessed be*
> *That hand that from it hath deliver'd me!*

> *Dangers in darkness, Devils, Hell and Sin,*
> *Did compass me while I this Vale was in.*
> *Yea Snares & Pits, & Traps & Nets did lie*
> *My Path about, that worthless silly I*
> *Might have been catch't entangled, and cast down:*
> *But since I live, let JESUS wear the Crown.*

Now as *Christian* went on his way, he came to a little ascent, which was cast up on purpose, that Pilgrims might see before them up there, therefore *Christian* went, and looking forward, he saw *Faithful* before him upon his Journey. Then said *Christian* aloud, Ho, ho, So, ho; stay, and I will be your Companion. At that *Faithful* looked behind him, to whom *Christian* cried, Stay, stay, till I come up to you: but *Faithful answered, No,* I am upon my Life, and the Avenger of Blood is behind me. At this *Christian* was somewhat moved, and putting to all his strength, he quickly got up with *Faithful,* and did also over-run him, so the *last was first.*[43] Then did *Christian* vain-gloriously smile, because he had gotten the start of his Brother, but not taking good heed to his feet, he suddenly stumbled and fell, and could not rise again, until *Faithful* came up to help him.

Christian over-takes Faithful

Then I saw in my dream they went very lovingly on together; and had sweet discourse of all things that had happened to them in their Pilgrimage; and thus *Christian* begun.

Chr. *My honoured and well beloved Brother* Faithful, *I am glad that I have overtaken you, and that God has tempered our Spirits, that we can walk as companions in this so pleasant a Path.*

Christian's fall makes Faithful and he go lovingly together

Faith. I had thought dear Friend, to have had your company quite from our Town, but you did get the start of me, wherefore I was forced to come this much of the way alone.

Chr. *How long did you stay in the City of* destruction, *before you set out after me on your Pilgrimage?*

Faith. Till I could stay no longer: for there was great talk presently after you were gone out, that our City would in short time with Fire from Heaven be burned down to the Ground.

Their talk about the Country *from whence they came*

Chr. *What? Did your Neighbours talk so?*

Faith. Yes, 'twas for a while in every body's mouth.

Chr. *What, and did no more of them but you come out to escape the danger?*

Faith. Though there was, as I said, a great talk thereabout, yet I do not think they did firmly believe it. For in the heat of the discourse I heard some of them deridingly speak of you, and of your desperate Journey, (for so they called this your Pilgrimage;) but I did believe, and do still, that the end of our city will be with Fire and Brimstone from above: and therefore I have made my escape.

Chr. *Did you hear no talk of Neighbour* Pliable?

Faith. Yes *Christian,* I heard that he followed you till he came at the Slough of *Despond;* where, as some said, he fell in; but I am sure he was soundly bedabbled with that kind of dirt.

Chr. *And what said the Neighbours to him?*

How Pliable *was accounted of when he got home*

Faith. He hath since his going back been had greatly in derision, and that among all sorts of People; some do mock and despise him, and scarce will any set him on work. He is now seven times worse than if he had never gone out of the City.

Chr. *But why should they be so set against him, since they also despise the way that he forsook?*

Faith. Oh, they say, Hang him; he is a turn Coat, he was not true to his profession; I think God has stirred up even his enemies to hiss at him, and make him a Proverb, because

Prov. 15.10 he hath forsaken the way.

Chr. *Had you no talk with him before you came out?*

Faith. I met him once in the Streets, but he leered away on the other side, as one ashamed of what he had done; so I spake not to him.

Chr. *Well, at my first setting out, I had hopes of that Man: but now I fear he will perish in the Overthrow of the*

City, for it is happened to him according to the true
Proverb, The Dog is turned to his vomit again and the Sow
that was washed, to her wallowing in the mire.

2 Pet. 2.22.
The Dog and
the Sow

Faith. They are my fears of him too, but who can hinder
that which will be?

Chr. Well Neighbour *Faithful,* said *Christian,* let us leave
him, and talk of things that more immediately concern our
selves. *Tell me now, what you have met with in the way as*
you came; for I know you have met with some things, or
else it may be writ for a wonder.

Faith. I escaped the Slough that I perceiv'd you fell into,
and got up to the Gate without that danger; only I met with
one whose name was *Wanton,* that had like to have done
me a mischief.

Chr. 'Twas well you escaped her Net; Joseph was hard
put to it by her, and he escaped her as you did, but it had
like to have cost him his Life.[44] But what did she do to you?*

Faithful
assaulted by
Wanton
Gen. 39.11,
12, 13

Faith. You cannot think (but that you know something)
what a flattering tongue she had, she lay at me hard to turn
aside with her, promising me all manner of content.

Chr. Nay, she did not promise you the content of a good
Conscience.*

Faith. You know that I mean, all carnal and fleshly
content.

Chr. Thank God you have escaped her: The abhorred of
the Lord shall fall into her Ditch.*

Prov. 22. 14

Faith. Nay, I know not whether I did wholly escape her
or no.

Chr. Why, I tro, you did not consent to her desires?*

Faith. No not to defile my self; for I remembered an
old writing that I had seen, which said, *her Steps take*
hold of Hell. So I shut mine Eyes, because I would not be
bewitched with her looks; then she railed on me, and I went
my way.

Prov. 5.5. Job
31.1

Chr. Did you meet with no other assault as you came?*

Faith. When I came to the foot of the Hill called *Diffi-*
culty, I met with a very aged Man, who asked me, *What*

He is assaulted *I was, and whither bound?* I told him that I am a Pilgrim,
by Adam *the* going to the Celestial City: Then said the old man, *Thou*
first *lookest like an honest fellow, wilt thou be content to dwell*
with me, for the wages that I shall give thee? Then I asked
him his name and where he dwelt? He said his name was
Eph. 4.22 *Adam the First,*[45] *and that he dwelt in the Town of Deceit.*
I asked him then, what was his work? And what the wages
he would give; He told me that his work was *many delights,*
and his wages, that I should be his Heir at last. I further
asked him, what House he kept, and what other Servants
he had? so he told me, *That his house was maintained with*
all the dainties in the world, and that his Servants were
those of his own begetting. Then I asked how many Children he had? He said that he had but three Daughters; *The*
1 John 2.15 *lust of the Flesh, the lust of the Eyes, and the pride of Life:*
and that I should marry them if I would. Then I asked how
long time he would have me to live with him? And he told
me, *as long as he lived himself.*

Chr. *Well, and what conclusion came the* Old man *and*
you at last?

Faith. Why at first I found my self somewhat inclinable
to go with the Man, for I thought he spake very fair; but
looking in his forehead, as I talked with him, I saw there
written, *Put off the old Man with his Deeds.*[46]

Chr. *And how then?*

Faith. Then it came burning hot into my mind: whatever
he said, and however he flattered, when he got me home to
his house, he would sell me for a slave. So I bid him forbear
to talk, for I would not come near the door of his House.
Then he revil'd me and told me, that he would send such a
one after me, that should make my way bitter to my Soul;
So I turned to go away from him; but just as I turned my
self to go thence, I felt him take hold of my flesh and give
me such a deadly twitch back that I thought he had pulled
Rom. 7.24 part of me after himself: This made me cry, *O wretched*
man! So I went on my way up the Hill.

Now when I had got about half way up I looked behind

me, and saw one coming after me, swift as the wind; so he overtook me just about the place where the Settle stands.

Chr. Just there, said Christian, *did I lay down to rest me; but being overcome there with sleep, I there lost this Roll out of my bosom.*

Faith. But good Brother hear me out. So soon as the man overtook me, he was but a word and a blow; for down he knocked me, and laid me for dead. But when I was a little come to my self again, I asked him wherefore he served me so? he said because of my secret inclining to *Adam the First:* and with that he struck me another deadly blow on the Breast, and beat me down backward; so I lay at his foot as dead as before. So when I came to my self again, I cried him mercy, but he said I know not how to show mercy, and with that knocked me down again. He had doubtless made an end of me, but that one came by, and bid him forbear.

Chr. Who was that that bid him forbear?

Faith. I did not know him at first, but as he went by, I perceived the holes in his hands and in his side, then I concluded that he was our Lord. So I went up the Hill.

Chr. That Man that overtook you was Moses, he spareth none, neither knoweth he how to show mercy to those that transgress his Law. The Thunder of Moses

Faith. I know it very well, it was not the first time that he has met with me, 'Twas he that came to me when I dwelt securely at home, and that told me he would burn my house over my head, if I stayed there.

Chr. But did you not see the house that stood there on the top of the hill on the side of which Moses *met you?*

Faith. Yes, and the Lions too, before I came at it; but for the Lions, I think they were asleep, for it was about Noon; and because I had so much of the day before me, I passed by the Porter, and came down the Hill.

Chr. He told me indeed that he saw you go by, but I wish you had called at the house; for they would have showed you so many Rarities, that you would scarce have

forgot them on the day of your death. But pray tell me, did you meet no body in the Valley of Humility?

Faithful
assaulted by Dis-
content

Faith. Yes, I met with one *Discontent,* who would willingly have persuaded me to go back again with him; his reason was, for that the Valley was altogether without *Honour;* he told me moreover, that there to go, was the way to disobey all my Friends, as *Pride, Arrogancy, Self-conceit, Worldly Glory,* with others, who he knew, as he said, would be very much offended, if I made such a fool of my self as to wade through this Valley.

Chr. *Well, and how did you answer him?*

Faithful's
answer to Dis-
content

Faith. I told him, that although these that he named might claim Kindred of me, and that rightly, (for indeed they were my Relations, *according to the flesh*) yet since I became a Pilgrim, they have disowned me, and I also have rejected them: and therefore they were to me now no more than if they had never been of my Lineage. I told him moreover, That as to this Valley he had quite mis-represented the thing: *for before Honour is Humility, and a haughty Spirit before a fall.*[47] Therefore said I, I had rather go through this Valley to the Honour that was so accounted by the wisest than choose that which he esteemed most worthy our affections.

Chr. *Met you with nothing else in that Valley?*

He is assaulted
with Shame

Faith. Yes, I met with *Shame,* but of all the men that I met with in my Pilgrimage, he, I think, bears the wrong name: the others would be said nay, after a little argumentation (and somewhat else,) but this bold-faced *Shame* would never have done.

Chr. *Why, what did he say to you?*

Faith. What! why he objected against Religion it self: he said it was a pitiful, low, sneaking business for a man to mind Religion: he said that tender Conscience was an unmanly thing: and that for a man to watch over his words and ways, so as to tie up himself from that hectoring Liberty, that the brave Spirits of the times accustom themselves unto would make him the Ridicule of the times. He objected also, that but few of the Mighty, Rich, or Wise, were ever of my opinion: nor any of them neither, before they were persuaded to be Fools, and to be of a voluntary fondness, to venture the loss of all, *for no body knows what.* He moreover objected the base and low estate and condition of those that were chiefly the Pilgrims of the times in which they lived: also their Ignorance, and want of understanding in all natural Science.[48] Yea, he did hold me to it at that rate also, about a great many more things than here I relate: as that it was a shame to sit whining and mourning under a Sermon, and a shame to come sighing and groaning home. That it was a shame to ask my Neighbour forgiveness for petty faults, or to make restitution where I have taken from any. He said also that Religion made a man grow strange to the great, because of a few Vices (which is called by finer names) and made him own and respect the base, because of the same Religious fraternity: And is not this, said he, a shame?

1 Cor. 1.26, Chap. 3.18. Phil. 3.7, 9. John 7.48

Chr. *And what did you say to him?*

Faith. Say! I could not tell what to say at first. Yea, he put me so to it, that my Blood came up in my Face: even this *Shame* fetch'd it up, and had almost beat me quite off. But at last I began to consider, *That that which is highly esteemed among Men, is had in an abomination with God.* And I thought again, this *Shame* tells me what men are, but it tells me nothing what *God* or the *Word* of God is. And I thought moreover, that at the day of doom we shall not be doomed to Death or Life, according to the hectoring Spirits of the World: but according to the Wisdom and Law of the highest. Therefore thought I, what God says is best indeed, is best, though all men in the World are against it. Seeing then that God prefers his Religion, seeing God prefers a tender Conscience, seeing they that make themselves Fools for the Kingdom of Heaven are wisest: and that the poor man that lovest Christ, is richer than the greatest man in the World that hates him: *Shame* depart, thou art an Enemy to my Salvation: shall I entertain thee against my Sovereign Lord? How then shall I look him in the face at his coming? should I now be ashamed of his Ways and Servants, how

Luke 16.15

Mark 8.3

can I expect the blessing? But indeed this *Shame* was a bold Villain; I could scarce shake him out of my Company; yea, he would be haunting of me, and continually whispering me in the Ear, with some one or other of the Infirmities that attend Religion: But at last I told him, 'twas but in vain to attempt further in this business; for those things that he disdained, in those did I see most glory: And so at last I got past that *importunate* one.

And when I had shaken him off, then I began to sing:

> *The Trials that those men do meet withal,*
> *That are obedient to the heavenly call,*
> *Are manifold and suited to the flesh.*
> *And come, and come, and come again afresh;*
> *That now or sometime else, we by them may*
> *Be taken, overcome, and cast away.*
> *O let the Pilgrims, let the Pilgrims then,*
> *Be vigilant, and quit themselves like Men.*

Chr. I am glad my Brother, that thou didst withstand this Villain so bravely; for of all, as thou sayest, I think he has the wrong Name, for he is so bold as to follow us into the Streets, and to attempt to put us to shame before all men; that is, to make us ashamed of that which is good; but if he was not himself audacious, he would never attempt to do as he does; but let us still resist him; for notwithstanding all his bravadoes, he promoted the Fool, and one else. *The Wise shall inherit Glory, said* Solomon, *but shame shall be the promotion of Fools.*

Prov. 3.35

Faith. I think we must cry to him for help against Shame, *that would have us to be valiant for Truth upon the earth.*[49]

Chr. You say true, But did you meet no body else in that Valley?

Faith. No not I, for I had Sun-shine all the rest of the way, through that, and also through the Valley of the shadow of death.

Chr. 'Twas well for you, I am sure it fared far otherwise with me. I had for a long Season, as soon almost as I entered into that Valley, a dreadful Combat with that foul Fiend *Apollyon*: Yea, I thought verily he would have killed me: especially when he got me down, and crush'd me under him, as if he would have crush'd me to pieces. For as he threw me, my sword flew out of my hand; nay he told me, *He was sure of me*: but *I cried to God, and he heard me, and delivered me out of all my troubles*. Then I entered into the Valley of the shadow of death, and had no light for almost half the way through it. I thought I should have been kill'd there, over and over: but at last, day broke, and the Sun rose, and I went through that which was behind with far more ease and quiet.

Moreover I saw in my dream, that as they went on, *Faithful*, as he chanced to look on one side, saw a man whose name is *Talkative*, walking at a distance besides them (for in this place there was room enough for them all to walk:) *he was a tall man, and something more comely* Talkative *at a distance than at hand*: To this man, *Faithful* addressed *described* himself in this manner:

Faith. *Friend, whither away? Are you going to the Heavenly Country?*

Talk. I am going to the same place.

Faith. *That is well: Then I hope we shall have your good company.*

Talk. With a very good will, will I be your companion.

Faith. *Come on then, and let us go together, and let us* Faithful *and* *spend our time in discoursing of things that are profitable.* Talkative *enter into discourse*

Talk. To talk of things that are good to me is very acceptable; with you, or with any other; and I am glad that I have met with those that incline to so good a work. For to speak the truth; there are but a few that care thus to spend their time (as they are in their travels) but choose much rather to be speaking of things to no profit, and this Talkative's *dis-* hath been a trouble to me. *like of bad discourse*

Faith. *That is indeed a thing to be lamented; for what thing so worthy of the use of the tongue and mouth of men on Earth, as are the things of the God of Heaven?*

Talk. I like you wonderful well, for your sayings are full of conviction; and I will add, what thing is so pleasant, and what so profitable, as to talk of the things of God?

What things so pleasant? (that is, if a man hath any delight in things that are wonderful) for instance; If a man doth delight to talk of the History, or the Mystery of things, or if a man doth love to talk of Miracles, Wonders or Signs, where shall he find things recorded so delightful, and so sweetly penned as in the holy Scriptures?

Faith. That's true: but to be profited by such things in our talk should be our chief design.

Talk. That is it that I said; for to talk of such things is most profitable, for by so doing, a man may get knowledge of many things: as of the vanity of earthly things, and the benefit of things above: (thus in general) but more particular, By this a man may learn the necessity of the New Birth, the insufficiency of our works, the need of Christ's righteousness, &c. Besides, by this a man may learn what it is to repent, to believe, to pray, to suffer, or the like: by this also a man may learn what are the great Promises and Consolations of the Gospel, to his own comfort. Further, by this a man may learn to refuse false Opinions, to vindicate the truth, and also to instruct the ignorant.

Talkative's fine discourse

Faith. All this is true, and glad am I to hear these things from you.

Talk. Alas, the want of this is the case that so few understand the need of Faith, and the necessity of a work of Grace in their Soul, in order to eternal Life, but ignorantly live in the works of the Law, by which a man can by no means enter the Kingdom of Heaven.

Faith. But by your leave, heavenly knowledge of these is the gift of God; no man attaineth to them by human industry, or only by the talk of them.

O brave Talkative

Talk. All that I know very well. For a man can receive nothing except it be given him from Heaven; all is of Grace not of works: I could give you a hundred Scriptures[50] for the confirmation of this.

Faith. *Well then, said* Faithful: *what is that one thing, that we shall at this time found our discourse upon?*

Talk. What you will: I will talk of things heavenly, or things earthly; things Moral, or things Evangelical; things sacred, or things prophane; things past, or things to come; things foreign, or things at home; things more essential, or things circumstantial; provided that all be done to our profit.

O brave Talkative

Faith. Now did *Faithful* begin to wonder, *and stepping to* Christian *(for he walked all this while by himself) he said to him, but softly, what a brave companion have we got! Surely this man will make a very excellent Pilgrim.*

Chr. At this Christian modestly smiled, and said, this man with whom you are so taken, will beguile with this tongue of his twenty of them that know him not.

Faithful beguiled by Talkative

Faith. *Do you know him then?*

Chr. Know him! Yes, better than he knows himself.

Faith. *Pray what is he?*

Christian makes a discovery of Talkative, telling Faithful who he was

Chr. His name is *Talkative,* he dwelleth in our Town; I wonder that you should be a stranger to him, only I consider that our Town is large.

Faith. *Whose Son is he? And whereabout doth he dwell?*

Chr. He is the Son of one *Say-well,* he dwells in *Prating-Row,*[51] and he is known of all that are acquainted with him, by the name of *Talkative* in *Prating-row,* and notwithstanding his fine tongue, he is but a sorry fellow.

Faith. *Well, he seems to be a very pretty man.*

Chr. This is to them that have not thorough acquaintance with him, for he is most abroad, near home he is ugly enough: your saying that he is a *pretty man,* brings to my mind what I have observed in the work of the Painter, whose Pictures show well at a distance, but very near, more displeasing.

Faith. *But I am ready to think that you do but jest, because you smiled.*

Chr. God forbid that I should jest (though I smiled) in this matter, or that I should accuse any falsely; I will give you a further discovery of him. This man is for any company, and any talk; as he talketh now with you, so will he talk when he is on the Ale-bench; And the more drink he hath in his Crown, the more of these things he hath in his mouth: Religion hath no place in his heart, or house, or conversation; all he hath lieth in his tongue, and his Religion is to make a noise therewith.

Faith. *Say you so! then I am in this man greatly deceived.*

Chr. Deceived! You may be sure of it. Remember the Proverb, *They say, and do not: but the Kingdom of God is not in Word, but in Power.* He talketh of Prayer, of Repentance, of Faith, and of the New birth but he knows only to talk of them. I have been in his Family, and have observed him both at home and abroad; and I know what I say of him is the truth. His house is as empty of Religion, *as the white of an Egg is of savour.* There is there neither Prayer, nor sign of Repentance for sin: Yea, the brute in his kind[52] serves God far better than he. He is the very stain, reproach and shame of Religion to all that know him; it can hardly have a good word in all the end of the Town where he dwells, through him. Thus say the common People that know him, *A Saint abroad, and a Devil at home.*[53] His poor family finds it so, he is such a churl, such a railer at, and so unreasonable with his Servants, that they neither know how to do for, or to speak to him. Men that have any dealings with him, say, it's better to deal with a *Turk* than with him, for fairer dealing they shall have at their hands. This *Talkative* (if it be possible) will go beyond them, defraud, beguile, and over-reach them. Besides, he brings up his Sons to follow his steps, and, if he finds in any of them *a foolish timorousness,* (for so he calls the first appearance of a tender conscience) he calls them fools and blockheads, and by no means will employ them in much, or speak to their commendations before others.[54] For my part I am of opinion, that he has, by his wicked life caused many to stumble and fall, and will be, if God prevents not, the ruin of many more.

Faith. *Well, my Brother, I am bound to believe you; not*

Matt. 23, 1 Cor. 4.20. Talkative talks but does not

His House is empty of Religion

He is a stain to Religion Rom. 2.24, 25

The Proverb that goes of him

Men shun to deal with him

*only because you say you know him, but also because like
a Christian, you make your reports of men. For I cannot
think that you speak these things of ill will, but because it
is even so as you say.*

Chr. Had I known him no more than you, I might perhaps, have thought of him as at the first you did: Yea, had
he received this report at their hands only that are enemies
to Religion, I should have thought it had been a slander.
(A lot that often falls from bad men's mouths upon good
men's names and professions:) But all these things, yea, and
a great many more as bad, of my own knowledge I can
prove him guilty of. Besides, good men are ashamed of him,
they can neither call him *Brother* nor *Friend;* the very name
of him among them, makes them blush they know him.

Faith. *Well, I see that* saying *and* doing *are two things,
and hereafter I shall better observe this distinction.*

Chr. They are two things indeed, and are as diverse, as
are the Soul and the Body. For as the Body without the
Soul is but a dead Carcass; so *saying,* if it be alone is but a
dead Carcass also. The Soul of Religion is the practick part.
*Pure Religion, and undefiled before God and the Father, is
this, to visit the fatherless and widows in their affliction,
and to keep himself unspotted from the World.* This *Talkative* is not aware of, he thinks that *hearing* and *saying* will
make a good Christian: and thus he deceives his own Soul.
Hearing is but the sowing of the Seed; talking is not sufficient to prove that fruit is indeed in the heart and life; and
let us assure our selves, that at the day of Doom men shall
be judged according to their fruit. It will not be said then,
Did you believe? But were you *Doers,* or *Talkers* only? and
accordingly shall they be judged. The end of the world is
compared to our Harvest, and you know men at harvest
regard nothing but fruit. Not that any thing can be accepted
that is not of Faith: But I speak this to show you how
insignificant the Profession of *Talkative* will be at that day.

Faith. *This brings me to mind that of* Moses, *by which
he describeth the Beast that is unclean. He is such an one
that parteth the hoof, but cheweth the Cud; not that parteth*

*The Carcass of
Religion*

James 1.27. *See
ver.* 23, 24, 25,
26

See Matt. 14.25

Lev. 11,
Deut. 14

Faithful convinced of the badness of *Talkative* *the Hoof only, or that cheweth the Cud only. The Hare cheweth the Cud, but yet is unclean because he parteth not the hoof. And this truly resembleth* Talkative: *he cheweth the Cud, he seeketh knowledge, he cheweth upon the Word, but he divideth not the hoof, he parteth not with the way of sinners; but as the Hare, he retaineth the foot of a dog or bear, and therefore is unclean.*[55]

Chr. You have spoke, for ought I know, the true Gospel sense of those Texts; and I will add another thing: *Paul* calleth some men, yea, and those great Talkers too, *Sounding-brass,* and *tinkling Cymbals:* that is, as he expounds 1 Cor. 13.1, 2, 3. Ch.14.7. *Talkative* like two things that sound without life them in another place, *things without life giving sound.* Things without life, that is, without the true Faith and Grace of the Gospel; and consequently, things that shall never be placed in the Kingdom of Heaven among those that are the Children of Life: Though their *sound* by their *talk* be as if it were the Tongue and Voice of an Angel.

Faith. *Well, I was not so fond of his Company at first, but I am as sick of it now. What shall we do to be rid of him?*

Chr. Take my advice, and do as I bid you, and you shall find that he will soon be sick of your company too, except God shall touch his heart and turn it.

Faith. *What would you have me to do?*

Chr. Why, go to him, and enter into some serious discourse about the *power of Religion,* and ask him plainly (when he has approved of it, for that he will) whether this thing be set up in his Heart, House or Conversation.

Faith. Then *Faithful* stepped forward again, and said to *Talkative: Come, what cheer? How is it now?*

Talk. Thank you, well. I thought we should have had a great deal of talk by this time.

Faith. *Well if you will we will fall to it now; and since you left it with me to state the question, let it be this: How doth the saving Grace of God discover its self, when it is in the heart of men?*

Talkative's false discovery of a work of grace *Talk.* I perceive then that our talk must be *about the power of things;* Well, 'tis a very good question, and I shall be willing to answer you. And take my answer in brief thus.

First, *Where the Grace of God is in the heart, it causeth there a great out-cry against sin*. Secondly, –

Faith. Nay, hold, let us consider of one at once: I think you should rather say, It shows it self inclining the Soul to abhor its sin.

Talk. Why, what difference is there between crying out against, and abhorring of sin?

Faith. Oh! a great deal; a man may cry against sin of policy, but he cannot abhor it, but by virtue of a godly antipathy against it: I have heard many cry out against sin in the Pulpit, who yet can abide it well enough in the heart, house and conversation. Joseph's *Mistress cried out with a loud voice, as if she had been very holy; but she would willingly, notwithstanding that, have committed uncleanness with him. Some cry out against sin, even as the mother cries out at her Child in her lap, when she calls it Slut, and naughty Girl, and then falls to hugging and kissing it.*

The crying out against sin, no sign of grace

Gen. 39.15

Talk. You lie at the catch[56] I perceive.

Faith. No not I, am only for setting things right. But what is the second thing whereby you will prove a discovery of a work of grace in the heart?

Talk. Great knowledge of Gospel-Mysteries.

Faith. This sign should have been first, but first or last, it is also false; for knowledge, great knowledge may be obtained in the Mysteries of the Gospel, and yet no work of grace in the Soul. Yea, if a man have all knowledge, he may yet be nothing; and so consequently be no child of God. When Christ *said,* Do you know all these things? *And the disciples had answered,* Yes: *He added,* Blessed are ye if ye do them. *He doth not lay the Blessing in the knowing of them, but in the doing of them. For there is a knowledge that is not attended with doing:* he that knoweth his Master's will and doth it not. *A man may know like an angel, and yet be no Christian: Therefore your sign is not true. Indeed to know is a thing that pleaseth Talkers and Boasters; but to do, is that which pleaseth God. Not that the heart can be good without knowledge; for without that the heart is naught: There is therefore knowledge and*

Great knowledge no sign of Grace. 1 Cor. 13

Knowledge and knowledge

True knowledge attended with endeavours

One good sign of grace

John 16.8. Rom. 7.24. John 16.9. Mark 16.16. Psalm 38.18. Jer. 31.19. Gal. 2.15. Acts 4.12. Matt. 5.6. Rev. 1.6

Rom. 10.10. Phil. 1.27. Matt. 5.9. John 24.15. Psalm 50.20. Job 42.5, 6. Ezek. 29.43

knowledge. Knowledge that resteth in the bare speculation of things, and knowledge that is accompanied with the grace of faith and love, which puts a man upon doing even the will of God from the heart: The first of these will serve the Talker, but about the other the true Christian is not content. Give me understanding and I shall keep thy Law, yea, shall I observe it with my whole heart. *Psal.*119.34.

Talk. You lie at the catch again, this is not for edification.

Faith. *Well if you please, propound another sign how this work of grace discovereth it self where it is.*

Talk. Not I, for I see we shall not agree.

Faith. *Well, if you will not, will you grant me leave to do it?*

Talk. You may use your liberty.

Faith. *A work of grace in the soul discovereth itself, either to him that hath it, or to standers by.*

To him that hath it, thus it gives him conviction of sin, especially of the defilement of his nature and the sin of unbelief (for the sake of which he is sure to be damned, if he findeth not mercy at God's hand by faith in Jesus Christ). This sight and sense of things worketh in him sorrow and shame for sin; he findeth moreover revealed in him the Saviour of the World, and the absolute necessity of closing with him for life; at the which he findeth hungerings and thirstings after him, to which hungerings, &c. the Promise is made. Now according to the strength or weakness of his faith in his Saviour, so is his joy and peace, so is his love to holiness, so are his desires to know him more, and also to serve him in this World. But though I say it discovereth it self thus unto him; yet it is but seldom that he is able to conclude, that this is a work of Grace, because his corruptions now, and his abused reason makes his mind to misjudge in this matter; therefore in him that hath this work there is required a very sound Judgement, before he can with steadiness conclude that this is a work of Grace.

To others it is thus discovered.

1. By an experimental[57] *confession of his faith in Christ.*
2. By a life answerable to that confession, to wit, a life of

holiness; heart-holiness, family-holiness, (if he hath a family) and by conversation-holiness[58] in the world: which in the general teacheth him inwardly to abhor his sin, and himself for that in secret, to suppress it in his Family, and so promote holiness in the World; not by talk only, as an Hypocrite or Talkative person may do: but by a practical subjection in faith and love to the power of the Word: and now Sir, as to this brief description of the work of Grace, and also the discovery of it, if you have ought to object, object: if not, then give me leave to propound to you a second question.

Talk. Nay, my part is not now to object, but to hear, let me therefore have your second question.

Faith. It is this, *Do you experience this first part of this description of it? and doth your life and conversation testify the same? or standeth your Religion* in word or tongue, and *not in* Deed *and* Truth: *pray you, if you incline to answer me in this, say no more than you know the God above will say* Amen *to; and also nothing but what your Conscience can justify you in.* For not he that commendeth himself is approved, but whom the Lord commendeth. *Besides, to say I am thus and thus, when my Conversation,*[59] *and all my Neighbours tell me I lie is great wickedness.*

Another good sign of grace

Talk. Then *Talkative* at first began to blush, but recovering himself, thus he replied. You come now to experience, to Conscience, and to God: and to appeal to him for justification of what is spoken: This kind of discourse I did not expect, nor am I disposed to give an answer to such questions, because, I count not my self bound thereto, unless you take upon you to be a *Catechiser;* and though you should so do, yet I may refuse to make you my Judge. But I pray you tell me, why you ask me such questions?

Talkative not pleased with Faithful's question

Faith. *Because I saw you forward to talk, and because I knew not that you had ought else but notion. Besides, to tell you all the truth, I had heard of you, that you are a man whose Religion lies in talk, and that your conversation*

The reasons why Faithful put him to that question

Faithful's *plain dealing to* Talkative *gives this your Mouth-profession the lie. They say you are a spot among Christians, and that Religion fareth the worse for your ungodly conversation, that some already have stumbled at your wicked ways, and that men are in danger of being destroyed thereby; your Religion and an Ale-house, and Covetousness, and Uncleanness, and Swearing, and Lying, and vain Company-keeping, &c. will stand together. That Proverb is true of you, which it said of a Whore; to wit, That she is a shame to all women, so you are a shame to all Professors.*

Talkative *flings away from* Faithful *Talk.* Since you are ready to take up reports, and to judge so rashly as you do; I cannot but conclude you are some peevish or melancholic man, not fit to be discoursed with and so adieu.

Chr. Then came up *Christian,* and said to his Brother, I told you how it would happen, your words and his lust could not agree; he had rather leave your company than A good riddance reform his life: but he is gone, as I said let him go; the loss is no man's but his own, he has saved us the trouble of going from him: for he continuing (as I suppose he will do) as he is would have been but a blot in our company: besides, the Apostle[60] says, *From such withdraw thy self.*

Faith. *But I am glad we had this little discourse with him, it may happen that he will think of it again; however I have dealt plainly with him; and so am clear of his blood if he perisheth.*

Chr. You did well to talk so plainly to him as you did; there is but little of this faithful dealing with men now-a-days, and that makes Religion to stink so in the Nostrils of many, as it doth; for they are these Talkative Fools, whose Religion is only in word, and are debauched and vain in their Conversation, that (being so much admitted into the fellowship of the godly) do puzzle the World, blemish Christianity, and grieve the sincere. I wish that all men would deal with such as you have done, then should they be either made more conformable to Religion, or the company of Saints would be too hot for them. Then did *Faithful* say,

How Talkative *at first lifts up his Plumes!*
How bravely doth he speak! How he presumes
To drive down all before him! but so soon
As Faithful *talks of* Heart-work *like the Moon,*
That's past the full, into the Wane he goes:
And so will all, but he that Heart-work *knows.*

Thus they went on talking of what they had seen by the way; and so made that way easy, which would otherwise no doubt have been tedious to them: for now they went through a Wilderness.

Now when they were got almost quite out of this Wilderness, *Faithful* chanced to cast his eye back, and espied one coming after them, and he knew him. Oh! said *Faithful* to his Brother, who comes yonder? Then *Christian* looked, and said, it is my good friend *Evangelist,* Aye, and my good friend too, said *Faithful;* for 'twas he that set me the way to the Gate. Now was *Evangelist* come up unto them, and thus saluted them. *Evangelist over-takes them again*

Evan. Peace be with you, dearly beloved, and peace be to your helpers.[61]

Chr. *Welcome, welcome, my good* Evangelist, *the sight of thy countenance brings to my remembrance, thy ancient kindness, and unwearied labouring for my eternal good.* *They are glad at the sight of him*

Faith. *And a thousand times welcome, said good* Faithful; *thy company, O sweet* Evangelist, *how desirable is it to us poor Pilgrims!*

Evan. Then said *Evangelist,* how hath it fared with you my friends, since the time of our last parting? What have you met with; and how have you behaved your selves?

Chr. *Then* Christian *and* Faithful *told him of all things that had happened to them in the way, and how, and with what difficulty they had arrived to that place.*

Evan. Right glad am I, said *Evangelist;* not that you have met with Trials, but that you have been Victors; and for that you have (notwithstanding many weaknesses) continued in the way to this very day. *His Exhortation to them*

I say, right glad am I of this thing, and that for mine own

John 4.36. Gal. 6.9. 1 Cor. 9.24, 25, 26, 27. Rev. 3.11

sake and yours; I have sowed, and you have reaped, and the day is coming when both he that sowed, and they that reaped shall rejoice together; that is, if you hold out; for in due time ye shall reap, if ye faint not. The Crown is before you, and it is an incorruptible one; so run that you may obtain it. Some there be that set out for this Crown, and after they have gone far for it, another comes in and takes it from them: hold fast therefore that you have, let no man take your Crown; you are not yet out of the Gun-shot of the Devil: you have not resisted unto blood, striving against sin. Let the Kingdom be always before you, and believe steadfastly concerning things that are invisible. Let nothing that is on this side the other world get within you; and above all look well to your own hearts, and to the lusts thereof; for they are deceitful above all things, and desperately wicked: set your faces like a flint, you have all power in heaven and earth on your side.[62]

They do thank him for his exhortation

Chr. *Then* Christian *thanked him for his exhortation, but told him withal, that they would have him speak further to them for their help the rest of the way; and the rather for that they well knew that he was a Prophet, and could tell them of things that might happen unto them; and also how they might resist and overcome them. To which request* Faithful *also consented. So* Evangelist *began as followeth.*

He predicteth what troubles they shall meet with in Vanity-Fair, *and encourageth them to steadfastness*

Evan. My Sons, you have heard in the words of the truth of the Gospel, that you must through many Tribulations enter into the Kingdom of Heaven. And again, that in every City, bonds and afflictions abide on you; and therefore you cannot expect that you should go long on your Pilgrimage without them in some sort or other. You have found something of the truth of these testimonies upon you already, and more will immediately follow: For now as you see, you are almost out of this Wilderness, and therefore you will soon come into a Town that you will by and by see before you; and in that Town you will hardly be beset with Enemies, who will strain hard but they will kill you: and be you sure that one or both of you must seal the testimony which you hold, with blood: but be you faithful unto death, and the King will give you a Crown of Life. He that shall die there, although his Death will be unnatural, and his pain perhaps great, he will yet have the better of his fellow; not only because he will be arrived at the Celestial city soonest, but because he will escape many miseries that the other will meet with in the rest of his Journey. But when you are come to the Town, and shall find fulfilled what I have here related, then remember your friend, and quit your selves like men; and commit the keeping of your souls to your God in well doing, as unto a faithful Creator.[63]

He whose lot it will be there to suffer will have the better of his brother

Then I saw in my Dream, that when they were got out of the wilderness, they presently saw a Town before them, and the name of that Town is *Vanity;* and at the town there is a Fair kept called *Vanity-Fair;* it is kept all the year long, it beareth the name of *Vanity-Fair,* because the Town where it is kept *is lighter than Vanity;* and also, because all that is there sold, or that cometh thither, is *Vanity.* As is the saying of the wise, *All that cometh is Vanity.*[64]

Isaiah 40.7. Eccl. 1.2, 11, 17

This Fair is no new erected business, but a thing of ancient standing; I will shew you the original of it.

Almost five thousand years agone, there were Pilgrims, walking to the Celestial City as these two honest persons are; and *Beelzebub, Apollyon* and *Legion,* with their Companions, perceiving by the Path that the Pilgrims made, that their way to the City lay through this *Town of Vanity,* they contrived here to set up a Fair; a Fair wherein should be sold of all sorts of *Vanity,* and that it should last all the year long. Therefore at this Fair are all such Merchandise sold, as Houses, Lands, Trades, Places, Honours, Preferments, Titles, Countries, Kingdoms, Lusts, Pleasures, and Delights of all sorts, as Whores, Bawds, Wives, Husbands, Children, Masters, Servants, Lives, Blood, Bodies, Souls, Silver, Gold, Pearls, precious Stones, and what not? And moreover, at this Fair there is at all times to be seen Jugglings, Cheats, Games, Plays, Fools, Apes, Knaves, and Rogues, and that of every kind.

The Antiquity of this Fair

The Merchandise of this Fair

Here are to be seen too, and that for nothing, Thefts,

Murders, Adulteries, False Swearers, and that of a blood red colour.

And as in other Fairs of less moment, there are several Rows and Streets under their proper Names where such Wares are vended; so here likewise, you have the proper Places, Rows, Streets, (*viz*. Countries and Kingdoms) where *The Streets of* the Wares of this Fair are soonest to be found: Here is the *the Fair* *Britain* Row, the *French* Row, the *Italian* Row, the *Spanish* Row, the *German* Row, where several sorts of Vanities are to be sold. But as in other *fairs,* some one Commodity is as the chief of all the Fair, to the Ware of *Rome* and her Merchandise is greatly promoted in this Fair: only our *English* Nation, with some others, have taken a dislike thereat.

Now as I said, the way to the Celestial City lies just through this *Town,* where this lusty Fair is kept; and he that will go to the City and yet not go through this Town *1 Cor. 5.10.* must needs *go out of the World.* The Prince of Princes *Christ went* himself, when here, went through this Town to his own *through this* *Fair.* Matt. 7.8. Country, and that upon a *fair-day* too: yea, and as I think, Luke 4. 5, 6, 7, it was *Beelzebub,* the chief Lord of this *Fair,* that invited him to buy of his *vanities;* yea, would have made him Lord of the Fair, would he but have done him Reverence as he went through the *Town.* Yea, because he was such a person of honour *Beelzebub* had him from *Street* to *Street,* and showed him all the Kingdoms of the world in a little time, that he might (if possible) allure that Blessed One, to *Christ bought* cheapen and buy some of his *Vanities.* But he had no mind *nothing in this* to the Merchandise, and therefore left the *Town,* without *Fair* laying out so much as one farthing upon these *Vanities.* This *Fair* therefore is an ancient thing, of long standing, and a very great *Fair.*

Now these Pilgrims, as I said, must needs go through this *The Pilgrims* *Fair.* Well so they did; but behold, even as they entered into *enter the Fair* the *Fair,* all the People in the *Fair* were moved, and the *The Fair in a* Town it self as it were in a Hubbub about them; and that *hubbub about* for several reasons; For *them*

First, The Pilgrims were clothed with such kind of *Raiment*, as was diverse from the *Raiment* of any that traded in that *Fair*. The people therefore of the *Fair* made a great gazing upon them: Some said they were fools, some they were Bedlams,[65] and some they were outlandish men.

The first cause of the hubbub

Secondly, and as they wondered at their *Apparel*, so they did likewise at their *Speech*; for few could understand what they said, they naturally spoke the Language of *Canaan*;[66] but they that kept the *Fair*, were the men of this world: so that from one end of the *Fair* to the other, they seemed *Barbarians* each to the other.

1 Corinthians 2.7, 8. *The second cause of the hubbub*

Thirdly, But that which did not a little amuse the Merchandisers, was, that these Pilgrims set very light by all their Wares, they cared not so much as to look upon them: And if they called upon them to buy, they would put their fingers in their ears and cry, *Turn away mine eyes from beholding Vanity*; and look upwards, signifying that their Trade and Traffic was in Heaven.

Third cause of the hubbub

Psalm 119.37. Phil. 3.19, 20

One chanced mockingly, beholding the carriages of the men, to say unto them, *What will you buy?* But they looking gravely upon him, said, *We buy the Truth*. At that, there was an occasion taken to despise the men the more; some mocking, some taunting, some speaking reproachfully, and some calling upon others to smite them. At last things came to an hubbub, and great stir in the *Fair;* insomuch that all order was confounded. Now was word presently brought to the *great one of the Fair*, who quickly came down, and deputed some of his most trusty Friends to take those men into examination, about whom the *Fair* was almost overturned. So the men were brought to examination; and they that sat upon them, asked them whence they came, whither they went, and what they did in such an unusual Garb? The men told them, that they were Pilgrims and Strangers in the world, and that they were going to their own Country, which was the heavenly *Jerusalem*, and that they had given no occasion to the men of the Town, nor yet to

Prov. 23.23

They are mocked

The Fair in a hubbub

They tell who they are, and whence they came

Heb. 11.12–16

the Merchandizers, thus to abuse them, and to let them in their Journey: except it was, for that, when one asked them They are not believed what they would buy, they said, they would *buy the Truth*. But they that were appointed to examine them, did not believe them to be any other than Bedlams and mad, or else such as came to put all things into confusion in the *Fair*. Therefore they took them and beat them, and besmeared They are put in the Cage them with dirt, and then put them into the Cage, that they might be made a spectacle to all the men of the *Fair*. There therefore they lay for some time, and were made the objects of any man's sport, or malice, or revenge. But the men Their behaviour in the Cage being patient, and not rendering railing for railing, but contrariwise blessing, and giving good words for bad, and kindness for injuries done: Some men in the *Fair* that were The men of the Fair do fall out among themselves about these two men more observing, and less prejudiced than the rest, began to check and blame the baser sort for their continual abuses done by them to the men: They therefore in angry manner let fly at them again, counting them as bad as the men in the Cage, and telling them that they seemed confederates, and should be made partakers of their Misfortunes. The other replied, that for ought they could see, the men were quiet and sober, and intended no body any harm; and that there were many that traded in their *Fair,* that were more worthy to be put into the Cage, yea, and Pillory too, than were the men that they had abused. Thus, after divers words had passed on both sides (the men behaving themselves all the while very wisely and soberly before them,) they fell to some blows among themselves, and did harm one to another. Then were these two poor men brought before They are made the Authors of this disturbance their Examiners again, and there charged as being guilty of the late hubbub that had been in the *Fair*. So they beat They are led up and down the Fair in Chains, for a terror to others them pitifully, and hanged Irons upon them, and led them in Chains up and down the *Fair,* for an Example and Terror to others, lest any should speak in their behalf, or join themselves unto them. But *Christian* and *Faithful* behaved themselves yet more wisely; and received the Ignominy and shame that was cast upon them, with so much meekness

and patience, that it won to their side (though but few in *Some of the men of the Fair won to them*
comparison of the rest) several of the men in the *Fair*.[67]
This put the other party yet into a greater rage, insomuch
that they concluded the death of these two men. Wherefore
they threatened that the Cage, nor Irons should serve their
turn, but that they should die for the abuse they had done, *Their Adversaries resolve to kill them*
and for deluding the men of the *Fair*. Then they were
remanded to the Cage again, until further order should be *They are again put into the Cage, and after brought to Trial*
taken with them. So they put them in, and made their feet
fast in the stocks.

Here therefore they called again to mind that they had
heard from their faithful friend *Evangelist,* and were the
more confirmed in their way and sufferings, by what he
told them would happen to them. They also now comforted
each other, that whose lot it was to suffer, even he should
have the best on't, therefore each man secretly wished that
he might have that Preferment: But committing themselves
to the all-wise dispose of him that ruleth all things, with
much content they abode in the condition in which they
were until they should be otherwise disposed of.

Then a convenient time being appointed, they brought
them forth to their Trial, in order to their Condemnation.
When the time was come, they were brought before their
enemies and Arraigned; the Judge's name was Lord *Hate-
good*:[68] Their Indictment was one and the same in substance, though somewhat varying in form; the Contents
whereof was this.

That they were enemies to, and disturbers of their Trade, *Their Indictment*
*that they had made Commotions and Divisions in the
Town, and had won a party to their own most dangerous
Opinions, in contempt of the Law of their Prince.*[69]

Then *Faithful* began to answer, that he had only set *Faithful's answer for himself*
himself against that which had set it self against him that
is higher than the highest. And said he, as for disturbance
I make none, being my self a man of Peace; the parties that
were won to us, were won by beholding our Truth and
Innocence, & they are only turned from the worse to the

Now faithful play the man speak for thy God:
Fear not the wickeds malice nor their rod:
Speak boldly man the truth is on thy side:
Die for it and to life in triumph ride:

better. And as to the King you talk of, since he is *Beelzebub*, the enemy of our Lord, I defy him and all his Angels.

Then Proclamation was made, that he that had ought to say for their Lord the King against the Prisoner at the Bar, should forthwith appear, and give in their Evidence. So there came in three Witnesses, to wit, *Envy*, *Superstition* and *Pickthank*:[70] They were then asked, If they knew the Prisoner at the Bar? And what they had to say for their Lord the King against him?

Then stood forth *Envy*, and said to this effect; My Lord,   Envy *begins*
I have known this man a long time, and will attest upon my Oath before this Honourable Bench, that he is –

Judge. Hold, give him his Oath: So they sware him: Then he said, My Lord, this man, notwithstanding his plausible name, is one of the vilest men in our Country; he neither regardeth Prince nor People, Law nor Custom; but doth all that he can to possess all men, with certain of his disloyal notions, which he in the general calls Principles of Faith and Holiness. And in particular, I heard him once my self affirm, *That Christianity and the Customs of our town of* Vanity, *were diametrically opposite, and could not be reconciled*. By which saying, my Lord, he doth at once, not only condemn all our laudable doings, but us in the doing of them.

Judge. Then did the Judge say unto him, hast thou any more to say?

Envy. My Lord, I could say much more, only I would not be tedious to the Court. Yet if need be, when the other Gentlemen have given in their evidence, rather than any thing shall be wanting that will dispatch him, I will enlarge my testimony against him. So he was bid stand by. Then they called *Superstition*, and bid him look upon the Prisoner; they also asked, what he could say for their Lord the King against him? Then they sware him, so he began.

Super. My Lord, I have no great acquaintance with this   Superstition
man, nor do I desire to have further knowledge of him;   *follows*
however this I know, that he is a very pestilent fellow,[71]
from some discourse that the other day I had with him in

this *Town;* for then talking with him, I heard him say, That our Religion was nought, and such by which a man could by no means please God: Which saying of his, my Lord, your Lordship very well knows, what necessarily thence will follow, to wit, that we still do worship in vain are yet in our sins, and finally shall be damned; and this is that which I have to say.

Then was *Pickthank* sworn, and did say what he knew, in behalf of their Lord the King against the Prisoner at the Bar.

Pickthank's tes-
timony

Pick. My Lord, and you Gentlemen all, this fellow I have known for a long time, and have heard him speak things that ought not to be spoke. For he hath railed on our noble Prince *Beelzebub,* and hath spoken contemptible of his honourable Friends, whose Names are, the Lord *Old-Man,* the Lord *Carnal delight,* the Lord *Luxurious,* the Lord *Desire of vain glory,* my old Lord *Lechery,* Sir *having Greedy,* with all the rest of our Nobility, and he hath said moreover, that if all men were of his mind, if possible, there is not one of these Noble men should have any longer a being in this Town. Besides, he hath not been afraid to rail on you my Lord, who are now appointed to be his Judge, calling you an ungodly Villain, with many other such like vilifying terms, with which he hath bespattered most of the Gentry of our Town. When this *Pickthank* had told his Tale, the Judge directed his Speech to the Prisoner at the Bar, saying, thou Runagate,[72] Heretic, and Traitor, hast thou heard what these honest Gentlemen have witnessed against thee?

Sins are all
Lords and great
ones

Faith. *May I speak a few words in my own defence?*

Judge. Sirrah, Sirrah, thou deservest to live no longer, but to be slain immediately upon the place; yet that all men may see our gentleness towards thee, let us hear what thou vile Runagate hast to say.

Faithful's
defence of
himself

Faith. 1. I say then in answer to what Mr. *Envy* hath spoken, I never said ought but this, *That what Rule, or Laws, or Custom, or People were flat against the Word of God, are diametrically opposed to Christianity.* If I have said amiss in this convince me in my error, and I am ready here before you to make my recantation.

2. As to the second, to wit, Mr *Superstition* and his charge against me, I said only this, *That in the worship of God there is required a Divine Faith, but there can be no divine faith without a divine revelation of the will of God. Therefore whatever is thrust into the Worship of God, that is not agreeable to Divine Revelation, cannot be done but by a human Faith, which Faith will not be profitable to Eternal Life.*

3. As to what Mr. *Pickthank* hath said, I say (avoiding terms, as that I am said to rail, and the like) that the Prince of this Town, with all the rabblement his Attendants, by this Gentleman named, are more fit for being in Hell, than in this Town and Country; *and so the Lord have mercy upon me.*

Then the Judge called to the Jury (who all this while stood by, to hear and observe;) Gentlemen of the Jury, you see this man about whom so great an uproar hath been made in this Town: you have also heard what these worthy Gentlemen have witnessed against him; also you have heard his reply and confession: It lieth now in your breath to hang him, or save his life: but yet I think meet to instruct you in our Law. *The Judge his speech to the Jury*

There was an act made in the days of *Pharaoh* the Great, Servant to our Prince, that, lest those of a contrary Religion should multiply and grow too strong for him, their Males should be thrown into the River. There was an Act also made in the days of *Nebuchadnezzar* the Great, another of his Servants, that whoever would not fall down and worship his golden Image, should be thrown into a Fiery Furnace. There was also an Act made in the days of *Darius*, that whoso for some time called upon any God but him should be cast into the Lions' Den. Now the substance of these Laws this Rebel has broken; not only in thought (which is not to be born) but also in word and deed; which must therefore needs be intolerable. *Exod. 1* *Dan. 3* *Dan. 6*

For that of *Pharaoh,* his law was made upon supposition,

to prevent mischief; no Crime yet being apparent; but here is a Crime apparent. For the second and third, you see he disputeth against our Religion; and for the Treason he hath confessed, he deserveth to die the death.

The Jury and their names

Then went the Jury out, whose names were, Mr. *Blindman*, Mr. *No-good*, Mr. *Malice*, Mr. *Love-lust*, Mr. *Heady*, Mr. *High-mind*, Mr. *Enmity*, Mr. *Liar*, Mr. *Cruelty*, Mr. *Hate-light*, and Mr. *Implacable*;[73] who every one gave in his private Verdict against him among themselves, and afterwards unanimously concluded to bring him in guilty before the Judge. And first among themselves, Mr. *Blindman*, the Foreman, said, *I see clearly that this man is an* Heretic. Then said Mr. *No-good*, *away with such a Fellow from the Earth*. *Ay*, said Mr. *Malice*, *for I hate the very looks of him*. Then said Mr. *Love-lust*, *I could never endure him. Nor I*, said Mr. *Liveloose*, *for he would always be condemning my way*. *Hang him, hang him*, said Mr. *Heady*, *A sorry Scrub* said Mr. *Highmind*. *My heart riseth against him*, said Mr. *Enmity*, *he is a Rogue*, said Mr. *Liar*, *Hanging is too good for him*, said Mr. *Cruelty*, *Let's dispatch him out of the way*, said Mr. *Hate-light*. Then said Mr. *Implacable*, *might I have all the world given me, I could not be reconciled to him, therefore let us bring him guilty of death*. And so they did, therefore he was presently condemned, to be had from the place from whence he came, and there to be put to the most cruel death that could be invented.

Every one's private Verdict

They conclude to bring him in guilty of death

The cruel death of Faithful

They therefore brought him out, to do with him according to their Law; and first they scourged him, then they buffeted him, then they lanced his flesh with knives; after that they stoned him with stones, then pricked him with their Swords; and last of all they burned him to ashes at the Stake.[74] Thus came *Faithful* to his end. Now I saw that there stood behind the multitude a Chariot and a couple of Horses,[75] waiting for *Faithful*, who (so soon as his Adversaries had dispatched him) was taken up into it, and straightway was carried up through the Clouds, with sound of Trumpet, the nearest way to the Celestial Gate. But as for *Christian*, he had some respite, and was remanded back

A Chariot and Horses wait to take away Faithful

Christian still a Prisoner

to Prison; so he there remained for a space: But he that over-rules all things, having the power of their rage in his own hand, so wrought it about, that *Christian* for that time escaped them and went his way.

And as he went he sang, saying,

> *Well* Faithful, *thou hast faithfully professed*
> *Unto thy Lord; with whom thou shalt be blessed;*
> *When* faithless *ones, with all their vain delight*
> *Are crying out under their Hellish plights;*
> *Sing* Faithful, *sing; and let thy name survive;*
> *For though they kill'd thee, thou art yet alive.*

The Song that Christian *made of* Faithful *after his death*

Now I saw in my Dream, that *Christian* went not forth alone, for there was one whose name was *Hopeful*, (Being so made by the beholding of *Christian* and *Faithful* in their words and behaviour, in their sufferings at the *Fair*,) who joined himself unto him, and entering into a brotherly Covenant, told him, that he would be his Companion. Thus one died to bear Testimony to the Truth, and another rises out of the Ashes to be a Companion with *Christian* in their Pilgrimage. This *Hopeful* also told *Christian*, that there were many more of the men in the *Fair* that would take their time, & follow after. So I saw that quickly, after they were got out of the *Fair*, they overtook one that was going before them, whose name was *By-ends*;[76] So they said to him, what Country-man, Sir? And how far go you this way? He told them, that he came from the Town of *Fair-speech*, and he was going to the Celestial City, (but told them not his name.)

Christian has another Companion

There are more of the men of the Fair *will follow*

They overtake By-ends

From Fair-speech, said Christian? *Is there any good that lives there?*

Prov. 26.25

By-ends. Yes, said *By-ends*, I hope.

Chr. Pray Sir, *what may I call you?* said *Christian*.

By-ends. I am a stranger to you, and you to me; If you be going this way, I shall be glad of your Company: if not, I must be content.

By-ends loth to tell his name

Chr. This Town of Fair-speech, *said* Christian, *I have*

Brave *Faithfull*, Bravely done in word and deed
Judge, Witnesses and Jury have instead
Of overcoming thee, but shewn their rage,
When they are dead thou'lt live from age to age.

heard of, and, as I remember, they say it's a wealthy place.

By-ends. Yes, I will assure you that it is, and I have very many rich kindred there.

Chr. Pray, who are your kindred there, if a man may be so bold?

By-ends. Almost the whole Town; and in particular, my Lord *Turn-about,* my Lord *Time-server,* my Lord *Fair-speech,* (from whose Ancestors that Town first took its name:) Also Mr. *Smooth-man,* Mr. *Facing both-ways,* Mr. *Anything,* and the Parson of our Parish, Mr. *Two-tongues,* was my Mother's own brother by Father's side: And to tell you the truth, I am become a Gentleman of Good Quality, yet my Great Grandfather was but a Waterman, looking one way, and rowing another, and I got most of my Estate by the same occupation.

Chr. Are you a married man?

By-ends. Yes, and my Wife is a very virtuous Woman, the Daughter of a virtuous Woman; she was my Lady *Faining's* Daughter, therefore she came of a very honourable Family, and is arrived to such a pitch of Breeding, that she knows how to carry it to all, even to Prince and Peasant. 'Tis true, we somewhat differ in Religion from those of the stricter sort, yet but in two small points: First, we never strive against Wind and Tide. Secondly, we are always most zealous when Religion goes in his Silver Slippers; we love much to walk with him in the Street, if the Sun shines and the People applaud him.

The Wife and kindred of By-ends

Where By-ends differs from others in Religion

Then *Christian* stepped a little aside to his fellow *Hopeful,* saying, It runs in my mind that this is one *By-ends* of *Fairspeech,* and if it be he, we have as very a Knave in our company, as dwelleth in all these parts. Then said *Hopeful, Ask him; methinks he should not be ashamed of his name.* So *Christian* came up with him again; and said, Sir, you talk as if you knew something more than all the World doth, and if I take not my mark amiss, I deem I have half a guess of you; is not your name Mr *By-ends* of *Fair-speech?*

By-ends. This is not my name, but indeed it is a Nickname that is given me by some that cannot abide me, and

I must be content to bear it as a reproach, as other good men have borne theirs before me.

How By-ends
got his name

Chr. *But did you never give an occasion to men to call you by this name?*

By-ends. Never, never! The worst that ever I did to give them an occasion to give me this name, was, that I had always the luck to jump in my judgement with the present way of the times, whatever it was, and my chance was to get thereby; but if things are thus cast upon me, let me count them a blessing, but let not the malicious load me therefore with reproach.

Chr. *I thought indeed that you were the man that I heard of; and to tell you what I think, I fear this name belongs to you more properly than you are willing we should think it doth.*

*He desires to
keep company
with* Christian.

By-ends. Well, if you will thus imagine, I can not help it. You shall find me a fair Company-keeper, if you will still admit me your Associate.

Chr. *If you will go with us, you must go against Wind and Tide, the which, I perceive, is against your opinion: You must also own Religion in his Rags, as well as when in his silver Slippers, and stand by him too, when bound in Irons, as well as when he walketh the Streets with applause.*

By-ends. You must not impose, nor Lord it over my Faith, leave me to my liberty, and let me go with you.

Chr. *Not a step further, unless you will do, in what I propound, as we.*

Then said *By-ends,* I shall never desert my old principles, By-ends *and*
Christian *part* since they are harmless and profitable. If I may not go with you, I must do as I did before you overtook me, even go by my self, until some overtake me that will be glad of my company.

Now I saw in my Dream, that *Christian* and *Hopeful* forsook him and kept their distance before him, but one of them looking back saw three men following Mr. *By-ends,* and behold, as they came up with him he made them a very *He has new
companions* low *Congee,*[77] and they also gave him a Compliment. The men's names were Mr. *Hold-the-World,* Mr. *Money-love,*

and Mr. *Save-all*; men that Mr. *By-ends* had formerly been acquainted with; for in their Minority they were School-fellows, and were taught by one Mr. *Gripe-man*,[78] a School-master in *Love-gain,* which is a Market-Town in the County of *Coveting* in the North. This School-master taught them the art of getting, either by violence, cozen-age,[79] flattery, lying, or by putting on a guise of Religion, and these four Gentlemen had attained much of the art of their Master, so that they could each of them have kept such a School themselves.

Well, when they had as I said, thus saluted each other, Mr. *Money-love* said to Mr. *By-ends,* who are they upon the Road before us? For *Christian* and *Hopeful* were yet within view.

By-ends. They are a couple of far Country men, that after their *mode* are going on Pilgrimage.

By-ends' Character of the Pilgrims

Money-love. Alas, why did they not stay, that we might have had their good company, for *they* and *we,* and *you* Sir, I hope are all going on a Pilgrimage.

By-ends. We are so indeed, but the men before us are so rigid, and love so much their own notions and do also lightly esteem the opinions of others; that let a man be never so godly, yet if he jumps not with them in all things, they thrust him quite out of their Company.

Mr. *Save-all.* That's bad but we read of some, *that are righteous overmuch,*[80] and such men's rigidness prevails with them to judge and condemn all but themselves, but I pray what, and how many were the things wherein you differed?

By-ends. Why they, after their head-strong manner, con-clude that it is their duty to rush on their Journey *all* weathers, and I am for waiting for *Wind* and *Tide.* They are for hazarding all for God at a Clap,[81] and I am for taking all advantages to secure my Life and Estate. They are for holding *their notions* though all other men be against them, but I am for Religion in what, and so far as the times, and my safety will bear it. They are for Religion, when in rags and contempt, but I am for him when he walks in his golden Slippers in the Sun-shine, and with applause.

Mr. *Hold-the-World*. Ay, and hold you there still, good Mr. *By-ends;* for my part, I can count him but a Fool, that having the liberty to keep what he has, shall be so unwise to lose it. Let us be as wise *as Serpents,* it's best to make hay while the Sun shines;[82] you see how the Bee lieth still all winter, and bestirs her only when she can have profit with pleasure. God sends sometimes Rain, and sometimes Sun-shine; if they be such fools to go through the first, yet let us be content to take fair weather along with us. For my part, I like that Religion best that will stand with the security of God's good Blessings unto us; for who can imagine, that is ruled by his reason, since God has bestowed upon us the good things of this Life, but that he would have us keep them for his sake. *Abraham* and *Solomon* grew rich in Religion. And *Job* says that a good man *shall lay up gold as dust.*[83] But he must not be such as the men before us, if they be as you have described them.

Mr. *Save-all*. I think that we are all agreed in this matter, and therefore there needs no more words about it.

Mr. *Money-love*. No there needs no more words about this matter indeed, for he that believes neither Scripture nor Reason[84] (and you see we have both on our side) neither knows his own liberty nor seeks his own safety.

Mr. *By-ends*. My Brethren, we are, as you see, going all on Pilgrimage, and for our better diversion from things that are bad, give me leave to propound unto you this question.

Suppose a Man; a Minister, or a Trades-man, &c. should have an advantage lie before him to get the good blessings of this life; Yet so as that he can by no means come by them except in appearance at least, he becomes extraordinary zealous in some points of Religion that he meddled not with before, may he not use this means to attain this end, and yet be a right honest man?

Mr. Money-love. *I see the bottom of your question, and with these Gentlemen's good leave, I will endeavour to shape you an answer. And first to speak to your question, as it concerns a* Minister *himself.* Suppose a Minister, a worthy man, possessed but of a very small benefice, and has in his eye a greater, more fat and plump by far; he has also now an opportunity of getting it; yet so as by being more studious by preaching more frequently, and zealously, and because the temper of the people requires it, by altering of some of his principles, for my part, I see no reason but a man may do this (provided he has a call). Ay, and more a great deal besides, and yet be an honest man. For why,

1. His desire of a greater Benefice is lawful (this cannot be contradicted) since 'tis set before him by Providence; so then he may get it if he can, *making no question for Conscience sake.*

2. Besides his desire after that Benefice, makes him more studious, a more zealous Preacher, &c. and so makes him a better man, Yea makes him better improve his parts, which is according to the mind of God.

3. Now as for his complying with the temper of his people, by dissenting, to serve them, some of his Principles: this argueth, 1. That he is of a self-denying temper. 2. Of a sweet and winning deportment. 3. And so more fit for the Ministerial Function.

4. I conclude then, that a Minister that changes a *Small* for a *Great,* should not for so doing be judged as covetous, but rather since he is improved in his parts, and industry, thereby be counted as one that pursues his call, and the opportunity put into his hand to do good.

And now to the second part of the question, which concerns the *Tradesman* you mentioned: suppose such a one to have but a poor employ in the world, but by becoming Religious he may mend his market, perhaps get a rich Wife,[85] or more and far better customers to his shops. For my part, I see no reason, but that this may be lawfully done. For why,

1. To become religious is a virtue, by what means soever a man becomes so.

2. Nor is it unlawful to get a rich wife, or more custom to my Shop.

3. Besides the man that gets these by becoming religious, gets that which is good of them that are good, by becoming good himself; so then here is a good wife, and good customers, and good gain, and all these by becoming religious, which is good. Therefore to become religious to get all these, is good and profitable design.

This answer, thus made by this Mr. *Money-love,* to Mr. *By-ends'* question was highly applauded by them all; wherefore they concluded upon the whole, that it was most wholesome and advantageous. And because, as they thought, no man was able to contradict it, and because *Christian* and *Hopeful* were yet within call they jointly agreed to assault them with the question as soon as they overtook them, and the rather, because they had opposed Mr. *By-ends* before. So they called after them and they stopped, and stood still till they came up to them but they concluded as they went, that not Mr. *By-ends,* but old Mr. *Hold-the-World* should propound the question to them, because as they supposed their answer to him would be without the remainder of that heat that was kindled betwixt Mr. *By-ends* and them, at their parting a little before.

So they came up to each other, and after a short salutation, Mr. *Hold-the-World* propounded the question to *Christian* and his Fellow and bid them to answer it if they could.

Chr. Then said *Christian,* even a Babe in Religion may answer ten thousand such questions. For if it be unlawful to follow Christ for Loaves,[86] as it is *John 6,* how much more is it abominable to make him and Religion a stalking Horse[87] to get and enjoy the World? Nor do we find any other than Heathens, Hypocrites, Devils, and Witches that are of this opinion.

1. *Heathens,* for when *Hamor* and *Shechem* had a mind to the daughter and Cattle of *Jacob,* and saw there was no ways for them to come at them, but by becoming Circumcised, they say to their companions, *If every Male of us be circumcised, as they are circumcised, shall not their Cattle and their Substance, and every Beast of theirs be ours.* Their

Daughters and their Cattle were that which they sought to obtain, and their Religion the stalking-horse they made use of to come at them. Read the whole story, *Genesis* 34.20, 21, 22, 23.

2. The Hypocritical Pharisees were also of this Religion, long prayers were their pretence, but to get Widows' Houses were their intent, and greater damnation was from God their Judgement, *Luke* 20.46, 47.

3. *Judas* the Devil was also of this Reason, he was religious for the Bag,[88] that he might be possessed of what was therein; but he was lost, cast away, and the very son of Perdition.

4. *Simon* the Witch was of this Religion, for he would have had the Holy Ghost that he might have got money therewith, and his sentence from *Peter's* mouth was according, *Acts* 8.19, 20, 21, 22.

5. Neither will it out of my mind, but that that man, that takes up Religion for the world, will throw away Religion for the world; for so surely as *Judas* designed the world in becoming Religious, so surely did he also sell religion and his Master for the same. To answer the question therefore affirmatively, as I perceive you have done and to accept of as authentic, such answer, is both Heathenish, Hypocritical and Devilish, and your reward will be according to your works. Then they stood staring one upon another, but had not therewith to answer *Christian*. *Hopeful* also approved of the soundness of *Christian's* answer, so there was a great silence among them. Mr. *By-ends* and his Company also staggered and kept behind, that *Christian* and *Hopeful* might outgo them. Then said *Christian* to his fellow, if these men cannot stand before the sentence of men, what will they do with the sentence of God? And if they are mute when dealt with by vessels of clay, what will they do when they shall be rebuked by the flames of a devouring fire?

Then *Christian* and *Hopeful* outwent them again, and went till they came at a delicate plain called *Ease,* where they went with much content; but that plain was but narrow, so they were quickly got over it. Now the further side

The Ease that Pilgrims have is but little in this life

Lucre-*Hill a*
dangerous Hill
of that Plain was a little Hill called *Lucre,* and in that *Hill* a *Silver Mine,* which some of them that had formerly gone that way because of the rarity of it had turned aside to see; but going too near the brim of the pit, the ground being deceitful under them, broke, and they were slain; some also had been maimed there, and could not to their dying day be their own men again.[89]

Demas *at the*
Hill Lucre

He *calls* to Chris-
tian *and* Hopeful
to come to him
Then I saw in my Dream, that a little off the Road, over against the *Silver Mine* stood *Demas* (Gentleman like) to call Passengers to come and see; who said to *Christian* and his fellow; Ho turn aside hither and I will show you a thing.[90]

Chr. What thing so deserving as to turn us out of the way to see it?

Dem. Here is a *Silver mine,* and some digging in it for Treasure, if you will come with a little pains you may richly provide for your selves.

Hopeful *tempted*
to go, but Chris-
tian *holds him*
back
Hope. Then said *Hopeful, let us go see.*

Chr. Not I, said *Christian,* I have heard of this place before now, and how many there have been slain; and besides, the Treasure is a snare to those that seek it; for it hindereth them in their Pilgrimage. Then *Christian* called

Hos. 4.18
to *Demas,* saying, *Is not this place dangerous? Hath it not hindered many in their* Pilgrimage?

Dem. Not very dangerous, except to those that are careless; but withal he blushed as he spake.

Chr. Then said *Christian* to *Hopeful,* let us not stir a step, but still keep on our way.

Hope. *I will warrant you, when* By-ends *comes up, if he hath the same invitation as us he will turn in thither to see.*

Chr. No doubt thereof, for his Principles send him that way, and a hundred to one but he dies there.

Dem. Then *Demas* called again, saying, but will you not come over to see?

Christian *round-*
eth up Demas.
2 Timothy 4.10
Chr. Then *Christian* roundly answered, saying, *Demas,* thou art an Enemy to the right ways of the Lord of this way, and hast been already condemned for thine own

turning aside, by one of his Majesty's Judges; and why seekest thou to bring us into the like condemnation? Besides, if we at all turn aside, our Lord the King will certainly hear thereof, and will there put us to shame, where we would stand with boldness before him.

Demas cried again that he also was one of their fraternity; and that if they would tarry a little, he also would walk with them.

Chr. Then said *Christian* what is thy name? Is it not the same by the which I have called thee?

Dem. Yes my name is Demas, *I am the son of* Abraham.

Chr. I know you, Gehazi *was your great grandfather, and* Judas *your father, and you have trod their steps; it is but a devilish prank that thou usest: Thy Father was hanged for a Traitor, and thou deservest no better reward. Assure thy self, that when we come to the King, we will do him word of this thy behaviour. Thus they went their way.*

By this time *By-ends* and his Companions were come again within sight, and they at the first beck went over to *Demas.* Now whether they fell into the Pit by looking over the brink thereof, or whether they went down to dig, or whether they were smothered at the bottom by the damps that commonly arise, of these things, I am not certain, but this I observed, that they were never seen again in the way.

Then sang *Christian,*

> By-ends *and* Silver Demas *both agree,*
> *One calls, the other runs that he may be*
> *A sharer in his Lucre, so these do*
> *Take up in this World, and no farther go.*

Now I saw, that just on the other side of this Plain, the Pilgrims came to a place where stood an old *Monument,* hard by the High way side, at the sight of which they were both concerned, because of the strangeness of the form thereof; for it seemed to them as if it had been a *Woman* transformed into the shape of a Pillar: here therefore they

2 Kings 5.20.
Matthew 26.14,
15, ch. 27, 1, 2,
3, 5, 6

By-ends goes
over to Demas

They see a
strange
Monument

stood looking and looking upon it, but could not for a time tell what they should make of the form thereof; at last *Hopeful* espied written above up on the head thereof, a writing in an unusual hand, but he being no Scholar called to *Christian* (for he was learned) to see if he could pick out the meaning: so he came, and after a little laying of Letters together, he found the same to be this, *Remember Lot's Wife*.[91] So he read it to his fellow; after which they

Genesis 19.26 both concluded that that was the Pillar of Salt into which *Lot's* Wife was turned for her looking back with a *covetous heart,* when she was going from *Sodom* for safety. Which sudden and amazing sight gave them occasion of this discourse.

Chr. Ah my Brother, this is a seasonable sight, it came opportunely to us after the Invitation which *Demas* gave us to come over to view the Hill *Lucre,* and had we gone over as he desired us, and as thou wast inclined to do (my Brother) we had for ought I know been made like this Woman a spectacle for those that shall come after, to behold.

Hope. I am sorry that I was so foolish, and am made to wonder that I am not now as *Lot's* Wife: for wherein was the difference 'twixt her sin and mine? She only looked back, and I had a desire to go see; let Grace be adored and let me be ashamed, that ever such a thing should be in mine heart.

Chr. Let us take notice of what we see here for time to come: This Woman escaped one Judgement; for she fell not by the destruction of *Sodom,* yet she was destroyed by another; as we see, she is turned into a Pillar of Salt.

Hope. True, and she may be to us both *Caution* and *Example; Caution,* that we should shun her sin, or a sign of what Judgement will overtake such as shall not be prevented by this caution: So *Korah, Dathan,* and *Abiram,* with the two hundred and fifty men, that perished in their

Numb. 26.9, 10 sin, did also become a Sign or Example to beware, but above all, I muse at one thing, to wit how *Demas* and his fellows can stand so confidently yonder to look for that treasure, which this Woman, but for looking behind her, after (for we read not that she stepped one foot out of the way) was turned into a Pillar of Salt, specially since the Judgement which overtook her, did make her an Example, within sight of where they are: for they cannot choose but see her, did they but lift up their eyes.

Chr. It is a thing to be wondered at, and it argueth that their hearts are grown desperate in that case, and I cannot tell who to compare them to so fitly, as to them that pick Pockets in the presence of the Judge, or that will cut purses under the Gallows. It is said of the men of *Sodom, that they were sinners* exceedingly, because they were *sinners before the Lord;* that is in his eye-sight, and notwithstanding the kindnesses that he had showed them, for the Land of Sodom was now like the Garden of *Eden heretofore.* This therefore provoked him the more to jealousy and made their plagues hot as the fire of the Lord out of Heaven could make it. And it is most rationally to be concluded, that such, even such as these are, they that shall sin in the sight, yea and that too in despite of such examples that are set continually before them to caution them to the contrary, must be partakers of severest Judgements. *Genesis 13.13* *Ver. 10*

Hope. Doubtless thou hast said the truth, but what a mercy is it, that neither thou, but especially I, am not made my self this example. This ministreth occasion to us to thank God, to fear before him, and always to remember *Lot's* wife.

I saw then that they went on their way to a pleasant River; which *David the King* called the *River of God;* but *John, the River of the water of Life.* Now their way lay just upon the bank of the River. Here therefore *Christian* and his Companion, walked with great delight; they drank also of the water of the River, which was pleasant and enlivening to their weary Spirits: Besides on the banks of the River, on either side, were *green Trees* for all manner of Fruit; and the Leaves they eat to prevent *A River.* Psal. 65.9. Rev. 22. Ezek. 47 *Trees by the River*

*The fruit, and
leaves of the Trees*

*A Meadow in
which they lie to
sleep.* Psal. 22,
Isa. 14.13
Surfeits, and other diseases that are incident to those that
heat their blood by Travels. On either side of the River was
also a Meadow curiously beautified with Lilies; and it was
green all the year long. In this Meadow they lay down and
slept, for here they might lie down safely. When they
awoke, they gathered again of the water of the River; and
then lay down again to sleep. Thus they did several days
and nights. Then they sang,

> *Behold ye how these Crystal Streams do glide,*
> *(To comfort Pilgrims) by the High-way side.*
> *The Meadows green; besides their fragrance smell,*
> *Yield dainties for them: and he that can tell*
> *What pleasant Fruit, yea, Leaves, these Trees do yield,*
> *Will soon sell all,*[92] *that he may buy this Field.*

So when they were disposed to go on (for they were not,
as yet, at their Journey's end) they eat and drank, and
departed.

Now I beheld in my Dream that they had journeyed far,
but the River and the way, for a time parted at which
they were not a little sorry, yet they durst not go out of
the way: Now the way from the River was rough, and
their feet tender by reason of their Travels; *So the Souls of*
Numb. 21.4 *the Pilgrims were much discouraged, because of the way.*
Wherefore still as they went on, they wished for a better
way. Now a little before them there was on the left hand
of the Road a *Meadow,* and a Stile to go over into it,
*By-path-
Meadow. One
temptation does
make way for
another*
and that *Meadow* is called *By-path Meadow.* Then said
Christian to his fellow, If this Meadow lieth along by
our way side, let's go on into it. Then he went to the Stile
to see and behold a Path lay along by the way on the
other side of the fence. 'Tis according to my wish, said
Christian, here is the easiest going; come good *Hopeful,*
and let us go over.

Hope. *But how if this Path should lead us out of the
way?*

Chr. That's not like, said the other; look doth it not go

along by the way side? So *Hopeful* being persuaded by his
fellow went after him over the Stile. When they were gone
over, and were got into the path they found it very easy for
their feet and withal, they looking before them spied a man
walking as they did, (and his name was *Vain-Confidence*)
so they called after him, and asked him whither that way
led? he said to the Celestial Gate. Look said *Christian*, did
I not tell you so? by this you may see we are right; so they
followed and he went before them. But behold, as night
came on, and it grew very dark, so he that went behind,
lost the sight of him that went before.

Strong Christian may lead weak ones out of the way

See what it is too suddenly to fall in with strangers

He therefore that went before (*Vain-confidence* by name)
not seeing the way before him, fell into a deep Pit, which
was on purpose there made by the Prince of those grounds
to catch *vain glorious* Fools withal, and was dashed in
pieces with his fall.

Isa. 9.16. A pit to catch the vain-glorious in

Now *Christian* and his fellow heard him fall. So they
called to know the matter, but there was none to answer,
only they heard a groaning. Then said *Hopeful,* where are
we now? Then was his fellow silent, as mistrusting that he
had led him out of the way. And now it began to rain and
thunder, and lighten in a very dreadful manner, and the
water rose amain.

Reasoning between Chris-tian and Hopeful

Then *Hopeful* groaned in himself, saying, *Oh that I had
kept on my way!*

Chr. Who could have thought that this Path should have
led us out of the way?

*Hope. I was afraid on't at the very first, and therefore
gave you that gentle caution. I would have spoke plainer,
but you are older than I.*

Chr. Good brother be not offended, I am sorry I have
brought thee out of the way, and that I have put thee into
such eminent danger; pray my Brother forgive me, I did not
do it of an evil Intent.

Christian's repentance for leading of his brother out of the way

*Hope. Be comforted my Brother, for I forgive thee; and
believe too, that this shall be for our good.*

Chr. I am glad I have with me a merciful Brother: But
we must not stand thus, let's try to go back again.

Hope. *But good Brother let me go before.*

Chr. No, if you please let me go first; that if there be any danger, I may be first therein, because by my means we are both gone out of the way.

Hope. *No said* Hopeful, *you shall not go first, for your mind being troubled may lead you out of the way again.* Then for their encouragement they heard the voice of one saying, *Let thine heart be towards the High-way, even the way that thou wentest, turn again.* But by this time the waters were greatly risen; by reason of which the way of going back was very dangerous. (Then I thought that it is easier going out of the way when we are in, than going in when we are out.) Yet they adventured to go back; but it was so dark, and the flood was so high, that in their going back they had like to have been drowned nine or ten times.

Jer. 31.21. They are in danger of drowning, as they go back

Neither could they with all the skill they had get again to the Stile that night. Wherefore at last, lighting under a little shelter, they sat down there until the daybreak: But being weary, they fell asleep. Now there was not far from the place where they lay, a *Castle* called *Doubting-Castle,* the owner whereof was *Giant Despair,*[93] and it was in his grounds they were now sleeping; wherefore he getting up in the morning early, and walking up and down in his Fields, caught *Christian* and *Hopeful* asleep in his grounds. Then with a grim and surly voice he bid them awake, and asked them whence they were? And what they did in his grounds? They told him they were Pilgrims, and that they had lost their way. Then said the *Giant,* you have this night trespassed on me, by trampling and lying on my Ground, and therefore you must go along with me, So they were forced to go, because he was stronger than they. They also had but little to say, for they knew themselves in a fault. The *Giant* therefore drove them before him, and put them into his Castle, into a very dark Dungeon, nasty and stinking to the spirit of these two men: Here then they lay from *Wednesday* Morning till *Saturday* Night without one bit of bread, or drop of drink or light, or any to ask how they did: They were therefore here in evil case, and were far

They sleep in the grounds of Giant Despair

He finds them in his ground and carries them to Doubting-Castle

The grievousness of their Imprisonment

from friends and acquaintance. Now in this place *Christian*   Psal. 88.16
had double sorrow, because 'twas through his unadvised
Counsel that they were brought into this distress.

Now *Giant Despair* had a Wife and her name was *Diffidence:*[94] So when he was gone to bed, he told his Wife what
he had done, to wit, that he had taken a couple of Prisoners,
and cast them into his *Dungeon,* for trespassing on his
Grounds. Then he asked her also what he had best to do
further to them. Then she counselled him, that when he
arose in the morning, he should beat them without mercy:
So when he arose, he getteth him a grievous Crab-tree
Cudgel, and goes down into the *Dungeon* to them; and
there falls first to rating of them as if they were dogs:
although they gave him never a word of distaste; then he
falls upon them, and beats them fearfully, in such sort that
they were not able to help themselves, or to turn them upon
the floor. This done he withdraws and leaves them, there   *On* Thursday
to condole their misery and to mourn under their distress: *Giant* Despair
so on that day, they spent the time in nothing but sighs and   *beats his*
bitter lamentations. The next night she talking with her   *Prisoners*
Husband about them further, and understanding that they
were yet alive, did advise him to counsel them to make
away themselves: So when morning was come, he goes to
them in a surly manner, as before, and perceives them to
be very sore with the stripes that he had given them the day
before; he told them, that since they were never like to
come out of that place, their only way would be, forthwith
to make an end of themselves; either with Knife, Halter, or   *On* Friday *Giant*
Poison.[95] For why, said he, should you choose life, seeing   Despair *coun-*
as it is attended with so much bitterness. But they desired   *sels them to kill*
him to let them go; with that he looked ugly upon them,   *themselves*
and rushing to them, had doubtless made an end of them
himself, but that he fell into one of his fits; (for he sometimes   *The Giant some-*
in Sun-shiny weather fell into fits) and lost (for a time) the   *times has fits*
use of his hands: wherefore he withdrew and left them (as
before) to consider what to do. Then did the prisoners
consult between themselves, whether 'twas best to take his
counsel or no: and thus they began their discourse.

The pilgrims now to gratifie the flesh
will seek its eas, but oh how they afresh
doe their bij plunge themselves new griefs into
who seeken to pleas the flesh themselves vndoe

Chr. Brother, said *Christian;* what shall we do? The life that we now live is miserable; for my part, I know not whether is best, to live thus, or die out of hand. *My Soul chooseth strangling rather than life:* and the Grave is more easy for me than this Dungeon: shall we be ruled by the Giant?

Christian crushed

Job 7.15

Hope. Indeed our present condition is dreadful, and death would be far more welcome to me than *thus* for ever to abide: but yet let us consider, the Lord of the country to which we are going, hath said, Thou shalt do no Murther, no not to another man's person; much more then are we forbidden to take his counsel to kill our selves. Besides he that kills another, can but commit murder upon his body; but for one to kill himself, is to kill body and soul at once. And moreover, my brother, thou talkest of ease in the Grave, but has thou forgotten to Hell whither for certain the murderers go? For no murderer hath eternal life, &c. And let us consider again, that all the Law is not in the hand of *Giant Despair:* Others, so far as I can understand, have been taken by him, as well as we; and yet have escaped out of his hand: Who knows, but that God that made the World, may cause that *Giant Despair* may die; or that, at some time or other, he may forget to lock us in; or, but he may in a short time have another of his fits before us, and may lose the use of his limbs; and if ever that would come to pass again, for my part, I am resolved to pluck up the heart of a man, and to try my utmost to get from under his hand. I was a fool that I did not try to do it before, but however, my Brother, let's be patient, and endure a while; the time may come that may give us a happy release: but let us not be our own murderers. With these words, *Hopeful* at present did moderate the mind of his Brother; so they continued together (in the dark) that day in their sad and doleful condition.

Hopeful *comforts him*

Well towards Evening the Giant goes down into the Dungeon again, to see if his Prisoners had taken his counsel; but when he came there, he found them alive; and truly, alive was all: for now, what for want of Bread and Water, and by reason of the wounds they received when he beat them, they could do little but breath: *But I say, he found them alive; at which he fell into a grievous rage, and told them, That seeing they had disobeyed his counsel, it should be worse with them than if they had never been born.*

At this they trembled greatly, and I think that Christian *fell into a Swound; but coming a little to himself again they renewed their discourse about the* Giant's *counsel; and whether yet they had best take it or no. Now* Christian *again seemed to be for doing it, but* Hopeful *made his second reply as followeth.*

Christian *still dejected*

Hope. My Brother, *said he,* remembrest thou not how valiant thou hast been heretofore? *Apollyon* could not crush thee, nor could all that thou didst hear or see, or feel in the Valley of the shadow of death; what hardship, terror and amazement hast thou already got through, and art thou now nothing but fears? Thou seest that I am in the dungeon with thee, a far weaker man by nature, than thou art; Also this *Giant* has wounded me as well as thee; and hath also cut off the Bread and Water from my mouth; and with that I mourn without the light; But let's exercise a little more patience. Remember how thou playedst the man at *Vanity-Fair,* and wast neither afraid of the Chain or Cage; nor yet of bloody Death: Wherefore let us (at least to avoid the shame, that becomes not a Christian to be found in) bear up with patience as well as we can.

Hopeful *comforts him again by calling former things to remembrance*

Now night being come again, and the Giant *and his Wife being in Bed, she asked him concerning the Prisoners, and if they had taken his counsel: To which he replied, They are sturdy Rogues, they choose rather to bear all hardship, than to make away themselves. Then said she, take them into the Castle-yard tomorrow, and show them the* Bones *and* Skulls *of those that thou hast already dispatched, and make them believe e're a week comes to an end, thou also wilt tear them in pieces as thou hast done their fellows before them.*

So when the morning was come, the Giant *goes to them again: and takes them into the Castle-yard, and shows*

them, as his Wife had bidden him. These, said he, were On Saturday *the*
Pilgrims, as you are, once, and they trespassed in my Giant threatened that shortly
grounds, as you have done, and when I thought fit, I tore *he would pull*
them in pieces; and so within ten days I will do you. Get *them in pieces*
*you down into your den again: and with that he beat them
all the way thither: they lay therefore all day on* Saturday
*in a lamentable case, as before. Now when night was come,
and when Mrs.* Diffidence *and her husband, the* Giant, *were
got to bed, they began to renew their discourse of their
Prisoners; and withal the old* Giant *wondered that he could
neither by his blows nor counsel, bring them to an end.
And with that his wife replied, I fear said she, that they live
in hopes that some will come to relieve them, or that they
have picklocks about them, by the means of which they
hope to escape. And sayst thou so, my dear, said the* Giant,
I will therefore search them in the morning.

Well, *on* Saturday *about midnight they began to* pray
and continued in prayer till almost break of day.

Now *a little before it was day, good* Christian, *as one
half amazed, brake out in this passionate speech,* What a
fool (quoth he) am I, thus to lie in a stinking Dungeon
when I may as well walk at liberty? I have a key in my A Key in *Chris-*
bosom, called Promise,[96] that will (I am persuaded) open tian's *bosom*
called Promise,
any Lock in *Doubting-Castle. Then said* Hopeful, *That's* *opens any Lock*
good news; good Brother pluck it out of thy bosom and *in* Doubting-
Castle
try. Then Christian *pulled it out of his bosom and began
to try at the Dungeon door, whose bolt (as he turned the
Key) gave back, and the door flew open with ease, and*
Christian *and* Hopeful *both came out. Then he went to the
outward door, that leads into the* Castle-yard, *and with his
Key opened that door also. After he went to the Iron-gate,
for that must be opened too, but that Lock went* damnable
*hard, yet the Key did open it; then they thrust open the gate
to make their escape with speed; but that gate as it opened
made such a cracking, that it waked* Giant Despair, *who
hastily rising to pursue the Prisoners, felt his limbs to fail,
for his fits took him again, so that he could by no means
go after them. Then they went on, and came to the King's*

*High-way; and so were safe, because they were out of his
Jurisdiction.*

*Now when they were gone over the Stile, they began to
contrive with themselves what they should do at that Stile,
to prevent those that shall come after from falling into the*
A Pillar erected *hands of* Giant Despair. *So they consented to erect there a*
by Christian and *Pillar, and to engrave upon the side thereof this Sentence,*
his fellow over this Stile is the way to *Doubting-Castle,* which is kept
by *Giant Despair,* who despiseth the King of the Celestial
Country, and seeks to destroy the Holy Pilgrims. *Many
therefore that followed after, read what was written, and
escaped the danger. This done, they sang as follows.*

> Out of the way we went, and then we found
> What 'twas to tread upon forbidden ground,
> And let them that come after have a care
> Lest they for trespassing, his Prisoners are,
> Whose Castle's *Doubting,* and whose name's *Despair.*

They went then till they came to the delectable Moun-
The delectable tains,[97] which Mountains belong to the Lord of the Hill of
Mountains which we have spoken before; so they went up to the
Mountains to behold the Gardens and Orchards, the Vine-
yards and Fountains of Water; where also they drank, and
They are washed themselves, and did freely eat of the Vineyards.
refreshed in the Now, there were on the tops of these Mountains, *Shepherds*
Mountains feeding their flocks, and they stood by the Highway-side.
The Pilgrims therefore went to them, and leaning upon
their staves; (as is common with weary Pilgrims, when they
Talks with the stand to talk with any by the way,) they asked, *Whose*
Shepherds *Delectable Mountains are these; and whose be the sheep
that feed upon them?*

Shep. These mountains are *Immanuel's Land,* and they
are within sight of his City; and the Sheep also are his, and
he laid down his life for them.

Chr. Is this the way to the Celestial City?

Shep. You are just in your way.

Chr. How far is it thither?

Mountains delectable they now ascend
Where shepherds be which to them do commend
Aluring things and things that cautious are
Pilgrims are stiddie kept by faith and feare

Shep. Too far for any, but those who shall get thither indeed.

Chr. *Is the way safe or dangerous?*

Shep. Safe for those for whom it is to be safe; *but trans-*
Hos. 14.9 *gressors shall fall therein.*

Chr. *Is there in this place any relief for pilgrims that are weary and faint in the way?*

Shep. The Lord of these Mountains hath given us a
Heb. 13.1, 2 charge *not to be forgetful to entertain strangers;* Therefore the good of the place is before you.

I also saw in my dream, that when the *Shepherds* perceived that they were wayfaring men, they also put questions to them, (to which they made answer as in other places) as whence came you? and how got you into the way? And by what means have you so persevered therein? for but few of them that begin to come hither, do show their faces on these Mountains. But when the Shepherds heard their answers, being pleased therewith, they looked
The Shepherds very lovingly upon them, and said, Welcome to the delec-
welcome them table Mountains.

The Shepherds, I say, whose names were *Knowledge, Experience, Watchful,* and *Sincere,* took them by the hand, and had them to their Tents, and made them partake of that which was ready at present. They said moreover, We would that you should stay here a while, to be acquainted with us, and yet more to solace yourselves with the good of these delectable Mountains. Then they told them that they were content to stay; and so they went to their rest that night, because it was very late.

Then I saw in my Dream, that in the Morning, the Shepherds called up *Christian* and *Hopeful* to walk with them upon the Mountains. So they went forth with them, and walked a while, having a pleasant prospect on every side. Then said the Shepherds one to another, Shall we
They are sure show these pilgrims some wonders? So when they had
wonders. The concluded to do it, they had them first to the top of an Hill
mountain of called *Error,* which was very steep on the farthest side,
Error and bid them look down to the bottom. So *Christian* and

Hopeful looked down, and saw at the bottom several men dashed all to pieces by a fall that they had had from the top. Then said *Christian,* What meaneth this? The shepherds answered, Have you not heard of them that were made to err, by hearkening to *Hymenius* and *Philetus,*[98] as concern- ing the faith of the Resurrection of the body? They answered, yea. Then said the shepherds, Those that you see lie dashed in pieces at the bottom of this mountain are they; and they have continued to this day unburied, as you see, for an Example to others to take heed how they clamber too high, or how they come too near the brink of this Mountain.

2 Tim. 2.17, 18

Then I saw that they had them to the top of another Mountain, and the name of that is *Caution,* and bid them look afar off; which, when they did, they perceived, as they thought, several men walking up and down among the Tombs that were there; and they perceived that the men were blind, because they stumbled sometimes upon the Tombs, and because they could not get out from among them.[99] Then said *Christian, What means this?*

Mount Caution

The shepherds then answered, Did you not see, a little below these Mountains, a *Stile* that led into a Meadow, on the left hand of this way? They answered, Yes. Then said the Shepherds, From that Stile there goes a path that leads directly to *Doubting Castle,* which is kept by *Giant Despair;* and these men (pointing to them among the Tombs) came once on pilgrimage, as you do now, even until they came to that same *Stile.* And because the right way was rough in that place, they chose to go out of it into that meadow, and there were taken by *Giant Despair,* and cast into *Doubting-Castle;* where after they had a while been kept in the dun- geon, he at last did put out their eyes, and led them among those Tombs, where he has left them to wander to this very day; that the saying of the wise man might be fulfilled, *He that wandereth out of the way of understanding, shall remain in the Congregation of the dead.* Then Christian and Hopeful looked upon one another, with tears gushing out, but yet said nothing to the Shepherds.

Prov. 21.16

Then I saw in my Dream, that the Shepherds had them to another place in a Bottom, where was a door on the side of a hill; and they opened the door, and bid them look in. They looked in therefore, and saw that within it was very dark and smoky; they also thought that they heard there a rumbling noise, as of fire, and a cry of some tormented, and that they smelt the scent of Brimstone. Then said *Christian, What means this?* The Shepherds told them, this is a by-way to Hell, a way that Hypocrites go in at; namely, such as sell their Birth-right, with *Esau;* such as sell their Master with *Judas;* such as blaspheme the Gospel, with *Alexander;* and that lie and dissemble, with *Ananias* and *Sapphira* his Wife.[100]

A By-way to Hell.

Then said *Hopeful* to the Shepherds, *I perceive that these had on them, even every one, a show of Pilgrimage, as we have now; had they not?*

Shep. Yes, and held it a long time, too.

Hope. *How far might they go on in Pilgrimage in their day; since they, notwithstanding, were thus miserably cast away?*

Shep. Some farther, and some not so far as these Mountains.

Then said the Pilgrims one to the other, *We had need to cry to the strong for strength.*

Shep. Aye, and you will have need to use it, when you have it too.

By this time the Pilgrims had a desire to go forwards, and the Shepherds a desire they should; so they walked together towards the end of the Mountains. Then said the Shepherds one to another, Let us here show the Pilgrims the Gates of the Celestial City, if they have skill to look through our Perspective-Glass.[101] The pilgrims lovingly accepted the motion: so they had them to the top of an high Hill, called *Clear,* and gave them their glass to look.

The Shepherds' Perspective-Glass
The Hill Clear

Then they tried to look; but the remembrance of that last thing that the Shepherds had shown them made their hands shake, by means of which impediment they could not look

steadily through the glass; yet they thought they saw something like the Gate, and also some of the Glory of the place.
Then they went away, and sang this Song.

The fruits of servile fear

> *Thus by the* Shepherds *Secrets are reveal'd,*
> *Which from all other men are kept conceal'd:*
> *Come to the* Shepherds *then, if you would see*
> *Things deep, things hid, and that mysterious be.*

When they were about to depart, one of the shepherds
gave them a *Note of the Way*. Another of them *bid them
beware of the Flatterer*. The third *bid them take heed that
they slept not upon the Enchanted Ground*. And the fourth
bid them God speed. So I awoke from my dream.[102]

A two-fold Caution

And I slept, and dreamed again, and saw the same two
Pilgrims going down the Mountains along the High-way
towards the City. Now a little below these Mountains on
the left hand, lieth the Country of *Conceit*, from which
Country there comes into the way in which the Pilgrims
walked, a little crooked Lane. Here, therefore, they met
with a very brisk Lad, that came out of that Country; and
his name was *Ignorance*. So Christian asked him, *from
what parts he came, and whither he was going?*

The Country of Conceit, out of which came Ignorance

Ign. Sir, I was born in the country that lieth off there, a
little on the left hand, and I am going to the Celestial City.

Christian and Ignorance have some talk

*Chr. But how do you think to get in at the Gate, for you
may find some difficulty there?*

Ign. As other good people do, said he.

*Chr. But what have you to show at that Gate, that the
Gate should be opened to you?*

Ign. I know my Lord's will, and have been a good Liver;
I pay every man his own; I pray, fast, pay Tithes, and give
Alms, and have left my Country for whither I am going.[103]

The ground of Ignorance's hope

*Chr. But thou camest not in at the wicket-gate that is at
the head of this way; Thou camest in hither through that
same crooked Lane, and therefore I fear, however thou
mayest think of thyself, when the reckoning-day shall come,*

thou wilt have laid to thy charge, that thou art a thief and a Robber, instead of getting admittance into the City.

Ign. Gentlemen, ye be utter strangers to me, I know you not; be content to follow the Religion of your Country, and I will follow the Religion of mine. I hope all will be well. And as for the Gate that you talk of, all the world knows that is a great way off of our Country. I cannot think that any man in all our parts doth so much as know the way to it; nor need they matter whether they do or no, since we have, as you see, a fine, pleasant, green Lane, that comes down from our Country, the next way into the way.

When *Christian* saw that the man was wise in his own conceit, he said to *Hopeful,* whisperingly, *there is more hopes of a Fool than of him.* And said, moreover, *when he that is a Fool walketh by the way, his wisdom faileth him, and he saith to every one that he is a fool.*

Prov. 26.12

Eccles. 10.3

How to carry it to a Fool

What, shall we talk farther with him, or outgo him at present, and so leave him to think of what he hath heard already, and then stop again for him afterwards, and see if by degrees we can do any good to him? Then said Hopeful,

> *Let Ignorance a little while now muse*
> *On what is said, and let him not refuse*
> *Good Counsel to embrace, lest he remain*
> *Still ignorant of what's the chiefest gain.*
> *God saith, those that no understanding have,*
> *(Although he made them,) them he will not save.*

Hope. He further added, it is not good, I think, to say so to him all at once; let us pass him by, if you will, and talk to him anon, *even as he is able to bear it.*

So they both went on, and *Ignorance* he came after. Now, when they had passed him a little way, they entered into a very dark Lane, where they met a man whom seven Devils had bound with seven strong Cords, and were carrying him back to the door that they saw on the side of the Hill. Now good *Christian* began to tremble, and so did *Hopeful* his Companion; Yet as the Devils led away the

Mat. 12.45.

Prov. 5.22

man, *Christian* looked to see if he knew him; and he thought it might be one *Turn-away,* that dwelt in the town of Apostacy. But he did not perfectly see his face, for he did hang his head like a Thief that is found; but being gone past, Hopeful looked after him, and espied on his back a paper with this Inscription, *Wanton Professor, and damnable Apostate.* Then said Christian to his fellow, Now I call to remembrance that which was told me of a thing that happened to a good man hereabout. The name of the man was *Little-Faith,* but a good man, and he dwelt in the Town of *Sincere.* The thing was this; At the entering in of this passage, there comes down from *Broad-way-gate,* a Lane, called *Dead-Man's Lane;* so called because of the Murders that are commonly done there. And this *Little-faith* going on Pilgrimage, as we do now, chanced to sit down there and slept. Now there happened at that time to come down the *Lane* from *Broad way-gate,* three sturdy Rogues; and their names were *Faint-heart, Mistrust,* and *Guilt,* (three Brothers) and they espying *Little-faith* where he was, came galloping up with speed. Now the good man was just awaked from his sleep, and was getting up to go on his Journey. So they came up all to him, and with threatening language bid him stand. At this, *Little-Faith* looked as white as a sheet, and had neither power to fight nor fly. Then said *Faint-heart*, deliver thy purse; but he making no haste to do it, (for he was loth to lose his Money) *Mistrust* ran up to him, and thrusting his hand into his Pocket, pulled out thence a bag of Silver. Then he cried out, Thieves, Thieves. With that, *Guilt* with a great Club that was in his hand struck *Little-Faith* on the head, and with that blow felled him flat to the ground, where he lay bleeding as one that would bleed to death. All this while the Thieves stood by. But at last, they hearing that some were upon the Road, and fearing lest it should be one *Great-Grace,* that dwells in the Town of *Good-confidence,* they betook themselves to their heels and left this good man to shift for himself who getting up, made shift to scramble on his way. This was the story.

The destruction of one Turn-away

Christian *telleth his Companion a story of* Little-faith

Broad-way gate. Dead-man's Lane

Little-faith *robbed by* Faint-heart, Mistrust & Guilt

They got away his Silver and knocked him down

Hope. *But did they take from him all that ever he had?*

Chr. No: The place where his Jewels were they never ransacked; so those he kept still. But, as I was told, the good man was much afflicted for his Loss, for the Thieves got most of his spending-money. That which they got not (as I said) were Jewels; also, he had a little odd money left, but scarce enough to bring him to his Journey's end. Nay, (if I was not misinformed) he was forced to beg as he went, to keep himself alive (for his jewels he might not sell). But beg and do what he could, *he went* (as we say) with *many a hungry belly* the most part of the rest of the way.

Hope. *But is it not a wonder they got not from him his Certificate, by which he was to receive his admittance at the Celestial Gate?*

Chr. 'Tis a wonder; but they got not that; though they missed it not through any good cunning of his; for he, being dismayed by their coming upon him, had neither power nor skill to hide any thing, so it was more by good providence, than by his endeavour that they missed of *that good thing*.

Hope. *But it must needs be a comfort to him they got not his Jewels from him?*

Chr. It might have been great comfort to him, had he used it as he should; But they that told me the story said that he made but little use of it all the rest of the way; and that because of the dismay that he had in their taking away his money: Indeed, he forgot it a great part of the rest of his Journey; and besides, when at any time it came into his mind, and he began to be comforted therewith, then would fresh thoughts of his Loss come again upon him, and these thoughts would swallow up all.

Hope. Alas, poor man! this could not but be a great grief unto him.

Chr. Grief? Aye, a grief indeed! would it not have been so to any of us, had we been used as he, to be robbed and wounded too, and that in a strange place, as he was? It is a wonder he did not die with grief, poor heart! I was told that he scattered almost all the rest of the way with nothing

Marginal notes:

Little-Faith *lost not his best things*

1 Pet. 4.18

He kept not his best things by his own cunning

2 Tim. 1.14

2 Pet. 1.9

He is pitied by both

but doleful and bitter Complaints. Telling also to all that overtook him, or that he overtook in the way as he went, where he was robbed, and how; who they were that did it, and what he had lost; how he was wounded, and that he hardly escaped with life.

Hope. But 'tis a wonder that his necessity did not put him upon selling, *or* pawning *some of his Jewels, that he might have wherewith to relieve himself in his Journey.*

Chr. Thou talkest like one upon whose head is the *shell* to this very day.[104] For what should he pawn them? or to whom should he sell them? In all that Country where he was robbed, his Jewels were not accounted of; nor did he want that relief which could from thence be administered to him. Besides, had his Jewels been missing at the Gate of the Celestial City, he had (and that he knew well enough) been excluded from an Inheritance there; and that would have been worse to him than the appearance and villainy of ten thousand thieves.

Christian *snibbeth his fellow for unadvised speaking*

Hope. Why art thou so tart, my brother? Esau sold his Birth-right, and that for a mess of Pottage, and that Birth-right was his greatest Jewel. And if he, why might not Little-faith *do so too?*

A discourse *about* Esau *and* Little Faith

Chr. Esau did sell his Birth-right indeed, and so do many besides, and by so doing exclude themselves from the chief Blessing, as also that *Caitiff* did; but you must put a difference betwixt *Esau* and *Little-Faith*, and also betwixt their Estates. *Esau's* Birth-right was Typical, but *Little-Faith's* Jewels were not so. *Esau's* belly was his God; but *Little-Faith's* belly was not so. *Esau's* want lay in his fleshly Appetite; *Little-Faith's* did not so. Besides, Esau could see no further than to the fulfilling of his lusts: *For I am at the point to die*, said he: *and what good will this Birth-right do me?* But *Little-Faith*, though it was his lot to have but a *little* faith, was by his *little faith* kept from such extravagances, and made to *see* and *prize* his Jewels more than to sell them, as *Esau* did his *Birth-right*. You read not any where that *Esau* had *Faith*, no, not so much as a little: Therefore no marvel, where the flesh only bears sway, (as

Esau *was ruled by his lusts*

Gen. 25.32

Esau *never had* Faith

it will in that man where no Faith is to resist) if he sells his *Birth-right* and his Soul and all, and that to the Devil of Hell; for it is with such as it is with the Ass, *Who in her*

Jer. 2.24 *occasion cannot be turned away.* When their minds are set upon their Lusts, they will have them, whatever they cost.

Little-faith *could not live upon* Esau's *Pottage* But *Little-Faith* was of another temper; his mind was on things Divine; his livelihood was upon things that were Spiritual, and from above: Therefore to what end should he that is of such a temper sell his Jewels (had there been any that would have bought them) to fill his mind with

A comparison between the Turtle-Dove *and the* Crow empty things? Will a man give a penny to fill his belly with hay? or can you persuade the *Turtle Dove* to live upon Carrion like the *Crow*? Though *faithless* ones can for carnal lusts, pawn or mortgage, or sell what they have, and themselves outright to boot; yet they that have Faith, *Saving Faith*, though but a little of it, cannot do so. Here, therefore, my Brother, is thy mistake.

Hope. *I acknowledge it; but yet your severe reflection had almost made me angry.*

Chr. Why, I did but compare thee to some of the Birds that are of the brisker sort, who will run to and fro in untrodden Paths with the shell upon their heads: but pass by that, and consider the matter under debate, and all shall be well betwixt thee and me.

Hope. *But,* Christian, *these three fellows, I am persuaded in my heart, are but a company of Cowards: would they have run else, think you, as they did, at the noise of one that was coming on the Road? Why did not* Little-Faith

Hopeful *swaggers* *pluck up a greater heart? He might, methinks, have stood one brush with them, and have yielded when there had been no remedy.*

Chr. That they are Cowards, many have said, but few

No great heart for God where there is but little Faith. We have more courage when out, than when we are in have found it so in the time of Trial. As for a great Heart, *Little-Faith* had none; and I perceive by thee, my Brother, hadst thou been the man concerned, thou art but for a brush, and then to yield. And verily, since this is the height of thy stomach,[105] now they are at a distance from us, should they appear to thee as they did to him, they might put thee to second thoughts.

But consider again, that they are but Journeymen Thieves, they serve under the King of the Bottomless-pit, who, if need be, will come to their aid himself, and his voice is *as the roaring of a Lion*. I myself have been engaged as this *Little-Faith* was, and I found it a terrible thing. These three Villains set upon me, and I beginning like a *Christian* to resist, they gave but a call, and in came their Master: I would, as the saying is, have given my Life for a penny, but that, as God would have it, I was clothed with Armour of Proof. Aye, and yet, though I was so harnessed, I found it hard work to quit myself like a man;[106] no man can tell what in that combat attends us, but he that hath been in the battle himself.

1 Pet. 5.8. Christian *tells his own experience in this case*

Hope. *Well, but they ran you see, when they did but suppose that one* Great-Grace *was in the way.*

Chr. True, they have often fled, both they and their Master, when *Great-Grace* hath but appeared; and no marvel, for he is the King's Champion: But I trow you will put some difference between *Little-Faith* and the *King's Champion*. All the King's Subjects are not his Champions, nor can they, when tried, do such feats of War as he. Is it meet to think that a little Child should handle Goliath as David did? or that there should be the strength of an *Ox* in a *Wren?* Some are strong, some are weak; some have great Faith, some have little: this man was one of the weak, and therefore he went to the walls.

The King's Champion

Hope. *I would it had been* Great-Grace, *for their sakes.*

Chr. If it had been he, he might have had his hands full, for I must tell you, that though *Great-Grace* is excellent good at his Weapons, and has, and can, so long as he keeps them at Sword's-point, do well enough with them; yet if they get within him, even *Faint-Heart, Mistrust,* or the other, it shall go hard but they will throw up his heels.[107] And when a man is down, you know, what can he do?

Whoso looks well upon *Great-Grace's* face, will see those

Scars and Cuts there that shall easily give demonstration of what I say. Yea, once I heard that he should say, (and that when he was in the combat,) We despaired even of life. How did these sturdy Rogues and their Fellows make *David* groan, mourn, and roar! Yea, *Heman* and *Hezekiah* too, though Champions in their days, were forced to bestir them when by these assaulted; and yet, notwithstanding, they had their Coats soundly brushed by them. *Peter* upon a time would go try what he could do; but though some do say of him that he is the Prince of the Apostles, they handled him so that they made him at last afraid of a sorry Girl.[108]

Besides, their King is at their whistle, he is never out of hearing; and if at any time they be put to the worst, he if possible comes in to help them: And of him it is said, *The Sword of him that layeth at him cannot hold; the Spear, the Dart, nor the Habergeon.*[109] *He esteemeth Iron as Straw, and Brass as rotten Wood. The Arrow cannot make him fly; sling-stones are turned with him into stubble. Darts are counted as stubble; he laugheth at the shaking of a spear.* What can a man do in this case? It is true, if a man could at every turn have *Job's* horse, and had skill and courage to ride him, he might do notable things. For his Neck is clothed with Thunder; he will not be afraid as the Grasshopper; the Glory of his Nostrils is terrible. He paweth in the Valley, rejoiceth in his Strength and goeth on to meet the Armed Men. He mocketh at fear, and is not affrighted; neither turneth he back from the Sword. The Quiver rattleth against him, the glittering Spear and the Shield. He swallows the ground with fierceness and rage; neither believes he that it is the sound of the trumpet. He says, among the Trumpets, Ha, ha! and he smelleth the Battle afar off, the Thundering of the Captains, and the shoutings.

But for such Footmen as thee and I are, let us never desire to meet with an Enemy, nor vaunt as if we could do better, when we hear of others that have been foiled, nor be tickled at the thoughts of our own manhood; for such commonly come by the worst when tried. Witness *Peter,* of whom I

Job 41.26. Leviathan's sturdiness

Job 39.19. The excellent Metal that is in Job's *Horse*

made mention before: He would swagger, aye, he would; He would, as his vain mind prompted him to say, do better and stand more for his Master than all men: but who so foiled and run down by those Villains as he?

When, therefore, we hear that such Robberies are done on the King's High-way, two things become us to do. First, to go out harnessed, and be sure *to take a shield with us:* for it was for want of that, that he who laid so lustily at *Leviathan*[110] could not make him yield. For, indeed, if that be wanting, he fears us not at all. Therefore he that had skill hath said, *Above all, take this Shield of Faith, wherewith ye* Ephes. 6 *shall be able to quench all the fiery darts of the wicked.*

'Tis good also that we desire of the King a Convoy, yea 'Tis good to that he will go with us himself. This made *David* rejoice have a Convoy when in the Valley of the shadow of death; and Moses was rather for dying where he stood, than to go one step without his God. O my Brother, if he will but go along with us, Exod. 33.15 what need we be afraid of ten thousands that shall set themselves against us? But without him, *the proud helpers* Psal. 3.5, 6, 7, 8. *fall under the slain.* Psal. 27.1, 2, Isa. 10.4

I for my part have been in the fray before now; and though (through the goodness of him that is best) I am as you see alive; yet I cannot boast of any Manhood, glad shall I be if I meet with no more such brunts; though I fear we are not got beyond all danger. However, since the Lion and the Bear have not as yet devoured me, I hope God will also deliver us from the next uncircumcised *Philistines.* Then sang *Christian,*

> *Poor* Little-Faith! hast been among the Thieves?
> Wast robb'd? Remember this, whoso believes,
> And get more Faith; then shall you Victors be
> Over ten thousand-else scarce over three.

So they went on, and Ignorance *followed.* They went A way and a then till they came at a place where they saw a way put way itself into *their way,* and seemed withal to lie as straight as the way which they should go; and here they knew not which of the two to take, for both seemed strait before them, therefore here they stood still to consider. And as they were thinking about the way, behold a man black of flesh[111] but covered with a very light Robe, come to them, and asked them why they stood there? They answered, they were going to the Celestial City, but knew not which of these ways to take. Follow me, said the man, it is thither that I am going. So they followed him in the way that but now came into the road, which by degrees turned and turned them so far from the city that they desired to go to, that in a little time their faces were turned away from it; yet they followed him. But by and by, before they were aware, he led them both within the compass of a Net, in which they were both so entangled that they knew not what to do; and with that *the white robe fell off the black man's back.* Then they saw where they were. Wherefore there they lay crying some time, for they could not get themselves out.

The Flatterer finds them

Christian and his fellow deluded

They are taken in a Net

Chr. Then said *Christian* to his fellow, Now do I see myself in an error. Did not the shepherds bid us beware of the Flatterer? As is the saying of the wise man, so we have found it this day: *A man that flattereth his Neighbour, spreadeth a Net for his Foot.*[112]

They bewail their condition

Prov. 29.6

Hope. They also gave us a note of directions about the Way, for our more sure finding thereof; but therein we have also forgotten to read, and have not kept ourselves from the Paths of the Destroyer. Here *David* was wiser than we; for saith he, *Concerning the works of men, by the word of thy Lips I have kept me from the paths of the Destroyer.* Thus they lay bewailing themselves in the net. At last they espied a Shining One coming towards them, with a Whip of small cords in his hand. When he was come to the place where they were, he asked them whence they came, and what they did there; they told him that they were poor Pilgrims, going to *Sion,* but were led out of their way by a black man, clothed in white, who bid us, said they, follow him, for he was going thither too. Then said he with the

Psal. 17.4

A shining one comes to them with a Whip in his Hand

whip, it is *Flatterer,* a false Apostle, that hath transformed himself into an Angel of Light. So he rent the Net, and let the men out. Then said he to them, Follow me, that I may set you in your way again; so he led them back to the way which they had left to follow the *Flatterer.* Then he asked them, saying, Where did you lie the last night? They said, With the Shepherds upon the delectable Mountain. He asked them then if they had not of the Shepherds, *a note of direction for the way?* They answered, Yes. But did you not, said he, when you were at a stand, pluck out and read your Note? They answered, No. He asked them, Why? They said they forgot. He asked, moreover, if the Shepherds did not bid them beware of the *Flatterer?* They answered, Yes. But we did not imagine, said they, *that this fine-spoken man had been he.*

Then I saw in my Dream, that he commanded them to *lie down;* which when they did, he chastised them sore, to teach them the good way wherein they should walk, and as he chastised them, he said, *As many as I love, I rebuke and chasten; be zealous, therefore, and repent.* This done, he bids them to go on their way, and take good heed to the other Directions of the Shepherds. So they thanked him for all his kindness, and went softly along the right way, singing,

> *Come hither, you that walk along the way;*
> *See how the Pilgrims fare that go astray:*
> *They catched are in an entangling Net,*
> *'Cause they good Counsel lightly did forget:*
> *'Tis true, they rescued were; but yet, you see,*
> *They're scourged to boot; Let this your caution be.*

Now after a while they perceived afar off, one coming softly, and alone all along the High way to meet them. Then said *Christian* to his fellow, Yonder is a man with his back towards *Sion,* and he is coming to meet us.

Hope. I see him; let us take heed to ourselves now, lest

Pro. 29.5. Dan. 11.32. 2 Cor. 11.13, 14

They are examined, and convicted of forgetfulness

Deceivers fine-spoken. Rom. 16.18

Dan. 25.1. 2 Chron. 6.26, 27

Rev. 3.19. *They are whipped and sent on their way*

he should prove a *Flatterer* also. So he drew nearer and nearer; and at last came up to them. His name was *Atheist,*
The Atheist
meets them
and he asked them whither they were going.

Chr. *We are going to Mount* Sion.

*He laughs
at them*
Then *Atheist* fell into a very great laughter.[113]

Chr. *What's the meaning of your laughter?*

Atheist. I laugh to see what ignorant persons you are, to take upon you so tedious a Journey; and yet are like to have nothing but your Travel for your Pains.

*They reason
together*
Chr. *Why, man? Do you think we shall not be received?*

Atheist. Received! There is not such a place as you dream of in all this World.

Chr. *But there is in the World to come.*

Atheist. When I was at home in mine own Country, I heard as you now affirm, and from that hearing went out to see, and have been seeking this City these twenty years,
Jer. 22.13.
Eccl. 10.15
but find no more of it than I did the first day I set out.

Chr. *We have both heard, and believe, that there is such a place to be found.*

Atheist. Had not I when at home believed, I had not come thus far to seek; but finding none, (and yet I should, had there been such a place to be found, for I have gone to
The Atheist
*takes up his
content in
this* World
seek it farther than you,) I am going back again, and will seek to refresh myself with the things that I then cast away for hopes of that which I now see is not.

Christian *pro-
voketh his Brother*
Chr. Then said *Christian* to *Hopeful*, his Companion, *Is it true which this man has said?*

Hopeful's *gra-
cious answer*
Hope. Take heed, he is one of the *Flatterers*. Remember what it cost us once already for our hearkening to such kind of fellows. What! no Mount Zion? Did we not see
2 Cor. 5.7
from the delectable Mountains, the Gate of the City? Also,
*A remembrance
of former chas-
tisements is an
help against pre-
sent temptations*
are we not now to walk by faith? Let us go on, lest the man with the Whip overtake us again.

You should have taught me that Lesson, which I will sound you in the ears withal: *Cease my Son to hear the Instructions that causeth to err from the Words of Know-*
Prov. 19.27.
Heb. 10.39
ledge. I say, my brother, cease to hear him, and let us believe to the saving of the Soul.

Chr. *My Brother, I did not put the question to thee, for that I doubted of the Truth of our Belief myself, but to prove thee, and to fetch from thee a fruit of the honesty of thy heart. As for this man, I know that he is blinded by the God of this world: Let thee and me go on, knowing that we have belief of the Truth; and no lie is of the Truth.*

A fruit of an honest heart. 1 Joh. 2.11

Hope. Now do I rejoice in hope of the glory of God. So they turned away from the man; and he laughing at them, went his way.

I then saw in my Dream that they went on until they came into a certain Country, whose Air naturally tended to make one drowsy, if he came a stranger into it. And here *Hopeful* began to be very dull, and heavy of Sleep: wherefore he said unto *Christian*, I do now begin to grow so drowsy that I can scarcely hold up mine eyes: let us lie down here, and take one nap.

They are come to the enchanted ground
Hopeful *begins to be drowsy*

Chr. *By no means, said the other; lest, sleeping, we never awake more.*

Christian *keeps him awake*

Hope. Why, my brother? sleep is sweet to the labouring man; we may be refreshed, if we take a nap.

Chr. *Do you not remember, that one of the Shepherds bid us beware of the enchanted ground? He meant by that, that we should beware of sleeping; wherefore let us not sleep, as do others; but let us watch and be sober.*

1 Thes. 5.6

Hope. I acknowledge myself in a fault, and had I been here alone, I had by sleeping run the danger of death. I see it is true that the wise man saith, *Two are better than one.* Hitherto hath thy Company been my mercy; *and thou shalt have a good reward for thy labour.*

He is thankful

Eccles. 4.9

Chr. N*ow then, said Christian, to prevent drowsiness in this place, let us fall into good discourse.*

To prevent drowsiness, they fall to good discourse. Good discourse prevents drowsiness

Hope. With all my heart said the other.

Chr. *Where shall we begin?*

Hope. Where God began with us, but do you begin, if you please.

Chr. *I will sing you first this Song.*

☞
*The Dreamer's
Note*

When Saints do sleepy grow, let them come hither,
And hear how these two Pilgrims talk together.
Yea, let them learn of them in any wise,
Thus to keep ope their drowsy, slumb'ring eyes.
Saints' Fellowship, if it be managed well,
Keeps them awake, and that in spite of Hell.

Chr. Then *Christian* began, and said, *I will ask you a question. How came you to think at first of doing what you do now?*

Hope. Do you mean, How came I at first to look after the good of my Soul?

Chr. *Yes, that is my meaning.*

Hope. I continued a great while in the delight of those things which were seen and sold at our *Fair*; things, which I believe now would have (had I continued in them still) drowned me in perdition and destruction.

Chr. *What things are they?*

Hope. All the Treasures and Riches of the World. Also I delighted much in Rioting, Revelling, Drinking, Swearing, Lying, Uncleanness, Sabbath-breaking, and what not, that tended to destroy the Soul. But I found at last, by hearing and considering of things that are Divine, which, indeed, I heard of you, as also of beloved *Faithful*, that was put to death for his Faith and Good-living in *Vanity Fair, That the end of these things is death.* And that for these things' sake, the wrath of God cometh upon the Children of Disobedience.

Rom. 6.21,
22, 23
Ephes. 5.6

Chr. *And did you presently fall under the power of this Conviction?*

Hopeful *at first
shut his eyes
against the light*

Hope. No: I was not willing presently to know the evil of sin, nor the Damnation that follows upon the commission of it; but endeavoured, when my Mind at first began to be shaken with the Word, to shut mine eyes against the light thereof.

Chr. *But what was the cause of your carrying of it thus to the first workings of God's blessed Spirit upon you?*

Reasons of the
resisting of light

Hope. The Causes were, 1. I was ignorant that this was the Work of God upon me. I never thought that by awakenings for sin, God at first begins the Conversion of a sinner. 2. Sin was yet very sweet to my flesh, and I was loath to leave it. 3. I could not tell how to part with mine old Companions, their presence and actions were so desirable unto me. 4. The hours in which convictions were upon me, were such troublesome and such heart-affrighting hours, that I could not bear, no not so much as the remembrance of them upon my heart.

Chr. *Then, as it seems, sometimes you got rid of your trouble.*

Hope. Yes, verily, but it would come into my mind again; and then I should be as bad, nay, worse than I was before.

Chr. *Why, what was it that brought your sins to mind again?*

Hope. Many things; as,

1. If I did but meet a good man in the streets; or,
2. If I have heard any read in the Bible; or,
3. If mine head did begin to ache; or,
4. If I were told that some of my Neighbours were sick; or,
5. If I heard the Bell toll for some that were dead; or,
6. If I thought of dying myself; or,
7. If I heard that sudden death happened to others.
8. But especially when I thought of myself, that I must quickly come to Judgment.

When he had lost his sense of sin, what brought it again

Chr. *And could you at any time, with ease, get off the guilt of sin, when by any of these ways it came upon you?*

Hope. No, not I, for then they got faster hold of my Conscience. And then, if I did but think of going back to sin, (though my mind was turned against it) it would be double torment to me.

Chr. *And how did you do then?*

Hope. I thought I must endeavor to mend my life; or else, thought I, I am sure to be damned.

Chr. *And did you endeavour to mend?*

When he could no longer shake off his guilt by sinful courses, then he endeavours to mend

Hope. Yes, and fled from not only my sins, but sinful company too, and betook me to religious Duties, as Praying, Reading, Weeping for sin, speaking Truth to my

Neighbours, &c. These things did I, with many others too much here to relate.

Chr. And did you think yourself well then?

Then he thought
himself well
Hope. Yes, for a while, but at the last my trouble came tumbling upon me again, and that over the neck of all my Reformations.

Chr. How came that about, since you were now reformed?

Reformation at
last could not
help, and why
Hope. There were several things brought it upon me; especially such sayings as these: *All our Righteousnesses are as filthy rags. By the works of the Law shall no flesh be justified. When ye have done all these things, say, We are*
Isa. 64.6. Gal.
2.6. Luke 17.10
unprofitable; with many more such like. From whence I began to reason with myself thus: If *All* my righteousnesses are as filthy rags; if by the deeds of the Law, no man can be justified; and if, when we have done *All,* we are yet unprofitable, then is it but a folly to think of Heaven by
His being a
debtor by the
Law troubled
him
the Law. I further thought thus; If a man runs 100 *l.* into the Shopkeeper's debt, and after that shall pay for all that he shall fetch; yet if his old debt stands still in the Book uncrossed, the shopkeeper may sue him for it, and cast him into prison, till he shall pay the debt.[114]

Chr. Well, and how did you apply this to your self?

Hope. Why, I thought thus with my self: I have by my sins run a great way into God's Book, and that my now reforming will not pay off that score; therefore I should think still, under all my present amendments: But how shall I be freed from that damnation that I brought my self in danger of by my former transgressions?

Chr. A very good Application: but pray go on.

Hope. Another thing that hath troubled me, even since my late amendments, is, that if I look narrowly into the best of what I do now, I still see sin, new sin, mixing itself
His espying bad
things in his best
duties troubled
him
with the best of that I do. So that now I am forced to conclude, that notwithstanding my former fond conceits of myself and duties, I have committed sin enough in one day to send me to hell, though my former life had been faultless.

Chr. And what did you do then?

Hope. Do! I could not tell what to do, till I brake my mind to *Faithful;* for he and I were well acquainted. And he told me, that unless I could obtain the Righteousness of a man that never had sinned, neither mine own, nor all the Righteousness of the World could save me.

This made him break his mind to Faithful *who told him the way to be saved*

Chr. *And did you think he spake true?*

Hope. Had he told me so when I was pleased and satisfied with my own amendments, I had called him Fool for his pains; but now, since I see mine own infirmity, and the sin which cleaves to my best performance I have been forced to be of his Opinion.

Chr. *But did you think when at first he suggested it to you, that there was such a man to be found, of whom it might justly be said, That he never committed Sin?*

Hope. I must confess the words at first sounded strangely; but after a little more talk and company with him, I had full conviction about it.

At which he started as present

Chr. *And did you ask him what man this was, and how you must be justified by him?*

Hope. Yes, and he told me it was the Lord Jesus, that dwelleth on the right hand of the Most High. And thus, said he, you must be justified by him, even by trusting to what he hath done by himself in the days of his Flesh, and suffered when he did hang on the Tree. I asked him further, how that man's Righteousness could be of that Efficacy, to justify another before God? And he told me, he was the mighty God, and did what he did; and died the Death also, not for himself but for me; to whom his doings, and the worthiness of them should be Imputed if I believed on him.

Heb. 10. Rev. 4. Col. 1. 2 Pet. 1 A more particular discovery of the way to be saved

Chr. *And what did you do then?*

Hope. I made my Objections against my believing; for that I thought he was not willing to save me.

He doubts of acceptation

Chr. *And what said* Faithful *to you then?*

Hope. He bid me go to him and see. Then I said it was Presumption. He said, No; for I was invited to come. Then he gave me a Book of *Jesus* his inditing, to encourage me the more freely to come. And he said concerning that book,

Matt. 11.28 He is better instructed

that every jot and tittle thereof stood firmer than heaven
and earth. Then I asked him what I must do when I came?
And he told me, I must entreat upon my knees, with all my
heart and Soul, the Father to reveal him to me. Then I asked
him further, how I must make my Supplication to him?
And he said, Go, and thou shalt find him upon a Mercy-
Seat, where he sits all the Year long, to give Pardon and
Forgiveness to them that come. I told him, that I knew not
what to say when I came. And he bid say to this effect: *God
be merciful to me a sinner, and make me to know and
believe in Jesus Christ; for I see, that if his Righteousness
had not been, or I have not Faith in that Righteousness, I
am utterly cast away: Lord, I have heard that thou art a
merciful God, and hast ordained that thy Son Jesus Christ
should be the Saviour of the world. And moreover, that
thou art willing to bestow him upon such a poor sinner as
I am (and I am a sinner indeed) Lord, take therefore this
opportunity, and magnify thy Grace in the salvation of my
soul, through thy Son Jesus Christ*, Amen.

Chr. *And did you do as you were bidden?*

Hope. Yes, over, and over, and over.

Chr. *And did the Father reveal the Son to you?*

Hope. Not at the first, nor second, nor third, nor fourth,
nor fifth; no, nor at the sixth time neither.

Chr. *What did you do then?*

Hope. What! why I could not tell what to do.

Chr. *Had you not thoughts of leaving off praying?*

Hope. Yes; an hundred times twice told.

Chr. *And what was the reason you did not?*

Hope. I believed that that was true which hath been told
me; to wit, that without the Righteousness of this Christ
all the World could not save me; and therefore thought I
with myself, if I leave off, I die; and I can but die at the
Throne of Grace. And withal this came into my mind, *If it
tarry, wait for it; because it will surely come, and will not
tarry.* So I continued praying until the Father showed me
his Son.

Chr. *And how was he revealed unto you?*

Matt. 24.35.
Psa. 95.6. Dan.
6.10. Jer. 29.12,
13. Exo. 25.22.
Lev. 16.9. Num.
7.8. Heb. 4.16.
He is bid to pray

He prays

*He thought to
leave off praying*

*He durst not
leave off praying
and why?*

Hab. 2.3.

Hope. I did not see him with my Bodily eyes, but with the eyes of my understanding; and thus it was. One day I was very sad, I think sadder than at any one time in my life; and this sadness was through a fresh sight of the greatness and vileness of my Sins. And as I was then looking for nothing but *hell,* and the everlasting damnation of my Soul, suddenly, as I thought, I saw the Lord Jesus looking down from Heaven upon me, and saying, *Believe on the Lord Jesus Christ, and thou shalt be saved.*[115]

But I Replied, Lord, I am a great, a very great sinner: And he answered, *My grace is sufficient for thee.*[116] Then I said, But, Lord, what is believing? And then I saw from that saying, *He that cometh to me shall never hunger, and he that believeth on me shall never thirst,* that believing and coming was all one; and that he that came, that is, that ran out in his heart and affections after Salvation by Christ, he indeed believed in Christ. Then the water stood in mine eyes, and I asked further, But, Lord, may such a great sinner as I am be indeed accepted of thee, and be saved by thee? And I heard him say, *And him that cometh to me, I will in no wise cast out.* Then I said, But how, Lord, must I consider of thee in my coming to thee, that my faith may be placed aright upon thee? Then he said, *Christ Jesus came into the World to save sinners. He is the end of the Law for righteousness to every one that believes. He died for our sins, and rose again for our justification. He loved us, and washed us from our sins in his own Blood.* He is the *Mediator* betwixt God and us, He ever *liveth to make intercession for us.* From all which I gathered, that I must look for Righteousness in his person, and for satisfaction[117] for my sins by his Blood; that what he did in obedience to his Father's Law, and in submitting to the penalty thereof, was not for himself, but for him that will accept it for his Salvation, and be thankful. And now was my heart full of joy, mine eyes full of tears, and mine affections running over with love to the name, People, and Ways of Jesus Christ.

Chr. *This was a Revelation of Christ to your Soul indeed.*

Marginal notes:

Eph. 1.18, 19

Christ is revealed to him and how

Acts 16.30, 31

Joh. 6.35

Joh. 6.37

But tell me particularly what effect this had upon your spirit.

Hope. It made me see that all the world, notwithstanding all the Righteousness thereof, is in a state of condemnation. It made me see that God the Father, though he be just, can justly justify the coming sinner. It made me greatly ashamed of the vileness of my former life, and confounded me with the sense of mine own ignorance; for there never came a thought into my heart before now that showed me so the beauty of Jesus Christ. It made me love a holy life, and long to do something for the Honour and Glory of the Lord Jesus. Yea, I thought that had I now 1000 gallons of blood in my body, I could spill it all for the sake of the Lord Jesus.

I saw then in my Dream, that *Hopeful* looked back, and saw *Ignorance,* whom they had left behind, coming after. *Look,* said he to *Christian, how far yonder youngster loitereth behind.*

Chr. Aye, aye, I see him: he careth not for our Company.

Hope. But I trow it would not have hurt him, had he kept pace with us hitherto.

Chr. That's true, but I warrant you, he thinketh otherwise.

Young Ignorance *Hope. That I think he doth; but, however let us tarry for*
comes up again *him.* So they did.

Then *Christian* said to him, *Come away Man, why do you stay so behind?*

Their Talk *Ign.* I take my pleasure in walking alone, even more a great deal than in company unless I like it the better.

Then said *Christian* to *Hopeful,* (but softly) *Did I not tell you he cared not for our company? But, however,* said he, *come up, and let us talk away the time in this solitary place.* Then directing his speech to *Ignorance* he said, *Come, how do you do? How stands it between God and your soul now?*

Ignorance's *Ign.* I hope, well; for I am always full of good motions,
hope, and the that come into my mind to comfort me as I walk.
ground of it.
Prov. 28.9 Chr. *What good motions? pray tell us.*

Ign. Why, I think of God and Heaven.

Chr. *So do the Devils and damned Souls.*

Ign. But I think of them, and desire them.

Chr. *So do many that are never like to come there.* The Soul of the sluggard desires and hath nothing.

Ign. But I think of them, and leave all for them.

Chr. *That I doubt, for leaving of* all is an hard matter; yea, a harder matter than many are aware of. But why, or by what, art thou persuaded that thou hast left all for God and Heaven?

Ign. My heart tells me so.

Chr. *The wise man says,* He that trusts his own heart is a fool. *What are good thoughts?*

Ignor. That is spoken of an evil heart, but mine is a good one.

Chr. *But how dost thou prove that?*

Ignor. It comforts me in hopes of Heaven.

Chr. *That may be through its deceitfulness; for a man's heart may minister comfort to him in the hopes of that thing for which he has yet no ground to hope.*

Ign. But my heart and life agree together; and therefore my hope is well grounded.

Chr. *Who told thee that thy heart and life agree together?*

Ign. My heart tells me so.

Chr. *Ask my fellow if I be a thief:* Thy *heart tells thee so: Except the Word of God beareth witness in this matter, other testimony is of no value.*

Ign. But is it not a good heart that hath good thoughts? And is not that a good life that is according to God's commandments?

Chr. *Yes, that is a good heart that hath good thoughts, and that is a good life, that is according to God's Commandments: But it is one thing indeed to have these, and another thing only to think so.*

Ign. Pray, what count you good thoughts, and a life according to God's commandments?

Chr. There are good thoughts of divers kinds, some respecting our selves, some God, some Christ, and some other things.

Ign. What be good thoughts respecting ourselves?

Chr. Such as agree with the Word of God.

Ign. When do our thoughts of our selves agree with the word of God?

Chr. When we pass the same Judgment upon ourselves which the Word passes. To explain my self: the Word of God saith of persons in a natural condition, There is none righteous, there is none that doth good. *It saith also* That every imagination of the heart of man is only evil, and that continually. *And again,* The Imagination of man's heart is evil from his Youth. *Now, then, when we think thus of our selves, having sense thereof, then are our thoughts good ones, because according to the word of God.*

Ign. *I will never believe that my heart is thus bad.*

Chr. Therefore thou never hadst one good thought concerning thy self in thy life. But let me go on: As the word passeth a judgment upon our hearts, so it passeth a Judgment upon our ways; and when the thoughts of our hearts and ways agree with the Judgment which the word giveth of both, then are both good, because agreeing thereto.

Ign. *Make out your meaning.*

Chr. Why, the word of God saith, That man's ways are crooked ways, not good but perverse; It saith, they are naturally out of the good way, that they have not known it. Now, when a man thus thinketh of his ways, I say, when he doth sensibly and with heart-humiliation thus think, then hath he good thoughts of his own ways, because his thoughts now agree with the judgment of the word of God.

Ign. *What are good thoughts concerning God?*

Chr. Even (as I have said concerning our selves) when our thoughts of God do agree with what the word saith of him. And that is, when we think of his Being and Attributes as the word hath taught: of which I cannot now discourse at large. But to speak of him with reference to us, then have we right thoughts of God, when we think that he knows us better than we know our selves, and can see sin in us when and where we can see none in our selves; when we think he knows our inmost thoughts, and that our heart, with all its

Marginal notes:

Rom. 3. Gen. 6.5

Psal. 125.5. Prov. 2.15. Rom. 3

depths, is always open unto his eyes; Also when we think that all our righteousness stinks in his nostrils, and that therefore he cannot abide to see us stand before him in any confidence, even in all our best performances.

Ign. Do you think that I am such a fool, as to think that God can see no further than I? or that I would come to God i' th' best of my performances?

Chr. Why how dost thou think in this matter?

Ign. Why, to be short, I think I must believe in Christ for Justification.

Chr. How! Think thou must believe in Christ, when thou seest not thy need of him! Thou neither seest thy original nor actual Infirmities, but hast such an Opinion of thyself, and of what thou doest, as plainly renders thee to be one that did never see the necessity of Christ's personal Righteousness to justify thee before God. How, then, dost thou say, I believe in Christ?

Ign. I believe well enough for all that.

Chr. How dost thou believe?

Ign. I believe that Christ died for sinners; and that I shall be justified before God from the Curse, through his gracious acceptance of my obedience to his Law. Or thus, Christ makes my Duties that are religious, acceptable to his Father by virtue of his Merits, and so shall I be justified.

Chr. Let me give an answer to this confession of thy Faith, 1. Thou believest with a fantastical[118] faith; for this faith is nowhere described in the Word. 2. Thou believest with a false Faith; because it taketh Justification from the personal Righteousness of Christ, and applies it to thy own. 3. This faith maketh not Christ a Justifier of thy person, but of thy actions; and of thy person for thy action's sake, which is false. 4. Therefore this faith is deceitful, even such as will leave thee under wrath in the day of God Almighty. For true Justifying faith puts the soul, as sensible of its lost condition by the Law, upon flying for refuge unto Christ's Righteousness; (which Righteousness of his is not an act of grace by which he maketh, for Justification, *thy* obedience accepted with God, but *his* personal obedience to the Law,

The faith of Ignorance

in doing and suffering for us what that required at our hands). This righteousness, I say, true faith accepteth; under the skirt of which the soul being shrouded, and by it, presented as spotless before God, it is accepted, and acquitted from condemnation.

Ign. What! would you have us trust to what Christ in his own person has done without us? This conceit would loosen the reins of our lust, and tolerate us to live as we list. For what matter how we live, if we may be justified by Christ's personal righteousness from all, when we believe it?

Chr. Ignorance is thy name, and as thy name is, so art thou: even this thy answer demonstrateth what I say. *Ignorant* thou art of what Justifying righteousness is, and as *ignorant* how to secure thy Soul through the faith of it from the heavy wrath of God. Yea, thou also art *ignorant* of the true effects of saving faith in this righteousness of Christ, which is to bow and win over the heart to God in Christ, to love his Name, his Word, Way and People, and not as thou *ignorantly* imaginest.

Hope. Ask him if ever he had Christ revealed to him from heaven.

Ignorance
jangles with
them

Ign. What? you are a man for Revelations! I do believe, that what both you and all the rest of you say about that matter, is but the fruit of distracted brains.

Hope. Why man! Christ is so hid in God from the natural apprehensions of the flesh, that he cannot by any man be savingly known, unless God the Father reveals him to them.

He speaks
reproachfully of
what he knows
not

Ign. That is your faith, but not mine; yet mine, I doubt not, is as good as yours: though I have not in my head so many whimsies as you.

Chr. Give me leave to put in a word: You ought not so slightly to speak of this matter: for this I will boldly affirm (even as my good companion hath done) that no man can

Mat. 11.18.
1 Cor. 12.3.
Eph. 1.18, 19

know Jesus Christ but by the revelation of the Father; yea, and faith too, by which the soul layeth hold upon Christ, (if it be right) must be wrought by the exceeding greatness of his Mighty Power; the working of which Faith, I perceive, poor *Ignorance,* thou art ignorant of. Be awakened, then, see thine own wretchedness, and fly to the Lord Jesus; and by his righteousness, which is the righteousness of God, (for he himself is God,) thou shalt be delivered from condemnation.

Ign. You go so fast, I cannot keep pace with you; do you go on before, I must stay a while behind.   *The Talk broke up*

Then they said;

> Well, Ignorance, *wilt thou yet foolish be,*
> *To slight good Counsel, ten times given thee?*
> *And if thou yet refuse it, thou shalt know,*
> *Ere long the evil of thy doing so.*
> *Remember, Man, in time, stoop, do not fear,*
> *Good counsel, taken well, saves; therefore hear.*
> *But if thou yet shalt slight it, thou wilt be*
> *The loser* (Ignorance) *I'll warrant thee.*

Then *Christian* addressed thus himself to his fellow.

Chr. Well, come my good *Hopeful,* I perceive that thou and I must walk by ourselves again.

So I saw in my Dream, that they went on apace before, and *Ignorance* he came hobbling after. Then said *Christian* to his Companion, *It pities me much for this poor man: it will certainly go ill with him at last.*

Hope. Alas, there are abundance in our Town in this condition; whole Families, yea, whole Streets, (and that of Pilgrims too;) and if there be so many in our parts, how many, think you, must there be in the place where he was born?

Chr. Indeed, the word saith, He hath blinded their eyes, lest they should see, &c. *But, now we are by ourselves, what do you think of such men? Have they at no time, think you, convictions of sin, and so, consequently, fears that their state is dangerous?*

Hope. Nay, do you answer that question yourself, for you are the elder man.

Chr. *Then I say, sometimes (as I think) they may, but*

they being naturally ignorant, understand not that such convictions tend to their good; and therefore they do desperately seek to stifle them, and presumptuously continue to flatter themselves in the way of their own hearts.

The good use of fear

Hope. I do believe, as you say, that fear tends much to men's good, and to make them right at their beginning to go on pilgrimage.

Job 28.28.
Psal. 111.10.
Prov. 1.7, ch.
9.10

Chr. Without all doubt it doth, if it be right; For so says the Word, The fear of the Lord is the beginning of Wisdom.

Hope. How will you describe right fear?

Right Fears

Chr. True or right fear is discovered by three things:

1. By its rise. It is caused by saving convictions for sin.

2. It driveth the Soul to lay fast hold of Christ for Salvation.

3. It begetteth and continueth in the Soul a great Reverence of God, his Word, and Ways, keeping it tender, and making it afraid to turn from them, to the right hand or to the left, to any thing that may dishonour God, break its Peace, grieve the Spirit, or cause the enemy to speak reproachfully.

Hope. Well said; I believe you have said the truth. Are we now almost got past the Enchanted Ground?

Chr. Why art thou weary of this discourse?

Hope. No, verily, but that I would know where we are.

Chr. We have not now above two miles further to go thereon. But let us return to our matter. Now, the ignorant know not that such conviction as tend to put them in fear, are for their good, and therefore they seek to stifle them.

Why ignorant Persons stifle convictions. In general. 2. Particular

Hope. How do they seek to stifle them?

Chr. 1. They think that those fears are wrought by the Devil (though indeed they are wrought of God,) and thinking so, they resist them, as things that directly tend to their Overthrow. 2. They also think that these fears tend to the spoiling of their Faith; when, (alas for them, poor men that they are) they have none at all; and therefore they harden their hearts against them. 3. They presume they ought not to fear, and therefore, in despite of them, wax presumptuously confident. 4. They see that those fears tend to take away from them their pitiful old self-holiness, and therefore they resist them with all their might.

Hope. I know something of this my self; for before I knew my self it was so with me.

Chr. *Well, we will leave at this time our Neighbour* Ignorance *by himself, and fall upon another profitable question.*

Hope. With all my heart; but you shall still begin.

Chr. *Well then, did you not know, about ten years ago, one* Temporary *in your parts, who was a forward man in Religion then?*

Talk about one Temporary. Where he dwells.

Hope. Know him! yes; he dwelt in *Graceless,* a town about two miles off of *Honesty,* and he dwelt next door to one *Turnback.*

Chr. *Right; he dwelt under the same roof with him. Well, that man was much awakened*[119] *once. I believe that then he had some sight of his sins, and of the wages*[120] *that were* due thereto.

He was towardly once

Hope. I am of your mind; for (my house not being above three miles from him) he would oft times come to me, and that with many tears. Truly I pitied the man, and was not altogether without hope of him; but one may see, it is not every one that cries, *Lord, Lord.*[121]

Chr. *He told me once, That he was resolved to go on Pilgrimage, as we go now; but all of a sudden he grew acquainted with one* Saveself, *and then he became a stranger to me.*

Hope. Now since we are talking about him, let us a little enquire into the reason of the sudden back-sliding of him and such others.

Chr. *It may be very profitable, but do you begin.*

Hope. Well then, there are in my Judgment, four reasons for it:

1. Though the Consciences of such men are awakened, yet their minds are not changed; therefore, when the power of guilt weareth away, that which provoked them to be religious ceaseth; Wherefore they naturally turn to their own course again; even as we see the Dog that is sick of

Reasons why towardly ones go back

what he hath eaten, so long as his Sickness prevails, he vomits and casts up all: not that he doth this of a free mind, (if we may say a Dog has a mind) but because it troubleth his stomach: but now, when his sickness is over, and so his stomach eased, his desires being not at all alienated from his vomit, he turns him about, and licks up all. And so it is true which is written, *The Dog is turned to his own vomit again.* Thus, I say, being hot for Heaven, by virtue only of the sense and fear of the torments of Hell, as their sense and fear of damnation chills and cools, so their desires for Heaven and Salvation cool also. So then it comes to pass, that when their guilt and fear is gone, their desires for Heaven and Happiness die, and they return to their course again.

2 Pet. 2.22

2. Another reason is, they have slavish fears that do over-master them: I speak now of the fears that they have of men; *For the fear of man bringeth a snare.* So then, though they seem to be hot for heaven so long as the flames of Hell are about their ears, yet, when that terror is a little over, they betake themselves to second thoughts, namely, that 'tis good to be wise and not to run (for they know not what) the hazard of losing all; or at least of bringing themselves into unavoidable and unnecessary troubles; and so they fall in with the *World* again.

Prov. 29.25

3. The shame that attends Religion, lies also as a block in their way; they are proud and haughty, and Religion in their eye is low and contemptible: therefore when they have lost their sense of hell and the wrath to come, they return again to their former course.

4. *Guilt,* and to meditate terror, are grievous to them; they like not to see their misery before they come into it; though perhaps the sight of at it first, if they loved that sight, might make them fly whither the righteous fly and are safe; but because they do, as I hinted before, even shun the thoughts of guilt and terror, therefore, when once they are rid of their awakenings about the terrors and wrath of God, they harden their hearts gladly, and choose such ways as will harden them more and more.

Chr. You are pretty near the business, for the bottom of all is, for want of a change in their mind and will. And therefore they are but like the Felon that standeth before the Judge, he quakes and trembles, and seems to repent most heartily but the bottom of all is the fear of the Halter: not that he hath any detestation of the offence, as is evident; because, let but this man have his liberty and he will be a Thief, and so a Rogue still, whereas, if his mind was changed, he would be otherwise.

Hope. Now I have showed you the reason of their going back, do you show me the manner thereof.

Chr. *So I will willingly.*

How the Apostate goes back

1. They drew off their thoughts, all that they may, from the remembrance of God, Death and Judgment to come.

2. Then they cast off by degrees private Duties, as Closet-prayer, curbing their lusts, Watching, sorrow for Sin, and the like.

3. Then they shun the company of lively and warm Christians.

4. After that, they grow cold to public Duty, as Hearing, Reading, Godly conference,[122] and the like.

5. They then begin to pick holes, as we say, in the coats of some of the Godly, and that devilishly, that they may have a seeming Colour to throw Religion (for the sake of some infirmities they have spied in them) behind their backs.

6. Then they begin to adhere to, and associate themselves with, carnal, loose, and wanton men.

7. Then they give way to carnal and wanton discourses in secret; and glad are they if they can see such things in any that are counted honest, that they may the more boldly do it through their example.

8. After this they begin to play with little sins openly.

9. And then, being hardened, they show themselves as they are. Thus, being launched again into the gulf of misery, unless a miracle of Grace prevent it, they everlastingly perish in their own deceivings.

Now I saw in my Dream, that by this time the pilgrims

were got over the Enchanted ground, and entering into
the Country of *Beulah*[123] whose Air was very sweet and
pleasant, the way lying directly through it, they solaced
themselves there for a season. Yea, here they heard continually the singing of Birds, and saw every day the flowers
appear in the earth, and heard the voice of the Turtle[124] in
the Land. In this Country the sun shineth night and day;
wherefore this was beyond the Valley of the *Shadow of
Death,* and also out of the reach of *Giant Despair,* neither
could they from this place so much as see *Doubting-Castle.*
Here they were within sight of the City they were going to;
also here met them some of the Inhabitants thereof. For in
this land the shining Ones commonly walked, because it
was upon the borders of heaven. In this land also the Con-
tract between the Bride and the Bridegroom was renewed;
yea, here, *as the Bridegroom rejoiceth over the Bride, so
doth God rejoice over them.* Here they had no want of
Corn and Wine; for in this place they met with abundance
of what they had sought for in all their Pilgrimage. Here
they heard voices from out of the City, loud voices, saying,
*Say ye to the Daughter of Zion, Behold, thy salvation
cometh, behold, his reward is with him.* Here all the Inhabitants of the Country called them *the holy People, the
Redeemed of the Lord; sought out,* &c.

Now, as they walked in this Land, they had more rejoicing than in parts more remote from the Kingdom, to which
they were bound; and drawing near to the City, they had
yet a more perfect view thereof: It was builded of Pearls
and precious Stones; also the streets thereof were paved
with Gold; so that, by reason of the natural glory of the
City, and the reflection of the Sun-beams upon it, *Christian*
with desire fell sick; *Hopeful* also had a fit or two of the
same Disease: wherefore here they lay by it a while, crying
out because of their pangs, *If you see my Beloved, tell him
that I am sick of love.*[125]

But, being a little strengthened, and better able to bear
their sickness, they walked on their way; and came yet
nearer and nearer, where were Orchards, Vineyards and

Marginal notes:
Isa. 62.4. Song 2.10, 11, 12

Angels

Isa. 62.5. ver. 8

Ver. 11

Ver. 12

Gardens, and their Gates opened into the Highway. Now, as they came up to these places, behold the Gardener stood in the way; to whom the Pilgrims said, Whose goodly Vineyards and Gardens are these? He answered, they are the King's, and are planted here for his own delight, and also for the solace of Pilgrims. So the Gardener had them into the Vineyards, and bid them refresh themselves with the dainties; he also showed them there the King's Walks and the Arbours where he delighted to be: And here they tarried and slept. *Deut. 23.24*

Now I beheld in my Dream, that they talked more in their sleep at this time, than ever they did in all their Journey; and, being in a muse thereabout, the Gardener said even to me, wherefore musest thou at the matter? It is the nature of the fruit of the Grapes of these Vineyards, to go down so sweetly as to cause the lips of them that are asleep to speak.

So I saw that when they awoke, they addressed themselves to go up to the city. But, as I said, the reflection of the sun upon the city (for the City was pure Gold) was so extremely glorious, that they could not as yet with open face behold it, but through an *Instrument* made for that purpose. So I saw, that as they went on, there met them two men in Raiment that shone like Gold, also their faces shone as the light. *Rev. 21.18. 2 Cor. 3.18*

These men asked the Pilgrims whence they came? and they told them. They also asked them where they had lodged, what difficulties, and dangers, what comforts and pleasures, they had met with in the way? and they told them. Then said the men that met them, You have but two difficulties more to meet with, and then you are in the City.

Christian then and his Companion asked the men to go along with them, so they told them that they would; But, said they, you must obtain it by your own Faith. So I saw in my dream, that they went on together till they came in sight of the Gate.

Now I further saw, that betwixt them and the Gate was a River, but there was no Bridge to go over; the River was very deep. At the sight therefore, of this River the Pilgrims were much stunned; but the men that went with them said, You must go through, or you cannot come at the Gate.

Death is not welcome to Nature, though by it we pass out of this World into Glory. 1 Cor. 15.51, 52

The Pilgrims then began to inquire if there was no other way to the Gate. To which they answered, Yes; but there hath not any, save two, to wit, *Enoch* and *Elijah*,[126] been permitted to tread that path since the foundation of the World, nor shall, until the last Trumpet shall sound. The Pilgrims then, especially *Christian,* began to despond in his mind, and looked this way and that, but no way could be found by them, by which they might escape the River. Then they asked the men if the waters were all of a depth? They

Angels help us not comfortably through Death

said no; yet they could not help them in that case; for, said they, *You shall find it deeper or shallower as you Believe in the King of the place.*

Then they addressed themselves to the Water, and entering, *Christian,* began to sink, and crying out to his good friend *Hopeful,* he said, I sink in deep waters, the Billows go over my head; all his Waves go over me, *Selah.*[127]

Then said the other, Be of good cheer, my Brother: I feel the bottom, and it is good. Then said *Christian,* Ah my friend, the sorrows of Death have compassed me about, I

Christian's conflict at the hour of Death

shall not see the Land that flows with Milk and Honey. And with that a great darkness and horror fell upon *Christian,* so that he could not see before him. Also here he in a great measure lost his senses, so that he could neither remember nor orderly talk of any of those sweet refreshments that he had met with in the way of his Pilgrimage. But all the words that he spoke still tended to discover that he had horror of mind, and heart-fears that he should die in that River, and never obtain entrance in at the Gate. Here also, as they that stood by perceived, he was much in the troublesome thoughts of the sins that he had committed, both since and before he began to be a Pilgrim. 'Twas also observ'd, that he was troubled with apparitions of Hobgoblins and evil Spirits; for ever and anon he would intimate so much by words. *Hopeful* therefore here had much ado to keep his Brother's head above water; yea, sometimes he would be quite gone down, and then, ere a while, he would rise up again half dead. *Hopeful* also would endeavour to comfort him, saying, Brother, I see the Gate, and Men standing by to receive us; but *Christian* would answer, 'Tis you, 'tis you they wait for; for you have been *Hopeful* ever since I knew you. And so have you, said he to *Christian*. Ah, brother, said he, surely if I was right he would now arise to help me; but for my sins he hath brought me into the snare, and hath left me. Then said *Hopeful*, My Brother, you have quite forgot the Text, where it is said of the wicked, *There is no band in their death, but their strength is firm; they are not troubled as other men, neither are they plagued like other men.*[128] These troubles and distresses that you go through in these Waters, are no sign that God hath forsaken you; but are sent to try you, whether you will call to mind that which heretofore you have received of his goodness, and live upon him in your distresses.

Then I saw in my dream, that *Christian*, was in a muse a while. To whom also *Hopeful* added these words, *Be of good cheer, Jesus Christ maketh thee whole.* And with that *Christian* brake out with a loud voice, Oh, I see him again; and he tells me, *When thou passest through the waters, I will be with thee; and through the Rivers, they shall not overflow thee.* Then they both took courage, and the Enemy was after that as still as a stone, until they were gone over. *Christian* therefore presently found ground to stand upon, and so it followed, that the rest of the River was but shallow. Thus they got over. Now upon the bank of the River on the other side, they saw the two shining men again, who there waited for them. Wherefore, being come out of the river, they saluted them, saying, *We are Ministering Spirits, sent forth to Minister for those that shall be heirs of Salvation.*[129] Thus they went along towards the Gate. Now you must note that the City stood upon a mighty hill, but the Pilgrims went up that hill with ease, because they had these two men to lead them up by the arms: they had likewise left their *mortal* Garments behind them in the River: for though they went in with them, they came out

Christian delivered from his fears in Death. Isa. 40.2

The Angels do wait for them so soon as they are passed out of this world. They have put off mortality

without them. They therefore went up here with much agility and speed, though the foundation upon which the city was framed was higher than the clouds. They therefore went up through the Region of the Air, sweetly talking as they went, being comforted, because they safely got over the River, and had such glorious Companions to attend them.

The talk that they had with the shining Ones was about the glory of the place; who told them that the beauty and glory of it was inexpressible. There, said they, is the Mount *Sion,* the heavenly *Jerusalem,* the innumerable company of *Angels,* and the Spirits of Just men made perfect.[130] You are going now, said they, to the Paradise of God, wherein you shall see the Tree of Life, and eat of the never-fading fruits thereof. And when you come there, you shall have white robes given you, and your walk and talk shall be every day with the King, even all the days of eternity. There you shall not see again such things as you saw when you were in the lower region upon earth; to wit, sorrow, sickness, affliction, and death; For the former things are passed away. You are going now to *Abraham,* to *Isaac* and *Jacob,* and to the Prophets; men that God hath taken away from the evil to come, and that are now resting upon their Beds, each one walking in his Righteousness. The men then asked, what must we do in the holy place? To whom it was answered, You must there receive the comfort of all your toil, and have joy for all your sorrow; you must reap what you have sown, even the fruit of all your Prayers and Tears, and Sufferings for the King by the way. In that place you must wear Crowns of Gold, and enjoy the perpetual sight and visions of the Holy One, *for there you shall see him as he is.* There also you shall serve him continually with praise, with shouting and thanksgiving, whom you desired to serve in the World, though with much difficulty, because of the Infirmity of your flesh. There your eyes shall be delighted with seeing, and your ears with hearing the pleasant voice of the mighty One. There you shall enjoy your friends again that are gone thither before you; and there you shall with

Heb. 12.22, 23, 24. Rev. 2.7, Rev. 3.4

Rev. 21.7

Isa. 57.1, 2. Isa. 65.14

Gal. 6.7

1 John 3.2

Now now look how the holi Pilgrims ride
Clouds are their chariots Angels are their guid
Who would not here for him all hazzards run
That thus provides for his when this worlds don

joy receive even every one that follows into the Holy place after you. There also you shall be clothed with Glory and Majesty, and put into an equipage fit to ride out with the King of Glory. When he shall come with sound of Trumpet in the Clouds, as upon the Wings of the Wind, you shall come with him; and when he shall sit upon the Throne of Judgment, you shall sit by him; yea, and when he shall pass Sentence upon all the workers of iniquity, let them be Angels or men, you also shall have a voice in that Judgment, because they were his and your enemies. Also, when he shall again return to the City, you shall go too, with sound of Trumpet, and be ever with him.

1 Thess. 4.13, 14, 15, 16. Jud. 14. Dan. 7.9, 10. 1 Cor. 6.2, 3

Now, while they were thus drawing towards the Gate, behold a company of the Heavenly Host came out to meet them: To whom it was said, by the other two shining Ones, These are the men that have loved our Lord, when they were in the World; and that have left all for his holy Name, and he hath sent us to fetch them, and we have brought them thus far on their desired Journey, that they may go in and look their Redeemer in the face with Joy. Then the Heavenly Host gave a great shout, saying, *Blessed are they that are called to the Marriage Supper of the Lamb.* There came out also at this time to meet them several of the King's Trumpeters, clothed in white and shining Raiment, who, with melodious noises and loud, made even the Heavens to echo with their sound. These Trumpeters saluted *Christian* and his Fellow with ten thousand welcomes from the World: and this they did with shouting and sound of Trumpet.

Rev. 19

This done, they compassed them round on every side; Some went before, some behind, and some on the right hand, and some on the left, (as it were to guard them through the upper Regions) continually sounding as they went, with melodious noise, in notes on high; so that the very sight was to them that could behold it, as if Heaven itself was come down to meet them. Thus therefore they walked on together, and, as they walked, ever and anon these Trumpeters even with joyful sound, would, by mixing their Music, with looks and gestures, still signify to *Chris-*

tian and his Brother, how welcome they were into their
company, and with what gladness they came to meet them:
and now were these two men, as it were in Heaven, before
they came at it; being swallowed up with the sight of Angels,
and with hearing of their melodious notes. Here also they
had the City itself in view; and they thought they heard all
the Bells therein to ring, to welcome them thereto: but
above all, the warm and joyful thoughts that they had about
their own dwelling there with such company, and that for
ever and ever; Oh! by what tongue or pen can their glorious
joy be expressed: Thus they came up to the Gate.

Now when they were come up to the Gate, there were
written over it, in Letters of Gold, *Blessed are they that do
his Commandments, that they may have right to the Tree
of Life; and may enter in through the Gates into the City.*   Rev. 22.14
Then I saw in my Dream, that the shining men bid them
call at the Gate: the which when they did, some from above
looked over the Gate, to wit, *Enoch, Moses,* and *Elijah,*
&c., to whom it was said, These pilgrims are come from
the City of *Destruction,* for the love that they bear to the
King of this place; and then the Pilgrims gave in unto them
each man his Certificate, which they had received in the
beginning: those therefore were carried in unto the King,
who, when he had read them, said, where are the men? To
whom it was answered, They are standing without the Gate.
The King then commanded to open the Gate, *That the righteous Nation* (said he) *that keepeth Truth, may enter in.*   Isa. 26.2
Now I saw in my Dream, that these two men went in at
the Gate; and lo, as they entered, they were transfigured;
and they had Raiment put on that shone like Gold. There
were also that met them with harps and crowns, and gave
them to them; the harps to praise withal, and the Crowns
in token of honour. Then I heard in my Dream, that all the
Bells in the City rang again for joy; and that it was said
unto them, *Enter ye into the joy of our Lord.*[131] I also heard
the men themselves, that they sang with a loud voice, saying,
*Blessing, Honour, Glory, and Power, be unto him that sit-
teth upon the Throne, and to the Lamb for ever and ever.*

Now just as the Gates were opened to let in the men, I look'd in after them; and behold, the City shone like the Sun; the Streets also were paved with Gold; and in them walked many men, with crowns on their heads, Palms in their hands, and golden harps, to sing praises withal.

There were also of them that had wings, and they answered one another without intermission, saying, *Holy, holy, holy is the Lord.* And after that they shut up the Gates, which when I had seen I wished myself among them.

Now while I was gazing upon all these things, I turned my head to look back and saw *Ignorance* come up to the River-side; but he soon got over, and that without half the difficulty which the other two men met with. For it happened, that there was then in that place one *Vain-hope,* a Ferry-man, that with his *Boat* helped him over; so he, as the other I saw, did ascend the hill, to come up to the Gate, only he came alone; neither did any man meet him with the least encouragement. When he was come up to the Gate, he looked up to the Writing that was above, and then began to knock, supposing that entrance should have been quickly administered to him; but he was asked by the men that looked over the top of the Gate, Whence come you? and what would you have? He answered, I have ate and drank in the presence of the King, and he has taught in our Streets.[132] Then they asked him for his certificate, that they might go in and show it to the King: so he fumbled in his bosom for one, and found none. Then said they, Have you none? but the man answered never a word. So they told the King, but he would not come down to see him, but commanded the two shining Ones that conducted *Christian* and *Hopeful* to the City, to go out and take *Ignorance,* and bind him hand and foot,[133] and have him away. Then they took him up, and carried him through the Air, to the door that I saw in the side of the hill, and put him in there. Then I saw that there was a way to hell, even from the Gates of Heaven, as well as from the City of Destruction. So I awoke, and behold it was a Dream.

Ignorance comes up to the River

Vain hope does ferry him over

The Conclusion

Now Reader I have told my Dream to thee;
See if thou canst interpret it to me.
Or to thy self, or Neighbours, but take heed
Of mis-interpreting: for that, instead,
Of doing good, will but thy self abuse.
By Mis-interpreting, evil ensues.
Take heed also, that thou be not extreme,
In playing with the out-side of my dream:
Nor let my figure, or similitude,
Put thee into a laughter, or a feud,
Leave this for Boys *or* Fools; *but as for thee,*
Do thou the substance of my matter see.

Put by the curtains; look within my Veil;
Turn up my Metaphors, and do not fail;
There, if thou seekest them such things to find,
As will be helpful to an honest mind.

What of my Dross *thou findest there, be bold*
To throw away, but yet preserve the Gold,
What if my Gold be wrapped up in Ore?
None throws away the Apple for the Core.
But if thou shalt cast all away in Vain,
I know not but 'twill make me dream again.

THE END

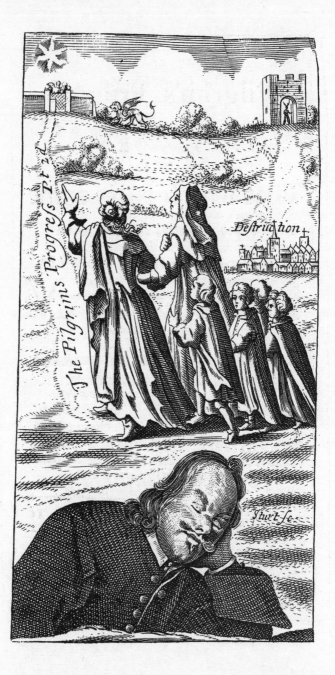

The Pilgrims Progres Pt 2d

Destruction

Sturt fc.

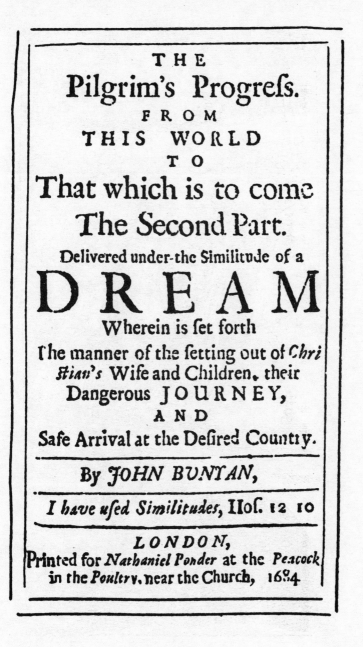

THE
Pilgrim's Progreſs.
FROM
THIS WORLD
TO
That which is to come
The Second Part.

Delivered under-the Similitude of a

DREAM

Wherein is ſet forth

The manner of the ſetting out of *Chri*
ſtian's Wife and Children, their
Dangerous JOURNEY,
AND
Safe Arrival at the Deſired Country.

By *JOHN BUNYAN*,

I have uſed Similitudes, Hoſ. 12. 10

LONDON,
Printed for *Nathaniel Ponder* at the *Peacock*
in the *Poultry,* near the Church, 1684.

THE
Author's Way of Sending forth
HIS
Second Part
OF THE
PILGRIM

Go, now my little Book, to every place,
Where my first Pilgrim, has but shown his Face:
Call at their door: if any say, who's there?
Then answer thou, Christiana is here.
If they bid thee come in, then enter thou,
With all thy boys. And then, as thou know'st how,
Tell who they are, also from whence they came;
Perhaps they'll know them, by their looks, or name
But if they should not, ask them yet again,
If formerly they did not entertain
One Christian a Pilgrim; If they say
They did: And was delighted in his way;
Then let them know that these related were
Unto him: yea, his wife and children are.

    Tell them, that they have left their house and home;
Are turned Pilgrims; seek a world to come:
That they have met with hardships in the way;
That they do meet with troubles night and day;
That they have trod on Serpents; fought with Devils,
Have also overcome a many evils.
Yea tell them also of the next[1] who have,
Of love to Pilgrimage, been stout and brave

Defenders of that way, and how they still
Refuse this World, to do their Father's will.
   Go tell them also of those dainty things
That Pilgrimage *unto the* Pilgrim *brings,*
Let them acquainted be, too, how they are
Beloved of their King, under his care;
What goodly Mansions[2] *he for them provides,*
Though they meet with rough Winds and swelling
        Tides,
How brave a calm they will enjoy at last,
Who to their Lord, and by his ways hold fast.
   Perhaps with heart and hand they will embrace
Thee, as they did my firstling, and will Grace
Thee and thy fellows with such cheer and fare,
As show will, they of Pilgrims *lovers are.*

1   Object

But how if they will not believe of me
That I am truly thine, 'cause some there be
That counterfeit the Pilgrim, and his name,
Seek by disguise to seem the very same.[3]
And by that means have wrought themselves into
The Hands and Houses of I know not who.

Answer

'Tis true, some have, of late, to Counterfeit
My Pilgrim, *to their own, my title set;*
Yea others, half my Name, and Title too;
Have stitched to their Book, to make them do;
But yet they by their Features do declare
Themselves not mine to be, whose ere they are.
   If such thou meetst with, then thine only way
Before them all, is, to say out thy say,
In thine own native Language, which no man
Now useth, nor with ease dissemble can.

If, after all, they still of you shall doubt,
Thinking that you like Gypsies, *go about,*
In naughty-wise the country to defile,
Or that you seek good People to beguile
With things unwarrantable: Send for me,
And I will Testify, you Pilgrims *be;*
Yea, I will Testify that only you
My Pilgrims *are; and that alone will do.*

2 Object

But yet, perhaps, I may enquire for him
Of those who wish him Damned life and limb,
What shall I do, when I at such a door
For *Pilgrims* ask, and they shall rage the more?

Answer

Fright not thyself, my Book, for such Bugbears,
Are nothing else but ground for groundless fears,
My Pilgrim's *book has travel'd Sea and Land,*
Yet could I never come to understand,
That it was slighted or turned out of Door
By any Kingdom, were they Rich or Poor.
    In France *and* Flanders, *where men kill each other,*
My Pilgrim *is esteem'd a Friend, a Brother.*
    In Holland, *too, 'tis said, as I am told,*
My Pilgrim *is with some, worth more than Gold.*
    Highlanders, *and* Wild-Irish *can agree*
My Pilgrim *should familiar with them be.*
    'Tis in New-England *under such advance,*
Receives there so much loving Countenance,
As to be Trimm'd, new-Cloth'd, & deck'd with gems,
That it might show its Features, and its Limbs,
Yet more; so comely doth my Pilgrim *walk,*
That of him thousands daily Sing and talk.[4]
    If you draw nearer home, it will appear
My Pilgrim *knows no ground, of shame, or fear:*

City, and Country will him Entertain,
With welcome, Pilgrim. *Yea, they can't refrain*
From smiling, if my Pilgrim *be but by,*
Or shows his head in any Company.

Brave Gallants do my Pilgrim *hug and love,*
Esteem it much, yea value it above
Things of greater bulk; yea, with delight
Say my Lark's *leg is better than a* Kite.[5]

Young Ladies, and young Gentle-women too,
Do not small kindness to my Pilgrim *show;*
Their Cabinets, their Bosoms, and their Hearts,
My Pilgrim *has, 'cause he to them imparts*
His pretty riddles in such wholesome strains,
As yields them profit double to their pains
Of reading. Yea, I think I may be bold
To say some prize him far above their Gold.

The very Children that do walk the street,
If they do but my holy Pilgrim *meet,*
Salute him will, will wish him well and say,
He is the only Stripling *of the Day.*

They that have never seen him, yet admire
What they have heard of him, and much desire
To have his Company, and hear him tell
Those Pilgrim *stories which he knows so well.*

Yea, some who did not love him at the first,
But call'd him Fool *and* Noddy, *say they must,*
Now they have seen & heard *him, him commend*
And to those whom they love, they do him send.

Wherefore my Second Part, *thou need'st not be*
Afraid to show thy Head: None can hurt thee,
That wish but well to him, that went before,
'Cause thou com'st after with a Second store
Of things as good, as rich, as profitable,
For Young, for Old, for Stagg'ring and for stable.

3   *Object*

But some there be that say he laughs too loud;
And some do say his Head is in a Cloud.
Some say, his Words and Stories are so dark,
They know not how, by them, to find his mark.[6]

Answer

One may (I think) say both his laughs & cries,
May well be guessed at by his wat'ry Eyes.
Some things are of that Nature as to make
One's fancy Chuckle while his Heart doth ache,
When Jacob saw his Rachel *with the Sheep,*
He did at the same time both kiss and weep.[7]

Whereas some say a Cloud is in his Head;
That doth but show his Wisdom's covered
With its own mantles: And to stir the mind
To a search after what it fain would find,
Things that seem to be hid in words obscure,
Do but the Godly mind the more allure;
To study what those Sayings should contain,
That speak to us in such a Cloudy strain.

I also know, a dark Similitude
Will on the Fancy more itself intrude,
And will stick faster in the Heart and Head,
Than things from Similes not borrowed.

Wherefore, my Book, let no discouragement
Hinder thy travels. Behold, thou art sent
To Friends, not Foes: to Friends that will give place
To thee, thy Pilgrims, *and thy words embrace.*

Besides, what my first Pilgrim *left conceal'd,*
Thou, my brave Second Pilgrim, *hast reveal'd;*
What Christian *left lock'd up, and went his way,*
Sweet Christiana *opens with her Key.*

4   *Object*

But some love not the method of your first,
Romance they count it; throw't away as dust,
If I should meet with such, what should I say?
Must I slight them as they slight me, or nay?

Answer

My Christiana, *if with such thou meet,*
By all means, in all Loving-wise, them greet;
Render them not reviling for revile;[8]
But, if they frown, I prithee on them smile,
Perhaps 'tis Nature, or some ill report,
Has made them thus *despise,* or thus *retort.*
Some love no Cheese, some love no Fish, & some
Love not their Friends, nor their own House or home;
Some start at Pig, slight Chicken, love not Fowl
More than they love a Cuckoo or an Owl.
Leave such, my Christiana, *to their choice,*
And seek those, who to find thee will rejoice;
By no means strive, but, in all humble wise,
Present thee to them in thy Pilgrim's *guise.*

   Go then, my little Book, and show to all
That entertain, and bid thee welcome shall,
What thou shalt keep close, shut up from the rest,
And wish what thou shalt show them may be bless'd
To them for good, and make them choose to be
Pilgrims, better by far than thee or me.

   Go, then, I say, tell all men who thou art:
Say, I am Christiana; *and my part,*
Is now with my four Sons, to tell you what
It is for men to take a Pilgrim's *lot;*

   Go also tell them who, and what they be
That now do go on pilgrimage with thee;
Say, Here's my neighbour Mercy, *she is one*
That has long-time with me a Pilgrim *gone;*

Come, see her in her Virgin *face, and learn*
'Twixt idle ones and Pilgrims *to discern.*
Yea let young Damsels learn of her to prize
The World which is to come, in any wise;
When little Tripping *Maidens follow God,*
And leave old doting sinners to his rod;
'Tis like those Days wherein the young ones cried
Hosanna *to whom the old ones did deride.*[9]

  Next tell them of old Honest, *who you found*
With his white hairs treading the Pilgrims' ground;
Yea, tell them how plain hearted this man *was;*
How after his good Lord he bare his Cross:
Perhaps with some grey Head this may prevail,
With Christ to fall in Love, and Sin bewail.

  Tell them also, how Master Fearing *went*
On Pilgrimage, and how the time he spent
In Solitariness, with Fears and Cries,
And how at last, he won the Joyful Prize.
He was a good man, though much down in spirit;
He is a good Man, and doth Life inherit.

  Tell them of Master Feeblemind *also,*
Who, not before, but still behind would go;
Show them also how he had like been slain,
And how one Great-Heart *did his life regain:*
This man was true of Heart; though weak in grace,
One might true Godliness read in his Face.

  Then tell them of Master Ready-to-halt,
A Man with Crutches, but much without fault:
Tell them how Master Feeblemind, *and he* (
Did love, and in Opinions *much agree.*
And let all know, though weakness was their chance,
Yet sometimes one could Sing, the other Dance.

  Forget not Master Valiant-for-the-Truth,
That man of courage, though a very Youth.
Tell every one his Spirit was so stout,
No man could ever make him face about,
And how Great-Heart *and he could not forbear*
But put down Doubting-Castle, slay Despair.

Overlook not Master Despondency,
Nor Much-afraid, *his Daughter, though they lie*
Under such mantles, as may make them look
(With some) as if their God had them forsook.
They softly went, but sure; and, at the end,
Found that the Lord of Pilgrims *was their friend.*
When thou hast told the World of all these things,
Then turn about, my book, and touch these strings
Which, if but *touched, will such Music make,*
They'll make a Cripple dance, a Giant quake.
Those Riddles that lie couch'd within thy breast,
Freely propound, expound: and for the rest
Of thy mysterious lines, let them remain,
For those whose nimble Fancies shall them gain.

  Now may this little Book a blessing be
To those who love this little Book and me;
And may its buyer have no cause to say,
His Money is but lost or thrown away.
Yea, may this Second Pilgrim *yield that Fruit,*
As may with each good Pilgrim's *fancy suit,*
And may it persuade some that go astray,
To turn their Foot and Heart to the right way,

Is the Hearty Prayer
of the Author,
JOHN BUNYAN

THE
Pilgrim's Progress
In the Similitude of a
DREAM.
The Second Part

Courteous Companions, sometime since, to tell you my dream that I had of *Christian* the Pilgrim, and of his dangerous journey towards the Celestial Country; was pleasant to me, and profitable to you. I told you then also what I saw concerning his *Wife* and *Children*, and how unwilling they were to go with him on Pilgrimage: Insomuch that he was forced to go on his Progress without them, for he durst not run the danger of that destruction which he feared would come by staying with them, in the City of Destruction: Wherefore, as I then showed you, he left them and departed.

Now it hath so happened, thorough the Multiplicity of Business,[1] that I have been much hindered, and kept back from my wonted Travels into those Parts whence he went, and so could not till now obtain an opportunity to make further inquiry after those whom he left behind, that I might give you an account of them. But having had some concerns that way of late, I went down again thitherward. Now, having taken up my Lodgings in a Wood[2] about a mile off the Place, as I slept, I dreamed again.

And as I was in my Dream, behold, an aged Gentleman came by where I lay; and, because he was to go some part of the way that I was travelling, me thought I got up and went with him. So, as we walked, and as Travellers usually do, it was as if we fell into discourse; and our talk happened to be about *Christian* and his Travels; For thus I began with the Old-man.

Sir, said I, *what Town is that there below, that lieth on the left hand of our way?*

Then said Mr. *Sagacity*,[3] for that was his name, it is the City of *Destruction*, a populous place, but possessed with a very ill conditioned, and idle sort of people.

I thought that was that city, quoth I, *I went once my self through that Town; and therefore know that this report you give of it is true.*

Sag. Too true, I wish I could speak truth in speaking better of them that dwell therein.

Well sir, quoth I, *Then I perceive you to be a well meaning man: and so one that takes pleasure to hear and tell of that which is good; pray, did you never hear what happened to a man sometime ago of this town, (whose name was* Christian,*) that went on a Pilgrimage up towards the higher Regions?*

Sag. Hear of him! Aye, and I also heard of the Molestations, Troubles, Wars, Captivities, Cries, Groans, Frights, and Fears, that he met with, and had in his Journey. Besides, I must tell you, all our Country rings of him; there are but few houses that have heard of him and his doings, but have sought after and got the *Records* of his Pilgrimage; yea, I think I may say, that that his hazardous Journey has got a many well-wishers to his ways: For though when he was here, he was *Fool* in every man's mouth, yet now he is gone, he is highly commended of all. For, 'tis said he lives bravely where he is: Yea, many of them that are resolved never to run his hazards, yet have their mouths water at his gains.

Christians are well spoken of when gone, tho' called Fools while they are here

They may, quoth I, *well think, if they think any thing that is true, that he liveth well where he is, for he now lives at, and in the Fountain of Life, and has what he has without Labour and sorrow, for there is no grief mixed therewith. [But, pray what talk have the people about him?]*[4]

Sag. Talk! The People talk strangely about him: some say that he *now walks in White*, that he has a Chain of Gold about his neck, that he has a Crown of Gold, beset

with Pearls upon his Head: Others say, that the shining Revel. 3.4, Chap. 6.11
ones that sometimes showed themselves to him in his Jour-
ney, are become his Companions, and that he is as familiar
with them where he is, as here one Neighbour is with
another. Besides, 'tis confidently affirmed concerning him, Zech. 3.7
that the King of the place where he is has bestowed upon
him already, a very rich and pleasant Dwelling at Court,
and that he every day eateth and drinketh, and walketh, and Luke 14.15
talketh with him, and receiveth of the smiles and favours of
him that is Judge of all there. Moreover, it is expected of
some, that his Prince, the Lord of that Country, will shortly
come into *these* parts, and will know the reason, if they can Jude 14, 15
give any, why his Neighbours set so little by him, and had
him so much in derision, when they perceived that he would
be a Pilgrim. For they say, that now he is so in the affections Christian's *King will take* Chris-tian's *part*
of his Prince, that his *Sovereign* is so much concerned with
the Indignities that were cast upon *Christian* when he
became a Pilgrim, that he will look upon all as if done unto
himself; and no marvel, for 'twas for the love that he had
to his Prince, that he ventured as he did. Luke 10.16

I dare say, quoth I; *I am glad on't; I am glad for the poor
man's sake, for that now he has rest from his Labour, and* Revel. 14.13
*for that he now reapeth the benefit of his Tears with Joy;
and for that he has got beyond the Gun-shot of his enemies,
and is out of the reach of them that hate him. I also am* Psal. 126.5, 6
*glad for that a Rumour of these things is noised abroad in
this Country; who can tell but that it may work some good
effect on some that are left behind? But pray, Sir, while it
is fresh in my mind, do you hear anything of his Wife and
Children? Poor hearts, I wonder in my mind what they do.*

Sag. Who? *Christiana,* and her sons? They are like to do *Good Tidings of* Christian's *Wife and Children*
as well as did *Christian* himself, for though they all played
the Fool at first, and would by no means be persuaded
by either the Tears or Entreaties of Christian, yet second
thoughts have wrought wonderfully with them, so they
have packed up, and are also gone after him.

Better, and better, quoth I: *But What! Wife and Children
and all?*

Sag. 'Tis true, I can give you an account of the matter, for I was upon the spot at the instant, and was thoroughly acquainted with the whole affair.

Then, said I, *a man it seems may report it for a truth?*

Sag. You need not fear to affirm it, I mean that they are all gone on Pilgrimage, both the good Woman and her four Boys. And being we are, as I perceive, going some considerable way together, I will give you an account of the whole of the matter.

This *Christiana,* (for that was her name from the day that she with her Children betook themselves to a *Pilgrim's* life,) after her Husband was gone *over the River,* and she could hear of him no more, her thoughts began to work in her mind; First, for that she had lost her husband, and for that the loving bond of that Relation was utterly broken betwixt them. For you know, said he to me, nature can do no less but entertain the living with many a heavy Cogitation, in the remembrance of the loss of loving relations. This therefore of her Husband did cost her many a Tear. But this was not all; for *Christiana* did also begin to consider with her self, whether her unbecoming behaviour towards her Husband, was not one cause that she saw him no more, and that in such sort he was taken away from her. And upon this came into her mind, by *swarms,* all her unkind, unnatural, and ungodly Carriages to her dear Friend; which also clogged her Conscience, and did load her with guilt. She was moreover much broken with recalling to remembrance the restless Groans, brinish Tears and self-bemoanings of her Husband, and how she did harden her heart against all his entreaties and loving persuasions (of her and her Sons) to go with him; yea, there was not any thing that *Christian* either said to her, or did before her, all the while that his burden did hang on his back, but it returned upon her like a flash of lightning, and rent the Caul of her Heart in sunder.[5] Specially that bitter out-cry of his, *What shall I do to be saved,* did ring in her ears most dolefully.

Then said she to her Children, Sons, we are all undone.

1 part pag. 158

Mark this, you that are Churls to your godly Relatives

1 part, page 12

I have sinned away your Father, and he is gone; he would have had us with him; but I would not go myself, I also have hindered you of Life. With that the Boys fell all into Tears, and cried out to go after their Father. Oh! said *Christiana*, that it had been but our lot to go with him, then had it fared well with us beyond what 'tis like to do now. For, tho' I formerly foolishly imagin'd concerning the Troubles of your Father, that they proceeded of a foolish Fancy that he had, or for that he was overrun with Melancholy Humours; yet now 'twill not out of my mind, but that they sprang from another cause; to wit, for that the Light of Light was given him, by the help of which, as I perceive, he has escaped the snares of death. Then they all wept again, and cried out: Oh, woe, worth the day![6]

James 1.23, 24, 25

The next night *Christiana* had a Dream, and, behold, she saw as if a broad Parchment was opened before her, in which were recorded the sum of her ways, and the crimes, as she thought, look'd *very black upon her*. Then she cried out aloud in her sleep, Lord, have mercy upon me a Sinner, and the little Children heard her.

Christiana's Dream

Luke 18.13

After this she thought she saw two very ill favoured ones standing by her Bed-side, and saying, *What shall we do with this Woman? For she cries out for Mercy, waking and sleeping: if she be suffered to go on as she begins, we shall lose her as we have lost her Husband.* Wherefore we must, by one way or other, seek to take her off from the thoughts of what shall be hereafter: else all the World cannot help it, but she will become a Pilgrim.

Mark this, this is the quintessence of Hell

Now she awoke in a great Sweat, also a trembling was upon her, but after a while she fell to sleeping again. And then she thought she saw *Christian,* her husband, in a place of bliss among many *Immortals,* with an *Harp* in his Hand, standing and playing upon it before one that sat on a Throne with a Rainbow about his Head. She saw also as if he bowed his Head with his Face to the Pav'd-work that was under the Prince's Feet, saying, *I heartily thank my Lord and King for bringing me into this place.* Then shouted a company of them that stood round about, and

Help against Discouragement

harped with their Harps; but no man living could tell what they said, but *Christian* and his Companions.[7]

Next Morning, when she was up, had prayed to God, and talked with her Children a while, one knocked hard at the door; to whom she spake out, saying, *If thou comest in God's name, come in.* So he said, *Amen,* and opened the Door, and saluted her with, *Peace be to this house.* The which when he had done, he said, *Christiana,* knowest thou wherefore I am come? Then she blushed and trembled, also her heart began to wax warm with desires to know from whence he came, and what was his Errand to her. So he said unto her; my name is *Secret,* I dwell with those that are high. It is talked of where I dwell, as if thou had'st a desire to go thither; also there is a report that thou art aware of the evil thou hast formerly done to thy Husband in hardening of thy Heart against his way, and in keeping of these thy Babes in their Ignorance. *Christiana,* the merciful one has sent me to tell thee that he is a God ready to forgive, and that he taketh delight to multiply pardon [to] offences. He also would have thee know that he inviteth thee to come into his presence, to his Table, and that he will feed thee with the Fat of his House, and with the heritage of *Jacob* thy father.

There is *Christian,* thy Husband, *that was,* with Legions more, his Companions, ever beholding that face that doth minister Life to beholders; and they will all be glad when they shall hear the sound of thy feet step over thy Father's Threshold.

Christiana at this was greatly abashed in herself, and bowing her head to the ground this *Visitor* proceeded and said, *Christiana!* Here is also a letter for thee, which I have brought from thy Husband's King. So she took it and opened it, but it smelt after the manner of the best Perfume, also it was Written in Letters of Gold. The Contents of the Letter was, *That the King would have her to do as did* Christian *her Husband: for that was the way to come to his City, and to dwell in his Presence with Joy, forever.* At this the good Woman was quite overcome. So she cried out

Convictions seconded with Fresh Tidings of God's readiness to Pardon

Song 1.3

Christiana quite overcome

to her *Visitor. Sir, will you carry me and my children with you, that we also may go and worship this King?*

Then said the Visitor, *Christiana! the bitter is before the sweet:* Thou must through troubles, as did he that went before thee, enter this Celestial City. Wherefore I advise thee, to do as did *Christian* thy Husband: go to the *Wicket Gate* yonder, over the Plain, for that stands in the head of the way up which thou must go; and I wish thee all good speed. Also I advise that thou put this Letter in thy Bosom. That thou read therein to thyself and to thy children until you have got it by root-of-heart.[8] For it is one of the Songs that thou must Sing while thou art in this House of thy Pilgrimage. Also this thou must deliver in at the *further* Gate.

Further Instruction to Christiana

Psal. 119.54

Now I saw in my Dream, that this Old Gentleman, as he told me this Story, did himself seem to be greatly affected therewith. He moreover proceeded and said, So *Christiana* called her Sons together, and began thus to Address herself unto them. My Sons, I have, as you may perceive, been of late under much exercise in my Soul about the Death of your Father; not for that I doubt at all of his Happiness: For I am satisfied now that he is well. I have also been much affected with the thoughts of my own State and yours, which I verily believe is by nature miserable: My Carriages also to your father in his distress is a great load to my Conscience. For I hardened both mine own heart and yours against him, and refused to go with him on Pilgrimage.

Christiana prays well for her Journey

The thoughts of these things would now kill me outright; but that for a Dream which I had last night, and but that for the encouragement which this Stranger has given me this Morning. Come, my Children, let us pack up, and be gone to the Gate that leads to the Celestial Country, that we may see your Father, and be with him, and his Companions in Peace, according to the Laws of that Land.

Then did her Children burst out into Tears for Joy that the Heart of their Mother was so inclined. So their visitor bid them farewell: and they began to prepare to set out for their Journey.

But while they were thus about to be gone, two of the Women that were *Christiana's* Neighbours came up to her House, and knocked at her Door. To whom she said as before, *If you come in God's name, come in.* At this the women were stunned, for this kind of Language, they used not to hear, or to perceive to drop from the lips of *Christiana.* Yet they came in; but behold, they found the good Woman preparing to be gone from her House.

Christiana's *new Language stuns her old Neighbours*

So they began and said, *Neighbour, pray what is your meaning by this?*

Christiana answered, and said to the eldest of them, whose name was Mrs. *Timorous,* I am preparing for a Journey. (This *Timorous* was daughter to him that met *Christian* upon the Hill *Difficulty:* and would have had him gone back for fear of the Lions.)

1 *Part, pag.* 48

Timorous. For what Journey I pray you?

Chris. Even to go after my good husband; and with that she fell a weeping.

Timo. I hope not so, good Neighbour, pray for your poor Children's sakes, do not so unwomanly cast away yourself.

Timorous *comes to visit* Christiana, *with* Mercy, *one of her Neighbours*

Chris. Nay, my children, shall go with me; not one of them is willing to stay behind.

Timo. I wonder in my very heart, what, or who has brought you into this Mind.

Chris. Oh, Neighbour, knew you but as much as I do, I doubt not but that you would go along with me.

Timo. Prithee, what new knowledge hast thou got that so worketh off thy mind from thy Friends, and that tempteth thee to go no body knows where?

Chris. Then *Christiana* replied, I have been sorely afflicted since my Husband's departure from me; but especially since he went *over the River.* But that which troubleth me most, is my churlish carriages to him when he was under his distress. Besides, I am *now* as he was *then;* nothing will serve me but going on Pilgrimage. I was a dreaming last

Death

night that I saw him. O that my Soul was with him. He
dwelleth in the presence of the King of the Country, he sits
and eats with him at his Table, he is become a Companion
of *Immortals*, and has a House now given him to dwell in,   2 Cor. 5.1, 2,
to which the best Palaces on Earth, if compared, seem to   3, 4
me but as a Dunghill. The Prince of the Place has also sent
for me, with promise of entertainment if I shall come to
him; his messenger was here even now, and has brought
me a Letter, which Invites me to come. And with that she
plucked out her Letter, and read it, and said to them, what
now will you say to this?

    Timo. *Oh the madness that has possessed thee and thy
Husband, to run yourselves upon such difficulties! You
have heard, I am sure, what your Husband did meet with,
even in a manner at the first step that he took on his way,
as our Neighbour* Obstinate *can yet testify; for he went
along with him; yea, and* Pliable *too, until they, like* wise
men, *were afraid to go any further. We also heard over and*   1 part, pag. 50,
above, how he met with the Lions, Apollyon, the shadow   61
of death, and many other things. Nor is the danger that he   *The reasonings*
met with at Vanity Fair *to be forgotten by thee. For if he,*   *of the flesh*
*though a man, was so hard put to it, what canst thou being
but a poor* Woman, *do? Consider also, that these four
sweet Babes are thy Children, thy Flesh and thy Bones.
Wherefore, though thou shouldest be so rash as to cast
away thyself: Yet for the sake of the fruit of thy Body, keep
thou at home.*

    But *Christiana* said unto her, Tempt me not, my Neigh-
bour: I have now a price put into my hands to get gain, and
I should be a Fool of the greatest size, if I should have no
heart to strike in with the opportunity. And for that you
tell me of all these Troubles that I am like to meet with in
the way, they are so far from being to me a discouragement,
that they show I am in the right. *The bitter must come
before the sweet,* and that also will make the sweet the
sweeter. Wherefore since you came not to my House, *in
God's name,* as I said, I pray you to be gone, and not to
disquiet me further.

Then *Timorous* also reviled her, and said to her Fellow, come, Neighbour *Mercy,* let's leave her in her own hands, since she scorns our Counsel and Company. But *Mercy* was at a stand, and could not so readily comply with her Neighbour: and that for a two fold-reason. First, her Bowels yearned[9] over *Christiana:* so she said within her self, if my Neighbour will needs be gone, I will go a little way with her, and help her. Secondly, her Bowels yearned over her own Soul, (for what *Christiana* had said, had taken some hold upon her mind.) Wherefore she said within her self again, I will yet have more talk with this *Christiana,* and, if I find Truth and Life in what she shall say, my self with my heart shall also go with her. Wherefore *Mercy* began thus to reply to her neighbour *Timorous.*

Mercy. Neighbour, *I did indeed come with you to see* Christiana *this Morning; and since she is, as you see, a taking of her last farewell of her Country, I think to walk this Sun-shine Morning, a little way with her to help her on the way.* But she told her not of her second Reason, but kept that to herself.

Timo. Well, I see you have a mind to go a fooling too: but take heed in time, and be wise: while we are out of danger, we are out; but when we are in, we are in. So Mrs. *Timorous* returned to her House, and *Christiana* betook her self to her Journey. But when *Timorous* was got home to her house she sends for some of her Neighbours, to wit, Mrs. *Bat's-Eyes,* Mrs. *Inconsiderate,* Mrs. *Light-mind,* and Mrs. *Know-nothing.* So when they were come to her House, she falls to telling of the story of *Christiana,* and of her intended Journey. And thus she began her Tale.

Timo. Neighbours, having had little to do this morning, I went to give *Christiana* a visit, and when I came at the door I knocked, as you know 'tis our Custom: And she answered, *If you come in God's Name, come in.* So in I went, thinking all was well: But, when I came in, I found her preparing her self to depart the Town, she, and also her Children. So I asked her what was her meaning by that? and she told me in short, That she was now of a mind to

Marginal notes:

Mercy's *Bowels* yearn over Christiana

Timorous *forsakes her; but* Mercy *cleaves to her*

Timorous *acquaints her Friends what the good* Christiana *intends to do* go on Pilgrimage, as did her husband. She told me also of a Dream that she had, and how the King of the Country where her Husband was, had sent an inviting Letter to come thither.

Then said Mrs. Know-Nothing, *And what! do you think she will go?*

Timo. Aye, go she will, whatever comes on't; and methinks I know it by this; for that which was my great Argument to persuade her to stay at home, (to wit, the Troubles she was like to meet with in the way) is one great Argument with her to put her forward on her Journey. For she told me in so many words, *The bitter goes before the sweet.* Yea, and for as much as it doth, it makes the sweet the sweeter.

Mrs. *Bat's-eyes.* Oh, this blind and foolish woman, said she, Will she not take warning by her husband's Afflictions? For my part, I see if he was here again, he would rest himself content in a whole Skin, and never run so many hazards for nothing.

Mrs. *Inconsiderate* also replied, saying, away with such Fantastical Fools from the Town; a good Riddance, for my part, I say, of her, Should she stay where she dwells, and retain this her mind, who could live quietly by her? for she will either be dumpish or unneighbourly, or talk of such matters as no wise Body can abide: Wherefore, for my part I shall never be sorry for her Departure; let her go, and let better come in her room: 'twas never a good World since these whimsical Fools dwelt in it.

Then Mrs. *Light-mind* added as followeth. Come, put this kind of Talk away. I was yesterday at Madam *Wanton's,* where we were as merry as the Maids. For who do you think should be there, but I, and Mr.s *Love-the-flesh,* and three or four more, with Mr. *Lechery,* Mrs. *Filth,* and some others. So there we had Music and Dancing, and what else was meet to fill up the pleasure. And I dare say my Lady herself is an admirable well bred Gentle-woman, and Mr. Lechery is as pretty a Fellow.

By this time *Christiana* was got on her way, and *Mercy*

Mrs. Know-nothing

Mrs. Bat's-eyes

Mrs. Inconsiderate

Mrs. Light-mind

Madam Wanton, *she that had like to a been too hard for* Faithful *in time past*

1 part, pag. 73

went along with her. So as they went, her children being there also, *Christiana* began to discourse. And, *Mercy,* said *Christiana,* I take this as an unexpected favour, that thou shouldest set forth out of Doors with me to accompany me a little in the way.

Mercy. Then said young Mercy, *(for she was but young,) If I thought it would be to purpose to go with you, I would never go near the Town any more.*

Chris. Well, *Mercy,* said *Christiana,* cast in thy Lot with me. I well know what will be the end of our Pilgrimage, my Husband is where he would not but be, for all the gold in the *Spanish* Mines. Nor shalt thou be rejected, though thou goest but upon *my Invitation.* The King who hath sent for me and my Children, is one that de-
lighteth in *Mercy.* Besides, if thou wilt, I will hire thee, and thou shalt go along with me as my servant. Yet we will have all things in Common betwixt thee and me, only go along with me.

Mercy. But how shall I be ascertained that I also should be entertained? Had I this hope but from one that can tell, I would make no stick at all, but would go, being helped by him that can help, though the way was never so tedious.

Christiana
allures her to the
Gate *which is*
Christ, *and*
promiseth there
to inquire
for her
Christiana. Well, loving *Mercy,* I will tell thee what thou shalt do, go with me to the *Wicket Gate,* and there I will further inquire for thee, and if there thou shalt not meet with encouragement, I will be content that thou shalt return to thy place. I will also pay thee for thy Kindness which thou showest to me and my Children, in the accompanying of us in our way as thou doest.

Mercy. Then will I go thither, and will take what shall follow, and the Lord grant that my Lot may there fall, even as the King of Heaven shall have his heart upon me.

Christiana, then was glad at heart, not only that she had a Companion, but also for that she had prevailed with this poor Maid to fall in love with her own Salvation. So they went on together, and *Mercy* began to weep. Then said *Christiana,* Wherefore weepeth my Sister so?

Mer. Alas! said she, who can but lament, that shall but rightly consider what a State and Condition my poor Relations are in, that yet remain in our sinful Town: and that which makes my grief the more heavy, is, because they have no Instructor, nor any to tell them what is to come.

Mercy grieves for her carnal Relations

Chris. Bowels becometh Pilgrims. And thou dost for thy Friends as my good *Christian* did for me when he left me: he mourned for that I would not heed nor regard him; but his Lord and ours did gather up his Tears, and put them into his Bottle;[10] and now both I, and thou, and these my sweet Babes, are reaping the Fruit and benefit of them. I hope, Mercy, that these Tears of thine will not be lost; for the Truth hath said, *That they that sow in tears shall reap in joy. And he that goeth forth and weepeth, bearing precious seed, shall doubtless come again with rejoicing, bringing his Sheaves with him.*

Christian's Prayers were answered for his Relations after he was dead

Psal. 126.5, 6

Then said *Mercy,*

> *Let the most blessed be my guide*
> *If't be his blessed Will,*
> *Unto his Gate, into his fold,*
> *Up to his Holy Hill.*

> *And let him never suffer me*
> *To swerve, or turn aside*
> *From his free grace and Holy ways,*
> *Whate'er shall me betide.*

> *And let him gather them of mine,*
> *That I have left behind;*
> *Lord make them pray they may be thine,*
> *With all their heart and mind.*

Now my old Friend proceeded, and said, But when *Christiana* came to the Slough of *Despond,* she began to be at a stand: for, said she, This is the place in which my dear

1 Part, page 17

*Their own carnal
Conclusions,
instead of the
word of life* Husband had like to have a been smothered with Mud. She perceived also, that notwithstanding the Command of the King to make this place for Pilgrims, good; yet it was rather worse than formerly. So I asked if that was true? Yes, said the Old Gentleman, too true. For many there be that pretend to be the King's Labourers; and that say they are for mending the King's High-ways, that bring *Dirt* and *Dung* instead of Stones, and so mar instead of mending.[11]

*Mercy the bold-
est at the Slough
of Despond*
Here *Christiana* therefore, with her Boys did make a stand: but said *Mercy,* Come, let us venture, only let us be wary. Then they looked well to the *Steps,* and made a shift to get staggeringly over.

Yet *Christiana* had like to a been in, and that not once nor twice. Now they had no sooner got over, but they thought they heard words that said unto them, *Blessed is she that believeth; for there shall be a performance of those*
Luke 1.45 *things which were told her from the Lord.*

Then they went on again; and said *Mercy* to *Christiana,* Had I as good ground to hope for a loving reception at the *Wicket Gate* as you, I think no Slough of *Despond* would discourage me.

Well, said the other, you know *your sore,* and I know *mine*: and, good friend, we shall all have enough evil before we come at our Journey's end.

For can it be imagined, that the people who design to attain such excellent Glories *as we do,* and that are so envied that Happiness *as we are,* but that we shall meet with what Fears and Snares, with what Troubles and Afflictions they can possibly assault us with, that hate us?

And now Mr. *Sagacity* left me to Dream out my Dream by my self. Wherefore, me-thought I saw *Christiana,* and *Mercy,* and the *Boys,* go all of them up to the Gate. To which when they were come, they betook themselves to a short debate about *how* they must manage their calling at
*Prayer should be
made with Con-
sideration, and
Fear: As well as in
Faith and Hope*
the Gate, and what should be said unto him that did open to them. So it was concluded, since *Christiana* was the eldest, that she should knock for entrance, and that she should speak to him that did open, for the rest. So *Chris-*

tiana began to knock, and as her poor Husband did she *knocked* and *knocked* again. But instead of any that answered, they all thought that they heard, as if a Dog came barking upon them. A Dog, and a great one too, and this made the Women and Children afraid. Nor durst they for a while to knock any more, for fear the *Mastiff* should fly upon them. Now therefore they were greatly tumbled up and down in their minds, and knew not what to do. Knock they durst not, for fear of the dog; go back they durst not, for fear that the Keeper of that Gate should espy them as they so went, and should be offended with them. At last they thought of knocking again, and knocked more vehemently than they did at the first. Then said the Keeper of the Gate, who is there? So the *Dog* left off to bark, and he opened unto them.

1 Part, pag. 27

The Dog, the Devil, an Enemy to Prayer

Christiana and her companions perplexed about Prayer

Then *Christiana* made low obeisance, and said, Let not our Lord be offended with his Handmaidens, for that we have knocked at his Princely Gate. Then said the Keeper, Whence come ye, and what is it that you would have?

Christiana answered, We are come from whence *Christian* did come, and upon the same *Errand* as he; to wit, to be, if it shall please you, graciously admitted by this Gate, into the way that leads unto the Celestial City. And I answer, my Lord, in the next place, that I am *Christiana*, once the Wife of *Christian*, that now is gotten above.

With that the Keeper of the Gate did marvel, saying, *What is she now become a Pilgrim, that but a while ago abhorred that Life?* Then she bowed her head, and said, yes; and so are these my sweet Babes also.

Then he took her by the hand, and led her in and said also, *Suffer the little Children to come unto me,*[12] and with that he shut up the Gate. This done, he called to a trumpeter that was above over the Gate, to entertain *Christiana* with shouting and the sound of Trumpet for joy. So he obeyed and sounded, and filled the Air with his Melodious Notes.

How Christiana *is entertained at the Gate*

Now all this while poor *Mercy* did stand without, trembling and crying for fear that she was rejected. But when

Christiana had gotten admittance for herself and her Boys, then she began to make Intercession for Mercy.

Chris. And she said, My Lord, I have a Companion that stands yet without, that is come hither upon the same account as my self. One that is much dejected in her mind, for that she comes, as she thinks, without sending for; whereas I was sent to, by my Husband's King to come.

Now *Mercy* began to be very impatient, for each Minute was as long to her as an hour, wherefore she prevented *Christiana* from a fuller interceding for her, by knocking at the Gate her self. And she knocked *then* so loud that she made *Christiana* to start. Then said the Keeper of the Gate who is there? And said *Christiana,* it is my Friend.

So he opened the Gate, and looked out; but *Mercy* was fallen down without in a Swoon, for she fainted, and was afraid, that no Gate should be opened to her.

Then he took her by the hand, and said, *Damsel,* I bid thee arise.[13]

O sir, she said, I am faint, there is scarce Life left in me. But he answered, that one once said, *When my soul fainted within me, I remembered the Lord: and my prayer came unto thee, into thy Holy Temple.* Fear not, but stand upon thy Feet, and tell me wherefore thou art come.

Mer. I am come for *that* unto which I was never invited, as my Friend *Christiana* was. *Hers* was from the King, and mine was but from *her:* Wherefore I fear I presume.

Did she desire thee to come with her to this Place?

Mer. Yes; and, as my Lord sees, I am come. And if there is any Grace and forgiveness of Sins to spare, I beseech that I thy poor Handmaid may be partaker thereof.

Then he took her again by the Hand, and led her gently in, and said: I pray for all them that believe on me,[14] by what means soever they come unto me. Then said he to those that stood by: Fetch something and give it *Mercy* to smell on, thereby to stay her fainting. So they fetched her a *Bundle* of *Myrrh,*[15] and a while after she was revived.

And now was *Christiana* and her Boys and *Mercy received* of the Lord at the head of the way, and spoken kindly unto by him.

Then said they yet further unto him, We are sorry for our Sins, and beg of our Lord his Pardon, and further information, what we must do.

I grant Pardon, said he, by word and deed; by word in the promise of Forgiveness: by deed in the way I obtained it. Take the first from my Lips with a kiss, and the other, as it shall be revealed. *Song 1.2. John 20.20*

Now I saw in my Dream that he spake many good words unto them, whereby they were greatly gladded. He also had them up to the top of the Gate, and showed them by what *deed* they were saved; and told them withal, that that sight they would have again as they went along in the way, to their comfort. *Christ Crucified seen afar off*

So he left them awhile in a Summer-Parlour[16] below, where they entered into talk by themselves. And thus *Christiana* began, *O Lord! How glad am I, that we are got in hither!* *Talk between the Christians*

Mer. So you well may; but I, of all, have cause to leap for joy.

Chris. I thought, one time, as I stood at the Gate (because I had knocked and none did answer) that all our Labour had been lost: Specially when that ugly Cur made such a heavy barking against us.

Mer. But my worst Fears was after I saw that you was taken in to his favour, and that I was left behind: Now, thought I, 'tis fulfilled which is Written. *Two women shall be grinding at the mill; the one shall be taken, and the other left.* I had much ado to forbear crying out, Undone, undone. *Mat. 24.41*

And afraid I was to knock any more; but when I looked up to what was Written over the Gate, I took courage. I also thought that I must either knock again or die. So I knocked; but I cannot tell how, for my spirit now *struggled* between life and death. *1 Part, pag. 28–9*

Christiana
thinks her Com-
panion prays
better than she.
Mat. 11.12
Chris. Can you not tell how you knocked? I am sure your knocks were so earnest that the very sound of them made me start, I thought I never heard such knocking in all my Life. I thought you would a come in by violent hands, or a took the Kingdom by storm.

Mer. Alas, to be in my case, who that so was could but a done so? You saw that the Door was shut upon me and there was a most cruel *Dog* there about. Who, I say, that was so faint hearted as I, would not a knocked with all their might? But pray, what said my Lord to my rudeness, was he not angry with me?

Christ pleased
with loud and
restless praises
Chris. When he heard your lumbering noise, he gave a wonderful Innocent Smile. I believe what you did pleas'd him well enough. For he showed no sign to the contrary. But I marvel in my heart why he keeps such a dog; had I known that afore, I should not have had heart enough to a ventured my self in this manner. But now we are in, we are in, and I am glad with all my heart.

Mer. I will ask if you please next time he comes down, why he keeps such a filthy Cur in his yard. I hope he will not take it amiss.

The Children are
afraid of the dog
Ay do, said the Children, and persuade him to hang him, for we are afraid he will bite us when we go hence.

So at last he came down to them again, and *Mercy* fell to the Ground on her Face before him and worshipped, and said, Let my Lord accept of the Sacrifice of praise which I now offer unto him, with the calves of my Lips.

So he said unto her, Peace be to thee, stand up.

Jer. 12.1, 2
But she continued upon her Face and said, *Righteous art thou, O Lord, when I pleaded with thee, yet let me talk*
Mercy expos-
tulates about
the dog
with thee of thy Judgements: Wherefore dost thou keep so cruel a Dog in thy Yard, at the sight of which such Women and Children as we are ready to fly from thy Gate for fear?

Devil
He answered, and said; *That Dog* has another Owner, he also is kept close in another man's ground; only my Pilgrims hear his barking. He belongs to the Castle which you see there at a distance: but can come up to the Walls of this Place. He has frighted many an honest pilgrim from

worse to better, by the great voice of his roaring. Indeed, he that owneth him doth not keep him out of any good will to me or mine; but with intent to keep the Pilgrims from coming to me, and that they may be afraid to come and knock at this Gate for entrance. Sometimes also he has broken out, and has *worried* some that I loved; but I take all at present patiently, I also give my Pilgrims timely help: So that they are not delivered to his power, to do with them what his Doggish nature would prompt him to. But what! My purchased one, I trow, hadst thou known never so much before hand, thou wouldst not have been afraid of a Dog.

A Check to the carnal fear of the Pilgrims

The Beggars that go from Door to Door, will, rather than lose a supposed Alms, run the hazard of the bawling, barking, and biting too of a Dog: And shall a dog, a dog in another Man's yard: a Dog whose barking I turn to the Profit of Pilgrims, keep any from coming to me? I deliver them from the Lions, their Darling from the power of the Dog.[17]

Mer. Then said *Mercy, I confess my ignorance: I spake what I understood not: I acknowledge that thou doest all things well.*

Christians when wise enough acquiesce in the wisdom of their Lord

Chris. Then *Christiana* began to talk of their Journey, and to inquire after the way. So he fed them, and washed their feet, and set them in the way of his Steps, according as he had dealt with her Husband before.

1 Part, pag. 31

So I saw in my Dream, that they walked on their way, and had the weather very comfortable to them.

Then *Christiana* began to sing, saying,

> *Bless'd be the day that I began,*
> *A pilgrim for to be;*
> *And blessed also be the man*
> *That thereto moved me.*

> *'Tis true, 'twas long ere I began*
> *To seek to live for ever:*
> *But now I run fast as I can:*
> *'Tis better late than never.*

Mar. 20.6

> *Our* Tears *to joy, our fears to Faith,*
> *Are turned, as we see;*
> *Thus our beginning (as one saith)*
> *Shows what our end will be.*[18]

Now there was, on the other side of the Wall that fenced in the way up which *Christiana* and her Companions was to go, a Garden; and that Garden belonged to him whose was that *Barking Dog,* of whom mention was made before. And some of the Fruit-Trees that grew in that Garden shot their Branches over the Wall; and being mellow, they that found them did gather them up and oft eat of them to their hurt. So *Christiana's* Boys, as Boys are apt to do, being pleased with the Trees, and with the Fruit that hung thereon, did *Pluck*[19] them, and began to eat. Their Mother did also chide them for so doing; but still the Boys went on.

The devil's garden

The Children eat of the Enemy's Fruit

Well, said she, my Sons, you Transgress, for that Fruit is none of ours: but she did not know that they did belong to the Enemy; I'll warrant you if she had she would a been ready to die for fear. But that passed, and they went on their way. Now, by that they were gone about two Bows-shot[20] from the place that led them into the way: they espied two very *ill-favoured ones* coming down apace to meet them. With that *Christiana,* and *Mercy* her Friend, covered themselves with their Veils, and so kept on their Journey: The Children also went on before, so that at last they met together. Then they that came down to meet them, came just up to the Women, as if they would embrace them; but *Christiana* said, Stand back, or go peaceably by as you should. Yet these two, as men that are deaf, regarded not *Christiana's* words, but began to lay hands upon them; at that *Christiana* waxing very wroth, spurned at[21] them with her feet. *Mercy* also, as well as she could, did what she could to shift them. *Christiana* again said to them, Stand back, and be gone, for we have no Money to lose being pilgrims, as ye see, and such too as live upon the Charity of our Friends.

Two ill favoured ones

They assault Christiana

The pilgrims struggle with them

Ill-fa. Then said one of the two Men, we make no assault

upon you for Money, but are come out to tell you, that if you will but grant one small request which we shall ask, we will make Women of you for ever.

Chris. Now *Christiana* imagining what they should mean, made answer again, *We will neither hear, nor regard, nor yield to what you shall ask, We are in haste, cannot stay; our Business is a Business of Life and Death.* So again she and her Companions made a fresh assay to go past Them. But they letted them in their way.

Ill-fa. And they said, We intend no hurt to your lives, 'tis an other thing we would have.

Chris. Aye, quoth *Christiana,* you would have us Body and Soul, for I know 'tis for that you are come; but we will die rather upon the spot, than to suffer ourselves to be brought into such Snares as shall hazard our well being hereafter. And with that they both *Shrieked* out, and cried, *She cries out* Murder, Murder; and so put themselves under those Laws that are provided for the Protection of Women. But the *Deut. 22.23,* men still made their approach upon them, with design to *26, 27* prevail against them: They therefore cried out again.

Now they being, as I said, not far from the Gate in at *'Tis good to cry* which they came, their voice was heard from whence they *out when we are* was, thither: Wherefore some of the House came out, and *assaulted* knowing that it was *Christiana's* Tongue, they made haste to her relief. But by that they were got within sight of them, the women were in a very great scuffle; the children also stood crying by. Then did he that came in for their relief *The* Reliever call out to the Ruffians, saying, What is that thing you do? *comes* Would you make my Lord's People to transgress? He also attempted to take them; but they did make their escape *The* Ill-ones *fly* over the wall into the Garden of the Man to whom the *to the devil for* great Dog belonged; so the Dog became their Protector. *relief* This Reliever then came up to the women, and asked them how they did. So they answered, We thank thy Prince, pretty well, only we have been somewhat affrighted; we thank thee also for that thou camest in to our help, for otherwise we had been overcome.

Reliever. So after a few more words, this *Reliever* said as

198   THE PILGRIM'S PROGRESS

The Reliever
talks to the
Women

followeth: *I marvelled much, when you was entertained at
the Gate above, being ye knew that ye were but weak
Women, that you petitioned not the Lord there for a Conductor; then might you have avoided these Troubles, and
Dangers: For he would have granted you one.*

mark this

 Chris. Alas said *Christiana,* we were so taken with our
present blessing, that Dangers to come were forgotten by
us; beside, who could have thought that so near the King's
Palace there could have lurked such naughty[22] ones: Indeed,
it had been well for us had we asked our Lord for one; but
since our Lord knew 'twould be for our profit, I wonder he
sent not one along with us.

We lose for want
of asking for

 *Relie. It is not always necessary to grant things not asked
for, lest by so doing they become of little esteem; but when
the want of a thing is felt, it then comes, under, in the Eyes
of him that feels it, that estimate, that properly is its due,
and so consequently will be thereafter used. Had my Lord
granted you a Conductor, you would not neither, so have
bewailed that oversight of yours, in not asking for one, as
now you have occasion to do. So all things work for good,
and tend to make you more wary.*

 Chris. Shall we go back again to my Lord, and confess
our folly and ask one?

 Relie. *Your confession of your folly, I will present him
with: To go back again, you need not. For in all places
where you shall come, you will find no want at all; for in
every of my Lord's Lodgings, which he has prepared for
the reception of his Pilgrims, there is sufficient to furnish
them against all attempts whatsoever. But as I said, He will
be inquired of by them, to do it for them: and 'tis a poor
thing that is not worth asking for.* When he had thus said,
he went back to his place, and the Pilgrims went on their

Ezek. 36.37

way.

The mistake of
Mercy

 Mer. Then said *Mercy,* what a sudden blank is here? I
made account that we had been past all danger, and that
we should never see sorrow more.

 Chris. Thy *Innocency,* my Sister, said *Christiana* to
Mercy, may excuse thee much; but as for me, my fault is

so much the greater, for that I saw this danger before I came out of the Doors, and yet did not provide for it where Provision might have been had. I am much to be blamed.

Christiana's Guilt

Mer. Then said Mercy, *how knew you this before you came from home? pray open to me this Riddle.*

Chris. Why, I will tell you. Before I set Foot out of Doors, one Night, as I lay in my Bed, I had a Dream about this. For methought I saw two men, as like these as ever any [in] the World could look, stand at my *Bed's-feet*, plotting how they might prevent my Salvation. I will tell you their very words, They said, ('twas when I was in my Troubles,) *What shall we do with this Woman? for she cries out waking and sleeping, for forgiveness, if she be suffered to go on as she begins, we shall lose her as we have lost her Husband.* This you know might a made me take heed, and have provided when Provision might a been had.

Christiana's Dream repeated

Mer. Well said *Mercy, as by this neglect we have an occasion ministered unto us to behold our own imperfections, so our Lord has taken occasion thereby, to make manifest the Riches of his Grace. For he, as we see, has followed us with un-asked kindness, and has delivered us from their hands that were stronger than we, of his mere good pleasure.*

Mercy makes good use of their neglect of duty

Thus now when they had talked away a little more time, they drew near to an House which stood in the way, which House was built for the relief of Pilgrims. As you will find more fully related in the first part of these Records of the *Pilgrim's Progress.* So they drew on towards the House, (the House of the Interpreter) and when they came to the Door, they heard a great talk in the House, they then gave ear, and heard, as they thought, *Christiana* mentioned by name. For you must know that there went along, even before her, a talk of her and her Children's going on Pilgrimage. And this was the more pleasing to them, because they had heard that she was *Christian's* Wife; that Woman who was sometime ago, so unwilling to hear of going on Pilgrimage. Thus therefore they stood still and heard the good people within commending her who they little

1 Part pag. 31

Talk in the Interpreter's house about Christiana's going on pilgrimage

She knocks at the Door thought stood at the Door. At last *Christiana* knocked, as she had done at the Gate before. Now, when she had knocked, there came to the Door a young Damsel named *Innocent,* and opened the Door and looked, and behold two Women was there.

The door is opened to them by Innocent

Dams. *Then said the Damsel to them, With whom would you speak in this place?*

Chris. *Christiana* answered, we understand that this is a Privileged place for those that are become Pilgrims, and we now at this Door are such: Wherefore we pray that we may be partakers of that for which we at this time are come; for the day, as thou seest, is very far spent, and we are loth tonight to go any further.

Dams. Pray what may I call your name, that I may tell it to my Lord within?

Chris. My name is *Christiana,* I was the wife of that Pilgrim that some years ago did travel this way, and these be his four children. This Maiden also is my Companion, and is going on Pilgrimage too.

Innocent. Then ran *Innocent* in, (for that was her name) and said to those within, Can you think who is at the Door! There is *Christiana* and her Children, and her Companion,

Joy in the house of the Interpreter that Christiana is turned Pilgrim all waiting for entertainment here. Then they leaped for Joy, and went and told their Master. So he came to the Door, and looking upon her, he said, *Art thou that* Christiana *whom* Christian, *the Good-man, left behind him, when he betook himself to a Pilgrim's Life?*

Chris. I am that Woman that was so hard-hearted as to slight my Husband's Troubles, and that left him to go on in his Journey alone, and these are his four Children; but now I also am come, for I am convinced that no way is right but this.

Inter. *Then is fulfilled that which also is written of the Man that said to his Son, go work to-day in my Vineyard; and he said to his father, I will not: but afterwards repented* Mat. 21.29 *and went.*

Chris. Then said *Christiana,* So be it: *Amen.* God made

it a true saying upon me, and grant that I may be found at
the last, of him in peace without spot and blameless.

Inter. *But why standest thou thus at the Door, come in
thou Daughter of* Abraham, *we was talking of thee but
now: For tidings have come to us before, how thou art
become a pilgrim. Come, Children, come in; come Maiden,
come in; so he had them all into the house.*

So when they were within, they were bidden sit down
and rest them; the which when they had done, those that
attended upon the Pilgrims in the House, came into the
room to see them. And one smiled, and another smiled,
and they all smiled for joy that *Christiana* was become a
Pilgrim. They also looked upon the boys; they stroked them *Old Saints glad*
over their Faces with the Hand, in token of their kind *to see the young*
reception of them; they also carried it lovingly to *Mercy,* *ones walk in*
and bid them all welcome into their Master's house. *God's ways*

After a while, because Supper was not ready, the *Inter-* *The Significant*
preter took them into his *Significant* Rooms, and showed *Rooms*
them what *Christian, Christiana's* Husband had seen some
time before. Here, therefore, they saw the *Man* in the Cage,
the *Man* and his Dream, the man that cut his way through
his Enemies, and the Picture of the biggest of them all:[23]
together with the rest of those things that were then so
profitable to *Christian.*

This done, and after those things had been somewhat
digested by *Christiana* and her Company: the *Interpreter*
takes them apart again and has them first into a Room,
*where was a man that could look no way but downwards,
with a Muck-rake in his hand. There stood also one over* *The man with*
his head with a Celestial Crown in his Hand, and proffered *the Muck-rake*
him that Crown, for his Muck-rake; but the man did neither *explained*
*look up nor regard; but raked to himself the Straws, the
small Sticks, and Dust of the Floor.*

Then said *Christiana, I persuade myself that I know
somewhat the meaning of this: For this is a Figure of a Man
of this World: Is it not, good Sir?*

Inter. Thou hast said the right, said he; and his

Muck-rake doth show his Carnal mind. And whereas thou seest him rather give heed to rake up Straws and Sticks, and the dust of the Floor, than to do what he says that calls to him from above with the Celestial Crown in his Hand; it is to show, That Heaven is but as a Fable to some, and that things here are counted the only things substantial. Now, whereas it was also showed thee that the man could look no way but downwards: It is to let thee know that earthly things when they are with Power upon Men's minds, quite carry their hearts away from God.

Chris. *Then said* Christiana, *O! deliver me from this Muck-rake.*

Christiana's prayer against the Muck-rake

Inter. That Prayer, said the *Interpreter,* has lain by till it is almost rusty: *Give me not Riches,* Is scarce the Prayer of one of ten thousand. Straws, and Sticks, and Dust, with most, are the great things now looked after.

Pro. 30.8

With that *Mercy* and *Christiana* wept, and said, It is, alas! too true.

When the *Interpreter* had shown them this, he has them into the very best Room in the House (a very brave room it was) so he bid them look round about, and see if they could find any thing profitable there. Then they looked round and round: For there was nothing to be seen but a very great *Spider* on the Wall: and that they overlooked.

Mer. Then said Mercy, *Sir, I see nothing;* but *Christiana* held her peace.

Of the Spider

Inter. But said the *Interpreter,* look again: she therefore looked again, and said, Here is not any thing, but an *ugly Spider,* who hangs by her Hands upon the Wall. Then said he, Is there but one spider in all this spacious Room? Then the water stood in *Christiana's* eyes, for she was a Woman quick of apprehension; and she said, Yes, Lord, there is here more than one. Yea, and *Spiders* whose Venom is far more destructive than that which is in her. The *Interpreter* then looked pleasantly on her, and said, Thou hast said the Truth. This made *Mercy* blush, and the Boys to cover their Faces: For they all began now to understand the Riddle.

Talk about the Spider

Pro. 30.28

Then said the *Interpreter* again, *The Spider taketh hold*

with her hands as you see, and is in Kings' Palaces. And wherefore is this recorded; but to show you, that, how full of the Venom of Sin soever you be, yet you may, by the hand of Faith, lay hold of, and dwell in the best Room that belongs to the King's House above?

The Interpretation

Chris. I thought, said *Christiana,* of something of this; but I could not imagine it at all. I thought that we were like *Spiders,* and that we looked like ugly Creatures, in what fine Room soever we were: But that by this *Spider,* that venomous and ill favoured Creature, we were to learn *how to act Faith,* came not into my mind. And yet she has taken hold with her hands, as I see, and dwells in the best Room in the House. God has made nothing in vain.[24]

Then they seemed all to be glad; but the water stood in their Eyes; Yet they looked one upon another, and also bowed before the *Interpreter.*

He had them then into another Room, where was a *Hen* and *Chickens,* and bid them observe a while. So one of the Chickens went to the Trough to drink, and every time she drank she lift up her head and her eyes towards Heaven. See, said he, what this little Chick doth, and learn of her to acknowledge whence your Mercies come, by receiving them with looking up. Yet again, said he, observe and look: So they gave heed, and perceived that the Hen did walk in a fourfold method towards her Chickens: 1. She had a *common call,* and that she hath all day long. 2. She had a *special call,* and that she had but sometimes. 3. She had a *brooding note,* and, 4. she had an *outcry.*

Of the Hen and Chickens

Now, said he, compare this *Hen* to your King, and these Chickens to his Obedient ones. For answerable to her, himself has his Methods, which he walketh in towards his People. By his common call, *he gives nothing;* by his special call, he always *has something to give,* he has also a brooding voice, *for them that are under his Wing;* and he has an out-cry, *to give the alarm when he seeth the Enemy come.* I choose, my Darlings, to lead you into the Room where such things are, because you are women, and they are easy for you.

Mat. 23.37

Chris. And Sir, said *Christiana,* pray let us see some more: So he had them into the Slaughter-house, where was a *Butcher* a killing of a Sheep; And behold the Sheep *Of the Butcher* was quiet, and took her Death patiently. Then said the *and the Sheep Interpreter:* you must learn of this Sheep, to suffer: And to put up [with] wrongs without murmurings and complaints. Behold how quietly she takes her Death, and without objecting she suffereth her Skin to be pulled over her Ears. Your King doth call you his Sheep.

Of the Garden After this, he led them into his Garden, where was great variety of Flowers: and he, said, do you see all these? So *Christiana* said, Yes. Then said he again, Behold the Flowers are divers in *Stature,* in *Quality,* in *Colour,* and *Smell,* and *Virtue;* and some are better than Some: Also where the Gardener has set them, there they stand, and quarrel not one with another.[25]

Of the Field Again, he had them into his Field, which he had sown with Wheat, and Corn: but when they beheld the tops of all was cut off, only the Straw remained. He said again, This Ground was Dunged, and Ploughed, and sowed, but what shall we do with the Crop? Then said *Christiana,* burn some, and make muck of the rest. Then said the *Interpreter* again, Fruit you see is that thing you look for; and for want of that you condemn it to the Fire, and to be trodden under foot of men: Beware that in this you condemn not yourselves.

Then, as they were coming in from abroad, they espied a little *Robin* with a great *Spider* in his mouth. So the *Of the* Robin *Interpreter* said, look here. So they looked, and *Mercy and the* Spider wondered, but *Christiana* said, What a disparagement is it to such a little pretty bird as the *Robin-red-breast* is, he being also a Bird above many, that loveth to maintain a kind of Sociableness with Man! I had thought they had lived upon crumbs of Bread, or upon other such harmless matter. I like him worse than I did.

The *Interpreter* then replied, This *Robin* is an Emblem very apt to set forth some Professors by; for to sight they are, as this *Robin,* pretty of Note, Colour, and Carriages, they seem also to have a very great Love for Professors that are sincere; and, above all other to desire to associate with them, and to be in their Company, as if they could live upon the good Man's crumbs. They pretend also, that therefore it is that they frequent the House of the Godly, and the appointments of the Lord: but when they are by themselves *as the Robin*, they can catch and gobble up *Spiders;* they can change their Diet, drink *Iniquity*, and swallow down Sin like Water.

So when they were come again into the House, because Supper as yet was not ready, *Christiana* again desired that the Interpreter would either *show* or *tell* of some other things that are Profitable. *Pray, and you will get at that which yet lies unrevealed*

Then the *Interpreter* began and said, *The fatter the Sow is, the more she desires the Mire; the fatter the Ox is, the more gamesomely he goes to the Slaughter; and the more healthy the lusty man is, the more prone he is unto Evil.*

There is a desire in Women, to go neat and find; and it is a comely thing to be adorned with that, that in God's sight is of great price.[26]

'Tis easier watching a night or two, than to sit up a whole year together: So 'tis easier for one to begin to profess well, than to hold out as he should to the end.

Every Ship-Master, when in a Storm, will willingly cast overboard that is of the smallest value in the Vessel; but who will throw the best out first? None but he that feareth not God.

One leak will sink a Ship, and one Sin will destroy a Sinner.

He that forgets his friend is ungrateful unto him; but he that forgets his Saviour is unmerciful to himself.

He that lives in sin, and looks for Happiness hereafter, is like him that soweth Cockle,[27] *and thinks to fill his barn with Wheat or Barley.*

If a man would live well, let him fetch his last day to him, and make it always his company-keeper.

Whispering, and change of thoughts, prove that Sin is in the World.

If the World, which God sets light by, is counted a
thing of that worth with men: what is Heaven that God
commendeth?

If the life that is attended with so many troubles, is so
loth to be let go by us, What is the Life above?

Every Body will cry up the goodness of Men; but who is
there that is, as he should be, affected with the Goodness
of God?

We seldom sit down to Meat; but we eat, and leave. So
there is in Jesus Christ more Merit and Righteousness than
the whole World has need of.

When the *Interpreter* had done, he takes them out into
his Garden again, and had them to a tree whose *inside* was
Of the Tree that all rotten and gone, and yet it grew and had Leaves. Then
is rotten at heart said *Mercy*, What means this? This tree, said he, whose
out-side is fair, and whose inside is rotten, is that to which
many may be compared that are in the Garden of God:
who with their mouths speak high in behalf of God, but
indeed will do nothing for him: whose leaves are fair; but
their heart Good for nothing but to be *Tinder* for the Devil's
Tinder-Box.[28]

Now Supper was ready, the Table spread, and all things
set on the Board: so they sat down, and did eat, when one
They are at had given thanks. And the *Interpreter* did usually entertain
Supper those that lodged with him with Music at Meals; so the
Minstrels played. There was also one that did Sing, And a
very fine voice he had.

His Song was this:

> *The Lord is only my Support,*
> *And he that doth me feed;*
> *How can I then want any thing*
> *Whereof I stand in need?*[29]

When the Song and Music was ended, the *Interpreter*
asked *Christiana*, *What it was that at first did move her*
thus to betake herself to a pilgrim's life?
Talk at Supper   *Christiana* answered: First, the loss of my husband came

into my mind, at which I heartily grieved: but all that was but natural Affection. Then after that came the Troubles, and Pilgrimage of my Husband's into my mind, and also how like a Churl I had carried it to him as to that. So guilt took hold of my mind, and would have drawn me into the *Pond*,[30] but that opportunely I had a Dream of the well-being of my Husband, and a Letter sent me by the King of that Country where my Husband dwells, to come to him. The Dream and the Letter together so wrought upon my mind, that they forced me to this way.

A Repetition of Christiana's Experience

Inter. *But met you with no opposition before you set out of Doors?*

Chris. Yes, a Neighbour of mine, one Mrs. *Timorous*. (She was a kin to him that would have persuaded my Husband to go back, for fear of the Lions.) She all-to-be-fooled me;[31] for, as she called it, my intended desperate adventure; she also urged what she could to dishearten me from it, the hardships and Troubles that my Husband met with in the way; but all this I got over pretty well. But a Dream that I had of two ill-looked ones, that I thought did Plot how to make me miscarry in my Journey, that hath troubled me much: Yea, it still runs in my mind, and makes me afraid of every one that I meet, lest they should meet me to do me a mischief, and to turn me out of my way. Yea, I may tell my Lord, tho' I would not have every body know it, that between this and the Gate by which we got into the way, we were both so sorely assaulted that we were made to cry out Murder; and the two that made this assault upon us, were like the two that I saw in my Dream.

Then said the *Interpreter,* Thy beginning is good; thy latter end shall greatly increase.[32] So he addressed himself to *Mercy*, and said unto her, *And what moved thee to come hither, Sweet-heart?*

Mercy. Then *Mercy* blushed and trembled, and for a while continued silent.

Interpreter. Then said he, be not afraid, only believe, and speak thy mind.

Mer. So she began and said, Truly Sir, my want of

Mercy's answer

Experience, is that that makes me covet to be in silence, and that also that fills me with fears of coming short at last. I cannot tell of visions and dreams, as my friend *Christiana* can; nor know I what it is to mourn for my refusing of the Counsel of those that were good relations.

Interpreter. *What was it then, dear heart, that hath prevailed with thee to do as thou hast done?*

Mer. Why, when our friend here, was packing up to be gone from our Town, I and another went accidentally to see her. So we knocked at the Door and went in. When we were within, and seeing what she was doing, we asked her what was her meaning. She said, she was sent for to go to her Husband; and then she up and told us how she had seen him in a Dream, dwelling in a curious place among *Immortals* wearing a Crown, playing upon a Harp, eating and drinking at his Prince's Table, and singing praises to him for bringing him thither, *&c.* Now, methought, while she was telling these things unto us, my heart burned within me. And I said in my Heart, if this be true, I will leave my Father and my Mother, and the Land of my Nativity, and will, if I may, go along with *Christiana.*

So I asked her further of the truth of these things, and if she would let me go with her: For I saw now that there was no dwelling, but with the danger of ruin, any longer in our Town. But yet I came away with a heavy heart; not for that I was unwilling to come away; but for that so many of my Relations were left behind. And I am come with all the desire of my heart, and will go, if I may, with *Christiana* unto her Husband, and his King.

Inter. Thy setting out is good, for thou hast given credit to the truth; thou art a *Ruth,* who did, for the love she bare to Naomi and to the Lord her God, leave Father and Mother, and the land of her Nativity, to come out and go with a people she knew not heretofore. *The Lord recompense thy work, and a full reward be given thee of the Lord God of* Israel, *under whose Wings thou art come to trust.*

Now Supper was ended, and Preparation was made for

Ruth 2.11, 12

Bed, the Women were laid singly alone, and the Boys by *They address themselves to bed* themselves. Now when *Mercy* was in bed, she could not sleep for joy, for that now her doubts of missing at last, *Mercy's good* were removed further from her than ever they were before. *night's rest* So she lay blessing and Praising God, who had such favour for her.

In the Morning they arose with the *Sun,* and prepared themselves for their departure: But the *Interpreter* would have them tarry a while, for, said he, you must orderly go from hence. Then said he to the Damsel that first opened unto them, Take them and have them into the Garden to the *Bath,* and there wash them, and make them clean from *The Bath* Sanctification the soil which they had gathered by travelling. Then *Innocent* the Damsel took them and led them into the Garden, and brought them to the *Bath,* so she told them that there they must wash and be clean, for so her Master would have *They wash in it* the Women to do that called at his House as they were going on *Pilgrimage.* Then they went in and washed, yea, they and the Boys, and all; and they came out of that *Bath,* not only sweet, and clean; but also much enlivened and strengthened in their Joints: So when they came in, they looked fairer a deal, than when they went out to the washing.[33]

When they were returned out of the Garden from the *Bath,* the *Interpreter* took them and looked upon them, and said unto them, *fair as the Moon.*[34] Then he called for the *Seal* wherewith they used to be *Sealed* that were washed in his *Bath.* So the *Seal* was brought, and he set his Mark *They are sealed* upon them, that they might be known in the Places whither they were yet to go. Now the seal was the contents and sum of the Passover which the children of *Israel* did eat, when they came out of the Land of *Egypt:* and the mark was set betwixt their Eyes. This seal greatly added to their Beauty, Exo. 13.8, 9, 10 for it was an Ornament to their Faces.[35] It also added to their gravity, and made their Countenances more like them of Angels.

Then said the *Interpreter* again to the Damsel that waited upon these Women, Go into the Vestry, and fetch out Garments for these People: So she went and fetched out

white Raiment, and laid it down before him; so he commanded them to put it on. *It was fine Linen, white and*
They are clothed *clean.*[36] When the Women were thus adorned, they seemed
to be a Terror one to the other; For that they could not see
that glory each one had in her self, which they could see in
each other. Now therefore they began to esteem each other
True humility better than themselves. For you are fairer than I am, said
one; and, You are more comely than I am, said another.
The Children also stood amazed, to see into what fashion
they were brought.

The *Interpreter* then called for a *Man-servant* of his, one
Great-heart, and bid him take *Sword,* and *Helmet* and
Shield,[37] and, Take these my Daughters, said he, and conduct them to the House called *Beautiful,* at which place
they will rest next. So he took his Weapons, and went
before them; and the *Interpreter* said, God speed. Those
also that belonged to the family, sent them away with many
a good wish. So they went on their way, and Sung,

> *This place hath been our second Stage:*
> *Here we have heard and seen*
> *Those good things that from Age to Age*
> *To others hid have been.*

> *The Dunghill-raker, Spider, Hen,*
> *The Chicken too to me*
> *Have taught a Lesson, let me then*
> *Conformed to it be.*

> *The Butcher, Garden, and the Field,*
> *The Robin and his bait,*
> *Also the Rotten-tree doth yield*
> *Me argument of weight*

> *To move me for to watch and pray,*
> *To strive to be sincere,*
> *To take my Cross up day by day,*
> *And serve the Lord with fear.*

Now I saw in my Dream, that they went on, and *Great-heart* went before them, so they went and came to the place where *Christian's* Burden fell off his Back, and tumbled into a Sepulchre. Here then they made a pause; and here *1 part pag. 41* also they blessed God. Now said *Christiana,* it comes to my mind what was said to us at the Gate, to wit, that we should have Pardon, by *Word* and *Deed:* by word, that is, by the promise; by *Deed,* to wit, in the way it was obtained. What the promise is, of that I know something; but what is it to have pardon by deed, or in the way that it was obtained, Mr *Great-Heart,* I suppose you know; wherefore if you please let us hear you discourse thereof.

Great-heart. Pardon by the deed done, is Pardon obtained by some one for another that hath need thereof; not *A comment* by the person pardoned, but in the way, *saith another,* in *upon what was* which I have obtained it. So then to speak to the question *said at the Gate,* more at large, the pardon that you and *Mercy* and these *or a discourse of* Boys have attained, was *obtained* by another; to wit, by *our being justi-* him that let you in at the Gate: And he hath obtained it in *fied by Christ* this double way; he hath performed Righteousness to cover you, and spilt his blood to wash you in.

Chris. *But if he parts with his Righteousness to us: What will he have for himself?*

Great-heart. He has more righteousness than you have need of, or than he needeth himself.

Chris. *Pray make that appear.*

Great-heart. With all my heart, but first I must premise that he of whom we are now about to speak, is one that has not his Fellow. He has two Natures in one person, plain to be *distinguished, impossible* to be *divided.* Unto each of these Natures a Righteousness belongeth, and each righteousness is essential to that Nature. So that one may as easily cause the Nature to be extinct, as to separate its Justice or Righteousness from it. Of *these* Righteousnesses therefore, we are not made partakers, for as that they, any of them, should be put upon us that we might be made just, and live thereby. Besides these there is a Righteousness which this Person has, as these two Natures are joined in one. And this is not the righteousness of the *God-head,* as distinguished from the *Manhood;* nor the Righteousness of the *Manhood,* as distinguished from the *Godhead;* but a Righteousness which standeth in the Union of both Natures: and may properly be called, the Righteousness that is essential to his being prepared of God to the capacity of the Mediatory[38] Office, which he was to be entrusted with. If he parts with his first Righteousness, he parts with his *God-head;* if he parts with his second Righteousness, he parts with the purity of his *Manhood;* if he parts with his third, he parts with that perfection that capacitates him to the office of Mediation. He has therefore another Righteousness which standeth in *performance,* or obedience to a revealed *Will* and that is what he puts upon Sinners, and that by which their Sins are covered. Wherefore he saith, *as by one man's disobedience many were made Sinners: so by the obedience of one shall many be made Righteous.*

Rom. 5.19

Chris. *But are the other Righteousnesses of no use to us?*

Great-heart. Yes, for though they are essential to his Natures and Office, and cannot be communicated unto another, yet it is by Virtue of them that the Righteousness that justifies, is for that purpose efficacious. The *Righteousness* of his *God-head* gives *Virtue* to his Obedience; the *Righteousness* of his *Man-hood* giveth capability to his obedience to Justify, and the righteousness that standeth in the Union of these two Natures to his Office, giveth Authority to that Righteousness to do the work for which it was ordained.

So then, here is a Righteousness that Christ, as God, has no need of, for he is God without it: here is a Righteousness that Christ, as Man, has no need of to make him so, for he is perfect Man without it. Again, here is a righteousness that Christ, as God-man, has no need of; for he is perfectly so without it. Here then is a Righteousness that Christ, as God, as Man, as God-man, has no need of, with Reference to himself, and therefore he can spare it, a justifying Righteousness, that he for himself wanteth not, and therefore he

giveth it away: Hence 'tis called the *gift of Righteousness.* Rom. 5.17
This Righteousness, since Christ Jesus the Lord has made
himself under the Law, *must* be given away: for the Law
Doth, not only bind him that is under it, *to do justly,* but
to use Charity: Wherefore he must, or *ought* by the Law, if
he hath two Coats,[39] to give one to him that hath none.
Now, our Lord indeed hath two *Coats,* one for himself,
and one to spare: wherefore he freely bestows one upon
those that have none. And thus *Christiana,* and *Mercy,* and
the rest of you that are here, doth your pardon come by
deed, or by the work of another man? Your Lord Christ is
he that has worked, and has given away what he wrought
for, to the next poor Beggar he meets.

But again, in order to Pardon by *deed,* there must something be paid to God as a price, as well as something
prepared to cover us withal. Sin has delivered us up to the
just Curse of a Righteous law: Now from this Curse we
must be justified by way of Redemption, a price being paid
for the harms we have done; and this is by the Blood of
your Lord: Who came and stood in your place, and stead,
and died your Death for your Transgressions: Thus has he Rom. 4.24
ransomed you from your Transgressions, by Blood, and
covered your polluted and deformed Souls with Righteousness: For the sake of which, God passeth by you,[40] and will Gala. 3.13
not hurt you when he comes to Judge the World.

Chris. *This is brave. Now I see that there was something* Christiana
to be learned by our being pardoned by word *and* deed. *affected with this way of*
Good Mercy, *let us labour to keep this in mind, and my* Redemption
Children do you remember it also. But, sir, was not this it
that made my good Christian's *burden fall from off his*
Shoulder, and that made him give three leaps for Joy?

Great-heart. Yes, 'twas the belief of this, that cut those *How the Strings*
Strings that could not be cut by other means, and 'twas to *that bound*
give him a proof of the Virtue of this, that he was suffered *Christian's burden to him*
to carry his Burden to the Cross. *were cut*

Chris. *I thought so, for though my heart was lightful and*
joyous before, yet it is ten times more lightsome and joyous
now. And I am persuaded by what I have felt, though I

have felt but little as yet, that if the most burdened Man in the World was here, and did see and believe, as I now do, 'twould make his heart the more merry and blithe.

Great-heart. There is not only comfort, and the ease of a Burden brought to us by the sight and Consideration of these; but an endeared Affection begot in us by it: for who can, if he doth but once think that Pardon comes not only by promise but thus; but be affected with the way and means of his Redemption, and so with the man that hath wrought it for him?

How affection to Christ is begot in the Soul

Chris. *True, methinks it makes my Heart bleed to think that he should bleed for me. Oh! thou loving one, Oh! thou Blessed one. Thou deservest to have me; thou hast bought me: Thou deservest to have me all, thou hast paid for me ten thousand times more than I am worth. No marvel that this made the Water stand in my Husband's Eyes, and that it made him trudge so nimbly on. I am persuaded he wished me with him; but, vile Wretch that I was, I let him come all alone. Oh,* Mercy, *that thy Father and Mother were here; yea, and Mrs.* Timorous *also. Nay, I wish now with all my Heart, that here was Madam* Wanton *too. Surely, surely, their hearts would be affected; nor could the fear of the one, nor the powerful lusts of the other, prevail with them to go home again, and to refuse to become good pilgrims.*

1 part pag. 41

Cause of admiration

Great-heart. You speak now in the warmth of your Affections; will it, think you, be always thus with you? Besides, this is not communicated to every one, nor to every one that did see your Jesus bleed. There was that stood by, and that saw the Blood run from the Heart to the Ground, and yet was so far off this, that instead of lamenting, they laughed at him, and instead of becoming his Disciples, did harden their Hearts against him. So that all that you have my Daughters, you have by peculiar impression made by a Divine contemplating upon what I have spoken to you. Remember that 'twas told you, that the *Hen* by her common call, gives no meat to her *Chickens.* This you have therefore by a special Grace.[41]

To be affected with Christ and with what he has done is a thing special

Now I saw in my Dream, that they went on until they were come to the place, that *Simple,* and *Sloth,* and *Presumption,* lay and slept in, when *Christian* went by on Pilgrimage. And behold they were hanged up in Irons[42] a little way off on the other side.

Mercy. Then said Mercy to him that was their Guide and Conductor, What are these three men? and for what are they hanged there?

Great-heart. These three men, were Men of very bad Qualities, they had no mind to be Pilgrims themselves, and whosoever they could, they hindered; they were for *Sloth* and *Folly* themselves, and whoever they could persuade with, they made so too, and withal taught them to presume that they should do well at last. They were asleep when *Christian* went by, and now you go by, they are hanged.

Mercy. But could they persuade any to be of their opinion?

Great-heart. Yes, they turned several out of the way. There was *Slow-pace* that they persuaded to do as they. They also prevailed with one *Short-wind,* with one *No-heart,* with one *Linger-after-Lust,* and with one *Sleepy-head,* and with a young woman her name was *Dull,* to turn out of the way and become as they. Besides, they brought up an ill report of your Lord, persuading others that he was a task-Master. They also brought up an evil report of the good Land, saying, 'twas not half so good as some pretend it was: They also began to vilify his Servants, and to count the best of them meddlesome, troublesome busy-bodies. Further, they would call the Bread of God's, *Husks;* the *Comforts* of his Children's, *Fancies;* the Travel and Labour of Pilgrims, things to no purpose.

Chris. Nay, said Christiana, if they were such, they shall never be bewailed by me, they have but what they deserve, and I think it is well that they stand so near the Highway that others may see and take warning. But had it not been well if their Crimes had been engraven in some Plate of Iron or Brass, and left her, even where they did their Mischiefs, for a caution to other bad Men?

Simple and Sloth *and* Presumption *hanged, and* why

Their crimes

Who they prevailed to turn out of the way

Behold here how the Slothfull are a Signe,
Hung up, cause holy ways they did decline.
See here too how the Child doth play ÿ man,
And weak grow strong, when Great heart leads
　　　　　　　　　　　　　　　　the Van.

Great-heart. So it is, as you well may perceive, if you will go a little to the Wall.

Mercy. No, no; let them hang, and their names Rot, and their Crimes live for ever against them; I think it a high favour that they were hanged afore we came hither: who knows else what they might have done to such poor Women as we are? Then she turned it *into* a Song, saying,

> *Now then you three hang there, and be a Sign*
> *To all that shall against the Truth combine.*
> *And let him that comes after, fear this end,*
> *If unto Pilgrims he is not a Friend.*
> > *And thou my Soul, of all such men beware,*
> > *That unto Holiness Opposers are.*

Thus they went on till they came to the foot of the Hill *Difficulty*, where again their good Friend Mr. *Great-heart* took an occasion to tell them what happened there when *Christian* himself went by. So he had them first to the Spring. *Lo,* saith he, *This is the spring that* Christian *drank of,* before he went up this Hill, and then 'twas clear and good; but now 'tis Dirty with the feet of some that are not desirous that Pilgrims here should quench their Thirst: Thereat *Mercy* said, *And why so envious tro?*[43] But said their guide, It will do, if taken up and put into a Vessel that is sweet and good; for then the dirt will sink to the bottom, and the water come out by itself more clear. Thus therefore Christiana and her companions were compelled to do. They took it up, and put it into an Earthen pot, and so let it stand till the Dirt was gone to the bottom, and then they drank thereof.

Next he showed them the two *by-ways* that were at the foot of the Hill, where *Formality* and *Hypocrisy* lost themselves. And, said he, these are dangerous Paths: Two were here cast away when *Christian* came by. And although, as you see these ways are since stopped up with *Chains, Posts,* and a *Ditch:* Yet there are those that will choose to adventure here rather than take the pains to go up this Hill.

(marginal notes:)
1 part pag. 45

Ezek. 34.18

'Tis difficult getting of good Doctrine in erroneous Times

By-paths though barred up will not keep all from going in them
1 part pag. 46

Pro. 13.15 Christiana. *The Way of Transgressors is hard. 'Tis a wonder that they can get into those ways, without danger of breaking their Necks.*

Great-heart. They will venture, yea, if at any time any of the King's servants do happen to see them, and do call upon them, and tell them that *they* are in the wrong way, and do bid them beware of the danger; then they will railingly Jer. 44.10, 17 return them answer, and say, *As for the Word that thou hast spoken unto us in the name of the King, we will not hearken unto thee; but we will certainly do whatsoever thing goeth out of our own mouths, &c.* Nay, if you look a little further, you shall see that these ways, are made cautionary enough, not only by these *Posts,* and ditch, and chain, but also by being hedged up: yet they will choose to go there.

The reason why some do choose to go in by-ways
Pro. 15.19 Christiana. *They are Idle, they love not to take Pains, up-hill-way is unpleasant to them. So it is fulfilled unto them as it is written, The way of the slothful man is a Hedge of Thorns. Yea, they will rather choose to walk upon a Snare, than to go up this Hill, and the rest of this way to the City.*

Then they set forward and began to go up the Hill, and up the Hill they Went; but before they got to the top, *Christiana* began to *Pant,* and said, I dare say this is a *The Hill puts the Pilgrims to it* breathing Hill;[44] no marvel if they that love their ease more than their Souls, choose to themselves a smoother way. Then said *Mercy,* I must sit down: also the least of the Children began to cry. Come, come, said Great-Heart, sit *They sit in the Arbour* not down here; for a little above is the Prince's *Arbour.* Then he took the little boy by the hand, and led him up thereto.

When they were come to the Arbour, they were very *1 part pag. 46* willing to sit down, for they were all in a pelting heat. Then said *Mercy,* How sweet is rest to them that labour! And how good is the Prince of Pilgrims to provide Mat. 11.28 such resting places for them! Of *this Arbour* I have heard much; but I never saw it before. But here let us beware of sleeping: for as I have heard, for that it cost poor *Christian* dear.

Then said Mr *Great-heart* to the little ones, Come, my pretty *Boys,* how do you do? What think you now of going on pilgrimage? Sir, said the least, I was almost beat out of heart; but I thank you for lending me a hand at my need. And I remember now what my Mother has told me, namely, that the way to Heaven is as up a Ladder, and the way to Hell is as down a Hill. But I had rather go up the Ladder to Life, than down the Hill to Death.

The little Boys answer to the guide, and also to Mercy

Then said *Mercy,* But the Proverb is, *To go down the Hill is easy.* But *James* said, (for that was his Name) The day is coming when in my opinion, *Going down the hill will be the hardest of all.* 'Tis a Good Boy, said his Master; thou hast given her a right answer. Then *Mercy* smiled, but the little boy did blush.

Which is hardest up Hill or down Hill

Chris. Come, said *Christiana,* will you eat a bit to sweeten your Mouths, while you sit here to rest your Legs? For I have here a piece of Pomegranate which Mr. *Interpreter* put into my Hand, just when I came out of his Doors; he gave me also a piece of an Honeycomb, and a little Bottle of Spirits. I thought he gave you something, said *Mercy,* because he called you a to-side. Yes, so he did, said the other. But Mercy, it shall be still as I said it should, when at first we came from home; thou shalt be a sharer in all the good that I have, because thou so willingly didst become my companion. Then she gave to them, and they did eat, both *Mercy,* and the Boys. And said *Christiana* to Mr. *Great-Heart,* Sir, will you do as we? But he answered, You are going on Pilgrimage, and presently I shall return; much good may what you have do to you. At home I eat the same every day. Now when they had eaten and drank, and had chatted a little longer, their guide said to them, The day wears away, if you think good, let us prepare to be going. So they got up to go, and the little boys went before; but *Christiana* forgot to take her Bottle of Spirits with her, so she sent her little Boy back to fetch it. Then said *Mercy,* I

They refresh themselves

Christiana forgets her Bottle of Spirits

think this is a *losing* place. Here *Christian* lost his *Roll,* and here *Christiana* left her Bottle behind her. Sir, what is the cause of this? So their guide made answer and said, The cause is *sleep,* or *forgetfulness:* some *sleep,* when they should keep *awake,* and some *forget* when they should *remember;* and this is the very cause why often at the *Mark this*resting-places, some Pilgrims in some things come off losers. Pilgrims should watch and remember what they have already received under their greatest enjoyments: But for want of doing so, oftentimes their rejoicing ends in Tears, and their Sun-shine in a Cloud: witness the story of *Chris-* 1 *part pag.* 49 *tian* at this place.

When they were come to the place where *Mistrust* and *Timorous* met *Christian* to persuade him to go back for fear of the Lions, they perceived as it were a Stage, and before it, towards the Road, a broad plate with a Copy of Verses Written thereon, and underneath, the reason of raising up of that Stage in that place, rendered. The Verses were these.

> Let him that sees this Stage take heed
> Unto his Heart and Tongue;
> Lest, if he do not, here he speed
> As some have long agone.

The words underneath the Verses were, *This Stage was built to punish those upon, who, through* Timorousness *or* Mistrust, *shall be afraid to go further on Pilgrimage. Also on this stage both* Mistrust *and* Timorous *were burned through the tongue with a hot Iron,*[45] for endeavouring to hinder Christian *in his journey.*

Then said *Mercy,* This is much like to the saying of the beloved, *What shall be given unto thee? or what shall be* Psal. 120.3, 4 *done unto thee? thou false Tongue? Sharp Arrows of the mighty, with Coals of* Juniper.

1 *part pag.* 50So they went on till they came within sight of the Lions. Now Mr. *Great-heart* was a strong man, so he was not

afraid of a Lion: But yet when they were come up to the place where the Lions were, the Boys, that went before, were glad to cringe behind, for they were afraid of the Lions; so they stepped back and went behind. At this their guide smiled, and said, How now, my Boys, do you love to go before when no danger doth approach, and love to come behind so soon as the Lions appear?

An Emblem of those that go on bravely, when there is no danger; but shrink when troubles come

Now, as they went on, Mr. *Great-heart* drew his Sword with intent to make a way for the Pilgrims in spite of the Lions. Then there appeared one that, it seems, had taken upon him to back the Lions. And he said to the Pilgrims' guide, What is the cause of your coming hither? Now the name of that man was *Grim,* or *Bloody-man*[46] because of his slaying of Pilgrims, and he was of the race of the *Giants.*

Of Grim *the* Giant, *and of his backing the* Lions

Great-heart. Then said the *Pilgrims'* guide, these Women and Children, are going on Pilgrimage, and this is the way they must go; and go it they shall, in spite of thee and the Lions.

Grim. This is not their way, neither shall they go therein. I am come forth to with stand them, and to that end will back the Lions.

Now to say the truth, by reason of the fierceness of the Lions, and of the *Grim*-carriage of him that did back them, this way had of late lain much un-occupied, and was almost grown over with Grass.

Christiana. Then said *Christiana,* tho' the Highways have been un-occupied heretofore, and tho' the Travellers have been made in times past, to walk thorough by-paths, it must not be so now I am risen, *Now I am Risen a Mother in* Israel.

Judg. 5.6, 7

Grim. Then he swore *by the Lions,* but it should; and therefore bid them turn aside, for they should not have passage there.

Great-heart. But their guide made first his approach unto *Grim,* and laid so heavily on him with his Sword, that he forced him to a retreat.

Grim. Then said he (that attempted to back the lions) will you slay me upon mine own Ground?

Great-heart. It is the King's High-way that we are in, and in his way it is that thou hast placed thy Lions; but these Women, and these Children, though weak, shall hold on their way in spite of thy Lions. And with that he gave him again, a down-right blow, and brought him upon his Knees. With this blow also he broke his Helmet, and with the next he cut off an Arm. Then did the *Giant Roar* so hideously, that his Voice frighted the Women, and yet they were glad to see him lie sprawling upon the Ground. Now the Lions were chained, and so of themselves could do nothing. Wherefore, when old *Grim* that intended to back them was dead, Mr. *Great-heart* said to the pilgrims, Come now and follow me, and no hurt shall happen to you from the Lions. They therefore went on; but the Women trembled as they passed by them, the Boys also looked as if they would die; but they all got by without further hurt.

A fight betwixt Grim and Great-heart

The Victory

They pass by the Lions

Now then they were within Sight of the *Porter's* lodge, and they soon came up unto it; but they made the more haste after this to go thither, because it is dangerous travelling there in the Night. So when they were come to the Gate, the guide knocked, and the Porter cried, *who is there;* But as soon as the Guide had said, *It is I,* he knew his Voice and came down. (For the Guide had oft before that, came thither as a Conductor of Pilgrims.) When he was came down, he opened the Gate, and seeing the Guide standing just before it (for he saw not the Women, for they were behind him) he said unto him, How now, Mr. *Great-Heart,* what is your business here so late at Night? I have brought, said he, some Pilgrims hither, where, by my Lord's commandment, they must Lodge. I had been here some time ago, had I not been opposed by the Giant that did use to back the Lions. But I, after a long and tedious combat with him, have cut him off, and have brought the Pilgrims hither in safety.

They come to the Porter's lodge

Porter. *Will you not go in, and stay till Morning?*

Great-heart. No, I will return to my Lord to-night.

Christiana. Oh Sir, I know not how to be willing you should leave us in our Pilgrimage, you have been so faithful, and so loving to us, you have fought so stoutly for us, you have been so hearty in counselling of us, that I shall never forget your favour towards us.

Mercy. Then said *Mercy,* O that we might have thy Company to our Journey's end! How can such poor Women as we, hold out in a way so full of Troubles as this way is, without a Friend, and Defender?

James. Then said *James,* the youngest of the Boys, Pray Sir be persuaded to go with us, and help us, because we are so weak, and the way so dangerous as it is.

Great-heart. I am at my Lord's Commandment. If he shall allot me to be your Guide quite thorough, I will willingly wait upon you; but here you failed at first; for when he bid me come thus far with you, then you should have begged me of him to have gone quite thorough with you, and he would have granted your request. However, at present I must withdraw; and so, good *Christiana, Mercy,* and my brave Children, Adieu.

Then the Porter, Mr. *Watchful,* asked *Christiana* of her country, and of her Kindred, and she said, *I came from the city of* Destruction, *I am a Widow Woman, and my Husband is dead, his name was* Christian, *the pilgrim.* How!, said the Porter, was he your husband? Yes, said she, and these are his Children: and this, pointing to *Mercy,* is one of my Towns-Women. Then the Porter rang his Bell, as at such times he is wont, and there come to the door one of the Damsels, whose name was *Humble-Mind.* And to her the Porter said, Go tell it within, that *Christiana,* the wife of *Christian* and her Children are come hither on Pilgrimage. She went in, therefore, and told it. But Oh what Noise for gladness was there within, when the Damsel did but drop that out of her Mouth?

So they came with haste to the Porter, for *Christiana* stood still at the Door; then some of the most grave said

Great-heart attempts to go back

The Pilgrims implore his company still

Help lost for want of asking for

1 part pag. 51

Christiana makes herself known to the Porter. He tells it to a damsel

Joy at the noise of the Pilgrims' coming

unto her, *Come in,* Christiana, *come in thou Wife of that Good Man, come in thou Blessed Woman, come in, with all that are with thee.* So she went in, and they followed her that were her Children, and her Companions. Now when they were gone in, they were had into a very large Room, where they were bidden to sit down: So they sat down, and the chief of the House were called to see and

Christians' *love is kindled at the sight of one another* welcome the Guests. Then they came in, and understanding who they were, did Salute each other with a kiss,[47] and said, Welcome ye Vessels of the Grace of God; welcome to us your Friends.

Now because it was somewhat late, and because the Pilgrims were weary with their Journey, and also made faint with the sight of the Fight, and of the terrible Lions: Therefore they desired, as soon as might be, to prepare to go to Rest. Nay, said those of the Family, refresh yourselves

Exo. 12.38. Joh. 1.29 first with a morsel of Meat. For they had prepared for them a Lamb, with the accustomed Sauce belonging thereto. For the Porter had heard before of their coming, and had told it to them within. So when they had Supped, and ended their prayer with a Psalm, they desired they might go to rest. But let us, said *Christiana,* if we may be so bold as to choose, be in that Chamber that was my husband's when

1 part pag. 57 he was here. So they had them up thither, and they all lay in a Room. When they were at Rest, *Christiana* and *Mercy* entered into discourse about things that were convenient.

Chris. Little did I think once, when my Husband went on Pilgrimage I should ever a followed.

Mercy. And you as little thought of lying in his Bed, and in his Chamber to Rest, as you do now.

Christ's Bosom is for all Pilgrims *Chris. And much less did I ever think of seeing his Face with Comfort, and of Worshipping the Lord the King with him, and yet now I believe, I shall.*

Mercy. Hark, don't you hear a Noise?

Christiana. Yes, 'tis, as I believe, a Noise of Music, for Joy that we are here.

Music *Mer.* Wonderful! Music in the House, Music in the Heart, and Music also in Heaven, for joy that we are here.[48]

Thus they talked a while, and then betook themselves to
sleep; so in the Morning, when they were awake *Christiana*
said to *Mercy,*

Mercy *did laugh
in her sleep*

Chris. *What was the matter that you did laugh in your
sleep to Night? I suppose you was in a Dream?*

Mercy. So I was, and a sweet Dream it was; but are you
sure I laughed?

Christiana. *Yes, you laughed heartily; but prithee* Mercy
tell me thy dream?

Mercy. I was a Dreamed that I sat all alone in a solitary
place, and was bemoaning of the hardness of my Heart.

Mercy's *Dream*

Now I had not sat there long, but methought many were
gathered about me to see me, and to hear what it was that
I said. So they hearkened, and I went on bemoaning the
hardness of my Heart. At this, some of them laughed at
me, some called me Fool, and some began to thrust me
about. With that, methought I looked up and saw one

*What her dream
was*

coming with Wings towards me. So he came directly to me,
and said *Mercy,* what aileth thee? Now when he had heard
me make my complaint, he said, *Peace be to thee;* he also
wiped my Eyes with his handkerchief, and *clad* me in *Silver
and Gold;* he put a Chain about my Neck, and Ear-rings in
mine Ears, and a beautiful Crown upon my Head. Then he

Ezek. 16.8, 9,
10, 11

took me by the hand, and said, *Mercy,* come after me. So
he went up, and I followed till we came at a Golden Gate.
Then he knocked, and when they within had opened, the
man went in and I followed him up to a Throne, upon
which one sat; and he said to me, *welcome, Daughter.* The
place looked bright, and twinkling like the stars, or rather
like the *Sun,* and I thought that I saw your Husband there;
so I awoke from my dream. But did I laugh?

Christiana. *Laugh! Aye, and well you might to see your
self so well. For you must give me leave to tell you, that I
believe it was a good Dream, and that, as you have begun
to find the first part true, so you shall find the second at
last.* God speaks once, yea twice, yet Man perceiveth it not,

Job 33.14, 15

in a Dream, in a Vision of the Night, when deep Sleep
falleth upon men, in slumbering upon the bed. *We need*

*not, when abed, lie awake to talk with God; he can visit us
while we sleep, and cause us then to hear his Voice. Our
Heart oftentimes wakes when we sleep, and God can speak
to that, either by Words, by Proverbs, by Signs, and Similitudes, as well as if one was awake.*[49]

Mercy. Well, I am glad of my Dream, for I hope ere long

*Mercy glad of
her dream*

to see it fulfilled, to the making of me laugh again.

*Christiana. I think it is now high time to rise, and to
know what we must do?*

Mercy. Pray, if they invite us to stay a while, let us
willingly accept of the proffer. I am the more willing to stay
a while here, to grow better acquainted with these maids:
methinks *Prudence, Piety,* and *Charity,* have very comely
and sober Countenances.

Chris. We shall see what they will do. So when they were
up and ready, they came down, and they asked one another
of their rest, and if it was Comfortable or not?

Mercy. Very good, said Mercy, *it was one of the best
Night's Lodging that ever I had in my life.*

Then said *Prudence* and *Piety,* If you will be persuaded
to stay here a while, you shall have what the House will

*They stay her
some time*

afford.

Charity. Aye, and that with a very good will, said
Charity. So they consented, and stayed there about a Month
or above, and became very Profitable one to another. And
because *Prudence* would see how *Christiana* had brought

Prudence *desires
to catechise*
Christiana's
children

up her Children, she asked leave of her to Catechise[50] them:
So she gave her free consent. Then she began at the youngest
whose name was *James.*

Pru. And she said, Come James, *canst thou tell me who*

James *catechised*

made thee?

Jam. God the Father, God the Son, and God the Holy-
Ghost.

Pru. Good Boy. And canst thou tell who saves thee?

Jam. God the Father, God the Son, and God the Holy
Ghost.

*Pru. Good Boy still. But how doth God the Father save
thee?*

Jam. By his Grace.

Pru. *How doth God the Son save thee?*

Jam. By his Righteousness, Death, and Blood, and Life.

Pru. *And how doth God the Holy Ghost save thee?*

Jam. By his *Illumination,* by his *Renovation,* and by his *Preservation.*

Then said *Prudence* to *Christiana,* You are to be commended for thus bringing up your Children. I suppose I need not ask the rest these Questions, since the youngest of them can answer them so well. I will therefore now apply myself to the next youngest.

Prudence. Then she said, Come *Joseph,* (for his name was *Joseph*) will you let me Catechise you?

Joseph
catechised

Joseph. With all my heart.

Pru. *What is Man?*

Joseph. A Reasonable Creature, so made by God, as my Brother said.

Pru. *What is supposed by this Word, saved?*

Joseph. That man by Sin has brought himself into a State of Captivity and Misery.

Pru. *What is supposed by his being saved by the Trinity?*

Joseph. That Sin is so great and mighty a Tyrant, that none can pull us out of its clutches but God; and that God is so good and loving to man, as to pull him indeed out of this Miserable State.

Pru. *What is God's design in saving of poor Men?*

Joseph. The glorifying of his Name, of his Grace, and Justice, etc. And the everlasting Happiness of his Creature.

Pru. *Who are they that must be saved?*

Joseph. Those who accept of his Salvation.

Pru. Good boy, *Joseph,* thy Mother hath taught thee well, and thou hast hearkened unto what she has said unto thee.

Then said *Prudence* to *Samuel,* who was the eldest but one,

Prudence. Come, *Samuel,* are you willing that I should Catechise you also?

Samuel
catechised

Sam. Yes, forsooth, if you please.

Pru. *What is heaven?*

Sam. A place and State most blessed, because God dwelleth there.

Pru. *What is Hell?*

Sam. A Place and State most woeful, because it is the dwelling-place of Sin, the Devil, and Death.

Prudence. *Why wouldest thou go to Heaven?*

Sam. That I may see God, and serve him without weariness; that I may see Christ, and love him everlastingly; that I may have that fullness of the Holy Spirit in me which I can by no means here enjoy.

Pru. *A very good boy also, and one that has learned well.*

Then she addressed her self to the eldest, whose Name was *Matthew;* and she said to him, Come, *Matthew,* shall I also Catechise you?

Mat. *With a very good Will.*

Pru. *I ask then, if there was ever any thing that had a being Antecedent to, or before God?*

Matthew
catechised

Mat. No, for God is Eternal, nor is there any thing, excepting himself, that had a being until the beginning of the first day. *For in six days the Lord made Heaven and Earth, the Sea, and all that in them is.*

Pru. *What do you think of the Bible?*

Mat. It is the Holy Word of God.

Pru. *Is there nothing Written therein, but what you understand?*

Mat. Yes, a great deal.

Pru. *What do you do when you meet with such places therein that you do not understand?*

Mat. I think God is wiser than I. I pray also that he will please to let me know all therein that he knows will be for my good.

Pru. *How believe you as touching the Resurrection of the Dead?*

Mat. I believe they shall rise, the same that was buried; the same in Nature, though not in Corruption. And I believe this upon a double Account. First, because God has promised it. Secondly, because he is able to perform it.

Then said *Prudence* to the Boys, You must still hearken to your Mother; for she can learn you more. You must also diligently give ear to what good talk you shall hear from others, for for your sakes do they speak good things. Observe also and that with carefulness, what the Heavens and the Earth do teach you; but especially be much in the Meditation of that Book which was the cause of your Father's becoming a Pilgrim. I for my part, my children, will teach you what I can while you are here, and shall be glad if you will ask me Questions that tend to Godly edifying.

Prudence's conclusion upon the Catechising of the Boys

Now by that these Pilgrims had been at this place a week, *Mercy* had a Visitor that pretended some good Will unto her, and his name was Mr. *Brisk;*[51] A man of some breeding, and that pretended to Religion; but a man that stuck very close to the World. So he came once or twice, or more, to *Mercy,* and offered love unto her. Now *Mercy* was of a fair Countenance, and therefore the more alluring.

Mercy has a sweet heart

Her mind also was, to be always busying of herself in doing, for when she had nothing to do for her self, she would be making of Hose and Garments for others, and would bestow them upon them that had need. And Mr. *Brisk* not knowing where or how she disposed of what she made, seemed to be greatly taken, for that he found her never Idle. I will warrant her a good Housewife, quoth he to himself.

Mercy's temper

Mercy then revealed the business to the Maidens that were of the House, and enquired of them concerning him: for they did know him better than she. So they told her that he was a very busy Young man, and one that pretended to Religion; but was, as they feared, a stranger to the Power of that which is good.

Mercy enquires of the Maids concerning Mr. Brisk

Nay then, said Mercy, *I will look no more on him; for I purpose never to have a clog*[52] *to my Soul.*

Prudence then replied, that there needed no great matter of discouragement to be given to him; her continuing so as she had begun to do for the Poor, would quickly cool his Courage.

So the next time he comes, he finds her at her old work, making things for the Poor. Then said he, What, always at it? Yes, said she, either for myself or for others. And what canst thou *earn* a day? quoth he. I do these things, said she, *That I may be Rich in good Works, laying up in store for myself a good Foundation against the time to come, that I may lay hold on Eternal Life.* Why, prithee, what doest thou with them? said he; Clothe the naked, said she. With that his Countenance fell. So he forbore to come at her again. And when he was asked the reason why, he said, *That* Mercy *was a pretty lass; but troubled with ill Conditions.*

When he had left her, *Prudence* said, Did I not tell thee that Mr. *Brisk* would soon forsake thee? yea, he will rise up an ill report of thee; For notwithstanding his pretence to Religion, and his seeming love to *Mercy:* Yet *Mercy* and he are of tempers so different, that I believe they will never come together.

Mercy. *I might a had Husbands afore now, though I spoke not of it to any; but they were such as did not like my Conditions, though never did any of them find fault with my Person: So they and I could not agree.*

Prudence. Mercy in our days is little set by, any further than as to its Name: the practice which is set forth by thy Conditions, there are but few that can abide.

Mercy. *Well, said Mercy, if no body will have me, I will die a Maid, or my Conditions shall be to me as a Husband. For I cannot change my Nature; and to have one who lies cross to me in this, that I purpose never to admit of, as long as I live. I had a Sister named* Bountiful, *that was married to one of these Churls; but he and she could never agree; but because my sister was resolved to do as she had begun, that is, to show Kindness to the Poor, therefore her husband first cried her down at the Cross*[53] *and then turned her out of his Doors.*

Pru. And yet he was a Professor, I warrant you?

Mer. Yes, such a one as he was, and of such as he, the World is now full: but I am for none of them all.

Talk between Mercy *and* Mr. Brisk

1 Tim. 6.17, 18, 19

He forsakes her, and why

Mercy *in the practice of* Mercy *rejected; While* Mercy *in the Name of* Mercy *is liked*

Mercy's *resolution*

How Mercy's *Sister was served by her Husband*

Now *Matthew* the eldest son of *Christiana*, fell Sick, *Matthew falls sick*
and his Sickness was sore upon him, for he was much
pained in his Bowels, so that he was with it, at times, pulled
as 'twere both ends together. There dwelt also not far
from thence one Mr. *Skill*, an ancient and well-approved
Physician. So *Christiana* desired it, and they sent for him,
and he came. When he was entered the room, and had a
little observed the Boy, he concluded that he was sick of
the Gripes. Then he said to his Mother, *What diet has* *Gripes of*
Matthew *of late fed upon?* Diet, said *Christiana*, nothing *Conscience*
but that which is wholesome. The Physician answered, *This* *The Physician's*
Boy has been tampering with something that lies in his *Judgement*
Maw undigested, and that will not away without means.
And I tell you he must be purged, or else he will die.

Samuel. Then said *Samuel, Mother, Mother, what was* *Samuel puts his*
that which my Brother did gather up and eat, as soon as *Mother in mind*
we were come from the gate that is the head of this way? *of the fruit his*
You know that there was an Orchard on the left hand, on *Brother did eat*
the other side of the Wall, and some of the Trees hung over
the Wall, and my Brother did pluck and did eat.

Christiana. True, my child, said *Christiana*, he did take
thereof, and did eat: naughty Boy as he was, I did chide
him, and yet he would eat thereof.

Skill. *I knew he had eaten something that was not whole-*
some Food. And that Food, to wit, that Fruit, is even the
most hurtful of all. It is the Fruit of Beelzebub's *Orchard.*
I do marvel that none did warn you of it; many have died
thereof.

Christiana. Then *Christiana* began to cry; and she said,
Oh, naughty Boy! and O careless Mother, what shall I do
for my Son?

Skill. *Come, do not be too much Dejected; the Boy may*
do well again, but he must purge and Vomit.

Christiana. Pray Sir try the utmost of your Skill with him
whatever it costs.

Skill. *Nay, I hope I shall be reasonable.* So he made him
a Purge; but it was too weak. 'Twas said it was made of the *Heb. 10.1, 2,*
Blood of a Goat, the Ashes of an Heifer, and some of the *3, 4*

Potion prepared

John 6.54, 55,
56, 57. Mark
9.49. *The Latin
I borrow*
Juice of Hyssop, &c. When Mr. *Skill* had seen that that Purge was too weak, he made him one to the purpose. It was made *Ex Carne et Sanguine Christi*[54] (you know Physicians give strange Medicines to their Patients) and it was made up into Pills with a Promise or two, and a proportionable quantity of Salt. Now, he was to take them three at a time, fasting, in half a quarter of a Pint of
Heb. 9.14

*The boy loth to
take the Physic*
Tears of Repentance. When this potion was prepared, and brought to the Boy, he was loth to take it, though torn with the Gripes, as if he should be pulled in pieces. *Come, come, said the Physician, you must take it.* It goes against my Stomach, said the Boy. *I must have you take it, said his*
Zech. 12.10
Mother. I shall Vomit it up again, said the Boy. Pray, sir, said *Christiana* to Mr. *Skill,* how does it taste? It has no ill taste, said the Doctor; and with that she touched one of the
*The Mother
tastes it, and
persuades him*
pills with the tip of her Tongue. Oh, *Matthew,* said she, this potion is sweeter than Honey. If thou lovest thy Mother, if thou lovest thy Brothers, if thou lovest *Mercy,* if thou lovest thy Life, take it. So with much ado, after a short Prayer for the blessing of God upon it, he took it, and it wrought kindly with him. It caused him to purge, it caused him to sleep, and to rest quietly, it put him into a fine heat and breathing sweat, and did quite rid him of his Gripes.

So in a little time he got up, and walked about with a
*A word of God
in the hand of
his Faith*
Staff, and would go from Room to Room, and talk with *Prudence, Piety,* and *Charity* of his Distemper, and how he was healed.

So when the Boy was healed, *Christiana* asked Mr. *Skill,* saying, Sir, what will content you for your pains and care
Heb. 13.11, 12,
13, 14, 15
to and of my child? And he said, You must pay the *Master of the College* of Physicians, according to rules made in that case and provided.

Chris. *But Sir, said she, what is this Pill good for else?*

Skill. It is a universal Pill, 'tis good against all the Diseases
*This Pill an Uni-
versal Remedy*
that Pilgrims are incident to, and when it is well prepared, it will keep good, *time* out of *mind.*

Chris. Pray Sir, make me up twelve Boxes of them: For if I can get these, I will never take other Physic.

Skill. These *Pills* are good to prevent Diseases, as well as to *cure* when one is Sick. Yea, I dare say it, and stand to it, that if a Man will but use this Physic as he should, *it will make him live for ever.* But, good *Christiana,* thou must give these Pills, *no other way;* but as I have prescribed: For if you do, they will do no good. So he gave unto *Christiana* Physic for herself, and her Boys, and for *Mercy;* and bid *Matthew* take heed how he ate any more *Green Plums,* and kissed them and went his way.[55]

Joh. 6.50

In a Glass of the Tears of Repentance

It was told you before, that *Prudence* bid the Boys, that if at any time they would, they should ask her some Questions that might be profitable, and she would say something to them.

Mat. Then *Matthew* who had been sick, asked her, *Why for the most part physic should be bitter to our Palates?*

Of Physic

Pru. To show how unwelcome the word of God, and the Effects thereof are to a Carnal Heart.

Of the Effects of Physic

Matthew. Why does Physic, if it does good, Purge,[56] and cause that we Vomit?

Prudence. To show that the Word when it works effectually, cleanseth the Heart and Mind. For look what the one doth to the Body, the other doth to the Soul.

Matthew. *What should we learn by seeing the Flame of our Fire go upwards? and by seeing the Beams, and sweet Influences of the Sun strike downwards?*

Of Fire and of the Sun

Prudence. By the going up of the Fire, we are taught to ascend to Heaven, by fervent and hot desires. And by the Sun sending his Heat, Beams, and sweet Influences downwards; we are taught, that the Saviour of the world, though high, reaches down with his Grace and Love to us below.

Matthew. *Where have the Clouds their Water?*

Of the Clouds

Pru. Out of the Sea.

Matthew. *What may we learn from that?*

Pru. That Ministers should fetch their Doctrine from God.

Mat. Why do they empty themselves upon the Earth?

Pru. To show that Ministers should give out what they know of God to the World.

Of the Rainbow   Mat. *Why is the Rainbow caused by the Sun?*

Prudence. To show that the Covenant of God's Grace is confirmed to us in Christ.

Mat. *Why do the Springs come from the Sea, to us, through the Earth?*

Prudence. To show that the Grace of God comes to us thorough the Body of Christ.

Mat. *Why do some of the Springs rise out of the tops of*
Of the Springs *high Hills?*

Prudence. To show that the Spirit of Grace shall spring up in *some* that are Great and Mighty, as well as in *many* that are Poor and low.

Of the Candle   Mat. *Why doth the Fire fasten upon the Candlewick?*

Pru. To show that unless Grace doth kindle upon the Heart, there will be no true Light of Life in us.

Matthew. *Why is the Wick and Tallow and all, spent to maintain the light of the Candle?*

Prudence. To show that Body and Soul and all, should be at the service of, and spend themselves to maintain in good Condition that Grace of God that is in us.

Mat. *Why doth the Pelican*[57] *pierce her own Breast with*
Of the Pelican *her Bill?*

Pru. To nourish her young ones with her Blood, and thereby to show that Christ the blessed, so loved his Young, his People, as to save them from Death by his Blood.

Mat. *What may one learn by hearing the Cock to*
Of the Cock *Crow?*

Prudence. Learn to remember *Peter's* Sin, and *Peter's* Repentance. The Cock's crowing shows also that day is coming on, let, then, the crowing of the Cock put thee in mind of that last and terrible Day of Judgement.

Now about this time their Month was out; wherefore they signified to those of the House, that 'twas convenient for them to up and be going. Then said *Joseph* to his
The weak may Mother, It is convenient that you forget not to send to the
sometimes call House of Mr. *Interpreter,* to pray him to grant that Mr.
the strong to
Prayers *Great-heart* should be sent unto us, that he may be our Conductor the rest of the way. Good *Boy,* said she, I had

almost forgot. So she drew up a Petition, and prayed Mr. *Watchful* the Porter to send it by some fit man to her good Friend Mr. *Interpreter;* who when it was come, and he had seen the contents of the Petition, said to the Messenger, Go tell them that I will send him.

When the Family where *Christiana* was, saw that they had a purpose to go forward, they called the whole House together, to give thanks to their King, for sending of them such profitable Guests as these. Which done, they said to *Christiana,* And shall we not show thee something, as our Custom is to do to Pilgrims, on which thou mayest meditate when thou art upon the way? So they took *Christiana,* her Children, and *Mercy,* into the Closet, and showed them one of the *Apples* that *Eve* did eat of, and that she also did give to her Husband, and that for the eating of which they were both turned out of Paradise, and asked her what she thought that was? Then *Christiana* said, 'Tis *Food or Poison,* I know not which; so they opened the matter to her, and she held up her hands and wondered.

Then they had her to a Place, and showed her *Jacob's Ladder.* Now at that time there were some Angels ascending upon it. So *Christiana* looked and looked to see the angels go up: so did the rest of the Company. Then they were going into another place, to show them something else: but *James* said to his mother, Pray, bid them stay here a little longer, for this is a curious sight. So they turned again, and stood feeding their Eyes with this *so pleasant a Prospect.* After this, they had them into a place where did hang up a *Golden Anchor,* so they bid *Christiana* take it down; for said they, you shall have it with you, for it is of absolute necessity that you should, that you may lay hold of that within the veil, and stand steadfast in case you should meet with turbulent weather: So they were glad thereof. Then they took them, and had them to the mount upon which *Abraham* our Father, had offered up *Isaac* his Son, and showed them the *Altar,* the *Wood,* the *Fire,* and the *Knife,* for they remain to be seen to this very Day. When they had seen it, they held up their hands, and blessed

They provide to be gone on their way

Eve's Apple

A sight of Sin is amazing. Gen. 3.6. Rom. 7.24

Jacob's Ladder

A sight of Christ is taking

Gen. 28.12. *Golden Anchor*

Joh. 1.51. Heb. 6.12, 19

Gen. 20

Of Abraham *offering up* Isaac

themselves, and said, Oh, What a man for love to his
Master, and for denial to himself, was *Abraham!* After they
had showed them all these things, *Prudence* took them
into the Dining-Room, where stood a pair of Excellent
Prudence's Virginals,[58] so she played upon them, and turned what she
Virginals   had showed them into this excellent Song, saying;

> Eve's *Apple we have showed you;*
> *Of that be you aware:*
> You have seen Jacob's *Ladder too,*
> *Upon which Angels are.*

> *An Anchor you received have;*
> *But let not these suffice,*
> *Until with* Abra'm *you have gave,*
> Your best, a Sacrifice.

Now about this time one knocked at the Door, So the
Porter opened, and behold, Mr. *Great-Heart* was there; but
Mr. Great-heart when he was come in, what Joy was there? For it came now
come again   afresh again into their minds, how but a while ago he had
slain old *Grim Bloody-man,* the Giant, and had delivered
them from the Lions.

Then said Mr. *Great-heart* to *Christiana* and to *Mercy,*
He brings a   My Lord has sent each of you a Bottle of Wine, and also
token from his   some parched Corn, together with a couple of Pomegran-
Lord with him   ates; he has also sent the boys some Figs, and Raisins to
refresh you in your way.[59]

Then they addressed themselves to their Journey, and
Prudence and *Piety* went along with them. When they came
to the gate, *Christiana* asked the Porter if any of late went
by. He said, No; only one, some time since, who also told
me, that of late there had been a great Robbery committed
Robbery   on the King's High-way, as you go. But, said he, the Thieves
are taken, and will shortly be Tried for their Lives. Then
Christiana and *Mercy* were afraid; but *Matthew* said,
Mother fear nothing, as long as Mr. *Great-Heart* is to go
with us, and to be our conductor.

Then said Christiana to the Porter, Sir, I am much obliged *Christiana takes* to you for all the Kindnesses that you have showed to me *her leave of the* since I came hither; and also for that you have been so *Porter* loving and kind to my Children. I know not how to gratify your Kindness; Wherefore pray, as a token of my respect to you, accept of this small mite. So she put a Gold Angel[60] in his Hand, and he made her a low obeisance, and said, Let thy garments be always White; and let thy Head want no Ointment.[61] Let *Mercy* live and not die, and let not her Works be few. And to the Boys he said, Do you fly Youthful *The Porter's* lusts, and follow after Godliness with them that are Grave, *blessing* and Wise, so shall you put gladness into your Mother's Heart, and obtain Praise of all that are sober minded. So they thanked the Porter and departed.

Now I saw in my Dream, that they went forward until they were come to the Brow of the Hill, where *Piety,* bethinking herself, cried out, *Alas!* I have forgot what I intended to bestow upon *Christiana* and her Companions. I will go back and fetch it. So she ran, and fetched it. While she was gone, *Christiana* thought she heard in a Grove a little way off on the Right-hand, a most curious Melodious Note, with Words much like these:

> *Through all my Life thy favour is*
> *So frankly showed to me,*
> *That in thy House for evermore*
> *My dwelling-place shall be.*

And listening still she thought she heard another answer it, saying,

> *For why, The Lord our God is good;*
> *His Mercy is for ever sure:*
> *His Truth at all times firmly stood:*
> *And shall from Age to Age endure.*[62]

So *Christiana* asked *Prudence* who 'twas that made those curious Notes? They are, said she, our Country Birds: they *Song 2.11, 12* sing these Notes but seldom, except it be at the Spring, when the Flowers appear, and the Sun shines warm, and then you may hear them all day long. I often, said she, go out to hear them; we also oft-times keep them tame in our House. They are very fine Company for us when we are *Melancholy*: also they make the Woods, and Groves, and Solitary places, places desirous to be in.

By this Time *Piety* was come again, so she said to *Christiana,* Look here, I have brought thee a *Scheme* of all those things that thou hast seen at our House: Upon which thou mayest look when thou findest thyself forgetful, and call those things again to remembrance for thy Edification, and comfort.

Piety *bestoweth something on them at parting*

Now they began to go down the Hill into the Valley of *Humiliation*. It was a steep Hill, and the way was slippery; but they were very careful; so they got down pretty well. When they were down in the Valley, *Piety* said to *Christiana,* This is the place where *Christian* your Husband met with the foul Fiend *Apollyon,* and where they had that dreadful fight that they had. I know you cannot but have heard thereof. But be of good Courage, as long as you have here Mr. *Great-heart* to be your Guide and Conductor, we hope you will fare the better. So when these two had committed the Pilgrims unto the Conduct of their Guide, he went forward, and they went after.

1 part pag. 59

Great-heart. Then said Mr. *Great-heart,* We need not be so afraid of this Valley: For here is nothing to hurt us, unless we procure it to our selves. 'Tis true, *Christian* did here meet with *Apollyon,* with whom he had also a sore Combat; but that *fray* was the fruit of those slips that he got in his going down the Hill. For they that get *slips there,* must look for *Combats here.* And hence it is, that this Valley has got so hard a name. For the common People, when they hear that some frightful thing has befallen such an one in such a place, are of an Opinion that that place is haunted with some foul Fiend, or evil Spirit; when, alas it is for the fruit of their doing, that such things do befall them there.

Mr. Great-heart *at the Valley of Humiliation*

1 part pag. 59

This Valley of *Humiliation* is of itself as fruitful a place as any the Crow flies over; and I am persuaded, if we could hit upon it, we might find somewhere hereabouts something that might give us an account why *Christian* was so hardly beset in this place.

The reason why Christian was so beset here

Then *James* said to his mother, Lo, yonder stands a Pillar, and it looks as if something was Written thereon: let us go and see what it is. So they went, and found there Written, *Let* Christian's *slips, before he came hither, and the Battles that he met with in this place, be a warning to those that come after.* Lo, said their Guide, did not I tell you that there was something hereabouts that would give Intimation of the reason why *Christian* was so hard beset in this place? Then turning to *Christiana,* he said: No disparagement to *Christian* more than to any others whose Hap and Lot it was. For 'tis easier going *up* than *down* this Hill, and that can be said but of few Hills in all these parts of the World. But we will leave the good Man, he is at rest, he also had a brave Victory over his Enemy; let him grant, that dwelleth above; that we fare no worse, when we come to be tried than he.

A Pillar with an Inscription on it

But we will come again to this Valley of *Humiliation*. It is the best and most fruitful piece of Ground in all those parts. It is fat Ground,[63] and as you see, consisteth much in Meadows: and if a man was to come here in the Summer-time, as we do now, if he knew not any thing before thereof, and if he also delighted himself in the sight of his Eyes, he might see that which would be delightful to him. Behold, how green this Valley is, also how beautified *with Lilies.* I have also known many labouring Men that have got good Estates in this Valley of *Humiliation.* (For God resisteth the Proud, but gives *more, more* Grace to the Humble.) For indeed it is a very fruitful Soil, and doth bring forth by handfuls. Some also have wished that the next way to their Father's House were here, that they might be troubled no more with either Hills or Mountains to go over; but the way is the way, and there's an end.

This Valley a brave place

Song 2.1

Jam. 4.6

1 Pet. 5.5

Men thrive in the Valley of Humiliation

Now, as they were going along, and talking, they espied

a Boy feeding his Father's Sheep. The Boy was in very mean Clothes, but of a very fresh and well-favoured Countenance, and as he sat by himself, he Sung. Hark, said Mr. Great-heart, to what the Shepherd's Boy saith. So they Hearkened, and he said,

> *He that is down, needs fear no fall;*
> *He that is low, no Pride:*
> *He that is humble, ever shall*
> Philip 4.12, 13 *Have God to be his Guide.*

> *I am content with what I have,*
> *Little be it or much;*
> *And, Lord, contentment still I crave,*
> *Because thou savest such.*

> Heb. 13.5 *Fulness to such a burden is,*
> *That go on Pilgrimage:*
> *Here little, and hereafter Bliss,*
> *Is best from Age to Age.*

Then said their *Guide,* do you hear him? I will dare to say, that this Boy lives a merrier Life, and wears more of that Herb called *Hearts-ease*[64] in his bosom, than he that is clad in Silk, and Velvet; but we will proceed in our Discourse.

Christ, when in the Flesh, had his Country-House in the Valley of Humiliation

In this Valley, our Lord formerly had his *Country-House;* he loved much to be here. He loved also to walk these Meadows, for he found the Air was pleasant. Besides here a man shall be free from the Noise, and from the hurryings of this Life, all States are full of Noise and Confusion; only the Valley of *Humiliation,* is that empty and Solitary Place. Here a man shall not be so let, and hindered in his Contemplation, as in other places he is apt to be. This is a Valley that nobody walks in but those that love a Pilgrim's Life. And tho' *Christian* had the hard hap to meet here with *Apollyon,* and to enter with him in a brisk encounter: Yet

I must tell you, that in former times men have met with Angels here, have found Pearls here, and have in this place *Hos. 12.4, 5* found the words of Life.

Did I say, our Lord had here in former days his Country-house, and that he loved here to walk? I will add, in this Place, and to the People that love and trace these Grounds, he has left a yearly revenue, to be faithfully paid them at certain Seasons, for their maintenance by the way, *Mat. 11.29* and for their further encouragement to go on in their Pilgrimage.

Samuel. Now as they went on, *Samuel* said to Mr. *Great-Heart: Sir, I perceive that in this Valley, my Father and* Apollyon *had their Battle; but whereabout was the Fight? for I perceive this Valley is large.*

Great-heart. Your father had that battle with *Apollyon* at a place yonder, before us, in a narrow Passage just beyond *Forgetful-Green:* And indeed that place is the most *Forgetful-Green* dangerous place in all these Parts. For if at any time the Pilgrims meet with any brunt, it is when they forget what Favours they have received, and how unworthy they are of them. This is the Place also where others have been hard put to it: But more of the place when we are come to it; for I persuade myself, that to this day there remains either some sign of the Battle, or some Monument to testify that such a Battle there was fought.

Mercy. Then said *Mercy*, I think I am as well in this Valley, as I have been anywhere else in all our Journey: The place methinks suits with my Spirit. I love to be in such *Humility a sweet* places where there is no rattling with Coaches, nor rum- *Grace* bling with Wheels: Methinks here one may without much Molestation, be thinking what he is, whence he came, what he has done, and to what the King has called him: Here one may think, and break at Heart, and melt in one's Spirit, until one's Eyes become as the *Fish Pools of Heshbon*. They *Song 7.4* that go rightly thorough this Valley of *Bacha* make it a Well, the Rain that God sends down from Heaven upon *Psal. 84.5, 6, 7.* them that are here also *filleth the Pools*. This Valley is that

Hos. 2.15 from whence also the King will give to his their Vineyards; and they that go through it, shall sing, (as Christian did, for all he met with Apollyon.)

An Experiment of it *Great-heart.* 'Tis true, said their Guide; I have gone thorough this Valley many a time, and never was better than when here.

I have also been a Conduct to several pilgrims, and they have confessed the same; To this man will I look, saith the King, even to him that is Poor, and of a contrite Spirit, and that trembles at my Word.

Now they were come to the place where the afore mentioned Battle was Fought. Then said the guide to *Christiana,* her Children, and *Mercy:* This is the place; on this ground Christian stood, and up there came Apollyon against him. And look, did I not tell you, here is some of your Husband's blood upon these stones to *The place where* this day: Behold also how here and there are yet to be *Christian and* seen upon the place, some of the Shivers of *Apollyon's* *the Fiend did* *fight, some signs* Broken *Darts.* See also how they did beat the Ground *of the Battle* with their Feet as they fought, to make good their Places *remains* against each other; how also with their by-blows, they did split the very Stones in pieces. Verily *Christian* did here play the Man, and showed himself as stout as could, had he been there, even *Hercules* himself. When *Apollyon* was beat, he made his retreat to the next Valley, that is called *The Valley of the shadow of Death,* unto which we shall come anon.

A Monument of Lo, yonder also stands a Monument on which is *the Battle* Engraven this Battle, and *Christian's* Victory, to his Fame, throughout all Ages: So because it stood just on the way-side before them, they stepped to it and read the Writing, which word for word was this:

> *Hard by, here was a Battle fought,*
> *Most strange, and yet most true.*
> *Christian and Apollyon fought*
> *Each other to subdue.*

> *The Man so bravely play'd the Man,*
> *He made the Fiend to fly:*
> *Of which a Monument I stand,*
> *The same to testify.*

*A Monument of
Christian's
Victory*

When they had passed by this place, they came upon the *1 Part pag. 65* Borders of the shadow of Death, and this Valley was longer than the other, a place also most strangely haunted with Evil things, as many are able to testify: but these Women and Children went the better thorough it, because they had day-light, and because Mr. *Great-heart* was their Conductor.

When they were entered upon this Valley, they thought they heard a groaning, as of dead men: a very great groaning. They thought also that they did hear Words of Lamen- *Groanings heard* tation spoken, as of some in extreme Torment. These things made the Boys to quake, the Women also looked pale and wan; but their Guide bid them be of Good Comfort.

So they went on a little further, and they thought that they felt the Ground begin to shake under them, as if some *The Ground* hollow Place was there: they heard also a kind of hissing as *shakes* of Serpents, but nothing as yet appeared. Then said the Boys, Are we not yet at the end of this Doleful place? But the Guide also bid them be of good Courage, and look well to their Feet lest haply, said he, you be taken in some Snare.

Now *James* began to be Sick; but I think the cause thereof *James sick with* was Fear, so his Mother gave him some of that Glass of *fear* Spirits that she had given her at the *Interpreter's* House, and three of the Pills that Mr. *Skill* had prepared, and the boy began to revive. Thus they went on till they came to about the middle of the Valley; and then *Christiana* said, Methinks I see something yonder upon the Road before us, a thing of such a shape such as I have not seen. Then said *The* Fiend *Joseph,* Mother, what is it? An ugly thing, Child; an ugly *appears* thing, said she. But, Mother, what is it like? said he. 'Tis like I cannot tell what, said she. And now it was but a little way off: Then said she, It is nigh. *The Pilgrims are*

Well, well, said Mr. *Great-heart,* let them that are most *afraid*

afraid keep close to me. So the *Fiend* came on, and the
Conductor met it; but when it was come to him, it vanished
to all their sights. Then remembered they what had been
said some time ago: *Resist the Devil, and he will flee
from you.*[65]

They went therefore on, as being a little refreshed: but
they had not gone far, before *Mercy,* looking behind her,
saw as she thought, something most like a Lion, and it
came at a great padding pace after; and it had a hollow
Voice of Roaring; and at every Roar it gave, it made the
Valley Echo, and their Hearts to ache, save the Heart of
him that was their Guide. So it came up, and Mr. *Great-
heart* went behind, and put the Pilgrims all before him. The
Lion also came on apace, and Mr. *Great-heart* addressed
himself to give him Battle: But when he saw that it was
determined that resistance should be made, he also drew
back and came no further.

Then they went on again, and their conductor went
before them, till they came to a place where was cast up a
pit, the whole breadth of the way; and before they could
be prepared to go over that, a great mist and a darkness
fell upon them,[66] so that they could not see. Then said the
Pilgrims, Alas! Now what shall we do? But their Guide
made answer, Fear not; stand still, and see what an end
will be put to this also; so they stayed there, because their
Path was marr'd. They then also thought that they did hear
more apparently the noise and rushing of the Enemies; the
fire also and the smoke of the pit were much easier to be
discerned. Then said *Christiana* to *Mercy,* Now I see what
my poor Husband went through: I have heard much of this
place, but I never was here afore now; poor man, he went
here all alone in the night; he had night almost quite
through the way, also these Fiends were busy about him,
as if they would have torn him in pieces. Many have spoke
of it; but none can tell what the Valley of the shadow of
death should mean until they come in themselves; *The heart
knows its own bitterness; and a stranger intermeddleth not
with its Joy:*[67] To be here is a fearful thing.

Side notes:
- Great-heart encourages them
- A Lion
- 1 Pet. 5.8, 9
- A pit and darkness
- Christiana *now knows what her Husband felt*

Great-heart. This is like doing business in great Waters, Great-heart's
or like going down into the deep; this is like being in the Reply
heart of the Sea, and like going down to the Bottoms of the
Mountains.[68] Now it seems as if the Earth with its bars
were about us for ever.[69] *But let them that walk in dark-*
ness and have no light, trust in the name of the Lord, and
stay upon their God.[70] For my Part, as I have told you
already, I have gone often through this Valley, and have
been much harder put to it than now I am, and yet you see
I am alive. I would not boast, for that I am not mine own
Saviour. But I trust we shall have a good deliverance. Come,
let us pray for light to Him that can lighten our darkness,
and that can rebuke, not only these, but all the Satans
in Hell.

So they cried and prayed, and God sent light and deliver- They pray
ance, for there was now no let in their way; no, not there,
where but now they were stopped with a pit.

Yet they were not got through the Valley; so they
went on still, and met with great stinks and loathsome
smells, to the great annoyance of them. Then said *Mercy* Mercy to
to *Christiana,* there is not such pleasant being here as at Christiana
the *Gate,* or at the Interpreter's, or at the House where we
lay last.

O but, said one of the Boys, *it is not so bad to go through* One of the Boys'
here, as it is to abide *here, always; and for ought I know,* Reply
one reason why we must go this way to the House prepared
for us is, that our home might be the sweeter to us.

Well said, *Samuel,* quoth the *Guide,* thou hast now spoke
like a man. Why, if ever I get out here again, said the *Boy,*
I think I shall prize Light, and good way better than I ever
did in all my life. Then said the *Guide,* We shall be out by
and by.

So on they went, and *Joseph* said, *Cannot we see to the*
end of this Valley as yet? Then said the *Guide,* Look to
your feet, for we shall presently be among the Snares.[71] So
they looked to their feet, and went on; but they were
troubled much with the Snares. Now, when they were come
among the Snares, they espied a man cast into the Ditch on

Heedless *is slain,*
and Takeheed
preserved

the left hand, with his flesh all rent and torn. Then said the Guide, That is one *Heedless,* that was a going this way; he has lain there a great while. There was one *Takeheed* with him, when he was taken, and slain, but *he* escaped their hands. You cannot imagine, how many are killed hereabouts, and yet men are so foolishly venturous, as to set out lightly on Pilgrimage, and to come without a *Guide.* Poor *Christian,* it was a wonder that he here escaped; but he was beloved of his God, also he had a good heart of his own, or else he could never have a-done it. Now they drew towards the end of this way; and just there where *Christian* had seen the Cave when he went by, out thence came forth *Maul*[72] a Giant. This *Maul* did use to spoil young Pilgrims with Sophistry; and he called *Great-heart* by his name, and said unto him, how many times have you been forbidden to do these things? Then said Mr. *Great-heart,* What things? What things! quoth the Giant; you know what things: but I will put an end to your trade. But, pray, said Mr. *Great-heart,* before we fall to it, let us understand wherefore we must fight. (Now the Women and Children stood trembling, and knew not what to do.) Quoth the giant, you rob the Country, and rob it with the worst of Thefts. These are but Generals, said Mr. *Great-heart;* come to particulars, man.

1 *Part pag.* 70.
Maul *a Giant*

He quarrels with
Great-heart

Then said the Giant, Thou practises the craft of a *Kidnapper,* thou gatherest up Women and Children, and carriest them into a strange Country, to the weakening of my Master's Kingdom. But now *Great-heart* replied, I am a Servant of the God of Heaven; my business is to persuade sinners to Repentance. I am commanded to do my endeavour to turn Men, Women, and Children, from darkness to light,[73] and from the power of Satan to God; and if this be indeed the ground of thy quarrel, let us fall to it as soon as thou wilt.

God's Ministers
counted as
Kidnappers

Then the Giant came up, and Mr. *Great-heart* went to meet him, and as he Went, he drew his *Sword,* but the *Giant* had a *Club.* So without more ado they fell to it, and at the first blow the *Giant* struck Mr. *Great-heart* down

The Giant *and*
Mr. Great-heart
must fight

upon one of his knees; with that the women and children cried out. So Mr. *Great-heart* recovering himself, laid about him in full lusty manner, and gave the *Giant* a wound in his arm; thus he fought for the space of an hour, to that height of heat, that the breath came out of the *Giant's* nostrils, as the heat doth out of a boiling Cauldron.

Weak folks' Prayers do sometimes help strong folks' Cries

Then they sat down to rest them, but Mr. *Great-heart* betook himself to Prayer; also the Women and Children did nothing but sigh and cry all the time that the Battle did last.

When they had rested them, and taken breath, they both fell to it again, and Mr. *Great-heart,* with a full blow, fetched the *Giant* down to the ground. Nay, hold, let me recover, quoth he. So Mr. *Great-heart* fairly let him get up; so to it they went again: and the Giant missed but little of all-to-breaking Mr. Great-Heart's Skull with his Club.

The Giant *struck down*

Mr. *Great-heart* seeing that, runs to him in the full heat of his spirit, and pierceth him under the fifth rib;[74] with that the *Giant* began to faint, and could hold up his Club no longer. Then Mr. *Great-heart* seconded his blow, and smit the head of the *Giant* from his shoulders. Then the Women and Children rejoiced, and Mr. *Great-heart* also praised God, for the deliverance he had wrought.

When this was done, they amongst them erected a Pillar, and fastened the *Giant's* head thereon, and wrote underneath in Letters that passengers might Read,

He is slain, and his head disposed of

> *He that did wear this head, was one*
> *That Pilgrims did misuse;*
> *He stopped their way, he spared none,*
> *But did them all abuse;*
> *Until that I, Great-heart, arose,*
> *The Pilgrims Guide to be;*
> *Until that I did him oppose*
> *That was their Enemy.*

Now I saw, that they went on to the Ascent that was a little way off cast up to be a Prospect for Pilgrims. (That

1 Part pag. 71

was the place from whence *Christian* had the first sight of
Faithful his Brother.) Wherefore here they sat down, and
rested, they also here did eat and drink, a and make merry;
for that they had gotten deliverance from this so dangerous an Enemy. As they sat thus and did eat, *Christiana*
asked the *Guide, If he had caught no hurt in the battle.*
Then said Mr. *Great-heart,* no, save a little on my flesh; yet
that also shall be so far from being to my Determent,
that it is at present a proof of my love to my Master, and
you, and shall be a means of Grace to increase my reward
2 Cor. 4 at last.

But was you not afraid, good Sir, when you see him come
Discourse of the *out with his Club?*
fights
It is my Duty, said he, to mistrust my own ability, that I
may have reliance on him that is stronger than all. *But*
what did you think when he fetched you down to the
ground at the first blow? Why, I thought, quoth he, that
so my master himself was served, and yet he it was that
conquered at last.

Mat. Here   Mat. *When you all have thought what you please, I think*
admires   *God has been wonderful good unto us, both in bringing us*
Goodness   *out of this Valley, and in delivering us out of the hand of*
this Enemy; for my part I see no reason why we should
distrust our God any more, since he has now, *and in*
such *a place as this, given us such testimony of his love*
as this.

Then they got up, and went forward. Now a little before
Old Honest   them stood an Oak; and under it, when they came to it,
asleep under an   they found an old *Pilgrim* fast asleep, they knew that he
Oak   was a *Pilgrim* by his *Clothes,* and his *Staff,* and his *Girdle.*

So the *Guide* Mr. *Great-heart* awaked him, and the old
Gentleman, as he lift up his eyes, cried out; What's the
matter? Who are you? and what is your business here?

Greath. Come, man, be not so hot; here is none but
Friends; yet the old man gets up and stands upon his guard,
and will know of them what they were. Then said the
Guide, My name is *Great-heart:* I am the guide of these
Pilgrims which are going to the Celestial Country.

Honest. Then said Mr. *Honest,* I cry you mercy; I fear'd that you had been of the Company of those that some time ago did rob *Little-faith* of his money; but now I look better about me, I perceive you are honester People.

One Saint some-times takes another for his Enemy

Greath. *Why, what would, or could you have done to a helped yourself, if we indeed had been of that Company?*

Talk between Great-heart and he

Hon. Done! Why, I would a fought as long as Breath had been in me: and had I so done, I am sure you could never have given me the worst on't; for a *Christian* can never be overcome, unless he shall yield of himself.

Greath. *Well said,* Father Honest, *quoth the Guide, for by this I know thou art a Cock of the right kind,*[75] for thou hast said the Truth.

Hon. And by this also I know that thou knowest what true Pilgrimage is; for all others do think that we are the soonest overcome of any.

Greath. *Well, now we are so happily met, pray let me crave your Name, and the name of the Place you came from?*

Whence Mr. Honest came

Hon. My name I cannot, but I came from the Town of *Stupidity;* it lieth about four Degrees beyond the City of *Destruction.*

Greath. *Oh! Are you that Country-man then? I deem I have half a guess of You, your name is Old* Honesty, *is it not?* So the old Gentleman blushed, and said, Not Honesty in the *Abstract,* but *Honest* is my Name, and I wish that my *Nature* shall agree to what I am called.

Hon. But, sir, said the old Gentleman, how could you guess that I am such a Man, since I came from such a place?

Greath. *I had heard of you before, by my Master; for he knows all things that are done on the Earth: But I have often wondered that any should come from your place; for your Town is worse than is the* City *of* Destruction *itself.*

Stupified ones are worse than those merely Carnal

Hon. Yes, we lie more off from the Sun, and so are more cold and Senseless; but was a man in a Mountain of Ice, yet if the Sun of Righteousness will arise upon him, his frozen Heart shall feel a Thaw; and thus it hath been with me.

Greath. I believe it, Father *Honest,* I believe it; for I know the thing is true.

Then the old Gentleman saluted all the Pilgrims with a holy Kiss of Charity,[76] and asked them of their Names, and how they had fared since they set out on their Pilgrimage.

Old Honest *and*
Christiana talk

Chris. Then said *Christiana,* My Name I suppose you have heard of; good *Christian* was my Husband, and these four were his Children. But can you think how the old Gentleman was taken, when she told them who she was? He skipped, he smiled, and blessed them with a thousand good Wishes, saying,

Hon. I have heard much of your Husband, and of his Travels and Wars which he underwent in his days. Be it spoken to your Comfort, the Name of your Husband rings all over these parts of the World: his Faith, his Courage, his Enduring, and his Sincerity under all, had made his

He also talks
with the Boys.
Old Mr.
Honest's Bless-
ing on them.
Mat. 10.3. Psal.
99.6. Gen. 39.
Acts

Name Famous. Then he turned him to the Boys, and asked them of their Names, which they told him: And then said he unto them, *Matthew,* be thou like Matthew the publican, not in Vice, but in Virtue. *Samuel,* said he, be thou like *Samuel* the Prophet, a man of Faith and Prayer. *Joseph,* said he, be thou like *Joseph* in *Potiphar's* House, Chaste, and one that flees from Temptation. And *James,* be thou like *James* the Just, and like *James* the Brother of our Lord.[77]

Then they told him of *Mercy,* and how she had left her Town and her Kindred to come along with *Christiana,* and

He blesseth
Mercy

with her Sons. At that the old *Honest* Man said, *Mercy* is thy Name? by *Mercy* shalt thou be sustained and carried thorough all those Difficulties that shall assault thee in thy way; till thou shalt come thither where thou shalt look the Fountain of Mercy in the face with Comfort.

All this while the Guide Mr. *Great-heart,* was very much pleased, and smiled upon his Companion.

Talk of one
Mr. Fearing

Now as they walked along together, the Guide asked the old Gentleman *if he did not know one Mr.* Fearing, *that came on Pilgrimage out of his Parts.*

Hon. Yes, very well, said he; he was a man that had the

Root of the Matter[78] in him, but he was one of the most troublesome Pilgrims that ever I met with in all my days.

Greath. *I perceive you knew him, for you have given a very right character of him.*

Hon. Knew him! I was a great Companion of his; I was with him most an end; when he first began to think upon what would come upon us hereafter, I was with him.

Greath. *I was his Guide from my Master's House, to the Gates of the Celestial City.*

Hon. Then you knew him to be a troublesome one?

Greath. I did so; but I could very well bear it; for Men of my calling, are oftentimes intrusted with the Conduct of such as he was.

Hon. Well then, pray let us hear a little of him, and how he managed himself under your Conduct?

Greath. Why he was always afraid that he should come short of whither he had a desire to go. Every thing frightened him that he heard any body speak of, if it had but the least appearance of Opposition in it. I heard that he lay roaring at the *Slough of Despond* for above a Month together; nor durst he, for all he saw several go over before him, venture, though they many of them offered to lend him their Hand. *He would not go back again neither.* The Celestial City, he said he should die if he came not to it; and yet he was dejected at every Difficulty, and stumbled at every Straw that any body cast in his way. Well, after he had lain at the *Slough of Despond* a great while, as I have told you; one sunshine Morning, I do not know how, he ventured, and so got over. But when he was over, he would scarce believe it. He had, I think, a *Slough of Despond* in his Mind, a *Slough* that he carried every where with him, or else he could never have been as he was. So he came up to the Gate, you know what I mean, that stands at the head of this way, and there also he stood a good while before he would adventure to knock. When the Gate was opened, he would give back, and give place to others, and say that he was not worthy. For, all he gat before some to the Gate, yet many of them went in before him. There the poor Man

Mr. Fearing's *troublesome Pilgrimage*

His behaviour at the Slough of Despond

His behaviour at the Gate

would stand shaking and shrinking; I dare say it would have pitied one's Heart to have seen him. Nor would he go back again. At last he took the Hammer that hanged on the Gate in his hand, and gave a small Rap or two; then one opened to him, but he shrunk back as before. He that opened stepped out after him, and said, Thou trembling one, what wantest thou? With that he fell to the ground. He that spoke to him wondered to see him so faint. So he said to him, *Peace be to thee,* up for I have set open the Door to thee; come in, for thou art blessed. With that he got up, and went in trembling; and when he was in, he

His behaviour at the Interpreter's Door

was ashamed to show his Face. Well, after he had been entertained there a while, as you know how the manner is, he was bid go on his way, and also told the way he should take. So he came till he came out to our House, but as he behaved himself at the Gate, so he did at my Master the *Interpreter's* Door. He lay there about in the Cold a good while, before he would adventure to call; *Yet he would not go back.* And the nights were long and cold then. Nay, he had a note of *Necessity* in his Bosom to my Master to receive him, and grant him the Comfort of his House, and also to allow him a stout and valiant Conduct, because he was himself so *Chicken-hearted* a Man; and yet for all that he was afraid to call at the Door. So he lay up and down there abouts, till, poor man, he was almost starved; yea, so great was his Dejection, that though he saw several others for knocking got in, yet he was afraid to venture. At last, I think I looked out of the Window, and perceiving a man to be up and down about the Door, I went out to him, and asked what he was: but, poor man, the water stood in his Eyes. So I perceived what he wanted. I went therefore in, and told it in the House, and we showed the thing to our Lord; So he sent me out again, to entreat him to come in; but I dare say, I had hard work to do it. At last he came in; and I will say that for my Lord, he carried it wonderful

How he was entertained there

lovingly to him. There were but a few good bits at the Table, but some of it was laid upon his Trencher. Then he presented the *Note,* and my Lord looked thereon and said, his Desire should be granted. So when he had been there a good while, he seemed to get some Heart, and to be a little more Comfortable. For my Master, you must know, is one of very tender Bowels, especially to them that are afraid, wherefore he carried it so towards him as might tend most to his Encouragement. Well, when he had had a sight of the things of the place, and was ready to take his journey to go to the City, my Lord, as he did to *Christian* before, gave him a Bottle of Spirits, and some comfortable things to eat. Thus we set forward, and I went before him; but the man was but of few Words, only he would sigh aloud.

He is a little encouraged at the Interpreter's house

When we were come to where the three Fellows were hanged, he said, that he doubted that that would be his end also. Only he seemed glad when he saw the Cross and the Sepulchre. There I confess he desired to stay a little to look; and he seemed for a while after to be a little *Cheery.* When he came to the Hill *Difficulty,* he made no stick at that, nor did he much fear the Lions: For you must know, that his Trouble *was not about such things as those,* his Fear was about his Acceptance at last.

He was greatly afraid when he saw the Gibbet, Cheery when he saw the Cross

I got him in at the House *Beautiful,* I think before he was willing; also, when he was in, I brought him acquainted with the Damsels that were of the Place, but he was ashamed to make himself much in Company, he desired much to be alone, yet he always loved good talk, and often would get behind the *Screen* to hear it; he also loved much to see *ancient* Things, and to be *pondering* them in his Mind. He told me afterwards, that he loved to be in those two Houses from which he came last, to wit, at the Gate, and that of the *Interpreters,* but that he durst not be so bold as to ask.

Dumpish at the house Beautiful

When we went also from the House *Beautiful,* down the Hill, into the Valley of *Humiliation,* he went *down as well as ever I saw a man in my Life,* for he cared not how mean he was, so he might be happy at last. Yea, I think there was a kind of Sympathy betwixt that Valley and him; for I never saw him better in all his Pilgrimage, than he was in that Valley.

He went down into, and was very Pleasant in the Valley of Humiliation

Lam. 3.27, 28, 29 Here he would lie down, embrace the Ground, and kiss the very Flowers that grew in this Valley. He would now be up every morning by break of Day, tracing and walking to and fro in this Valley.

But when he was come to the entrance of the Valley of *Much perplexed* the Shadow of Death, I thought I should have lost my Man; *in the Valley of* not for that he had any Inclination to go back, that he *the Shadow of* always abhorred, but he was ready to die for Fear. O, the *Death* *Hobgoblins* will have me, the *Hobgoblins* will have me, cried he; and I could not beat him out on't. He made such a noise, and such an outcry here, that, had they but heard him, 'twas enough to encourage them to come and fall upon us.

But this I took very great notice of, that this Valley was as quiet when we went thorough it, as ever I knew it before or since. I suppose, those Enemies here, had now a special Check from our Lord, and a command not to meddle until Mr. *Fearing* had passed over it.

It would be too tedious to tell you of all; we will therefore *His Behaviour at* only mention a Passage or two more. When he was come *Vanity-Fair* at *Vanity Fair,* I thought he would have fought with all the men in the Fair, I feared there we should have been both knocked o' the Head, so hot was he against their Fooleries; upon the enchanted Ground, he was also very wakeful. But when he was come at the *River* where was no Bridge, there again he was in a heavy case; now, now, he said, he should be drowned for ever, and so never see that Face with Comfort, that he had come so many miles to behold.

And here also I took notice of what was very remarkable, the Water of that River was lower at this time than ever I saw it in all my Life; so he went over at last, not much above wet-shod.[79] When he was going up to the Gate, Mr. Great-heart began[80] to take leave of him, and to wish him *His Boldness* a good Reception above; So he said, *I shall, I shall.* Then *at last* parted we asunder, and I saw him no more.

Hon. *Then it seems he was well at last.*

Greath. Yes, yes, I never had doubt about him, he was a
man of a choice Spirit, only he was always kept very low, Psal. 88. Rom.
and that made his Life so burthensome to himself, and so 14.21. 1 Cor.
troublesome to others. He was, above many, tender of Sin; 8.13
he was so afraid of doing Injuries to others, that he often
would deny himself of that which was lawful, because he
would not offend.

Hon. *But what should be the reason that such a good
Man should be all his days so much in the dark?*

Greath. There are two sorts of Reasons for it; one is, The *Reason why*
wise God will have it so, some must *Pipe,* and some must *good men are so*
Weep.[81] Now Mr. *Fearing* was one that played upon *this* *in the dark.*
Bass. He and his Fellows sound the *Sackbut,* whose Notes Mar. 11.16, 17,
are more doleful than the Notes of other Music are: though 18
indeed, some say, the Bass is the Ground of Music. And for
my part, I care not at all for that Profession, which begins
not in heaviness of Mind. The first string that the Musician
usually touches, *is the Bass,* when he intends to put all in
tune; God also plays upon this string first, when he sets the
Soul in tune for himself. Only there was the imperfection
of Mr. *Fearing,* he could play upon no other Music but
this, till towards his latter end.

I make bold to talk thus Metaphorically, for the ripening
of the Wits of young Readers, and because in the Book of
the Revelations, the Saved are compared to a company of Revel. 8.2,
Musicians that play upon their *Trumpets* and Harps, and *Chap. 14.2, 3*
sing their Songs before the Throne.

Hon. *He was a very zealous man, as one may see by
what Relation you have given of him. Difficulties, Lions,
or Vanity Fair, he feared not at all; 'twas only Sin, Death,
and Hell, that was to him a Terror;* because he had some
Doubts about his Interest in that Celestial Country.

Greath. You say right. *Those* were the things that were his *A Close about*
Troublers; and they, as you have well observed, arose from *him*
the weakness of his Mind there about, not from weakness of
Spirit as to the practical part of a Pilgrim's Life. I dare believe
that as the Proverb is, he could have bit a Firebrand, had it

stood in his Way:[82] But the things with which he was oppressed, no man ever yet could shake off with ease.

Christiana's
Sentence

Christiana. *Then said* Christiana, *This relation of Mr.* Fearing *has done me Good. I thought nobody had been like me, but I see there was some Semblance 'twixt this good man and I, only we differed in two things. His Troubles were so great they brake out, but mine I kept within. His also lay so hard upon him, they made him that he could not knock at the Houses provided for Entertainment; but my Trouble was always such, as* made me knock the louder.

Mercy's
Sentence

Mer. If I might also speak my Heart, I must say that something of him has also dwelt in me. For I have ever been more afraid of the Lake and the loss of a place in *Paradise,* than I have been of the loss of other things. Oh, thought I, may I have the Happiness to have a Habitation *there,* 'tis enough, though I part with all the World to win it.

Matthew's
Sentence

Mat. *Then said* Matthew, *Fear was one thing that made me think that I was far from having that within me which accompanies Salvation, but if it was so with such a good man as he, why may it not also go well with me?*

James's Sentence

Jam. No fears, no Grace, said *James.* Though there is not always Grace where there is the fear of Hell, yet, to be sure there is no Grace where there is no fear of God.

Greath. *Well said, James; thou hast hit the Mark, for the fear of God is the beginning of Wisdom;*[83] and to be sure they that want the beginning, *have neither* middle, *nor* end. *But we will here conclude our discourse of Mr.* Fearing, *after we have sent after him this Farewell.*

Their Farewell
about him

> *Well, Master* Fearing, *thou didst fear*
> *Thy God: and wast afraid*
> *Of doing any thing, while here,*
> *That would have thee betray'd.*
> *And didst thou fear the Lake and Pit?*
> *Would others do so too:*
> *For, as for them that want thy Wit,*
> *They do themselves undo.*

Now I saw, that they still went on in their Talk. For after Mr. *Greatheart* had made an end with Mr. *Fearing*, Mr. *Honest* began to tell them of another, but his Name was Mr. *Selfwill*. He pretended himself to be a *Pilgrim*, said Mr. *Honest*; but I persuade my self he never came in at the Gate that stands at the head of the way.

Of Mr. Self-will

Greath. *Had you ever any talk with him about it?*

Hon. Yes, more than once or twice; but he would always be like himself, *self-willed*. He neither cared for man, nor Argument, nor yet Example; what his Mind prompted him to, that he would do, and nothing else could he be got to.

Old Honest *had talked with him*

Greath. *Pray, what Principles did he hold, for I suppose you can tell?*

Hon. He held that a man might follow the Vices, as well as the Virtues of the Pilgrims; and that if he did both, he should be certainly saved.

Self-will's *Opinions*

Greath. *How? If he had said, 'tis possible for the best to be guilty of the Vices, as well as to partake of the Virtues of Pilgrims, he could not much a been blamed. For indeed we are exempted from no Vice absolutely, but on condition that we Watch and Strive. But this I perceive is not the thing. But if I understand you right, your meaning is, that he was of that Opinion, that it was allowable so to be?*

Hon. Aye, aye, so I mean, and so he believed and practised.

Greath. *But what ground had he for his so saying?*

Hon. Why, he said he had the Scripture for his warrant.

Greath. *Prithee, Mr.* Honest, *present us with a few Particulars.*

Hon. So I will. He said, To have to do with other men's Wives had been practised by *David*, God's Beloved, and therefore he could do it. He said to have more Women than one, was a thing that *Solomon* practised, and therefore he could do it. He said, that *Sarah*, and the godly Midwives of *Egypt* lied, and so did save *Rahab*, and therefore he could do it. He said that the Disciples went at the bidding of their Master, and took away the Owner's *Ass*, and therefore he could do so too. He said that *Jacob* got the

Inheritance of his Father in a way of Guile and Dissimulation, and therefore he could do so too.[84]

Greath. *High base! Indeed, and are you sure he was of this Opinion?*

Hon. I heard him plead for it, bring Scripture for it, bring Arguments for it, &c.

Greath. *An Opinion that is not fit to be, with any Allowance, in the World.*

Hon. You must understand me rightly. He did not say that any man might do this; but that they who had the Virtues of those that did such things, might also do the same.

Greath. *But what more false than such a Conclusion? For this is as much as to say, that because good men heretofore have sinned of Infirmity, therefore he had allowance to do it of a presumptuous Mind. Or if, because a Child, by the blast of the Wind, or for that it stumbled at a stone, fell down and defiled itself in Mire, therefore he might wilfully lie down and wallow like a Boar therein. Who could a thought that any one could so far a been blinded* I Pet. 2.8 *by the power of Lust? But what is written must be true: they Stumble at the Word, being disobedient; whereunto also they were appointed.*

His supposing that such may have the godly Man's Virtues, who addict themselves to their Vices, is also a Delusion as strong as the other. 'Tis just as if the Dog should say, I have, or may have the Qualities of the Child, because I lick up its stinking Excrements. To eat up the Sin of God's people, as a dog licks up filth, is no sign that one Hos. 4. 8 *is possessed with their Virtues. Nor can I believe that one that is of this Opinion, can at present have Faith or Love in him. But I know you have made strong Objections against him; prithee what can he say for himself?*

Hon. Why, he says, To do this by way of Opinion, seems abundantly more Honest, than to do it, and yet hold contrary to it in Opinion.

Greath. *A very wicked Answer, for though to let loose the Bridle to Lusts, while our Opinions are against such*

*things, is bad; yet to sin and plead a Toleration so to do, is
worse: the one stumbles Beholders accidentally, the other
leads them into the Snare.*

Hon. There are many of this man's mind, that have not
this man's mouth, and *that* makes going on Pilgrimage of
so little esteem as it is.

Greath. *You have said the Truth, and it is to be lamented.
But he that feareth the King of Paradise, shall come out of
them all.*

Christiana. There are strange Opinions in the World. I
know one that said, 'twas time enough to repent when they
come to die.

Greath. *Such are not over Wise. That man would a been
loth, might he have had a week to run twenty miles in for
his Life, to have deferred that Journey to the last hour of
that Week.*

Hon. You say right, and yet the generality of them that
count themselves Pilgrims, do indeed do thus. I am, as you
see, an old Man, and have been a traveller in this Road
many a day; and I have taken notice of many things.

I have seen some that have set out as if they would drive
all the World afore them: Who yet have, in a few days, died
as they in the Wilderness, and so never got sight of the
promised Land.[85]

I have seen some that have promised nothing at first
setting out to be Pilgrims, and that one would have thought
could not have lived a day, that have yet proved very good
Pilgrims.

I have seen some, that have run hastily forward, that
again have, after a little time, run just as fast back again.

I have seen some who have spoke very well of a Pilgrim's Life at first, that after a while, have spoken as much
against it.

I have heard some, when they first set out for Paradise,
say positively, there is such a place, who, when they have
been almost there, have come back again, and said there is
none.

I have heard some vaunt what they would do in case they

should be opposed, that have, even at a false Alarm fled Faith, the Pilgrim's way, and all.

Fresh News of trouble   Now as they were thus on their way, there came one running to meet them, and said, Gentlemen, and you of the weaker sort, if you love Life, shift for your selves, for the Robbers are before you.

1 Part pag. 125   *Greath.* Then said Mr. *Great-heart,* They be the three that set upon *Littlefaith* heretofore. Well, said he, we are Great-heart's Resolution ready for them: so they went on their way. Now they looked at every Turning when they should a met with the Villains. But whether they heard of Mr. *Great-heart,* or whether they had some other Game, they came not up to the Pilgrims.

Christiana *wisheth for an Inn*   *Chris. Christiana* then wished for an Inn for herself and her Children; because they were weary. Then said Mr. *Honest,* There is one a little before us, where a very honour-Rom. 16.23. Gaius able Disciple, one *Gaius,* dwells. So they all concluded to turn in thither; and the rather, because the old Gentleman *They enter into his House* gave him so good a Report. So when they came to the Door they went in, not knocking, for Folks use not to knock at the Door of an Inn. Then they called for the Master of the House, and he came to them. *So they asked if they might lie there that Night?*

Gaius *Entertains them, and how*   *Gaius.*[86] Yes Gentlemen, if you be true Men, for my House is for none but Pilgrims. Then was *Christiana, Mercy,* and the boys the more glad, for that the Innkeeper was a Lover of Pilgrims. So they called for Rooms; and he showed them one for *Christiana* and her children and *Mercy,* and another for Mr. *Great-heart* and the old Gentleman.

Greath. Then said Mr. Great-heart, *good* Gaius, *what hast thou for Supper? for these pilgrims have come far to day, and are weary.*

Gaius. It is late, said *Gaius,* so we cannot conveniently go out to seek Food; but such as we have you shall be welcome to, if that will content.

Greath. We will be content with what thou hast in the House, for as much as I have proved thee, thou art never destitute of that which is convenient.

Then he went down and spake to the cook, whose name was *Taste-that-which-is-good,* to get ready Supper for so many Pilgrims. This done, he comes up again, saying, come, my good Friends, you are welcome to me, and I am glad that I have an House to entertain you; and while Supper is making ready, if you please, let us entertain one another with some good Discourse. So they all said, content.

Gaius his Cook

Gaius. Then said *Gaius, Whose Wife is this aged Matron, and whose Daughter is this young Damsel?*

Greath. This Woman is the Wife of one *Christian,* a Pilgrim of former times; and these are his four Children. The Maid is one of her Acquaintance; one that she hath persuaded to come with her on Pilgrimage. The Boys take all after their Father, and covet to tread in his Steps. Yea, if they do but see any place where the old Pilgrim hath lain, or any print of his Foot, it ministreth Joy to their Hearts, and they covet to lie or tread in the same.

Talk between Gaius and his Guests

Mark this

Gaius. Then said *Gaius,* Is this *Christian's* Wife, and are these *Christian's* Children? I knew your Husband's Father, yea, also his Father's Father. Many have been good of this stock; their Ancestors dwelt first at *Antioch. Christian's* Progenitors (I suppose you have heard your Husband talk of them) were very worthy men. They have, above any that I know, showed themselves men of great Virtue and Courage for the Lord of the Pilgrims, his ways, and them that loved him. I have heard of many of your Husband's Relations that have stood all Trials for the sake of the Truth. *Stephen,* that was one of the first of the Family from whence your Husband sprang, was knocked o' th' Head with Stones. *James,* another of this Generation, was slain with the edge of the Sword. To say nothing of *Paul* and *Peter,* men anciently of the Family from whence your Husband came. There was *Ignatius,* who was cast to the Lions; *Romanus,* whose Flesh was cut by pieces from his bones; and *Polycarp,* that played the man in the Fire. There was he that was hanged up in a Basket in the Sun for the Wasps to eat; and he whom they put into a Sack, and cast him into

Act. 11.26

Of Christian's Ancestors

Acts 7.59, 60. Cha. 12.

the Sea, to be drowned.[87] 'Twould be impossible, utterly to count up all of that Family who have suffered Injuries and Death, for the love of a Pilgrim's Life. Nor can I, but be glad to see that thy Husband has left behind him four such Boys as these. I hope they will bear up their Father's name, and tread in their Father's steps, and come to their Father's end.

Greath. Indeed Sir, they are likely Lads, they seem to choose heartily their Father's Ways.

Gaius. That is it that I said, wherefore *Christian's* family is like still to spread abroad upon the face of the Ground, and yet to be numerous upon the face of the Earth. Where-

Advice to Christiana about her Boys fore let *Christiana* look out some Damsels for her sons, to whom they may be Betrothed, &c., that the Name of their Father, and the House of his Progenitors, may never be forgotten in the World.

Hon. 'Tis pity his Family should fall, and be extinct.

Gaius. Fall it cannot, but be diminished it may; but let *Christiana* take my advice, and that is the way to up-hold it.

And *Christiana,* said *This* Innkeeper, I am glad to see

Mercy and Matthew Marry thee and thy Friend *Mercy* together here, a lovely Couple. And may I advise, take *Mercy* into a nearer Relation to thee. If she will, let her be given to *Matthew* thy eldest son. 'Tis the way to preserve you a Posterity in the Earth.[88] So this Match was concluded, and in process of time they were married. But more of that hereafter.

Gaius also proceeded, and said, I will now speak on the behalf of the Women, to take away their Reproach. For as Death and the Curse came into the world by a Woman, so also did Life and Health; *God sent forth his Son, made of*

Gen. 3. Gal. 4 *a Woman.* Yea, to show how much they that came after did abhor the Act of the Mother, this Sex, in the old Testament,

Why Women of old so much desired Children coveted Children, if happily this or that Woman might be the Mother of the Saviour of the World. I will say again, that when the Saviour was come, Women rejoiced in him,

Luke 2 before either Man or Angel. I read not that ever any man did give unto Christ so much as one Groat; but the Women followed him, and ministered to him of their Substance. 'Twas a woman that washed his Feet with Tears, and a Woman that anointed his Body to the Burial. They were Women who wept when he was going to the Cross, and Women that followed him from the Cross, and sat by his Sepulchre when he was buried. They were Women that was first with him at his Resurrection-*morn,* and Women that brought Tiding first to his Disciples that he was risen from the Dead. Women therefore are highly favoured,[89] and show by these things that they are sharers with us in the Grace of Life.

Chap. 8.2, 3. Chap. 7.37, 50. Joh. 11.2. Chap. 12.3. Luke 23.27

Matt. 27.55, 56, 61. Luke 24.22, 23

Now the Cook sent up to signify that Supper was almost ready, and sent one to lay the Cloth, the Trenchers, and to set the Salt and Bread in order.

Supper ready

Then said *Matthew, the sight of this Cloth, and of this forerunner of a Supper, begetteth in me a greater Appetite to my Food than I had before.*

Gaius. So let all ministering Doctrines *to* thee in this Life, beget in thee a greater desire to sit at the Supper of the great King in his Kingdom; for all Preaching, Books, and Ordinances[90] here, are but as the laying of the Trenchers, and the setting of Salt upon the Board, when compared with the Feast that our Lord will make for us when we come to his House.

What to be gathered from laying of the Board with the Cloth and Trenchers

So Supper came up, and first a *Heave-shoulder* and a *wave-Breast*[91] were set on the Table before them; to show that they must begin their *Meal* with Prayer and Praise to God. The *heave-Shoulder David* lifted his Heart up to God with, and with the *wave-Breast, where his Heart lay,* he used to lean upon his Harp when he played. These two Dishes were very fresh and good, and they all ate heartily well thereof.

Levit. 7.32, 33, 34. Chap. 10.14, 15. Psal. 25.1. Heb. 13.15

The next they brought up was a Bottle of Wine, red as Blood. So *Gaius* said to them, Drink freely, this is the Juice of the true Vine, that makes glad the Heart of God and Man. So they drank and were merry.

Deut. 32.14. Judg. 9.13. Joh. 15.1

The next was a Dish of Milk well crumbed. But *Gaius* said, *Let the Boys have that, that they may grow thereby.*

1 Pet. 2.1, 2. A Dish of Milk

Then they brought up in course a Dish of *Butter* and
Of Honey and *Honey.* Then said *Gaius,* Eat freely of *this,* for this is good
Butter to cheer up, and strengthen your Judgements and Under-
Isa. 7.15 standings. This was our Lord's Dish when he was a Child.
*Butter and Honey shall he eat, that he may know to refuse
the Evil, and choose the Good.*

Then they brought them up a dish of Apples, and they
A Dish of were very good tasted Fruit. Then said *Matthew,* May we
Apples eat Apples, since they were such, by, and with which, the
Serpent beguiled our first Mother?

Then said *Gaius,*

> *Apples were they* with *which we were beguil'd,*
> *Yet* Sin, *not Apples hath our Souls defil'd:*
> *Apples forbid, if ate, corrupts the Blood:*
> *To eat such, when commanded, does us good.*
> *Drink of his Flagons then, thou Church, his Dove,*
> *And eat* his *Apples, who are sick of Love.*[92]

Then said *Matthew, I made the Scruple, because I a while
since was sick with eating of Fruit.*

Gaius. Forbidden Fruit will make you sick, but not what
our Lord has tolerated.

While they were thus talking, they were presented with
Song 6.11. another Dish; and 'twas a dish of *Nuts.* Then said some at
A Dish of Nuts the Table, *Nuts* spoil tender Teeth, especially the Teeth of
Children. Which when *Gaius* heard, he said,

> *Hard* Texts[93] *are Nuts, (I will not call them Cheaters,)*
> *Whose* Shells *do keep their* Kernels *from the* Eaters:
> *Ope then the Shells, and you shall have the Meat,*
> *They here brought are for you to crack and Eat.*

Then were they very Merry, and sat at the Table a long
time, talking of many Things. Then said the Old Gentleman, My good Landlord, while we are cracking your *Nuts,*
if you please, do you open this Riddle.

A man there was, though some did count him mad,
The more he cast away, the more he had.

A Riddle put forth by old Honest

Then they all gave good heed, wondering what good *Gaius* would say, so he sat still a while, and then thus replied:

He that bestows his Goods upon the Poor,
Shall have as much again, and ten times more.

Gaius *opens*

Then said *Joseph*, I dare say Sir, I did not think you could a found it out.

Joseph *wonders*

Oh! said *Gaius,* I have been trained up in this way a great while. Nothing teaches like Experience; I have learned of my Lord to be kind, and have found by experience that I have gained thereby. *There is that scattereth, and yet increaseth; and there is that withholdeth more than is meet, but it tendeth to Poverty: There is that maketh himself Rich, yet hath nothing; there is that maketh himself poor, yet hath great Riches.*

Prov. 11.24. Chap. 13.7

Then *Samuel* whispered to *Christiana* his Mother, and said, Mother, this is a very good man's House: let us stay here a good while, and let my Brother *Matthew* be married here to *Mercy*, before we go any further.

The which *Gaius* the Host overhearing, said, *With a very good Will, my Child.*

So they stayed there more than a Month, and *Mercy* was given to *Matthew* to Wife.

Matthew *and* Mercy *are Married*

While they stayed here, *Mercy* as her Custom was, would be making Coats and Garments to give to the Poor, by which she brought up a very good Report upon the Pilgrims.

But to return again to our Story. After Supper, the lads desired a Bed, for that they were weary with Travelling. Then *Gaius* called to show them their Chamber, but said *Mercy*, I will have them to Bed. So she had them to Bed, and they slept well: but the rest sat up all Night. For *Gaius* and they were such suitable company, that they could not tell how to part. After much talk of their Lord, themselves,

The Boys go to Bed, the rest sit up

and their Journey; old Mr. *Honest,* he that put forth the
Riddle to *Gaius,* began to *nod.* Then said *Great-heart,*
What Sir, you begin to be drowsy, come rub up,[94] now
here's a *Riddle* for you. Then said Mr. *Honest,* Let's
hear it.

Then said Mr. *Great-heart,*

> *He that will kill, must first be overcome:*
> *Who live abroad would, first must die at home.*

Ha, said Mr. *Honest,* it is a hard one, hard to expound,
and harder to practise. But come Landlord, said he, I will,
if you please, leave my part to you: do you expound it, and
I will hear what you say.

No, said *Gaius,* it was put to you, and 'tis expected you
should answer it.

Then said the Old Gentleman,

> *He first by Grace must conquer'd be,*
> *That Sin would mortify;*
> *And who, that lives, would convince me,*
> *Unto himself must die.*

It is right, said *Gaius,* good Doctrine and Experience
teaches this. For first, until Grace displays itself, and over-
comes the Soul with its Glory, it is altogether without heart
to oppose Sin. Besides, if Sin is Satan's Cords, by which the
soul lies bound, how should it make Resistance before it is
loosed from that infirmity?

Secondly, Nor will any one that knows either Reason or
Grace, believe that such a man can be a living Monument
of Grace, that is a Slave to his own Corruptions.

And now it comes in my mind, I will tell you a Story,
worth the hearing. There were two Men that went on
Pilgrimage, the one began when he was young, the other
when he was old. The young Man had strong Corruptions
to grapple with, the old Man's were weak with the decays
of Nature. The young man trod his steps as even as did the

old one, and was every way as light as he; who now, or which of them, had their Graces shining clearest, since both seemed to be alike?

Hon. *The young Man's, doubtless. For that which heads* A Comparison *it against the greatest Opposition, gives best demonstration that it is strongest. Specially when it also holdeth pace with that which meets not with half so much; as to be sure old Age does not.*

Besides, I have observed that old men have blessed themselves with this mistake; Namely, taking the decays of Nature, for a gracious Conquest over Corruptions, and so A Mistake have been apt to beguile themselves. Indeed, old men that are gracious are best able to give Advice to them that are young, because they have seen most of the emptiness of things: but yet, for an old and a young to set out both together, the young one has the advantage of the fairest discovery of a work of Grace within him, though the old Man's Corruptions are naturally the weakest.

Thus they sat talking till break of day. Now, when the Family was up, *Christiana* bid her son *James* that he should read a Chapter; so he read the 53d of *Isaiah*. When he had done, Mr. *Honest* asked why it was said *That the Saviour* Another *is said to come out of a dry Ground, and also, that he had* Question *no Form nor Comeliness in him?*

Greath. Then said Mr. *Great-heart*, To the first I answer, because, The Church of the Jews, of which Christ came, had then lost almost all the Sap and Spirit of Religion. To the second I say, The Words are spoken in the Person of the Unbelievers, who, because they want that Eye, that can see into our Prince's Heart, therefore they judge of him by the meanness of his Outside.

Just like those that know not that precious Stones are covered over with a homely *Crust;* who when they have found one, because they know not what they have found, cast it again away, as men do a common Stone.

Well, said *Gaius,* Now you are here, and since, as I know, Mr. *Great-heart* is good at his Weapons, if you please, after we have refreshed ourselves, we will walk into the Fields,

Giant Slay-good
assaulted and
slain

to see if we can do any good. About a mile from hence there is one *Slay-good,* a *Giant,* that doth much annoy the King's Highway in these parts. And I know whereabout his Haunt is, he is master of a number of Thieves: 'twould be well if we could clear these Parts of him.

So they consented and went, Mr. *Great-heart* with his *Sword, Helmet,* and *Shield;* and the rest with Spears and Staves.

He is found with
one Feeble-
mind *in his*
hands

When they came to the place where he was, they found him with one *Feeble-mind* in his Hands, whom his Servants had brought unto him, having taken him in the Way; now the Giant was rifling of him, with a purpose after that to pick his Bones. For he was of the nature of *Flesh-eaters.*

Well, so soon as he saw Mr. *Great-heart,* and his Friends, at the Mouth of his Cave, with their Weapons, he demanded what they wanted?

Greath. We want thee: for we are come to revenge the Quarrel of the many that thou hast slain of the Pilgrims, when thou hast dragged them out of the King's Highway: wherefore come out of thy Cave. So he armed himself and came out, and to Battle they went, and fought for above an Hour, and then stood still to take Wind.

Slay-good. *Then said the Giant, Why are you here on my Ground?*

Greath. To revenge the Blood of Pilgrims, as I also told thee before; so they went to it again, and the Giant made Mr. *Great-heart* give back, but he came up again, and in the greatness of his Mind, he let fly with such stoutness at the Giant's Head and Sides, that he made him let his Weapon fall out of his Hand. So he smote him and slew

Feeble-mind
rescued from the
Giant

him, and cut off his Head, and brought it away to the *Inn.* He also took *Feeble-mind* the Pilgrim, and brought him with him to his Lodgings. When they were come home, they showed his Head to the Family, and set it up as they had done others before, for a Terror to those that should attempt to do as he, hereafter.

Then they asked Mr. *Feeble-mind* how he fell into his hands?

Feeble. Then said the poor man, I am a sickly man, as *How* Feeble- you see, and because Death did usually once a day, *knock* mind *came to be* *at my Door,* I thought I should never be well at home. So I *a Pilgrim* betook myself to a Pilgrim's Life, and have travelled hither from the Town of *Uncertain*, where I and my Father were born. I am a man of no strength at all, of Body, nor yet of Mind, but would, if I could, though I can but *crawl,* spend my life in the Pilgrim's way. When I came at the Gate that is at the head of the Way, the Lord of that place did entertain me freely. Neither objected he against my weakly Looks, nor against my *feeble Mind;* but gave me such things as were necessary for my Journey, and bid me hope to the end. When I came to the House of the *Interpreter,* I received much Kindness there: and because the Hill *Difficulty* was judged too hard for me, I was carried up that by one of his Servants. Indeed I have found much Relief from Pilgrims, though none was willing to go so softly as I am forced to do. Yet still as they came on, they bid me be of good Cheer, and said, that it was the will of their Lord that Comfort 1 Thess. 5.14 should be given to the *feeble-minded,* and so went on their *own* pace. When I was come up to *Assault-Lane,* then this *Giant* met with me, and bid me prepare for an *Encounter;* but, alas, feeble one that I was, I had more need of a *Cordial.* So he came up and took me. I conceited[95] he would not kill me; also when he had got me into his Den, since I went not with him *willingly,* I believed I should come out alive again. For I have heard, that not any Pilgrim that is *Mark this* taken captive by violent Hands, if he keeps Heart-whole towards his Master, is by the Laws of Providence to die by the Hand of the Enemy. *Robbed* I looked to be, and Robbed[96] to be sure I am; but I am as you see, escaped with Life, for the which I thank my King as Author, and you, as the Means. Other Brunts I also look for, but this I have resolved on, to wit, to *run* when I can, to *go* when I cannot *Mark this* *run,* and to *creep* when I cannot *go.* As to the main, I thank him that loved me, I am fixed; my way is before me, my Mind is beyond the *River* that has no Bridge, though I am, as you see, but of a *feeble Mind.*

Hon. *Then said old Mr.* Honest, *Have not you sometime ago, been acquainted with one Mr.* Fearing, *a* Pilgrim?

Feeble. Acquainted with him; Yes. He came from the Town of *Stupidity,* which lieth *four Degrees* to the Northward of the City of *Destruction,* and as many off, of where I was born: Yet we were well acquainted, for indeed he was mine Uncle, my Father's Brother. He and I have been much of a Temper: he was a little shorter than I, but yet we were much of a Complexion.[97]

Mr. Fearing *Mr.* Feeble-mind's *Uncle* Feeble-mind *has some of Mr.* Fearing's *Features*

Hon. *I perceive you knew him, and I am apt to believe also that you were related one to another; for you have his whitely look, a Cast like his with your Eye, and your Speech is much alike.*

Feeble. Most have said so, that have known us both: and, besides, what I have read in him, I have for the most part, found in my self.

Gaius *comforts him*

Gaius. *Come Sir, said good* Gaius, be of good Cheer; you are welcome to me, and to my House; and what thou hast a mind to, call for freely; and what thou wouldst have my Servants do for thee, they will do it with a ready Mind.

Feeble. Then said Mr. *Feeble-mind,* This is unexpected Favour, and as the Sun, shining out of a very dark Cloud. Did Giant *Slay-good* intend me this Favour when he stopped me, and resolved to let me go no further? Did he intend, that after he had rifled my Pockets, I should go to *Gaius mine Host?* Yet so it is.

Notice to be taken of Providence

Now, just as Mr. *Feeble-mind* and *Gaius* were thus in talk; there comes one running, and called at the Door, and told, That about a Mile and a half off, there was one Mr. *Not-right,* a Pilgrim, struck dead upon the place where he was, with a *Thunder-bolt.*

Tidings how one Not-right *was slain with a Thunder-bolt, and Mr.* Feeble-mind's *Comment upon it*

Feeble. Alas! said Mr. *Feeble-mind,* is he slain, he overtook me some days before I came so far as hither, and would be my Company-keeper. He was also with me when *Slay-good* the Giant took me, but he was nimble of his Heels, and escaped. But it seems, he escaped to die, and I was took to live.

What, one would think, doth seek to slay outright,
Ofttimes, delivers from the saddest Plight.
That very Providence, *whose Face is* Death,
Doth oft times to the lowly, Life bequeath.
I was taken, he did escape and flee;
Hands Cross'd[98] *gave Death to him, and Life to me.*

Now, about this time *Matthew* and *Mercy* were married;
also *Gaius* gave his daughter *Phebe* to *James, Matthew's*
Brother, to Wife; after which time, they yet stayed about
ten days at *Gaius'* House, spending their time, and the
Seasons, like as Pilgrims use to do.

When they were to depart, *Gaius* made them a Feast,
and they did eat and drink, and were merry. Now the
Hour was come that they must be gone; wherefore Mr.
Great-heart called for a Reckoning. But *Gaius* told him
that at his House, it was not the Custom for *Pilgrims* to
pay for their Entertainment. He boarded them by the year,
but looked for his Pay from the good *Samaritan,* who had
promised him, at his return, whatsoever Charge he was at
with them, faithfully to repay him. Then said Mr. *Great-
heart* to him,

Greath. *Beloved, thou dost faithfully, whatsoever thou
dost, to the Brethren, and to Strangers, who have borne
Witness of thy Charity before the Church, whom if thou
(yet) bring forward on their Journey, after a Godly sort,
thou shalt do well.*

Then Gaius took his Leave of them all, and of his Children, and particularly of Mr. *Feeble-mind*. He also gave
him something to drink by the way.

Now Mr. *Feeble-mind,* when they were going out of the
Door, made as if he intended to linger. The which, when
Mr. *Great-heart* espied, he said, Come, Mr. *Feeble-mind,*
pray do you go along with us: I will be your *Conductor,*
and you shall fare as the rest.

Feeble. *Alas, I want a suitable Companion, you are all
lusty and strong, but I, as you see, am weak; I choose
therefore rather to come behind, lest, by reason of my many*

The Pilgrims prepare to go forward

Luke 10.33, 34, 35. How they greet one another at part-ing. 1 Joh. 5.6

Gaius his last kindness to Feeble-mind

Feeble-mind for going behind

Infirmities, I should be both a Burden to myself and to you. I am, as I said, a man of a weak and feeble Mind, and shall be offended and made weak at that which others can bear. I shall like no Laughing; I shall like no gay Attire; I shall

His Excuse for it

like no unprofitable Questions. Nay, I am so weak a Man, as to be offended with that which others have a liberty to do. I do not yet know all the Truth; I am a very ignorant Christian man; *sometimes if I hear some rejoice in the Lord, it troubles me because I cannot do so too. It is with me as it is with a weak Man among the strong, or as with a sick Man among the healthy, or as a Lamp despised, (He that is ready to slip with his Feet, is as a Lamp despised in the*

Job 12.5

Thought of him that is at ease.) So that I know not what to Do.

Greath. But Brother, said Mr. *Great-heart,* I have it in *Commission,* to comfort the *feeble-minded,* and to support

Great-heart's
Commission.
1 Thess. 5.14
Rom. 14. 1 Cor.
8, Chap. 9.22.
A Christian
Spirit

the weak. You must needs go along with us; we will wait for you, we will lend you our help, we will deny ourselves of some things, both *Opinionative* and *Practical,* for your sake; we will not enter into Doubtful Disputations before you; we will be made all things to you rather than you shall be left behind.

Now, all this while they were at *Gaius'* door; and behold, as they were thus in the heat of their Discourse, Mr. *Ready-*

Psa. 38.17.
Promises

to-halt came by, with his *Crutches* in his hand, and he also was going on Pilgrimage.

Feeble. *Then said Mr.* Feeble-mind *to him, Man! How camest thou hither? I was but now complaining that I had not a suitable Companion, but thou art according to my*

Feeble-mind
glad to see
Ready-to-halt
come by

Wish. Welcome, welcome, good Mr. Ready-to-halt, *I hope thou and I may be some help.*

Readyto. I shall be glad of thy Company, said the other; and, good Mr. *Feeble-mind,* rather than we will part, since we are thus happily met, I will lend thee one of my Crutches.

Feeble. *Nay, said he, though I thank thee for thy good Will, I am not inclined to halt afore I am Lame. Howbeit, I think when occasion is, it may help me against a Dog.*

Readyto. If either my *self,* or my Crutches can do thee a pleasure, we are both at thy Command, good Mr. *Feeblemind.*

Thus therefore they went on, Mr. *Great-heart,* and Mr. *Honest* went before, *Christiana* and her Children went next, and Mr. *Feeble-mind* and Mr. *Ready-to-halt* came behind with his Crutches. Then said Mr. *Honest,*

Hon. *Pray Sir, now we are upon the Road, tell us some profitable things of some that have gone on Pilgrimage before us.*   *New Talk*

Greath. With a good Will. I suppose you have heard how *Christian* of old did meet with *Apollyon* in the Valley of *Humiliation,* and also what hard work he had to go thorough the Valley of the Shadow of Death. Also I think you cannot but have heard how *Faithful* was put to it by *Madam Wanton,* with *Adam* the first, with one *Discontent,* 1 Part *from* pag. and *Shame;* four as deceitful Villains, as a man can meet 73 to pag. 78 with upon the Road.

Hon. *Yes, I have heard of all this; but indeed good* Faithful *was hardest put to it with* Shame, *he was an unwearied one.*

Greath. Aye; for, as the pilgrim well said, He of all men had the wrong name.

Hon. *But pray, sir, where was it that* Christian *and* Faithful *met* Talkative? *That same was also a notable one.*

Greath. He was a confident Fool, yet many followed his ways.

Hon. *He had like to a beguiled* Faithful?

Greath. Aye, but *Christian* put him into a way quickly to find him out. Thus they went on till they came to the 1 Part pag. 89 place where *Evangelist* met with *Christian* and *Faithful,* and prophesied to them what should befall them at *Vanity-Fair.*

Greath. Then said their *Guide,* hereabouts did *Christian* and *Faithful* meet with *Evangelist,* who prophesied to them of what troubles they should meet with at Vanity-Fair.

Hon. *Say you so! I dare say it was a hard Chapter that then he did read unto them?*

Greath. 'Twas so, but he gave them Encouragement

1 Part pag. 90,
&c. withal. But what do we talk of them, they were a couple of Lion-like Men; they had set their faces like Flint.[99] Don't you remember how undaunted they were when they stood before the Judge?

Hon. *Well:* Faithful *bravely suffered.*

Greath. So he did, and as brave things came on't; For *Hopeful,* and some others, as the Story relates it, were Converted by his Death.

Hon. *Well, but pray go on; for you are well acquainted with things.*

Greath. Above all that *Christian* met with after he had passed thorough *Vanity Fair,* one *By-ends* was the arch
1 Part pag. 102 one.

Hon. *By-Ends: What was he?*

Greath. A very arch Fellow, a downright Hypocrite; one that would be Religious, which way ever the World went, but so cunning, that he would be sure never to lose, nor suffer for it.

He had his *Mode* of Religion for every fresh Occasion, and his Wife was as good at it as he. He would turn and change from Opinion to Opinion; yea, and plead for so doing, too. But, so far as I could learn, he came to an ill End with his *By-Ends,* nor did I ever hear that any of his Children were ever of any Esteem with any that truly feared God.

They are come within sight of Vanity. Psa. 21.16

Now by this time they were come within sight of the Town of *Vanity,* where *Vanity-Fair* is kept. So when they saw that they were so near the Town, they consulted with one another how they should pass thorough the Town; and some said one thing, and some another. At last Mr. *Great-heart* said, I have, as you may understand, often been a *Conductor* of Pilgrims thorough this Town. Now, I am acquainted with one Mr. *Mnason,*[100] a *Cyprusian* by nation,

They enter into one Mr. Mnason's to Lodge

an old disciple, at whose House we may Lodge. If you think good, said he, we will turn in there?

Content, said Old *Honest;* Content, said *Christiana;* Content, said Mr. *Feeble-mind;* and so they said all. Now you must think it was *Even-tide,* by that they got to the outside of the Town, but Mr. *Great-Heart* knew the way to the Old Man's House. So thither they came; and he called at the Door, and the old Man within knew his Tongue as soon as ever he heard it; so he opened the door, and they all came in. Then said *Mnason* their Host, How far have ye come to-day? So they said, from the House of *Gaius* our Friend. I promise you, said he, you have gone a good Stitch,[101] you may well be a weary; sit down. So they sat down.

Greath. *Then said their Guide, Come, what Cheer Sirs? I dare say you are welcome to my Friend.*

Mna. I also, said Mr. *Mnason,* do bid you Welcome; and whatever you want, do but say, and we will do what we can to get it for you.

Hon. *Our great Want a while since, was Harbour, and good Company, and now I hope we have both.* They are glad of entertainment

Mna. For Harbour, you see what it is, but for good Company, that will appear in the Trial.

Greath. *Well, said Mr. Great-heart, will you have the Pilgrims up into their Lodging?*

Mna. I will, said Mr. *Mnason.* So he had them to their respective Places; and also showed them a very fair Dining-room, where they might be, and sup together, until the time should come to go to Rest.

Now when they were seated in their places, and were a little cheery after their Journey, Mr. *Honest* asked his Landlord if there was any store of good People in the Town?

Mna. We have a few, for indeed they are but a few, when compared with them on the other Side.

Hon. *But how shall we do to see some of them? for the Sight of good Men to them that are going on Pilgrimage, is like the appearing of the Moon and Stars to them that are sailing upon the Seas.* They desire to see some of the good People in the Town

Mna. Then Mr. *Mnason* stamped with his Foot, and his daughter *Grace* came up; so he said unto her, *Grace* go you, tell my Friends, Mr. *Contrite,* Mr. *Holy-man,* Some sent for Mr. *Love-saint,* Mr. *Dare-not-lie,* and Mr. *Penitent;* that I have a Friend or two at my House, that have a mind this evening to see them.

So *Grace* went to call them, and they came; and after Salutation made, they sat down together at the Table.

Mna. Then said Mr. *Mnason* their Landlord, My Neighbours, I have, as you see, a company of *Strangers* come to my House, they are *Pilgrims:* They come from afar, and are going to Mount *Zion.* But who, quoth he, do you think this is? pointing with his Finger to *Christiana.* It is *Christiana,* the wife of *Christian,* the famous Pilgrim, who, with *Faithful* his Brother, was so shamefully handled in our Town. At that they stood amazed, saying, we little thought to see *Christiana* when *Grace* came to call us; wherefore this is a very comfortable Surprise. They then asked her of her welfare, and if these young Men were her Husband's Sons. And when she had told them they were; they said, The King, whom you love and serve, make you as your Father, and bring you where he is in Peace.

Some Talk   *Hon.* Then Mr. *Honest (when they were all sat down)*
betwixt Mr.   asked *Mr.* Contrite and the rest, in what posture their Town
Honest and   was at present.
Contrite

The Fruit of   *Cont.* You may be sure we are full of Hurry, in Fair time.
Watchfulness   'Tis hard keeping our Hearts and Spirits in any good Order, when we are in a cumbered[102] Condition. He that lives in such a place as this is, and has to do with such as we have, has Need of an Item, to caution him to take heed, every Moment of the Day.

Hon. But how are your Neighbors now for quietness?

Persecution not   *Cont.* They are much more moderate now than formerly.
so hot at Vanity   You know how *Christian* and *Faithful* were used at our
Fair as formerly   Town; but of late, I say, they have been far more moderate. I think the Blood of *Faithful* lieth with load upon them till now; for since they burned him, they have been ashamed to burn any more. In those days we were afraid to walk the Streets, but now we can show our Heads. *Then* the Name of a Professor was odious; *now,* specially in some parts of

our Town, (for you know our Town is large,) Religion is counted Honourable.

Then said Mr. Contrite *to them, Pray how fareth it with you in your Pilgrimage? how stands the Country affected towards you?*

Hon. It happens to us, as it happeneth to Wayfaring men: sometimes our way is clean, sometimes foul; sometimes up hill, sometimes down hill; We are seldom at a Certainty. The Wind is not always on our Backs, nor is every one a friend that we meet with in the Way. We have met with some notable Rubs already; and what are yet behind we know not; but for the most part, we find it true that has been talked of old: *A good Man must suffer Trouble.*[103]

Cont. *You talk of Rubs, what Rubs have you met withal?*

Hon. Nay, ask Mr. *Great-heart,* our Guide; for he can give the best Account of that.

Greath. We have been beset three or four times already: First *Christiana* and her Children were beset by two Ruffians, that they feared would take away their Lives; We was beset by Giant *Bloody-man,* Giant *Maul,* and Giant *Slay-good.* Indeed, we did rather beset the last, than were beset by him. And thus it was: after we had been some time at the house of *Gaius mine Host, and of the whole Church,* we were minded upon a time to take our Weapons with us, and go see if we could light upon any of those that are Enemies to Pilgrims; (for we heard that there was a notable one thereabouts). Now *Gaius* knew his Haunt better than I, because he dwelt thereabout. So we looked, and looked, till at last we discerned the Mouth of his Cave: then we were glad, and pluck'd up our Spirits. So we approached up to his *Den;* and lo when we came there, he had dragged by mere force into his Net, this *poor man,* Mr. *Feeble-mind,* and was about to bring him to his End. But when he saw us, supposing, as we thought, he had another Prey, he left the poor man in his Hole, and came out. So we fell to it full sore, and he lustily laid about him; but, in conclusion, he was brought down to the Ground, and his Head cut off, and set up by the Way-side for a Terror to such as should after practise such Ungodliness. That I tell you the Truth, here is the man himself to affirm it, who was as a Lamb taken out of the Mouth of the Lion.

Feeble. *Then said Mr.* Feeble-mind, *I found this true, to my Cost and Comfort; to my Cost, when he threatened to pick my bones every moment; and to my Comfort, when I saw Mr.* Great-heart *and his Friends with their Weapons approach so near for my* Deliverance.

Mr. Holy-man's
Speech

Holym. Then said Mr. *Holy-man,* there are two things that they have need to possess who go on Pilgrimage, *Courage,* and an *unspotted Life.* If they have not *Courage,* they can never hold on their way; and if their Lives be *loose,* they will make the very Name of a *Pilgrim* stink.

Mr. Love-saint's
Speech

Loves. Then said Mr. *Love-saint;* I hope this Caution is not needful amongst you. But truly there are many that go upon the Road, that rather declare themselves Strangers to Pilgrimage, than Strangers and Pilgrims in the Earth.

Mr. Dare-not-lie
his Speech

Dareno. *Then said Mr.* Dare-not-lie, *'Tis true; they neither have the Pilgrim's Weed, nor the Pilgrim's Courage; they go not uprightly, but all* awry *with their Feet; one shoe goeth* inward, *another* outward; *and their Hosen out behind;* there a *Rag,* and there a *Rent,* to the disparagement of their Lord.

Mr. Penitent *his
Speech*

Penit. These things, said Mr. *Penitent,* they ought to be troubled for, nor are the Pilgrims like to have that grace put upon them and their pilgrim's Progress, as they desire, until the way is cleared of such Spots and Blemishes.

Thus they sat talking and spending the time, until Supper was set upon the Table, unto which they went and refreshed their weary Bodies; so they went to Rest. Now they staid in this Fair a great while, at the house of this Mr. *Mnason,* who in process of time gave his Daughter *Grace* unto *Samuel, Christiana's* Son, to Wife, and his Daughter *Martha* to *Joseph.*

The time as I said, that they staid here, was long, (for it was not now as in former times.) Wherefore the *Pilgrims* grew acquainted with many of the good people of the

Town, and did them what *Service* they could. *Mercy*, as she was wont, laboured much for the Poor, wherefore their Bellies and Backs blessed her, and she was there an Ornament to her Profession. And, to say the truth, for *Grace*, *Phebe*, and *Martha*, they were all of a very good Nature, and did much good in their place. They were also all of them very Fruitful; so that *Christian's* name, as was said before, was like to live in the World.

While they lay here, there came a *Monster* out of the Woods, and slew many of the people of the Town. It would also carry away their Children, and teach them to suck its Whelps. Now, no man in the town durst so much as face this *Monster;* but all fled when they heard the noise of his coming. *A Monster*

The *Monster* was like unto no one Beast upon the Earth. Its Body was like a Dragon, and it had seven Heads and ten Horns.[104] *It made great havoc of Children, and yet it was governed by a Woman.* This *Monster* propounded Conditions to men; and such men as loved their Lives more than their Souls, accepted of those Conditions. So they came under. *Rev. 17.3. His Shape. His Nature*

Now this Mr. *Great-heart*, together with these who came to visit the Pilgrims at Mr. *Mnason's* House, entered into a Covenant to go and engage this Beast, if perhaps they might deliver the People of this Town, from the Paws and Mouths of this so devouring a Serpent.

Then did Mr. *Great-heart*, Mr. *Contrite*, Mr. *Holy-man*, Mr. *Dare-not-lie*, and Mr. *Penitent*, with their Weapons go forth to meet him. Now the Monster at first was very Rampant, and looked upon these Enemies with great Disdain; but they so belaboured him, being sturdy men at Arms, that they made him make a Retreat; so they came home to Mr. *Mnason's* House again. *How he is engaged*

The *Monster*, you must know, had his certain Seasons to come out in, and to make his attempts upon the Children of the People of the Town. At these Seasons did these valiant Worthies watch him in, and did still continually assault him; in so much that in process of time he became

not only wounded, but lame. Also he has not made that
havoc of the Townsmen's children as formerly he had done;
and it is verily believed by some that this Beast will die of
his Wounds.

This therefore made Mr. *Great-heart* and his Fellows, of
great Fame in this Town, so that many of the People that
wanted their taste of things, yet had a reverent Esteem and
Respect for them. Upon this account, therefore, it was, that
these Pilgrims got not much hurt here. True, there were
some of the baser sort, that could see no more than a
Mole, nor understand any more than a Beast; these had no
reverence for these men, nor took they notice of their
Valour or Adventures.

Well, the time grew on that the Pilgrims must go on their
way; wherefore they prepared for their Journey. They sent
for their Friends, they conferred with them, they had some
time set apart; therein to commit each other to the Protection of their Prince. There were again, that brought them
of such things as they had, that were fit for the weak, and
the strong, for the Women, and the men; and so *laded* them
with such things as was necessary.

Then they set forward on their way, and their Friends
accompanying them so far as was convenient, they again
committed each other to the Protection of their King, and
parted.

They therefore that were of the Pilgrims' Company went
on, and Mr. *Great-heart* went before them. Now, the
Women and Children being weakly, they were forced to go
as they could bear; by this means Mr. *Ready-to-halt,* and
Mr. *Feeble-mind,* had more to sympathize with their Condition.

When they were gone from the Townsmen, and when
their Friends had bid them farewell, they quickly came to
the place where *Faithful* was put to death. Therefore they
made a stand, and thanked him that had enabled him to bear
his Cross so well; and the rather, because they now found
that they had a benefit by such a Manly Suffering as his was.

1 Part p. 101   They went on therefore after this, a good way further,

talking of *Christian* and *Faithful,* and how *Hopeful* joined himself to *Christian* after that *Faithful* was dead.

Now they were come up with the *Hill Lucre,* where the *Silver-mine* was, which took *Demas* off from his Pilgrimage, and into which, as some think, *By-ends* fell and perished; wherefore they considered that. But when they were come to the old Monument that stood over against the *Hill Lucre,* to wit, to the Pillar of Salt, that stood also within view of *Sodom* and its stinking lake; they marvelled, as did *Christian* before, that men of that Knowledge and ripeness of Wit as they was, should be so blinded as to turn aside here. Only they considered again, that Nature is not affected with the Harms that others have met with, especially if that thing upon which they look, has an attracting Virtue upon the foolish Eye.[105]

I saw now that they went on till they came at the River that was on this Side of the delectable Mountains. To the River where the fine Trees grow on both sides, and whose Leaves, if taken inwardly, are good against Surfeits;[106] where the Meadows are green all the year long, and where they might lie down safely. 1 Part p. 113 Psal. 23

By this River side in the meadows, there were Cotes and Folds for Sheep, a House built for the *nourishing* and bringing up of those Lambs, the Babes of those Women that go on Pilgrimage. Also there was here one that was entrusted with them, who could have compassion, and that could gather these Lambs with his Arm, and carry them in his Bosom, and gently lead those that were with young. Now, to the Care of *this Man Christiana* admonished her four Daughters to commit their little ones; that by these waters they might be housed, harboured, succoured, and nourished, and that none of them might *be lacking in time to come.* This *man,*[107] if any of them go astray, or be lost, he will bring them again; he will also bind up that which was broken, and will strengthen them that are sick. Here they will never want Meat and Drink and Clothing, here they will be kept from Thieves and Robbers, for this man will die before one of those committed to his Trust shall be Heb. 5.2. Isa. 40.11 Jer. 23.4. Ezek. 34.11, 12, 13, 14, 15, 16

John 10.16 lost. Besides, here they shall be sure to have good *Nurture* and Admonition, and shall be taught to walk in right Paths, and that you know is a Favour of no small account. Also here, as you see, are delicate *Waters,* pleasant *Meadows,* dainty *Flowers,* Variety of *Trees,* and such as bear *wholesome Fruit.* Fruit, not like that which *Matthew* ate of, that fell over the wall out of *Beelzebub's* garden; but Fruit that procureth Health where there is none, and that continueth and increaseth it where it is.

So they were content to commit their little Ones to him; and that which was also an encouragement to them so to do, was, for that all this was to be at the Charge of the King, and so was as an Hospital to young Children, and *Orphans.*

They being come to By-path Stile, have a mind to have a pluck with Giant Despair

Now they went on: And when they were come to *By-path* Meadow, to the Stile over which *Christian* went with his Fellow *Hopeful,* when they were taken by *Giant Despair* and put into *Doubting* Castle: They sat down, and consulted what was best to be done, to wit, now they were so strong, and had got such a man as Mr. *Great-heart* for

1 Part p. 116 their Conductor, whether they had not best to make an Attempt upon the Giant, demolish his Castle, and if there were any Pilgrims in it, to set them at liberty before they went any further. So one said one thing, and another said the contrary. One questioned if it was lawful to go upon *unconsecrated* ground, another said they might, provided their end was good; but Mr. *Great-heart* said, Though that Assertion offered last cannot be universally true, yet I have a Commandment to resist Sin, to overcome Evil, to fight the good Fight of Faith: and I pray, with whom should I fight this good fight, if not with *Giant Despair?* I will therefore attempt the taking away of his Life, and the demolishing of *Doubting* Castle. Then said he, Who will go with me? Then said old *Honest*, I will. And so will we

1 John 2.13, 14 too, said *Christiana's* four sons, *Matthew, Samuel, James,* and *Joseph;* for they were young men and strong.

So they left the Women in the Road, and with them Mr.

Feeble-mind, and Mr. *Ready-to-halt* with his Crutches, to
be their Guard, until they came back; for in that place
though *Giant Despair* dwelt so near, they keeping in the
road, *A little child might lead them.*   Isa. 11.6

So Mr. *Great-heart, old Honest,* and the four young
men, went to go up to *Doubting* Castle, to look for *Giant
Despair.* When they came at the Castle Gate, they knocked
for entrance with an unusual Noise. At that the old *Giant*
comes to the Gate, and *Diffidence* his Wife follows. Then
said he, Who and what is he that is so hardy, as after
this manner to molest the *Giant Despair?* Mr. *Great-heart*
replied, It is I, *Great-heart,* one of the King of the Celestial
Country's Conductors of Pilgrims to their Place. And I
demand of thee that thou open thy Gates for my Entrance:
prepare thyself also to Fight, for I am come to take away
thy head; and to demolish *Doubting* Castle.

Now *Giant Despair,* because he was a *Giant,* thought no
man could overcome him: and again, thought he, Since   Despair *has over-*
heretofore I have made a Conquest of Angels, shall *Great-*   *come Angels*
heart* make me afraid? So he harnessed himself, and went
out. He had a Cap of Steel upon his Head, a Breast-plate
of Fire girded to him, and he came out in Iron-Shoes, with
a great Club in his Hand. Then these six men made up to
him, and beset him behind and Before; also, when *Diffi-*
dence* the *Giantess* came up to help him, old Mr. *Honest*
cut her down at one Blow. Then they fought for their Lives,
and *Giant Despair* was brought down to the Ground, *but
was very loth to die.* He struggled hard, and had, as they   Despair *is loth*
say, as many Lives as a Cat; but *Great-heart* was his death,   *to die*
for he left him not till he had severed his Head from his
shoulders.

Then they fell to demolishing *Doubting* Castle, and that   Doubting-
you know might with ease be done, since *Giant Despair*   Castle
was dead. They was seven days in destroying of that; and   *demolished*
in it of Pilgrims, they found one Mr. *Despondency,* almost
starved to Death, and one *Much-afraid* his Daughter:
these two they saved alive. But it would have made you a

wondered to have seen the dead Bodies that lay here and there in the Castle Yard, and how full of dead men's Bones the Dungeon was.

When Mr. *Great-heart* and his Companions had performed this Exploit, they took Mr. *Despondency,* and his daughter *Much-afraid,* into their Protection, for they were honest People, though they were Prisoners in *Doubting Castle* to that Tyrant *Giant Despair.* They, therefore, I say, took with them the Head of the Giant (for his Body they had buried under a heap of Stones,) and down to the road and to their Companions they came, and showed them what they had done. Now, when *Feeblemind* and *Ready-to-halt* saw that it was the head of *Giant Despair* indeed, they were very jocund and merry. Now *Christiana,* if need was, could play upon the *Viol,* and her Daughter *Mercy* upon the *Lute:* so, since they were so merry disposed, she played them a Lesson,[108] and *Ready-to-halt* would dance. So he took *Despondency's* daughter, named *Much-afraid,* by the Hand, and to Dancing they went in the Road. True, he could not Dance without one Crutch in his Hand, but I promise you, he footed it well: also the Girl was to be commended, for she answered the Music handsomely.

They have Music and Dancing for Joy

As for Mr. *Despondency,* the Music was not so much to him, he was for feeding rather than dancing, for that he was almost starved. So *Christiana* gave him some of her Bottle of Spirits for present Relief, and then prepared him something to eat; and in a little time the old Gentleman came to himself, and began to be finely revived.

Now I saw in my Dream, when all these things were finished, Mr. *Great-heart* took the Head of *Giant Despair,* and set it upon a Pole by the Highway side, right over against the Pillar that *Christian* erected for a *Caution* to Pilgrims that came after, to take heed of entering into his Grounds.

Then he writ under it upon a *Marble* stone these Verses following:

The doubting Castle be demolished,
And the Gyant dispair hath lost his head
Sin can rebuild the Castle, make't remaine;
And make despair the Gyant live againe

A Monument of
Deliverance

This is the Head of him, *Whose* Name *only*
In former times, did Pilgrims *terrify.*
His Castle's *down, and* Diffidence *his Wife*
Brave Master Great-heart *has bereft of Life.*
Despondency, *his Daughter* Much-afraid,
Great-heart, *for them, also the Man has play'd.*
Who hereof doubts, if he'll but cast his Eye
Up hither, may his Scruples satisfy.
This Head, also when doubting Cripples dance,
Doth show from Fears they have Deliverance.

When these men had thus bravely showed themselves
against *Doubting Castle,* and had slain *Giant Despair,* they
went forward, and went on till they came to the *Delectable*
Mountains, where *Christian* and *Hopeful* refreshed themselves with the Varieties of the Place. They also acquainted
themselves with the Shepherds there, who welcomed them
as they had done *Christian* before, unto the delectable
Mountains.

Now the Shepherds seeing so great a train follow Mr.
Great-heart, (for with him they were well acquainted,) they
said unto him, Good Sir, you have got a goodly company
here; pray where did you find all these?

Then Mr. *Great-heart* replied,

The Guide's
Speech to the
Shepherds

First here's Christiana *and her train,*
Her Sons, and her Sons' wives, who, like the Wain,[109]
Keep by the Pole, and do by Compass steer,
From Sin to Grace, else they had not been here.
Next here's old Honest *come on Pilgrimage,*
Ready-to-halt too, who I dare engage
True-hearted is, and so is Feeble-mind,
Who willing was, not to be left behind.
Despondency, *good man, is coming after,*
And so also is Much-afraid, *his daughter.*
May we have Entertainment here, or must
We further go? Let's know whereon to trust.

Then said the Shepherds; This is a comfortable Company; *Their Entertain-*
you are welcome to us; for we have for the *Feeble,* as well *ment.* Matt.
as for the *Strong;* our Prince has an Eye to what is done to 25.40
the least of these. Therefore Infirmity must not be a block
to our Entertainment. So they had them to the Palace Door,
and then said unto them, Come in *Mr. Feeble-mind;* come
in *Mr. Ready-to-halt;* Come in, *Mr. Despondency,* and *Mrs.*
Much-afraid his Daughter. These Mr. *Great-heart* said the
Shepherds to the Guide, we call in by name, for that they
are most subject to draw back; but as for you, and the rest
that are *strong,* we leave you to your wonted Liberty. Then
said Mr. *Great-heart,* This day I see that Grace doth shine
in your Faces, and that you are my Lord's Shepherds indeed; *A Description of*
for that you have not *pushed* these Diseased neither with *False Shepherds.*
Side nor Shoulder, but have rather strewed their way into Ezek. 34.21
the Palace with Flowers, as you should.

So the Feeble and weak went in, and Mr. *Great-heart*
and the rest did follow. When they were also set down, the
Shepherds said to those of the weakest sort, What is it that
you would have? For said they, all things must be managed
here, to the supporting of the weak, as well as to the
warning of the Unruly.

So they made them a Feast of things, easy of Digestion,
and that were pleasant to the Palate and nourishing; the
which when they had received, they went to their rest, each
one respectively unto his proper place. When Morning was
come, because the mountains were high, and the day clear;
and because it was the Custom of the Shepherds to show
the Pilgrims, before their departure, some Rarities; therefore, after they were ready, and had refreshed themselves,
the Shepherds took them out into the Fields, and showed
them first, what they had shown to *Christian* before.

Then they had them to some new places. The first was to
Mount-Marvel, where they looked, and beheld a man at a
Distance, *that tumbled the Hills about with Words.*[110] Then *Mount-*Marvel.
they asked the Shepherds what that should mean? So they 1 Part p. 133
told them, that that man was the son of one *Great-grace,*
of whom you read in the first part of the Records of the

Pilgrim's Progress. And he is set there to teach Pilgrims

Mar. 11.23, 24 how to believe down, or to tumble out of their ways, what Difficulties they should meet with, by faith. Then said *Mr. Great-heart,* I know him, he is a man above many.

Then they had them to another place, called *Mount*
Mount-Innocent *Innocent.* And there they saw a man clothed all in White; and two men, *Prejudice* and *Ill-will,* continually casting dirt upon him. Now behold the Dirt, whatsoever they cast at him, would in a little time fall off again, and his garment would look as clear as if no Dirt had been cast thereat.

Then said the Pilgrims, what means this? The Shepherds answered, This Man is named *Godlyman,* and this Garment is to show the Innocency of his Life. Now, those that throw Dirt at him, are such as hate his *Well-Doing,* but, as you see the Dirt will not stick upon his Clothes, so it shall be with him that liveth Innocently in the World. Whoever they be that would make such men dirty, they labour all in vain; for God, by that a little time is spent will cause that their *Innocence* shall break forth as the Light, and their Righteousness as the Noon day.

Mount-Charity Then they took them, and had them to *Mount-Charity,* where they showed them a man that had a bundle of Cloth lying before him, out of which he cut Coats and Garments, for the Poor that stood about him; yet his Bundle or Roll of Cloth was never the less.

Then said they, What should this be? This is, said the Shepherds, to show you, that he who has a Heart to give of his Labour to the Poor, shall never want wherewithal. He that watereth shall be watered himself. And the Cake that the Widow gave to the Prophet did not cause that she had the less in her Barrel.[111]

The Work of
one Fool, and
one Want-wit They had them also to the place where they saw one *Fool,* and one *Want-wit,* washing an *Ethiopian*[112] with intention to make him white, but the more they washed him, the blacker he was. Then they asked the Shepherds what that should mean. So they told them, saying, Thus it is with the vile Person; all means used to get such a one a

good Name, shall in Conclusion tend but to make him more abominable. Thus it was with the *Pharisees;* and so it shall be with all Hypocrites.

Then said *Mercy* the Wife of *Matthew* to *Christiana* her Mother, Mother, I would, if it might be, see the Hole in the Hill; or that, commonly Called, the *By-way* to Hell. So her Mother brake her mind to the Shepherds. Then they went to the Door; it was in the side of an Hill, and they opened it, and bid *Mercy* hearken a while. So she hearkened, and heard one saying, *Cursed be my Father for holding of my Feet back from the way of Peace and Life;* and another said, *Oh that I had been torn in pieces before I had, to save my Life, lost my Soul;* and another said, *If I were to live again, how would I deny myself, rather than to come to this place.* Then there was as if the very Earth groaned, and quaked under the Feet of this young Woman for fear; so she looked white, and came trembling away, saying, Blessed be he and she that is delivered from this Place.

1 Part p. 126

Mercy has a mind to see the hole in the Hill

Now, when the Shepherds had shown them all these things, then they had them back to the Palace, and entertained them with what the House would afford. But *Mercy* being a young, and breeding Woman, longed for something that she saw there, but was ashamed to ask. Her Mother-in-law then asked her what she ailed, for she looked as one not well. Then said *Mercy, There is a Looking glass hangs up in the Dining-room,* off which I cannot take my mind; if therefore I have it not, I think I shall Miscarry. Then said her Mother, I will mention thy Wants to the Shepherds, and they will not deny it thee. But she said, I am ashamed that these men should know that I longed. Nay, my Daughter, said she, it is no Shame, but a Virtue, to long for such a thing as that; so *Mercy* said, Then Mother, if you please, ask the Shepherds if they are willing to sell it.

Mercy longeth, and for what

Now the Glass was one of a thousand.[113] It would present a man, one way with his own Feature exactly; and turn it but another way, and it would show one the very Face and Similitude of the Prince of Pilgrims himself. Yes, I have talked with them that can tell, and they have said that they

It was the Word of God

Jam. 1.23

1 Cor. 13.12 have seen the very Crown of Thorns upon his Head, by looking in that Glass; they have therein also seen the holes 2 Cor. 3.18 in his Hands, his Feet, and his Side. Yea such an excellency is there in this Glass, that it will show him to one where they have a mind to see him; whether living or dead, whether in Earth or Heaven, whether in a State of Humiliation, or in his Exaltation, whether coming to Suffer, or coming to Reign.

1 Part p. 124   *Christiana* therefore went to the Shepherds apart. (Now the Names of the Shepherds were *Knowledge, Experience, Watchful,* and *Sincere*) and said unto them, There is one of my Daughters, a breeding Woman, that, I think doth long for something that she hath seen in this House, and she thinks that she shall miscarry if she should by you be denied.

Experience. Call her, call her, She shall assuredly have *She doth not* what we can help her to. So they called her, and said to *lose her Longing* her, *Mercy,* what is that thing thou wouldst have? Then she blushed, and said, The great Glass that hangs up in the Dining-room: so *Sincere* ran and fetched it, and with a joyful Consent it was given her. Then she bowed her Head and gave Thanks, and said, by this I know that I have obtained Favour in your Eyes.

They also gave to the other young Women such things as they desired, and to their Husbands great Commendations for that they joined with Mr. *Great-heart* in the slaying of *Giant-Despair,* and the demolishing of *Doubting-Castle.*

How the   About *Christiana's* Neck, the Shepherds put a Bracelet, *Shepherds adorn* and so did they about the Necks of her four Daughters; *the Pilgrims* also they put Ear-rings in their Ears, and Jewels on their Fore-heads.[114]

When they were minded to go hence, They let them go in Peace, but gave not to them those certain Cautions which before was given to *Christian* and his Companion. The Reason was, for that these had *Great-heart* to be their 1 Part p. 127 Guide, who was one that was well acquainted with things,

and so could give them their Cautions more seasonably, to
wit, even when the Danger was nigh the approaching.

What Cautions *Christian* and his Companions had
received of the Shepherds, they had also lost by that the
time was come that they had need to put them in practice. 1 Part p. 136
Wherefore here was the Advantage that this Company had
over the other.

From hence they went on Singing, and they said,

> *Behold, how* fitly *are the Stages set!*
> *For their Relief, that Pilgrims are become;*
> *And how they* us *receive without* one *let,*
> *That make the* other *Life our* Mark *and Home,*
> *What* Novelties *they have, to us they give,*
> *That we,* though *Pilgrims, joyful lives may Live,*
> *They do upon us too such things bestow,*
> *That show we Pilgrims are, where'er we go.*

When they were gone from the Shepherds, they quickly
came to the Place where *Christian* met with one *Turn-away*
that dwelt in the Town of *Apostasy.* Wherefore of him Mr.
Great-heart their Guide did now put them in Mind; saying, 1 Part p. 129
This is the place where *Christian* met with one *Turn-away,*
who carried with him the Character of his Rebellion at his
Back. And this I have to say concerning this man, He would
hearken to no Counsel, but once a falling, persuasion could
not stop him. When he came to the place where the Cross *How one* Turn-
and Sepulchre was, he did meet with one that did bid him away *managed*
look there, but he gnashed with his Teeth, and stamped, Heb. 10.26, 27,
and said he was resolved to go back to his own Town. 28, 29
Before he came to the Gate, he met with *Evangelist,* who
offered to lay Hands on him, to turn him into the way
again; but this *Turn-away resisted him,* and having done
much *despite* unto him, he got away over the wall, and so
escaped his Hand.

Then they went on; and just at the place where *Little-
Faith* formerly was Robbed, there stood a man with his

One Valiant-for-
Truth *beset with
Thieves*
Sword drawn, and his Face all Bloody. Then said Mr. *Great-heart,* What art thou? The man made Answer, saying, I am one whose Name is *Valiant-for-Truth.* I am a Pilgrim, and am going to the Celestial City. Now, as I was in my way, there were three men did beset me, and propounded unto me these three things: 1. Whether I would become one of them? 2. Or go back from whence I came? 3. Or die upon the place? To the first I answered, I had

Prov. 1.10, 11,
12, 13, 14
been a true Man a long Season, and therefore it could not be expected that I should now cast in my Lot with Thieves. Then they demanded what I would say to the Second. So I told them that the Place from whence I came, had I not found Incommodity there, I had not forsaken it at all; but finding it altogether unsuitable to me, and very unprofitable for me, I forsook it for this Way. Then they asked me what I said to the third. And I told them, my Life cost more dear far, than that I should lightly give it away. Besides, you have nothing to do thus to put things to my Choice; wherefore at your Peril be it if you meddle. Then these three, to wit, *Wild-head, Inconsiderate,* and *Pragmatic,* drew upon me, and I also drew upon them.

*How he behaved
himself, and put
them to flight*
So we fell to it, one against three, for the space of above three hours. They have left upon me, as you see, some of the Marks of their Valour, and have also carried away with them some of mine. They are but just now gone. I suppose they might, as the saying is, hear your Horse dash, and so they betook them to flight.

Greath. *But here was great Odds, three against one.*

Valiant. 'Tis true, but *little* and *more,* are nothing to him

Psal. 27.3.
*Great-heart
wonders at his
Valour*
that has the Truth on his side. *Though an Host should encamp against me, said one, My Heart shall not fear. Though War should rise against me, in this will I be Confident, etc.* Besides, said he, I have read in some Records, that one man has fought an Army; and how many did *Samson* slay with the Jaw-bone of an Ass!

Greath. *Then said the Guide, Why did you not cry out, that some might have come in for your Succour?*

Valiant. So I did, to my King, who I knew could hear, and afford invisible Help, and that was sufficient for me.

Greath. *Then said* Great-heart *to Mr.* Valiant-for-truth, *Thou hast worthily behaved thy self; Let me see thy Sword; so he showed it him.*

Has a mind to see his Sword, and spends his Judgement on it

When he had taken it in his Hand, and looked thereon awhile, he said, Ha! *It is a right* Jerusalem *Blade.*

Isa. 2.3

Valiant. It is so. Let a man have one of *these Blades,* with a Hand to wield it, and skill to use it, and he may venture upon an Angel with it. He need not fear its holding, if he can but tell how to lay on. Its Edges will never blunt. It will cut *Flesh,* and *Bones,* and *Soul,* and *Spirit,* and all.

Ephes. 6.12, 13, 14, 15, 16, 17

Heb. 4.12

Greath. *But you fought a great while, I wonder you was not weary?*

Valiant. I fought till my sword did cleave to my Hand, and then they were joined together, as if a Sword grew out of my Arm; and when the Blood ran thorough my Fingers, then I fought with most Courage.

2 Sa. 23.10. *The Word. The Faith. The Blood*

Greath. *Thou hast done well, thou hast resisted unto Blood,*[115] *striving against Sin. Thou shalt abide by us, come in, and go out with us; for we are thy Companions.*

Then they took him and washed his Wounds, and gave him of what they had, to refresh him: and so they went together. Now, as they went on, because Mr. *Great-heart* was delighted in him, (for he loved one greatly that he found to be a man of his Hands,) and because there was with his Company, them that was feeble and weak; Therefore he questioned with him about many things; as first, *what Country-man he was?*

Valiant. I am of *Dark-land;* for there was I born, and there my Father and Mother are still.

What country man Mr. Valiant *was*

Greath. *Dark-land,* said the Guide, *Doth not that lie on the same Coast with the City of* Destruction?

Valiant. Yes it doth. Now that which caused me to come on Pilgrimage was this. We had one Mr. *Tell-true* came in to our parts, and he told it about, what *Christian* had done, that went from the City of *Destruction.* Namely, how he

How Mr. Valiant *came to go on Pilgrimage*

had forsaken his *Wife* and *Children,* and had betaken himself to a *Pilgrim's* life. It was also confidently reported how he had killed a Serpent that did come out to resist him in his Journey; and how he got through to whither he intended. It was also told what Welcome he had at all his Lord's Lodgings, especially when he came to the Gates of the Celestial City. For there, said the man, he was received with sound of Trumpet, by a company of shining ones. He told also how all the Bells in the City did ring for Joy at his Reception, and what Golden Garments he was clothed with; with many other things that now I shall forbear to relate. In a word, that man so told the Story of *Christian* and his Travels, that my heart fell into a burning haste to be gone after him, nor could father or mother stay me. So I got from them, and am come thus far on my Way.

Greath. *You came in at the Gate, did you not?*

He begins right

Valiant. Yes, yes. For the same man also told us, that all would be Nothing, if we did not begin to enter this way at the Gate.

Christian's
Name famous

Greath. *Look you, said the Guide, to* Christiana, *The Pilgrimage of your Husband, and what he has gotten thereby, is spread abroad far and near.*

Valiant. Why, is this *Christian's* wife?

Greath. Yes, That it is; and these also are her four Sons.

Valiant. What! and going on Pilgrimage too?

Greath. *Yes, verily they are following after.*

He is much
rejoiced to see
Christian's *Wife*

Valiant. It glads me at Heart! Good man! How Joyful will he be, when he shall see them that would not go with him, yet to enter after him, in at the Gates into the City?

Greath. *Without doubt it will be a Comfort to him; For, next to the Joy of seeing himself there, it will be a Joy to meet there his Wife and his Children.*

Valiant. But now you are upon that, pray let me hear

Whether we shall
know one another
when we come to
Heaven

your Opinion about it. Some make a Question whether we shall know one another when we are there?

Greath. *Do they think they shall know themselves then?*

Or that they shall rejoice to see themselves in that Bliss?
And if they think they shall know and do these; Why not
know others, and rejoice in their Welfare also?

Again, since Relations are our second self, though that
State will be dissolved there, yet why may it not be ration-
ally concluded that we shall be more glad to see them there,
than to see they are wanting?

Valiant. Well, I perceive whereabouts you are as to this.
Have you any more things to ask me about my beginning
to come on Pilgrimage?

Greath. *Yes, Was your Father and Mother willing that*
you should become a Pilgrim?

Valiant. Oh, no. They used all means imaginable to persuade me to stay at Home.

Greath. *Why, what could they say against it?*

Valiant. They said it was an idle Life, and if I my self   *The great*
were not inclined to Sloth and Laziness, I would never   *stumbling-Blocks*
countenance a Pilgrim's Condition.   *that by his*
                                                            Friends were laid
                                                            in his way

Greath. *And what did they say else?*

Valiant. Why, They told me, That it was a dangerous
Way, yea, the most dangerous Way in the World, said they,
is that which the Pilgrims go.

Greath. *Did they show you wherein this way is so*
dangerous?

Valiant. Yes. And that in many Particulars.

Greath. *Name some of them.*

Valiant. They told me of the Slough of *Despond*, where   *The first*
Christian was well nigh smothered. They told me that there *Stumbling-Block*
were Archers standing ready in *Beelzebub-Castle* to shoot
them who should knock at the *Wicket*-Gate for Entrance.
They told me also of the Wood, and dark Mountains, of
the Hill *Difficulty*, of the Lions, and also of the three Giants,
Bloody-man, Maul, and *Slay-good.* They said moreover,
that there was a foul *Fiend* haunted the Valley of *Humili-*
ation, and that *Christian* was, by him, almost bereft of Life.
Besides, said they, You must go over the *Valley of the*
Shadow of Death, where the *Hobgoblins* are, where the
Light is Darkness, where the Way is full of Snares, Pits,

Traps, and Gins. They told me also of *Giant-Despair*, of *Doubting-Castle*, and of the *Ruins* that the Pilgrims met with here. Further, they said, I must go over the enchanted Ground, which was dangerous; And that after all this, I should find a River, over which I should find no Bridge, and that that River did lie betwixt me and the Celestial Country.

Greath. *And was this all?*

The Second   Valiant. No, they also told me that this way was full of *Deceivers*, and of Persons that lay await there, to turn good men out of the Path.

Greath. *But how did they make that out?*

The Third   Valiant. They told me that Mr. *Worldly Wiseman* did lie there in wait to deceive. They said also, that there was *Formality* and *Hypocrisy* continually on the Road. They said also that *By-ends*, *Talkative*, or *Demas*, would go near to gather me up; That the *Flatterer* would catch me in his Net, or that, with green-headed[116] *Ignorance* I would presume to go on to the Gate, from whence he was sent back to the Hole that was in the side of the Hill, and made to go the By-way to Hell.

Greath. *I promise you, This was enough to discourage. But did they make an end here?*

The Fourth   Valiant. No, stay. They told me also of many that had tried that way of old, and that had gone a great way therein, to see if they could find something of the Glory there, that so many had so much talked of from time to time; and how they came back again, and befooled themselves for setting a Foot out of Doors in that Path, to the Satisfaction of all the Country. And they named several that did so, as *Obstinate* and *Pliable*, *Mistrust* and *Timorous*, *Turn-away* and old *Atheist*, with several more; who, they said, had, some of them, gone far to see what they could find, but not one of them had found so much Advantage by going, as amounted *to the weight of a Feather*.

Greath. *Said they any thing more to discourage you?*

The Fifth   Valiant. Yes, they told me of one Mr. *Fearing*, who was a Pilgrim, and how *he* found his way so Solitary, that he never had a comfortable Hour therein, also, that Mr. *Despondency* had like to been starved therein; Yea, and also, which I had almost forgot, that *Christian* himself, about whom there has been such a Noise, after all his Ventures for a Celestial Crown, was certainly drowned in the black River, and never went a foot further, however it was smothered up.

Greath. *And did none of these things discourage you?*

Valiant. No; they seemed but as so many Nothings to me.

Greath. *How came that about?*

Valiant. Why, I still believed what Mr. *Tell-true* had said, and that carried me beyond them all.

Greath. *Then this was your Victory, even your Faith?*

Valiant. It was so, I believed, and therefore came out, got into the Way, fought all that set themselves against me, and, by believing, am come to this Place.

How he got over these Stumbling-Blocks

> *Who would true Valour see,*
> *Let him come hither;*
> *One here will Constant be,*
> *Come Wind, come Weather.*
> *There's no Discouragement,*
> *Shall make him once Relent,*
> *His first avow'd Intent*
> To be a Pilgrim.
>
> *Who so beset him round,*
> *With dismal Stories,*
> *Do but themselves confound;*
> *His strength the more is.*
> *No Lion can him fright,*
> *He'll with a Giant Fight,*
> *But he will have a right,*
> To be a Pilgrim.

Hobgoblin, *nor foul* Fiend
Can daunt *his Spirit;*
He knows he at the end
Shall Life Inherit.
Then Fancies fly away,
He'll not fear what men say;
He'll labour Night and Day
To be a Pilgrim.

1 Part p. 139   By this time they were got to the *enchanted Ground,* where the Air naturally tended to make one *Drowsy.* And that place was all grown over with Briars and Thorns; excepting *here* and *there,* where was an *enchanted Arbour,* upon which, if a man sits, or in which if a man sleeps, 'tis a question, say some, whether ever he shall rise or wake again in this World. Over this Forest therefore they went, both one with an other, and Mr. *Great-heart* went before, for that he was the Guide, and Mr. *Valiant-for-truth* came behind, being there a guard, for fear lest peradventure some *Fiend,* or *Dragon,* or *Giant,* or *Thief,* should fall upon their Rear, and so do Mischief. They went on here each man with his Sword drawn in his Hand; for they knew it was a dangerous place. Also they cheered up one another as well as they could. *Feeble-mind,* Mr. *Great-heart* commanded should come up after him; and Mr. *Despondency* was under the Eye of Mr. *Valiant.*

Now they had not gone far, but a great Mist and a Darkness fell upon them all; so that they could scarce, for a great while, see the one the other. Wherefore they were forced for some time, to feel for one another by Words; for they walked not by sight.

But any one must think, that here was but sorry going for the best of them all; but how much worse for the Women and Children, who both of *Feet* and *Heart* were but Tender. Yet so it was, that, through the encouraging Words of him that led in the Front, and of him that brought them up behind, they made a pretty good shift to wag along.[117]

The Way also here was very wearisome thorough Dirt and Slabbiness.[118] Nor was there, on *all* this Ground, so much as one *Inn* or *Victualling-House* wherein to refresh the feebler sort. Here, therefore, was *grunting,* and *puffing,* and *sighing:* While one tumbleth over a Bush, another sticks fast in the Dirt, and the Children, some of them, lost their Shoes in the Mire. While one cries out, I am down, and another, Ho, Where are you? and a third, the Bushes have got such fast hold on me, I think I cannot get away from them.

Then they came at an *Arbour,* warm, and promising much Refreshing to the Pilgrims; for it was finely wrought above-head, beautified with *Greens,* furnished with *Benches* and *Settles.* It also had in it a soft Couch whereon the weary might lean. This, you must think, all things considered, was tempting; for the Pilgrims already began to be foiled with the badness of the way: but there was not one of them that made so much as a motion to stop there. Yea, for ought I could perceive, they continually gave so good heed to the Advice of their Guide, and he did so faithfully tell them of *Dangers,* and of the *Nature* of Dangers when they were at them, that usually, when they were nearest to them, they did most pluck up their Spirits, and hearten one another to deny the Flesh. This *Arbour* was called *The Slothful's Friend,* and was made on purpose to allure, if it might be, some of the Pilgrims there, to take up their Rest, when weary.

An Arbour *on the Enchanting Ground*

The Name of the Arbour

I saw them in my Dream, that they went on in this their *solitary* Ground, till they came to a place at which a man is apt to lose his Way. *Now,* though when it was light, their Guide could well enough tell how to miss those ways that led wrong, yet in the dark he was put to a stand. But he had in his Pocket a Map of all ways leading to, or from the Celestial City; wherefore he struck a Light (for he never goes also without his Tinder-box), and takes a view of his Book or Map,[119] which bids him to be careful in that place to turn to the right-hand-way. And had he not been careful here to look in his Map, they had all, in probability, been

The way difficult to find

The Guide has a Map of all ways leading to or from the City

smothered in the Mud; for just a little before them, and
that at the end of the cleanest Way too, was a Pit, none
knows how deep, full of nothing but Mud, there made on
purpose to destroy the Pilgrims in.

Then thought I with my self, who, that goeth on Pilgrim-
God's Book age, but would have one of these Maps about him, that he
may look, when he is at a *stand,* which is the way he must
take.

They went on then in this *enchanted* Ground, till they
came to where there was another *Arbour,* and it was built
An Arbour and by the High-way-side. And in that *Arbour* there lay two
two asleep men whose Names were *Heedless* and *Too-bold*. These two
therein went thus far on Pilgrimage; but here being wearied with
their Journey, they sat down to rest themselves, and so fell
fast asleep. When the Pilgrims saw them, they stood still,
and shook their Heads; for they knew that the Sleepers
were in a pitiful Case. Then they consulted what to do,
whether to go on and leave them in their Sleep, or to step
The Pilgrims try to them and try to wake them. So they concluded to go to
to wake them them and wake them; that is, if they could; but with this
Caution, namely, to take heed that they themselves did not
sit down nor embrace the offered Benefit of that *Arbour.*

So they went in and spake to the men, and called each
by his Name, (for the Guide, it seems, did know them) but
there was no Voice nor Answer. Then the Guide did shake
them, and do what he could to disturb them. Then said one
of them, *I will pay you when I take my Money;* At which
the guide shook his Head. *I will fight so long as I can hold
my Sword in my Hand,* said the other. At that, one of the
Their Endeavour Children laughed.
is fruitless. Prov.
23.34, 35   Then said *Christiana,* what is the meaning of this? The
Guide said, *They talk in their Sleep.* If you strike them, beat
them, or whatever else you do to them, they will answer
you after this fashion; or as one of them said in old time,
when the Waves of the Sea did beat upon him, and he slept
as one upon the Mast of a Ship, *When I awake I will seek
it yet again.* You know, when men talk in their Sleeps, they
say any thing; but their Words are not governed either by

Faith or Reason. There is an *Incoherency* in their Words *now*, as there was before betwixt their going on Pilgrimage and sitting down here. This then is the Mischief on't, when *heedless* ones go on Pilgrimage, 'tis twenty to one, but they are served thus. For this *enchanted* Ground is one of the last refuges that the Enemy to Pilgrims has; wherefore it is, as you see, placed almost at the end of the Way, and so it standeth against us with the more Advantage. For when, thinks the Enemy, will these Fools be so desirous to sit down as when they are weary, and when so like to be weary as when almost at their Journey's end? Therefore it is, I say, that the *enchanted* Ground is placed so nigh to the Land *Beulah,* and so near the end of their Race. Wherefore let Pilgrims look to themselves, lest it happen to them as it has done to these that, as you see, are fallen asleep, and none can awake them.

Then the Pilgrims desired with trembling to go forward; only they prayed their Guide to strike a Light, that they might go the rest of their way by the help of the light of a Lantern. So he struck a light, and they went by the help of that through the rest of this way, though the Darkness was very great. *The light of the Word. 2 Pet. 1.19*

But the Children began to be sorely weary, and they cried out unto him that loveth Pilgrims, to make their way more Comfortable. So by that they had gone a little further, a Wind arose that drove away the Fog, so the Air became more clear. *The Children cry for weariness*

Yet they were not off (by much) of the *enchanted* Ground; only now they could see one another better, and the way wherein they should walk.

Now when they were almost at the end of this Ground, they perceived that a little before them was a *solemn* Noise, as of one that was much concerned. So they went on and looked before them: and behold they saw, as they thought, *a Man upon his Knees,* with Hands and Eyes lift up, and speaking, as they thought, earnestly to one that was above. They drew nigh, but could not tell what he said; so they went softly till he had done. When he had done, he got up, *Standfast upon his Knees in the Enchanted Ground*

and began to run towards the Celestial City. Then Mr.
Great-heart called after him, saying, So-ho, Friend, let us
have your Company if you go, as I suppose you do, to the
Celestial City. So the man stopped, and they came up to
him. But as soon as Mr. *Honest* saw him, he said, I know
this man. Then said Mr. *Valiant-for-truth,* Prithee, who
The Story of is it? It is one, said he, that comes from where-abouts I
Standfast dwelt, his name is *Stand-fast,* he is certainly a right good
Pilgrim.

So they came up one to another; and presently *Stand-fast*
said to old *Honest,* Ho, Father *Honest,* are you there? Aye,
said he, that I am, as sure as you are there. Right glad am
I, said Mr. *Stand-fast,* that I have found you on this Road.
And as glad am I, said the other, that I espied you on your
Knees. Then Mr. *Standfast* blushed, and said, But why, did
Talk betwixt you see me? Yes, that I did, quoth the other, and with my
him and Mr. Heart was glad at the Sight. Why, what did you think? said
Honest *Stand-fast.* Think, said old *Honest,* what should I think? I
thought we had an honest Man upon the Road, and therefore should have his Company by and by. If you thought
not amiss, said Standfast, how happy am I! But if I be not
as I should, 'tis I alone must bear it. That is true, said the
other; But your fear doth further confirm me that things
are right betwixt the Prince of Pilgrims and your Soul. For
he saith, *Blessed is the man that feareth always.*

Valiant. Well, but Brother, I pray thee tell us what was
it that was the cause of thy being upon thy Knees, even
They found him now? Was it for that some special Mercy laid Obligations
at Prayer upon thee, or how?

Stand. Why we are as you see, upon the *enchanted
Ground*; and as I was coming along, I was musing with
myself of what a dangerous Road, the Road in this place
What it was that was, and how many that had come even thus far on Pilgrim-
fetched him age, had here been stopped, and been destroyed. I thought
upon his Knees also of the manner of the Death with which this place
destroyeth Men. Those that die here, die of no violent
Distemper: the Death which such die is not grievous to
them. For he that goeth away in a *Sleep,* begins that Journey

with Desire and Pleasure. Yea, such acquiesce in the Will
of that Disease.

Hon. Then Mr. Honest *interrupting of him said, did you
see the two Men asleep in the Arbour?*

Stand. Aye, aye, I saw *Heedless,* and *Too-bold* there; and
for ought I know, there they will lie till they Rot. But let   Prov. 10.7
me go on with my Tale? As I was thus Musing, as I said,
there was one in very pleasant Attire, *but old,* who presented herself to me, and offered me three things, to wit,
her *Body,* her *Purse,* and her *Bed.* Now the Truth is, I was
both aweary and sleepy. I am also as poor as an *Owlet,*[120]
and that, perhaps, the *Witch* knew. Well, I repulsed her
once and twice, but she put by my Repulses, and smiled.
Then I began to be angry; but she mattered that nothing at
all. Then she made Offers again, and said, if I would be
ruled by her, she would make me great and happy. For,
said she, I am the Mistress of the World, and men are made
happy by me. Then I asked her name, and she told me it
was *Madam Bubble.*[121] This set me further from her; but   *Madam* Bubble,
she still followed me with Enticements. Then I betook me,   *or this vain
as you see, to my Knees, and with Hands lift up, and cries,   World*
I prayed to him that had said, he would help. So, just as
you came up, the Gentlewoman went her way. Then I
continued to give thanks for this my great Deliverance; for
I verily believe she intended no good, but rather sought to
make stop of me in my Journey.

*Hon. Without doubt her Designs were bad. But stay,
now you talk of her, methinks I either have seen her, or
have read some story of her.*

Stand. Perhaps you have done both.

*Hon. Madam Bubble! Is she not a tall comely Dame,
something of a swarthy Complexion?*

Stand. Right, you hit it, she is just such an one.

*Hon. Doth she not speak very smoothly, and give you a
Smile at the end of a Sentence?*

Stand. You fall right upon it again, for these are her very
Actions.

Hon. Doth she not wear a great Purse by her Side, and

*is not her Hand often in it, fingering her Money, as if that
was her Heart's delight?*

Stand. 'Tis just so. Had she stood by all this while, you
could not more amply have set her forth before me, nor
have better described her Features.

Hon. Then he that drew her Picture was a good
Limner,[122] and he that wrote of her, said true.

The World *Greath.* This Woman is a *Witch*, and it is by Virtue of
her *Sorceries* that this Ground is *enchanted;* whoever doth
lay his Head down in *her Lap*, had as good lay it down on
that Block over which the Axe doth hang; and whoever lay
their Eyes upon her Beauty, are counted the Enemies of
Jam. 4.4. 1 John
2.15 God. This is she that maintaineth in their Splendour, all
those that are the Enemies of Pilgrims. Yea, this is she that
has bought off many a man from a Pilgrim's Life. She is a
great *Gossiper;* she is always, both she and her daughters,
at one Pilgrim's Heels or another, now Commending, and
then preferring the excellences of this Life. She is a bold
and impudent Slut; she will talk with any Man. She always
laugheth poor Pilgrims to scorn, but highly commends the
Rich. If there be one cunning to get Money in a Place, she
will speak well of him, from House to House. She loveth
Banqueting, and Feasting, mainly well; she is always at one
full Table or another. She has given it out in some places
that she is a Goddess, and therefore some do Worship her.
She has her times and open places of Cheating; and she will
say and avow it, that none can show a Good comparable
to hers. She promiseth to dwell with Children's Children,
if they will but love and make much of her. She will cast
out of her Purse, Gold like Dust, in some places and to
some Persons. She loves to be sought after, spoken well of,
and to lie in the Bosoms of Men. She is never weary of
commending her Commodities, and she loves them most
that think best of her. She will promise to some Crowns,
and Kingdoms, if they will but take her Advice; yet many
has she brought to the Halter, and ten thousand times more
to Hell.

Stand. *O! said* Standfast, *What a Mercy is it that I did resist her; for whither might she a drawn me?*

Greath. Whither! Nay, none but God knows whither. But in general, to be sure, she would a drawn thee *into many foolish and hurtful Lusts, which drown men in Destruction and Perdition.*   1 Tim. 6.9

'Twas she that set *Absalom* against his Father, and *Jeroboam* against his Master. 'Twas she that persuaded *Judas* to sell his Lord, and that prevailed with *Demas*[123] to forsake the Godly Pilgrim's Life. None can tell of the Mischief that she doth. She makes Variance betwixt Rulers and Subjects, betwixt Parents and Children, 'twixt Neighbour and Neighbour, 'twixt a Man and his Wife, 'twixt a Man and himself, 'twixt the Flesh and the Heart.

Wherefore, good Master *Stand-fast,* be as your Name is, and when you have done all, *stand.*[124]

At this Discourse there was among the Pilgrims a mixture of Joy and Trembling, but at length *they brake* out and Sang,

> *What Danger is the Pilgrim in,*
> *How many are his Foes?*
> *How many ways there are to Sin,*
> *No living Mortal knows.*
> *Some of the Ditch shy are, yet can*
> *Lie tumbling in the Mire:*
> *Some, though they shun the Frying-pan*
> *Do leap into the Fire.*

After this, I beheld, until they were come into the Land of *Beulah,* where the Sun shineth Night and Day. Here, because they was weary, they betook themselves a while to Rest. And because this Country was common for Pilgrims, and because the Orchards and Vineyards that were here   1 Part, pag. 156
belonged to the King of the Celestial Country; therefore they were licensed to make bold with any of his things.

But a little while soon refreshed them here; for the Bells

did so ring, and the Trumpets continually sound so Melodiously, that they could not sleep, and yet they received as much refreshing, as if they had slept their Sleep ever so soundly. Here also all the noise of them that walked the Streets was, *More pilgrims are come to Town.* And another would answer, saying, And so many went over the Water, and were let in at the Golden Gates Today. They would cry again, There is now a Legion of Shining ones, just come to Town, by which we know that there are more Pilgrims upon the Road, for here they come to wait for them, and to comfort them after all their Sorrow. Then the Pilgrims got up, and walked to and fro: But how were their Ears now filled with heavenly Noises, and their Eyes delighted with Celestial Visions? In this Land they *heard* nothing, *saw* nothing, *felt* nothing, *smelt* nothing, *tasted* nothing, that was offensive to their Stomach or Mind; only when they tasted of the Water of the River, over which they were *Death bitter to* to go, they thought that it tasted a little Bitterish to the *the Flesh, but* Palate, but it proved sweeter when 'twas down.

sweet to the
Soul. Death has In this place there was a Record kept of the Names of
its Ebbings and them that had been Pilgrims of old, and a History of all the
Flowings like the famous Acts that they had done. It was here also much
Tide discoursed, how the *River* to some had had its *flowings,* and what *ebbings* it has had while others have gone over. It has been in a manner *dry* for some, while it has overflowed its Banks for others.

In this place, the Children of the Town would go into the King's Gardens, and gather Nosegays for the Pilgrims, and bring them to them with much Affection. Here also grew *Camphire,* with *Spikenard* and *Saffron, Calamus,* and *Cinnamon,* with all its Trees of *Frankincense, Myrrh,* and *Aloes,* with all *chief* Spices.[125] With these the Pilgrims' Chambers were perfumed while they stayed here; and with these were their Bodies anointed, to prepare them to go over the *River* when the time appointed was come.

Now, while they lay here, and waited for the good Hour, there was a Noise in the Town, that there was a *Post* come

from the Celestial City, with Matter of great Importance, *A Message of Death sent to Christiana*
to one *Christiana,* the Wife of *Christian* the Pilgrim. So
Enquiry was made for her, and the House was found out
where she was, so the Post presented her with a Letter; The
Contents whereof was, *Hail, Good Woman; I bring thee* *His Message*
Tidings that the Master calleth for thee, and expecteth
that thou shouldst stand in his Presence, in Clothes of
Immortality, within these ten Days.

When he had read this Letter to her, he gave her therewith
a sure Token that he was a true Messenger, and was come
to bid her make haste to be gone. The Token was, *An* *How welcome is Death to them that have nothing to do but to die*
Arrow with a Point sharpened with Love, let easily into
her Heart, which by degrees wrought so effectually with
her, that at the time appointed she must be gone.

When *Christiana* saw that her time was come, and that
she was the first of this Company that was to go over: she
called for Mr. *Great-heart* her Guide, and told him how
Matters were. So he told her he was heartily glad of the *Her Speech to her Guide*
News, and could a been glad had the Post come for him.
Then she bid that he should give Advice how all things
should be prepared for her Journey.

So he told her, saying, Thus and thus it must be, and we
that Survive will accompany you to the River-side.

Then she called for her Children, and gave them her *To her Children*
Blessing; and told them that she had read with Comfort the
Mark that was set in their Foreheads, and was glad to see
them with her there, and that they had kept their Garments
so white. Lastly, She bequeathed to the Poor that little she
had, and commanded her Sons and her Daughters to be
ready against the Messenger should come for them.

When she had spoken these Words to her Guide and to
her Children, she called for Mr. *Valiant-for-truth,* and said
unto him, Sir, you have in all places showed yourself true- *To Mr. Valiant*
hearted; be Faithful unto Death, and my King will give you
a Crown of Life. I would also entreat you to have an Eye
to my Children, and if at any time you see them faint, speak
comfortably to them. For my Daughters, my Sons' Wives,

they have been Faithful, and a fulfilling of the Promise upon
To Mr.
Stand-fast
To old Honest them, will be their end. But she gave Mr. *Stand-fast* a Ring.

Then she called for old Mr. *Honest,* and said of him,
Behold an Israelite indeed, in whom is no Guile.[126] Then
said *he,* I wish you a fair Day when you set out for Mount
Sion, and shall be glad to see that you go over the River
dry-shod. But she answered, Come *Wet,* come *Dry,* I long
to be gone; for however the Weather is in my Journey, I
shall have time enough when I come there to sit down and
rest me, and dry me.

Then came in that good Man Mr. *Ready-to-halt* to see
To Mr. Ready-
to-Halt her. So she said to him, Thy Travel hither has been with
Difficulty; but that will make thy Rest the sweeter. But
watch, and be ready; for at an Hour when you think not,
the Messenger may come.

After him, came in Mr. *Despondency,* and his Daughter
To Despon-
dency, *and his*
Daughter *Much-afraid.* To whom she said, You ought with Thankful-
ness for ever, to remember your Deliverance from the
Hands of Giant *Despair,* and out of *Doubting-Castle.* The
effect of that Mercy is, that you are brought with Safety
hither. Be ye watchful, and cast away Fear; be sober and
hope to the End.

To Feeble-mind Then she said to Mr. *Feeble-Mind,* Thou wast delivered
from the Mouth of Giant *Slay-good,* that thou mightest live
in the Light of the Living for ever, and see thy King with
Comfort. Only I advise thee to repent thee of thy aptness
to fear and doubt of his Goodness before he sends for thee;
lest thou shouldest, when he comes, be forced to stand
before him for that Fault with Blushing.

Her last Day,
and manner of
Departure Now the day drew on that *Christiana* must be gone. So
the Road was full of People to see her take her Journey.
But behold, all the Banks beyond the River were full of
Horses and Chariots, which were come down from above
to accompany her to the City-Gate. So she came forth, and
entered the *River,* with a *Beckon* of Farewell, to those that
followed her to the River side. The last word that she was
heard to say were, *I come Lord, to be with thee and bless*
thee.

So her Children and Friends returned to their Place, for those that waited for *Christiana,* had carried her out of their Sight. So she went, and called, and entered in at the Gate with all the Ceremonies of Joy that her Husband *Christian* had done before her.

At her Departure her Children wept, but Mr. *Great-heart,* and Mr. *Valiant,* played upon the well tuned Cymbal and Harp for Joy. So all departed to their respective Places.

In process of time there came a *Post* to the Town again, and his Business was with Mr. *Ready-to-halt.* So he enquired him out, and said to him, I am come in the Name of Him whom thou hast Loved and Followed, though upon *Crutches.* And my Message is to tell thee, that he expects thee at his Table to Sup with him in his Kingdom the next Day after *Easter.* Wherefore prepare thyself for this Journey. *[margin: Ready-to-Halt Summoned]*

Then he also gave him a Token[127] that he was a true Messenger, saying, *I have broken thy golden Bowl,* and loosed *thy silver cord.* *[margin: Eccles. 12.16]*

After this, Mr. *Ready-to-halt* called for his Fellow Pilgrims, and told them, saying, I am sent for, and God shall surely visit you also. So he desired Mr. *Valiant* to make his *Will.* And because he had nothing to bequeath to them that should Survive him, but his *Crutches,* and his good *Wishes,* therefore thus he said, *These Crutches I bequeath to my Son that shall tread in my Steps: with an hundred warm Wishes that he may prove better than I have done.* *[margin: Promises. His Will]*

Then he thanked Mr. *Great-heart* for his Conduct, and his Kindness, and so addressed himself to his Journey. When he came to the brink of the River, he said, Now I shall have no more need of these *Crutches,* since yonder are Chariots and Horses for me to ride on. The last Words he was heard to say, was, *Welcome Life.*[128] So he went his Way. *[margin: His last words]*

After this, Mr. *Feeble-mind* had Tidings brought him, that the Post sounded his Horn at his Chamber Door. Then he came in, and told him, saying, I am come to tell thee that thy Master has need of thee, and that in a very little time thou must behold his Face in Brightness. And take this *[margin: Feeble-mind Summoned]*

Eccles. 12.3 as a Token of the Truth of my Message. *Those that look out at the Windows shall be darkened.*

Then Mr. *Feeble-mind* called for his Friends, and told them what Errand had been brought unto him, and what Token he had received of the truth of the Message. Then he said, since I have nothing to bequeath to any, to *He makes no* what purpose should I make a Will? As for my *feeble Will* *Mind,* that I will leave behind me, for that I shall have no need of it in the place whither I go; nor is it worth bestowing upon the poorest Pilgrim: Wherefore when I am gone, I desire that you, Mr. *Valiant,* would bury it in a dunghill. This done, and the Day being come on which he was to *His last words* depart; he entered the *River* as the rest. His last Words were, *Hold out Faith and Patience.* So he went over to the other Side.

When Days had many of them passed away, Mr. *Despon-* *Mr. Despon-* *dency* was sent for. For a *Post* was come and brought this *dency* Message to him: *Trembling Man, these are to summon thee summoned* *to be ready with thy King, by the next Lord's day, to shout for Joy for thy Deliverance from all thy Doubtings.*

And said the Messenger, that my Message is true, take this for a Proof. So he gave him *The Grasshopper to be a* *Eccles. 12.5. His* *Burden unto him.* Now Mr. *Despondency's* Daughter *Daughter goes* whose name was *Much-afraid,* said, when she heard what *too* was done, that she would go with her Father. Then Mr. *Despondency* said to his Friends; Myself, and my Daughter, you know what we have been, and how troublesomely we have behaved ourselves in every Company. My will and my *His Will* Daughter's is, that our *Desponds* and slavish Fears, be by no man ever received, from the day of our *Departure,* for ever; for I know that after my Death they will offer themselves to others. For, to be plain with you, they are Ghosts,[129] the which we entertained when we first began to be Pilgrims, and could never shake them off after. And they will walk about and seek Entertainment of the Pilgrims, but for our Sakes, shut the Doors upon them.

His last words   When the time was come for them to depart, they went up to the Brink of the river. The last Words of Mr. *Despon-*

dency were, *Farewell Night, Welcome Day*. His Daughter went through the River singing, but none could understand what she said.

Then it came to pass, a while after, that there was a *Post* in the Town that enquired for Mr. *Honest*. So he came to his House where he was, and delivered to his Hand these Lines: *Thou art Commanded to be ready against this Day seven Night, to present thyself before thy Lord, at his Father's House*. And for a Token that my Message is true, *All thy Daughters of Music shall be brought low*. Then Mr. *Honest* called for his Friends, and said unto them, I Die, but shall make no Will. As for my Honesty, it shall go with me; let him that comes after be told of this. When the Day that he was to be gone, was come, he addressed himself to go over the *River*. Now the *River* at that time overflowed the Banks in some places. But Mr. *Honest* in his Life time, had spoken to one *Good-conscience* to meet him there, the which he also did, and lent him his Hand, and so helped him over. The last words of Mr. *Honest* were, *Grace Reigns*. So he left the World.

After this it was noised abroad that Mr. *Valiant-for-truth* was taken with a Summons, by the same *Post* as the other; and had this for a Token that the Summons was true, *That his Pitcher was broken at the Fountain*. When he understood it, he called for his Friends, and told them of it. Then said he, I am going to my Father's, and though with great Difficulty I am got hither, yet now I do not repent me of all the Trouble I have been at to arrive where I am. *My Sword* I give to him that shall succeed me in my Pilgrimage, and my *Courage* and *Skill* to him that can get it. My *Marks* and *Scars* I carry with me, to be a Witness for me, that I have fought his Battles, who now will be my Rewarder. When the Day that he must go hence, was come, many accompanied him to the River side, into which as he went, he said, *Death, where is thy Sting?* And as he went down deeper, he said, *Grave, where is thy Victory?*[130] So he passed over, and all the Trumpets sounded for him on the other side.

Mr. Honest summoned

Eccles. 12.4

He makes no Will

Good conscience helps Mr Honest over the River

Mr Valiant summoned

Eccl. 12.6

His Will

His last words

Mr. Stand-fast *is*
summoned
Then there came forth a Summons for Mr. *Stand-fast*.
(This Mr. *Stand-fast* was he whom the rest of the Pilgrims
found upon his Knees in the *enchanted* Ground.) For the
Post brought it him open in his Hands. The Contents
whereof were, *That he must prepare for a Change of Life,
for his Master was not willing that he should be so far from
him any longer.* At this Mr. *Stand-fast* was put into a Muse;
Nay, said the Messenger, you need not doubt of the Truth
of my Message; for here is a Token of the Truth thereof,

Eccl. 12.6. *He
calls for Mr.
Great-Heart*
Thy Wheel is broken at the Cistern. Then he called to him
Mr. *Greatheart,* who was their Guide, and said unto him,
Sir, Although it was not my hap to be much in your good
Company during the Days of my Pilgrimage, yet, since the

*His Speech to
him*
time I knew you, you have been profitable to me. When I
came from home, I left behind me a Wife, and five small
Children. Let me entreat you, at your Return, (for I know
that you go, and return to your Master's House, in hopes
that you may yet be a Conductor to more of the Holy
Pilgrims,) that you send to my Family, and let them be
acquainted with all that hath, and shall happen unto me.
Tell them moreover, of my happy Arrival to this Place, and
of the present late blessed Condition I am in. Tell them also
of *Christian* and *Christiana* his Wife, and how *She* and her

*His Errand to
his Family*
Children came after her Husband. Tell them also of what
a happy End she made, and whither she is gone. I have little
or nothing to send to my Family, unless it be Prayers and
Tears for them; of which it will suffice that you acquaint
them, if peradventure they may prevail. When Mr. *Stand-
fast* had thus set things in order, and the time being come
for him to haste him away; he also went down to the River.
Now there was a great Calm at that time in the River,
wherefore Mr. *Stand-fast,* when he was about halfway in,
stood a while, and talked with his Companions that had
waited upon him thither. And he said,

This River has been a Terror to many; yea, the thoughts

His last words.
Jos. 3.17
of it also have often frighted me. But now methinks I stand
easy, my Foot is fixed upon that, upon which the Feet

of the Priests that bare the Ark of the Covenant stood while *Israel* went over this *Jordan*. The Waters indeed are to the Palate Bitter, and to the Stomach cold; yet the thoughts of what I am going to, and of the Conduct that waits for me on the other side, do lie as a glowing Coal at my Heart.

I see myself now at the *end* of my Journey; my *toilsome* Days are ended. I am going to see *that* Head that was Crowned with Thorns, and *that* Face which was spit upon, for me.

I have formerly lived by Hearsay, and Faith, but now I go where I shall live by sight, and shall be with him in whose Company I delight myself.

I have loved to hear my Lord spoken of, and wherever I have seen the print of his Shoe in the Earth, there I have coveted to set my Foot too.

His Name has been to me as a *Civet-Box;* yea, sweeter than all Perfumes. His voice to me has been most sweet, and his Countenance, I have more desired than they that have most desired the Light of the Sun. His Word I did use to gather for my Food, and for Antidotes against my Faintings. He hath held me, and hath kept me from mine Iniquities; yea, my steps hath he strengthened in his Way.

Now while he was thus in Discourse, his Countenance changed, his *strong men*[131] bowed under him, and after he had said, *Take me, for I come unto thee,* he ceased to be seen of them.

But Glorious it was to see how the open Region was filled with Horses and Chariots, with Trumpeters and Pipers, with Singers, and Players upon stringed Instruments, to welcome the Pilgrims as they went up, and followed one another in at the beautiful Gate of the City.

As for *Christian's* children, the four Boys that *Christiana* brought with her, with their Wives and Children, I did not stay where I was, till they were gone over. Also, since I came away, I heard one say, that they were yet alive, and so would be for the Increase of the Church, in that Place where they were for a time.

Shall it be my Lot to go that way again,[132] I may give those that desire it, an Account of what I here am silent about; meantime I bid my Reader *Adieu*.

FINIS

Notes

Abbreviations

GA   *Grace Abounding to the Chief of Sinners*, ed. John Stach-niewski with Anita Pacheco (Oxford: Oxford World's Classics, 1998)

MW   *The Miscellaneous Works of John Bunyan*, general editor Roger Sharrock (13 vols.; Oxford: Clarendon Press, 1976–94)

Owens   *The Pilgrim's Progress*, ed. W. R. Owens (Oxford: Oxford World's Classics, 2003)

Sharrock *The Pilgrim's Progress*, ed. J. B. Wharey, 2nd edn., revised Roger Sharrock (Oxford: Clarendon Press, 1960)

References to the Bible are to the Authorized (King James) Version of 1611, though Bunyan sometimes quotes from the Geneva Bible of 1560, or from memory.

THE AUTHOR'S APOLOGY FOR HIS BOOK

1. *Apology*: This is used more in the older sense of justification or vindication than an excuse.

2. *writing of the Way . . . our Gospel-Day*: The book Bunyan was working on may have been *The Heavenly Foot-Man,* based on 1 Corinthians 9: 24, but not published until 1698. Although 'Gospel Day' refers to the present era, after Christ, *The Heavenly Foot-Man* does warn that 'the gates of Heaven may be shut shortly' (*MW* 5.151).

3. *pull'd*: The image is from spinning, pulling the wool from the distaff to make thread.

4. *Dark clouds . . . the bright bring none*: Bunyan is playing on the meaning of 'dark' as 'obscure' as well as full of rain.

5. *How does the Fowler . . . Of all his postures?*: Sharrock notes the

similarity of this description of bird-catching tricks to that of Joseph Strutt in *Sports and Pastimes of the People of England*.

6. *If that a Pearl may in a Toad's-head dwell*: Toads were supposed to be poisonous, but to have a jewel in their head that could cure the swelling from a poisonous bite (Thomas Lupton, *One Thousand Notable Things* (1579); see also Duke Senior in Shakespeare, *As You Like It*, 2.1.12–14).

7. *Were not God's Laws ... Metaphors?*: Bunyan learned to read the Old Testament typologically, that is, to see in characters and events of the Old Testament a foreshadowing of the person and work of Christ. Although the value of metaphor seems to be an argument between Bunyan's friends, there was also an argument during the Restoration between Anglicans and Dissenters about the desirability of plain speech. Bunyan's admirer John Owen was attacked by Samuel Parker for his use of 'fulsome and luscious metaphors'.

8. *by Pins and Loops ... the Light and Grace that in them be*: A series of examples from the Old Testament that may be interpreted typologically. Bunyan devoted a whole book, *Solomon's Temple Spiritualized* (1688), to this method, which, he argues, shows us 'the more exactly how the *New* and *Old Testament*, as to the spiritualness of the worship, was as one and the same' (*MW* 7.8).

9. *Sound words I know Timothy is to use*: 'If any man teach otherwise, and consent not to wholesome words ...' (1 Timothy 6: 3).

10. *Dialogue-wise*: The obvious example of such a dialogue is Arthur Dent's *Plain Man's Pathway to Heaven* (1601, much reprinted), one of the two books of popular devotion Bunyan's first wife brought with her as a dowry (see *GA*, p. 9).

11. *he that taught us first to Plough ... his Design?*: An allusion to Isaiah 25: 24–6: 'Doth the ploughman plough all day to sow? ... For his God doth instruct him to discretion.'

12. *picking-meat*: A dainty cut of meat.

13. *A Man i'th'Clouds*: This could be a reference to early science fiction, such as Wilkins, *The Discovery of a New World* (1640) or Godwin's *A Man in the Moon*; but the cloud is also a biblical reference to the presence of God, in Exodus 13: 21 for example, or Revelation 1: 7.

THE FIRST PART

1. *I lighted on a certain place where was a Den: and I laid me down in that place to sleep*: The marginal note identifying the den as a 'gaol' first appears in the third edition (1679). The prison in Doubting Castle is also called a den, cf. *OED* 3b, 'a small confined room or abode, esp. one unfit for human habitation'. Another *OED* definition, 1, 'the lair of a wild beast' is suggested by the lion at the bottom of the 'sleeping portrait'. Richard L. Greaves (*Glimpses of Glory: John Bunyan and English Dissent* (Palo Alto, Calif.: Stanford University Press, 2002), pp. 216–27) suggests that the book was begun *c.* 1668, during Bunyan's first imprisonment. The details of lying down to dream in the wilderness recall Jacob in Genesis 28: 11–13, and in alluding to this Bunyan invites comparison with the authority of the patriarch of the chosen people (see Beth Lynch, *John Bunyan and the Language of Conviction* (Cambridge: D. S. Brewer, 2004), pp. 88–9).

2. *a man clothed with rags ... What shall I do?*: The details of the man's appearance are explained theologically by the marginal references. The rags are a sign of spiritual poverty and the impossibility of pleasing God by human attempts at righteousness (Isaiah 64: 6); the burden is sin (Psalm 38: 4). With '*What shall I do?*' compare Acts 2: 37, where after Peter's sermon the crowd ask, 'What shall we do?' See also *GA*, p. 17, 'On this word I mused, and could not tell what to do.'

3. *my bowels*: In this period the bowels were regarded as the seat of tender emotion.

4. *distemper*: The word meant any sort of illness, but particularly (as here) a disturbance of the mind.

5. *Evangelist*: The figure of Evangelist, the minister of the Gospel who shows the pilgrim the way, could have been based on Bunyan's own pastor in the 1650s, John Gifford, but also represents something of Bunyan's own ministry.

6. *Fly from the wrath to come*: In *Come, and Welcome, to Jesus Christ* (1678), Bunyan discusses flying to Christ 'when all Refuge fails, and a man is made to see that there is nothing left him but Sin, Death, and Damnation' (*MW* 8.258).

7. *Wicket-gate*: A wicket is a narrow gate. The key biblical allusion, apart from those in the margins, is Luke 13: 24, 'Strive to enter in at the strait gate', expounded at length in Bunyan's *The Strait Gate* (1676; *MW* 5). Bunyan recounts a dream in *Grace Abounding*

where he tries to get through a mountain to the sunlight where the people of God are, and eventually finding 'a narrow gap, like a little doorway in the wall' (*GA*, p. 19). He interprets the gap as 'Jesus Christ, who is the way to God the Father'.

8. *(for that was his name)*: This is one of the few examples in the book where Bunyan delays telling us the name of a character. We learn later that Christian was originally called Graceless. There are several moments of transformation for Christian in the text, but this is the first and arguably the most important.

9. *fantastical*: Holding irrational or illusory ideas.

10. *slough . . . Despond*: A *slough* is a boggy place, particularly referring to a ditch near a road or an almost impassably muddy place in a road. *Despond*, despondency or despair, was a recurrent feeling for Bunyan during his long conversion experience; in *Grace Abounding* Bunyan compares himself to a child fallen into a mill-pit, who could find no handhold or foothold to get out, or sinking 'into a gulf, as a house whose foundation is destroyed' (*GA*, p. 57).

11. *plat*: Any flat area or surface.

12. *the Law-giver*: Bunyan's Lutheran theology here, and in the episode of Mr Worldly Wiseman which follows, stresses the limitations of the Law, in the biblical sense of the Ten Commandments and other Old Testament instructions, in helping us out of despair. This is argued in his early text *The Doctrine of the Law and Grace Unfolded* (1659). Without Help Christian cannot get out.

13. *Mr. Worldly Wiseman*: This episode is the chief addition to the second edition. He may in part be a satirical portrait of the Bedfordshire Anglican minister Edward Fowler, whose theology Bunyan attacks in *A Defence of the Doctrine of Justification by Faith* (1672), and some of whose views also appear in the figures of Ignorance and By-ends (see T. L. Underwood's introduction to *MW* 4.xx–xxv, and Isabel Rivers, *Reason, Grace and Sentiment: A Study of the Language of Religion and Ethics in England 1660–1780*, vol. 1: *Whichcote to Wesley* (Cambridge: Cambridge University Press 1991), ch. 3). Bunyan's position is that obedience to the moral Law (hence the references to Legality and Morality and the terrible vision of Mount Sinai) and receiving the grace of God are quite different, and that Fowler confuses them. Bunyan here adds a critique of the fashionability of such ideas in 'credit and good fashion' (p. 23).

14. *afraid to venture further, lest the hill should fall on his head*: The fear of the hill falling recalls Bunyan's fear that the steeple at Elstow would fall on his head while he was watching the bell-ringers (*GA*,

p. 13). Christian's burden feels heavier because he is becoming more conscious of his own sin – 'When God brings sinners into the Covenant of Grace, he doth first kill them with the Covenant of Works' (*The Doctrine of the Law and Grace Unfolded*; MW 2.137). The hill is an allusion Mount Sinai, where Moses received the Ten Commandments in Exodus 19–20, heralded by thunder and lightning.

15. *with that he opened the gate*: Note that Good-will pulls Christian in as well as opening the gate to him, as an indication that grace is an active force in this stage of conversion. This contrasts with the dream vision in *Grace Abounding*, where Bunyan has to squeeze through 'a narrow gap, like a little doorway in the Wall' between him and the godly people of Bedford sitting in the sun. *Mount Zion* is Jerusalem, which becomes the figure of the kingdom of heaven in the New Testament, e.g. Hebrews 12: 22, Revelation 14: 1. The *gate* represents Jesus ('I am the door', John 10: 9); Bunyan had recently written about its narrowness in *The Strait Gate*. ('*The Gate which is Christ*' appears in the marginal notes to the second part.)

16. *Butt down upon*: Probably in the sense of projecting out from the place where they are; a rare usage.

17. *the house of the Interpreter*: This episode continues Christian's instruction in a series of pictures reminiscent of the emblem-book tradition, a Europe-wide phenomenon of allegorical albums accompanied by (usually verse) explanations of each illustration. Bunyan himself wrote one later, *A Book for Boys and Girls* (1686).

18. *the picture of a very grave person*: This is an epitome of the Puritan pastor or Evangelist, with a possible reference to Bunyan's own first pastor, John Gifford. '*The law of truth was written upon its lips*' is an unacknowledged reference to Malachi 2: 6. Sharrock points out the similarities with pictures in Geoffrey Whitney, *A Choice of Emblems* (1586), vol. 2, p. 225, and Francis Quarles, *Emblemes* (1635), frontispiece and vol. 4, p. 190.

19. *Then he took him by the hand ... fit for the King of Glory to inhabit*: The dusty parlour reinforces the contrast between law and Gospel. 'Dust' is a common biblical word for the flesh, or life without the Spirit, or death (Genesis 2: 7, 3: 19); 'water' often signifies baptism, or the Spirit (John 7: 37–8).

20. *a man in an iron Cage*: A picture of the despair of the apostate – a 'professor' in Bunyan, and Puritan thought more generally, is one who professes faith but does not always live up to it. Two cases particularly affected Bunyan. One was Francis Spira, an

Italian Protestant who went over to Catholicism under pressure, and was unable to find his way back to faith despite his struggles. He is referred to in *GA*, p. 45, and *The Barren Fig-Tree, or the Doom and Downfall of the Fruitless Professor* (1673): 'Now to have the heart so hardened . . . this is a bar put in by the Lord God . . . This was the burden of *Spira's* complaint, *I cannot do it: O now I cannot do it*' (*MW* 5.58). The other was John Child, a member of Bunyan's congregation, who left it in 1659, conformed to the Church of England, and committed suicide in remorse in 1684. 'I laid the reins on the neck of my lusts' (below) is a quasi-proverbial phrase, like 'I gave full rein'; the horse as a symbol of lust that needs reining in is common in this time: it appears in Spenser's *Faerie Queene*, for example.

21. *and that wall was called Salvation*: Bunyan has adapted the Isaiah image from salvation being a city wall to it being a wall either side of the way; at this stage, then, there is no way that Christian can stray from the path.

22. *a Cross . . . a sepulchre*: The cross and the sepulchre are both empty, so it is after Easter, and therefore not a crucifix that Christian sees. He experiences release from his burden of sin by Christ's sacrifice, the standard Reformed (and Pauline) doctrine: Jesus 'should die to give the justice of his Father *satisfaction,* and so to take away the curse that was due to us wretched *sinners*' (*The Doctrine of the Law and Grace Unfolded*; *MW* 2. 96).

23. *three shining ones*: Angels. They give Christian three gifts: forgiveness, a garment of righteousness for his rags, and a roll, a document which is a guarantee that he will be accepted at the gate to the Celestial City.

24. *Every fat must stand upon his own bottom*: A proverbial expression, here meaning 'mind your own business'. A 'fat' means a fool, a meaning now obsolete.

25. *Formalist . . . Hypocrisy*: A formalist is someone who only has the appearance of religion; he is thus paired with Hypocrisy. He is not necessarily a ritualist.

26. *two lions*: The lions represent civil and ecclesiastical persecution. In the Preface to *Grace Abounding*, written in prison, Bunyan says, '*I stick between the Teeth of the Lions in the Wilderness.*' The fact that the lions are chained suggests a period after Bunyan's release, when the restrictions on Nonconformists were partly lifted.

27. *what house is this*: The House Beautiful is often associated with Houghton Manor House, built by Mary Sidney around 1615; in

Bunyan's time it was owned by the Earl of Aylesbury, a considerable collector (see Charles Harper, *The Bunyan Country* (London: Cecil Palmer, 1928), pp. 87 ff., and John Pestell, *Travel with John Bunyan* (Epsom: Day One Publications, 2002), p. 85). There is no evidence of Bunyan actually going inside the house. However, allegorically, it represents the support given by the congregation of believers.

28. *Then said Charity ... four small children*: This exchange with Charity was added in the second edition. Bunyan had four children by his first wife.

29. *conversation*: Behaviour as opposed to talk (*OED* 6, now obsolete).

30. *precise*: A common accusation against Puritans. 'The *Precisian* is he, whose pureness is, not to swear before a Magistrate' (Giles Widdowes, *The Schysmatical Puritan* (Oxford, 1630); Widdowes was a supporter of Archbishop Laud). See Lawrence A. Sasek, *Images of English Puritanism* (Baton Rouge: Louisiana State University Press, 1989), pp. 284–96.

31. *all manner of furniture ... wear out*: The Christian's armour, as described by Paul in Ephesians 6: 13–18, is alluded to at various points in the narrative, and contributes to the iconography of Christian in some of the illustrations. In the encounter with Apollyon below, Christian realizes that there is no armour at the back.

32. *They also showed him ... up to the prey*: Christian is here shown the biblical equivalent of the cabinet of curiosities, a common feature of rich men's houses in the period, not just the Earl of Aylesbury's. See P. Fumerton, *Cultural Aesthetics* (Chicago: University of Chicago Press, 1991). For Moses' rod, see Exodus 4: 2–5; for Jael's killing Sisera, see Judges 4: 21; for Gideon's use of trumpets and pitchers, see Judges 7: 19–22; for Shamgar's ox goad, see Judges 3: 31; for David and Goliath, see 1 Samuel 17: 38–51; and for the man of sin, see 2 Thessalonians 2: 3–8.

33. *Immanuel's Land*: Emmanuel, which means 'God is with us', is used of Jesus in Matthew 1: 23. His land is described as common land; in the seventeenth century much common land was being enclosed by local landowners for their own use, so this passage may have a political edge to it.

34. *a loaf of bread, a bottle of wine and a cluster of raisins*: The provisions allude to the 'two hundred loaves of bread, and an hundred bunches of raisins, and an hundred of summer fruits, and a bottle of wine' brought to David by Ziba in 2 Samuel 16: 1; 'the wine, that such as be faint in the wilderness may drink' (v. 2).

35. *Apollyon*: The name comes from the Greek for destroyer, the 'angel of the bottomless pit' in Revelation 9: 11. His bear-feet and lion's mouth come from the beast of Revelation 13: 2, and his scales from Leviathan in Job 41: 15, 'His scales are his pride.' Leviathan is seen by Bunyan and others as a type of the devil: 'The Wiles and Temptations of the Devil, who is that great and dogged Leviathan' (*The Saints Knowledge of Christ's Love*, 1692; MW 13.345).

36. *non-age*: Nonage, immaturity, below the legal age of consent.

37. *Thou didst faint . . . all thou sayest and doest*: Apollyon's arguments are very similar to Bunyan's own concerns about his sinfulness in *Grace Abounding*, and thus form the clearest examples of Bunyan's use of allegory to express his own psychomachia (spiritual struggle).

38. *as God would have it . . . through him that loved us*: 'As God would have it' carries the inescapable echo of 'as luck would have it'. Bunyan's Christian universe does not have luck. Because the sword of the spirit is the Word of God, Christian's quoting from Scripture is a wielding of the sword.

39. *thorough*: The obvious modern equivalent would be 'through', but there seems to be an element of 'thorough' in Apollyon's absence, so I have preferred the original form.

40. *another, call'd the Valley of the shadow of Death . . . a very solitary place*: Bunyan's picture of the Valley of the Shadow of Death is an extension of Psalm 23: 4, quoted by Christian at p. 69 (see Hannibal Hamlin, *Psalm Culture and Early Modern English Literature* (Cambridge: Cambridge University Press, 2004), pp. 162–8). As with the encounter with Apollyon, Christian is struggling with the same temptations as Bunyan did; 'then darkness seized upon me, whole floods of Blasphemies' (*GA*, p. 29).

41. *Quag*: Like the modern 'quagmire', this is a marshy place which doesn't take one's weight. David's adultery with Bathsheba (2 Samuel 11–12, Psalm 51) led him deeper into sin when he tried to get her husband killed. If the Slough of Despond is psychological, the quag is moral, and grace rather than effort is needed to escape.

42. *Pope*: Bunyan's reference to Giant Pope is heavily influenced by his knowledge of Foxe's *Acts and Monuments*, which he read in prison, and which details the burning of Protestants by Catholics in England and Europe. Although the Reformation had dealt a blow to papal power in England, the Popish Plot and the Exclusion

Crisis were, soon after the publication, to revive the fear of Catholicism in England.

43. *the Avenger of Blood … so the last was first*: The 'Avenger of Blood' refers to Deuteronomy 19: 6, 'Lest the avenger of the blood pursue the slayer, while his heart is hot, and overtake him'; but, in context, the slayer is innocent, because he caused death accidentally. 'Many that are first shall be last; and the last shall be first', a saying of Jesus about the kingdom of God, appears in all three Synoptic Gospels (Matthew 19: 30, Mark 10: 31, Luke 13: 30).

44. *Joseph … it had like to have cost him his Life*: Wanton is here identified with Potiphar's wife in the story of Joseph in Egypt (Genesis 39), and serves as the book's main example of sexual temptation.

45. *Adam the First*: In Paul's theology, the sin of Adam, the first man, has to be cancelled by Christ, the 'second Adam'; see Romans 5: 14–15, 1 Corinthians 15: 21–2. In Bunyan's typological view, 'as Adam is called the Image of God; so also is Christ himself called and reckoned as the answering Antitype of such an Image' (*The Ten First Chapters of Genesis*, 1692; *MW* 13.116). He lives in the Town of Deceit because Adam and Eve were deceived by the serpent.

46. *Put off the old Man with his Deeds*: A reference to Colossians 3: 9–10, 'Lie not one to another, seeing that ye have put off the old man with his deeds; and have put on the new man.' In the rest of Faithful's narrative, the old man is variously linked with the flesh and the Law of Moses.

47. *before Honour is Humility, and a haughty Spirit before a fall*: A combination of two half-verses from Proverbs 15: 33 and 16: 18.

48. *to be Fools … want of understanding in all natural Science*: 1 Corinthians 4: 10 talks of believers being 'fools for Christ's sake' as part of a wider contrast between 'the wisdom of this world' and that of the Spirit and the cross. The reference to 'natural Science' is likely to refer to the most fashionable sort of worldly wisdom available at the time. The Royal Society had been founded in 1660 and was mostly composed of bishops, aristocrats and gentlemen. However, the phrase 'natural science' goes back to the fifteenth century.

49. *valiant for Truth upon the earth*: A phrase from Jeremiah 9: 3, where it is used with a negative; and thus leads into the Talkative episode. It gives Bunyan the name of the character Valiant-for-Truth in the second part.

50. *a hundred Scriptures*: Of the 'hundred', the most obvious is

Ephesians 2: 8, treated in Bunyan's *Saved by Grace* (1676; *MW* 8). Ironically, there he discusses Paul's point that to be saved by grace is part of 'God's design to cut off boasting' (p. 211); but in Talkative's mouth the talk of grace sounds remarkably like boasting.

51. *Prating-Row*: 'Prating' is chattering, empty talk. In a paragraph devoted to 'you whose religion lieth only in your tongues', Bunyan says 'A prating tongue will not unlock the gates of heaven' (*The Strait Gate*; *MW* 5.124). The whole section is relevant to the Talkative episode.

52. *the brute in his kind*: The argument that animals give glory to God by doing things according to their nature; an argument that the satirical poet Rochester uses against the argument that men are distinguished by their rationality in 'A Satyr against Mankind' (written 1674–5; see *The Complete Works*, ed. Frank H. Ellis (London: Penguin Books, 1994), pp. 72–7), itself criticized by a court sermon of Edward Stillingfleet in 1675.

53. *A Saint abroad, and a Devil at home*: A proverbial expression.

54. *he brings up his Sons ... before others*: These ideas on the way servants and children are (and should be) treated are dealt with in more detail in Bunyan's *Christian Behaviour* (1663; *MW* 3.28–32).

55. *This brings me to mind ... therefore is unclean*: Faithful's allegorical reading of the Old Testament to extract Christian truth ('Gospel sense') is a constant habit of Christians, at least since Augustine. Bunyan's extended exercise in this vein, *Solomon's Temple Spiritualized*, begins by defending this practice of reading for 'Figures, Patterns and Shadows of things in the Heavens' because they 'are already committed to God by sacred story', and therefore 'it is duty to us to leave off to lean to common understandings' (*MW* 7.8).

56. *lie at the catch*: Talkative accuses Faithful of waiting to catch him out.

57. *experimental*: Based on experience – not with the modern sense of trying it out to see if it works.

58. *heart-holiness ... conversation-holiness*: Sharrock points out the frequency of such compounds in Bunyan and other Puritan writers.

59. *Conversation*: Behaviour.

60. *the Apostle*: St Paul, in 1 Timothy 6: 5, 'Perverse disputings of men of corrupt minds ... from such withdraw thyself', and possibly in 2 Timothy 3: 5, 'Having a form of godliness, but denying the

power thereof: from such turn away.' There is something of the
Paul–Timothy relationship in Christian and Faithful.

61. *peace be to your helpers*: A reference to 1 Chronicles 12: 18, where
Amasai greets David, 'peace, peace be unto thee, and peace be to
thine helpers; for thy God helpeth thee.'

62. *I say, right glad am I ... on your side*: Evangelist pulls together
a number of biblical texts in this paragraph, apart from those
mentioned in the margin: Owens notes Hebrews 12: 4 and 11: 1,
Jeremiah 17: 9, Isaiah 50: 7 and Matthew 28: 18.

63. *My Sons ... as unto a faithful Creator*: Again Evangelist's discourse is full of biblical phrases: Acts 14: 22 and 20: 23, Revelation
6: 9 and 2: 10. It is very similar to Bunyan's preaching habits, as
recorded in his sermon-treatises.

64. *the name of that Town is Vanity ... All that cometh is Vanity*:
Vanity Fair is based on the large fairs that Bunyan may have seen,
either in Stourbridge in Cambridgeshire or London's Bartholomew
Fair. 'Vanity' is from Ecclesiastes (from the Old Testament Wisdom literature, so 'the wise'), meaning emptiness as well as self-
regard. Bunyan's emphasis on its corrosive commercialism (souls
for sale) is his own, as is the link with the temptation of Christ in
the wilderness.

65. *Bedlams*: Madmen (from the Bethlehem Hospital in London,
transferred to Moorfields in 1676, and a paying spectacle).

66. *the Language of Canaan*: Literally, the language of the Promised
Land. Puritans were often criticized, especially in the Restoration,
for their use of metaphoric language to describe spiritual experience (see ch. 8 of N. H. Keeble, *The Literary Culture of Nonconformity in Later Seventeenth-Century England* (Leicester:
Leicester University Press, 1987)). The phrase comes from Isaiah
19: 18, also the source of the 'city of destruction'.

67. *But the men being patient ... several of the men in the Fair*: The
effect of the meek behaviour of martyrs is often commented on
by Foxe. Sharrock notes that in 1670 two Bedford bailiffs were
imprisoned for refusing to distrain the goods of Nonconformists.

68. *Lord Hate-good*: This character is based on a number of bullying
judges of the period, particularly Sir John Kelynge, before whom
Bunyan appeared (see 'A Relation of My Imprisonment' in *GA*,
which also reproduces the terms of Bunyan's own indictment),
and Judge Jeffreys.

69. *their Prince*: 'The prince of this world' is Jesus' title for the Devil
in John's Gospel (e.g. 14: 30). Bunyan, according to his own

account, was indicted because he 'devilishly and perniciously abstained from coming to church . . . to the great disturbance and distraction of the good subjects of this kingdom, contrary to the laws of our sovereign lord the king' (*GA*, p. 106).

70. *Pickthank*: A telltale; literally, one who curries favour (picks a thank).

71. *pestilent fellow*: The phrase used of St Paul in his trial in Acts 24: 5. The New Testament trials are as important a source for this section as Foxe and Bunyan's recollections of his own trial.

72. *Runagate*: Old spelling of 'renegade'; Thomas S. Freeman points out that the phrase comes from Foxe's account of the trial of the Scots reformer George Wishart ('A Library in Three Volumes: Foxe's "Book of Martyrs" in the Writings of John Bunyan', *Bunyan Studies*, 5 (1994), pp. 48–57).

73. *Mr. Blindman . . . Mr. Implacable*: The grim humour of the names of the jurymen may owe something to the false jury put forward by Sir Symon Synod in Richard Overton's *The Araignment of Mr Persecution* (1645).

74. *They therefore brought him out . . . at the Stake*: The account of Faithful's torture and death is indebted to many of Foxe's accounts; and the woodcut illustration which accompanies it is also in the style of the editions Bunyan would have known. Echoes of Christ's Passion are also to be noted ('buffeted': Matthew 26: 27; 'scourged': Matthew 27: 26).

75. *a Chariot and a couple of Horses*: The chariot and horses refer to 2 Kings 2: 11, where the prophet Elijah is taken directly up into heaven.

76. *By-ends*: Literally, secondary considerations; but the combination of his home town, his upward social mobility and his friends suggests that he is representative of those who compromised with the Restoration church, 'when Religion goes in his Silver Slippers' (p. 103). By-ends is unusually uncomfortable with his 'Nickname', as he puts it. (For a discussion of the By-ends episode, see Nick Davis, 'The Problem of Misfortune in *The Pilgrim's Progress*', in Vincent Newey (ed.), *The Pilgrim's Progress: Critical and Historical Views* (Liverpool: Liverpool University Press, 1980)). The water-man joke is proverbial.

77. *Congee*: A bow (from the French, and thus, even at this stage, associated with the royal court).

78. *Gripe-man*: A slang word for a miser or usurer (*OED* 6).

79. *cozenage*: Cheating.

80. *righteous overmuch*: Ironically, a phrase from Ecclesiastes 7: 16.

81. *hazarding all for God at a Clap*: A reference to Acts 15: 26, 'Men that have hazarded their lives for the name of our Lord Jesus Christ'; 'at a Clap' means at once, without waiting for an opportune moment.

82. *wise as Serpents ... make hay while the Sun shines*: A bizarre mixture of the biblical (Christ's words to his disciples, Matthew 10: 16) and a folk proverb.

83. *Job says ... lay up gold as dust*: These are actually the words of Eliphaz, one of Job's comforters, in Job 22: 24. This may indicate that it is meant to be another example of these men twisting Scripture to their own advantage. However, in his commentary on Genesis, Bunyan suggests that Job 'is a holy collection of those proverbs and sayings of the ancients' (*MW* 12.121), which may indicate that to him it does not much matter who says what.

84. *Scripture nor Reason*: A common combination in Restoration divines like Fowler with whom Bunyan disagreed (see Rivers, *Reason, Grace and Sentiment*, ch. 3).

85. *perhaps get a rich Wife*: Bunyan was to explore this further in *Mr Badman*, where Badman pretends to religion in order to marry a rich wife.

86. *unlawful to follow Christ for Loaves*: In John 6: 26, shortly after the feeding of the five thousand, Jesus rebukes those who only followed him because of the bread.

87. *a stalking Horse*: A horse that one hides behind when hunting.

88. *Judas the Devil ... he was religious for the bag*: Judas carried the bag, i.e. the purse, for the disciples (John 12: 6).

89. *some of them ... be their own men again*: Although there are New Testament denunciations of 'filthy lucre', this incident may refer to Samuel's sons, who turned aside after lucre (1 Samuel 8: 3).

90. *I will show you a thing*: 'Demas hath forsaken me, having loved this present world,' writes St Paul in 2 Timothy 4: 10 (noted in the margin further down).

91. *Remember Lot's Wife*: Bunyan returns to Lot's wife in *The Heavenly Footman*, again in the context of an image of the Christian life as a journey; the figure of Lot, who did not even look where she was, is like Christian as he leaves home (*MW* 5.176–7).

92. *Will soon sell all*: An allusion to Matthew 13: 44, where the kingdom of heaven is compared to treasure found in a field. The finder 'for joy thereof goeth and selleth all that he hath, and buyeth that field'.

93. *Giant Despair*: He is a combination of fairy-tale giant and angry landowner (Bunyan consistently distrusts landowners). In *Grace*

Abounding, Bunyan describes a long period of despair when he feared that he had committed the unforgivable sin: 'These words were to my Soul like Fetters of Brass of my Legs' (*GA*, p. 40). Bunyan's experience in jail may also inform the description of their isolation.

94. *Diffidence*: Added in the second edition; 'wanting confidence or faith' (*OED*).

95. *to make an end of themselves; either with Knife, Halter, or Poison*: In *GA* Bunyan reports no temptation to suicide; however, in Spenser's *The Faerie Queene*, i.ix.51, the figure of Despair holds out a rusty dagger to Red-Cross and tells him to end it all.

96. *a key . . . called Promise*: They remember the key after a period of prayer. The image comes from Matthew 16: 19; there is an account of Scripture promises in *GA*, pp. 69–70, which has the image of the bosom and suggests that the promise is John 6: 37. There is also an allusion to Paul's escape from prison in Acts 12: 10. 'Bunyan's deconstruction of romance's mythical conventions here comes in the form of a magic key that is nothing less than the Word' (Michael Davies, *Graceful Reading: Theology and Narrative in the Works of John Bunyan* (Oxford: Oxford University Press, 2002), p. 283).

97. *delectable Mountains*: There is no agreement on the source of this, the last of the edifying stopping-places on the way to the Celestial City. The Chiltern Hills in Bedfordshire are hardly mountainous. However, some of the enigmatic exchanges between the shepherds and the pilgrims might indicate that they have reached the higher levels of predestinarian theology, and thus made 'progress' (see A. Richard Dutton, ' "Interesting but Tough": Reading *The Pilgrim's Progress*', *Studies in English Literature*, 18 (1978), pp. 439–56, and Davies, *Graceful Reading*, pp. 243 ff.).

98. *Hymenius and Philetus*: The error of Hymeneus and Philaetus in 2 Timothy 2: 17–18 was to say the resurrection has already happened, and so there would be no hope for the pilgrims. 'That the resurrection is past with good men already' is listed as a Quaker error in a later edition of *Grace Abounding*, and was also a belief of some Ranters; Bunyan deals with it at more length in *The Resurrection of the Dead* (1665: *MW* 3, and see J. Sears McGee's Introduction, pp. xlvi ff.).

99. *the men were blind . . . from among them*: In Mark 5: 2 there is a man 'with an unclean spirit' who lives around the tombs; Bunyan compares himself to this man, 'yielding to desparation' in *GA* (p. 53).

100. *Esau ... Ananias and Sapphira his Wife*: All biblical examples: Esau in Genesis 25, Judas in the Gospels, Alexander in 2 Timothy 4: 14–15 and Ananias and Sapphira in Acts 5.

101. *Perspective-Glass*: A seventeenth-century term for a telescope.

102. *I awoke from my dream*: As this does not correspond to any break in the narrative, it may refer to a break in composition, possibly occasioned by Bunyan's release from prison.

103. *I know my Lord's will . . . whither I am going*: There are echoes here of the Pharisee in Jesus' parable of the Pharisee and the publican (Luke 18: 10–14), expounded at length by Bunyan in *A Discourse upon the Pharisee and the Publican* (1685; MW 10), although Ignorance is also compared to the fool-figure in Proverbs.

104. *upon whose head is the shell to this very day*: Proverbial for immature, like a chick just hatched. Little-Faith is an example of the weak believer (of whom there are more in the second part) who, despite everything, has enough spiritual insight to survive as a Christian. Esau's selling of his birthright (see below) is 'typical' in that he is the type, or pattern, of those who give up eternal life for present gratification. In *Grace Abounding*, Bunyan tells how he was afraid that he had 'sold Christ' and, like Esau, would be unable to repent.

105. *stomach*: Bravery.

106. *quit myself like a man*: Compare Faithful's playing the man, and Paul's exhortation to 'quit you like men', 1 Corinthians 16: 13.

107. *throw up his heels*: Make him fall, as in wrestling.

108. *make David groan ... afraid of a sorry Girl*: David's groaning could be a reference to many of the Psalms: Owens convincingly identifies Psalm 38: 6, 8 and 9. Heman is the author of Psalm 88. For Hezekiah's reaction to the siege of Jerusalem, see 2 Chronicles 32. The story of Peter denying Christ while questioned by a girl after Christ's arrest is given in three of the Gospels; see Matthew 26: 69–75.

109. *Habergeon*: A sleeveless jacket of armour, usually of chain mail.

110. *Leviathan*: From Job 41, as are the previous quotations; associated with the whale, but also with the Devil: 'who is that great and dogged Leviathan' (*The Saints Knowledge of Christ's Love*, MW 13. 344).

111. *a man black of flesh*: This figure of the Flatterer is discussed in some detail in Sharrock, p. 335. He is later revealed as a false minister, like Satan in 2 Corinthians 11: 14, 'transformed into an angel of light'.

112. *A man that ... spreadeth a Net for his Foot*: The net is an example

of a biblical metaphor turned into a reality within Bunyan's allegory.

113. *Then Atheist fell into a very great laughter*: Atheist's laughter is characteristic of most depictions of atheism in the period; Bacon's 1625 essay 'Of Atheism' blames the 'custom of profane scoffing in holy matters, which doth by little and little deface the reverence of religion'.

114. *and cast him into prison, till he shall pay the debt*: Imprisonment for debt was very common in Bunyan's day.

115. *I saw the Lord Jesus . . . thou shalt be saved*: This contrasts with the early episode in *Grace Abounding* where Bunyan sees 'the Lord Jesus looking down upon me, as being very hotly displeased with me' (*GA*, p. 10). Much of Hopeful's subsequent account of his conversion parallels that of Bunyan, as related in *Grace Abounding*.

116. *My grace is sufficient for thee*: 2 Corinthians 12: 9; compare *GA*, p.59, where it is repeated three times.

117. *satisfaction*: Part of Bunyan's Reformed theology of the sacrifice of Christ; 'the Eternal Justice of God, could not consent ot the salvation of the Sinner, without a Satisfaction for the Sin committed' (*A Defence of the Doctrine of Justification by Faith*; *MW* 4.39).

118. *fantastical*: Imaginary.

119. *awakened*: A commonly used term for a soul touched by preaching for the first time: 'I found my spirit did lean most after awakening and converting-Work' (*GA*, p. 81).

120. *the wages*: An allusion to Romans 6: 23, 'the wages of sin is death'.

121. *not every one that cries, Lord, Lord*: The verse (in Matthew 7: 21) concludes 'shall enter into the kingdom of heaven'.

122. *Hearing, Reading, Godly conference*: Hearing sermons, reading the Bible and talking about it with other Christians (as they are doing at this moment in the text), a key part of Puritan practice.

123. *Beulah*: Hebrew for 'married', but referring to the land around Jerusalem in the vision of its future glory in Isaiah 62: 4.

124. *the voice of the Turtle*: A quotation from the Song of Songs 2: 12; in modern translations it becomes a turtledove.

125. *If you see my Beloved, tell him that I am sick of love*: From Song of Songs 5: 8, allegorically interpreted as the love of Christ and his Church. The language here is combined with the vision of the New Jerusalem in Revelation 21.

126. *Enoch and Elijah*: They were both directly taken up into heaven (Genesis 5: 24, 2 Kings 2: 11).

127. *I sink in deep waters . . . Selah*: From Psalm 88: 7, combined with phrases from Psalms 69: 2 and 42: 7; Bunyan rejected the conventional view that a peaceful death was a sign of eternal salvation.

128. *There is no band in their death . . . like other men*: Psalm 73: 4–5, noted in the margins of some early editions.

129. *Ministering Spirits . . . heirs of Salvation*: From Hebrews 1: 14.

130. *the Spirits of Just men made perfect*: The verses from Hebrews gave Bunyan 'great refreshment' (*GA*, pp. 74–5).

131. *Enter ye into the joy of our Lord*: An echo of the reward for the faithful servants in the parable of the talents, Matthew 25: 21–3.

132. *I have ate and drank . . . he has taught in our Streets*: From Luke 13: 26, which goes on 'But he [the master of the house] shall say, I tell you, I know you not whence ye are; depart from me, all ye workers of iniquity.'

133. *bind him hand and foot*: From Matthew 22: 13; as in the previous note, the conclusion of the verse gives the action, 'take him away, and cast him into outer darkness'.

THE SECOND PART: THE AUTHOR'S WAY OF SENDING FORTH HIS SECOND PART OF THE PILGRIM

1. *next*: Sharrock emends to 'rest', but as 'next' makes sense I have retained it.

2. *Mansions*: A reference to the House Beautiful and the House of the Interpreter, but with an allusion to John 14: 2, 'In my Father's house are many mansions.'

3. *some there be . . . to seem the very same*: Bunyan's principal target here seems to be *The Second Part of the Pilgrim's Progress* by T.S., the General Baptist Thomas Sherman (1682), though he was not pretending to be Bunyan, nor were others like Benjamin Keach, who wrote *Travels of True Godliness* (1683). Ponder had problems with piracy of Bunyan's own text. (For Sherman, see Davies, *Graceful Reading*, pp. 292 ff., and Susan Cook, 'Pilgrim's Progresses: Derivative Texts and the Seventeenth-Century Reader', in David Gay *et al.* (eds.), *Awakening Words: John Bunyan and the Language of Community* (Newark: Delaware University Press, 2000), pp. 186–201.)

4. *My Pilgrim's book has travel'd . . . thousands daily Sing and talk*:

Apart from the bestselling success of the first part in England, there was an American edition in 1681, a Dutch translation in 1682, a French translation in 1685 and a Welsh edition in 1687. There are no Gaelic editions that have survived from this period, though there were early printings of the English version in Scotland. 'Deck'd with gems' probably refers to the binding of the book.

5.   *my Lark's leg is better than a Kite*: Proverbial ('Kite' being the bird of prey). Larks were a delicacy in early modern England; nobody eats kites.

6.   *But some there be . . . to find his mark*: The objections in this section are those that Thomas Sherman makes (see note 3 above).

7.   *kiss and weep*: An allusion to Genesis 29: 10–11, where Jacob sees Rachel for the first time, 'And Jacob kissed Rachel, and lifted up his voice, and wept.'

8.   *Render them not reviling for revile*: See 1 Peter 2: 23, 'When he [Jesus] was reviled, [he] reviled not again.'

9.   *old doting sinners . . . Hosanna to whom the old ones did deride*: 'Doting: to be weak-minded from old age' (*OED* I.2). 'Deride': an allusion to Matthew 21: 15, 'when the chief priests and scribes saw the wonderful things that he [Jesus] did, and the children crying in the temple, and saying, Hosanna to the Son of David; they were sore displeased'.

THE SECOND PART

1.   *Multiplicity of Business*: As well as Bunyan's pastoral and preaching responsibilities, he published seven books after the first part, including *Mr Badman* and *The Holy War*.

2.   *a Wood*: Contrasting to the 'Den', the 'Gaol', of the first part.

3.   *Mr. Sagacity*: This character reminds us of Wiseman, one of the two speakers in the dialogue form of *Mr Badman*, but he does not survive as a device for long in this narrative.

4.   *[But, pray . . . about him?]*: This sentence has weak textual authority, but it does make sense of Sagacity's 'Talk!' as a response, indicating that the original compositor may have skipped over a line in the manuscript.

5.   *rent the Caul of her Heart in sunder*: A phrase from Hosea 13: 8, 'I [God] will rend the caul of their heart.' Hosea's prophecy runs a continuous parallel between Israel's disloyalty to God and a woman's disloyalty to her husband. A caul is a membrane covering a foetus.

6. *woe, worth the day*: Ezekiel 30: 2. 'Woe worth . . .' is a Middle English phrase meaning 'may evil happen' or 'cursed be'.

7. *Then shouted a company . . . and his Companions*: See Revelation 14: 2–3, 'I heard the voice of harpers harping with their harps: And they sung as it were a new song before the throne . . . and no man could learn that song but the hundred and forty and four thousand, which were redeemed from the earth.'

8. *by root-of-heart*: By memory. The phrase appears in Chapman's play *Bussy D'Ambois* (1607).

9. *her Bowels yearned*: A biblical phrase (e.g. 1 Kings 3: 26) meaning 'she felt strongly'. See also note 3 to the first part (p. 317).

10. *did gather up his Tears, and put them into his Bottle*: See Psalm 56: 8, 'put thou my tears into thy bottle'; true prayers may not be answered immediately, but they are not wasted.

11. *many there be . . . mar instead of mending*: The attack on false ministers ('that pretend to be the King's Labourers') seems to be against those who are too strict and exclusive, rather than those, like Worldly Wiseman in the first part, who offer a merely legal way out of despondency.

12. *Suffer the little Children to come unto me*: The words of Jesus when the disciples tried to stop people bringing their children to him, Mark 10: 14.

13. *Damsel, I bid thee arise*: An allusion to Jesus' words to Jairus' daughter in Mark 5: 41.

14. *I pray for all them that believe on me*: An echo of the words of Jesus in John 17: 20; another instance in which the Keeper of the Gate is identified with Jesus.

15. *a Bundle of Myrrh*: A reference to the Song of Songs 1: 13, 'a bundle of myrrh is my wellbeloved to me'; the beloved is identified with Christ in the usual Christian allegorical reading of this book of the Bible.

16. *Summer-Parlour*: A room for use in the summer.

17. *their Darling from the power of the Dog*: From Psalm 22: 20. The Devil is the dog's owner. Although Mercy has been 'purchased' by Christ's blood, she can still feel threatened by the dog.

18. *Bless'd be the day . . . what our end will be*: Christiana's song is in Common Metre, like most of the Psalms in Thomas Sternhold's *Whole Book of Psalms* (1562) and similar Psalm paraphrases (e.g. Psalm 18, 'But blessed be the living Lord/Most worthy of all praise'). Bunyan's congregation were divided about singing in worship, however, and did not do so until 1691.

19. *Pluck*: The first edition has 'Plash', meaning to bend down (often

used of hedge-laying); the second edition reading has a more obvious allusion to Genesis 3.

20. *two Bows-shot*: The distance an arrow might travel from a bow, so about 200 metres.

21. *spurned at*: struck against.

22. *naughty*: A much stronger word in this period; more like 'evil' than a word that might be used of a child.

23. *the biggest of them all*: Evangelist.

24. *by this Spider . . . God has made nothing in vain*: The spider venom as sin image is developed in a long dialogue poem in *A Book for Boys and Girls* (*MW* 6.214 ff.), e.g. '*Spider*: My venom's good for something, 'cause God made it/Thy sin hath spoiled thy nature, doth degrade it.'

25. *he led them into his Garden . . . one with another*: Owens points out how often Bunyan compares the people of God in the Church to a garden.

26. *of great price*: A reference to the exhortation to women in 1 Peter 3 not to be adorned with gold but with 'a meek and quiet spirit, which is in the sight of God of great price' (3: 4). In view of the proverbial tone of the Interpreter's speech, there may also be a hint of Proverbs 31: 10, the price of a virtuous women is 'far above rubies'.

27. *Cockle*: A weed that grows in cornfields. The proverb is quoted by Berowne in *Love's Labours Lost*, 4.3.357.

28. *Tinder for the Devil's Tinder-Box*: Bunyan had come to a similar conclusion in his *The Barren Fig-Tree*, an extended treatment of Matthew 3: 10. See *MW* 5.62–4.

29. *The Lord is only my Support . . . in need*: This is the first verse of Psalm 23, as paraphrased by William Whittingham, one of the translators of the Geneva Bible; Bunyan might have read it in the 1562 Scottish Metrical Psalter, or heard it sung somewhere, though his own congregation did not sing until after his death.

30. *Pond*: Possibly a version of the Slough of Despond; there is an example of a woman (E.C.) who attempted to drown herself in a pond before her conversion in *Spiritual Experiences of Sundry Believers*, gathered by Henry Walker (1652).

31. *all-to-be-fooled me*: Called me a fool.

32. *Thy beginning . . . greatly increase*: See Job 8: 7.

33. *Then they went in and washed . . . when they went out to the washing*: Sanctification (becoming more holy) is pictured in the first part as the sprinkling of water to help with sweeping up the dust; here the bath inevitably recalls baptism, though Bunyan

himself did not regard baptism as essential (see Richard L. Greaves, *John Bunyan* (Courtenay Studies in Reformation Theology, 2; Abingdon: Sutton Courtenay, 1969), pp. 135–44). In his 1688 work *The Water of Life*, Bunyan sees water as an image of the Spirit which 'maintains these things once planted in the Soul, by its continual waterings of them *in* the Soul' (*MW* 7.205), a process of sanctification.

34. *fair as the Moon*: Song of Songs 6: 10.

35. *he called for the Seal . . . an Ornament to their Faces*: As well as the Exodus reference, there is the sense of Ephesians 1: 13, 'ye were sealed with that holy Spirit of promise'.

36. *fine Linen, white and clean*: In Revelation 19: 8, the Church, the bride of Christ, is 'arrayed in fine linen, clean and white: for the fine linen is the righteousness of saints'.

37. *Sword, and Helmet and Shield*: Although Great-heart takes on some of the role of Evangelist as guide, he also wears the armour of God that Christian has in the First Part.

38. *Mediatory*: Jesus is the 'one mediator between God and men' (1 Timothy 2: 5).

39. *two Coats*: Bunyan is taking Christ's command in Luke 3: 11, 'He that hath two coats, let him impart to him that hath none', as an allegory of Christ's own dual nature.

40. *passeth by you*: A reference to the Passover, Exodus 12: 23.

41. *by a special Grace*: The Calvinist doctrine that 'effectual calling' is only for the elect, although others might hear.

42. *they were hanged up in Irons*: Executed prisoners were often publicly hung in chains in Bunyan's time.

43. *why so envious tro?*: 'Tro' is here an interrogative particle.

44. *a breathing Hill*: One that makes one out of breath as one climbs it.

45. *were burned through the tongue with a hot Iron*: Boring through the tongue was a punishment for offences of speech, such as blasphemy. There are European examples in Foxe, but it seems to have been particularly targeted at Quakers in New England, and it was part of the vicious punishment given to the Quaker James Naylor in 1655, when he was accused of claiming to be Christ. It was rare in England.

46. *Grim, or Bloody-man*: Like the 'Bloodmen' that attack Mansoul in Bunyan's *The Holy War*, this character may allude to the increased political and legal pressures on Nonconformists during the 1680s (see Greaves, *Glimpses of Glory*, ch. 12, 'Nonconformity and the Tory Backlash').

47. *they . . . did Salute each other with a kiss*: In Romans 16: 16, in a

chapter which names several women and men of the early Church, Paul commands, 'Salute one another with an holy kiss.'

48. *Music in the House . . . for joy that we are here*: Although Bunyan's congregation, like many Nonconformist churches, did not sing hymns in services until some years after his death, he was keen on music. The John Bunyan Museum in Bedford has an iron fiddle, and a flute made out of a chair leg belonging to him, and there are tunes written out in *A Book for Boys and Girls* which may be Bunyan's own compositions (*MW 6*).

49. *Our Heart . . . as if one was awake*: As well as being a defence of the dream vision aspect of the book, this alludes to Song of Songs 5: 2, 'I sleep, but my heart waketh: it is the voice of my beloved . . .'

50. *Catechise*: Catechizing, instruction by learning a question-and-answer form of Christian doctrine and practice, was widespread among Puritans, and there are numbers of catechisms in print, both official (such as in the Book of Common Prayer or the Westminster Assembly's *Shorter Catechism*) or by individual teachers, such as Bunyan's own *Instruction for the Ignorant* (1675; *MW 8*).

51. *Brisk*: Largely a pejorative word in the seventeenth century, with overtones of flirtatiousness (Owens).

52. *clog*: Impediment.

53. *cried her down at the Cross*: A kind of illegal divorce, whereby a man might disown his wife's debts, or even sell her, at the market cross. According to Offor (*The Works of John Bunyan*, ed. George Offor, 3 vols. (Glasgow, Edinburgh and London: Blackie and Son, 1854), vol. 3, p. 201), it was still practised in Bedfordshire in the seventeenth century; and it supplies the opening incident of Thomas Hardy's *The Mayor of Casterbridge*.

54. *Ex Carne et Sanguine Christi*: 'Of the body and blood of Christ'; Latin, very unusually for Bunyan.

55. *and went his way*: Matthew's healing follows the stages of repentance and, effectively, conversion. 'Beelzebub's Orchard' seems to allude to the fruit eaten by Eve and Adam in Eden. Sharrock notes that 'Mathew's Pills' were a well-known patent remedy in the Restoration.

56. *Purge*: Purging was one of the principal procedures in seventeenth-century medicine.

57. *the Pelican*: This bird was (erroneously) believed to feed its young with blood from its breast, and thus became a popular emblem of Christ in literature and art.

58. *Virginals*: An early keyboard instrument.

59. *a Bottle of Wine . . . to refresh you in your way*: The refreshments

may allude to a number of biblical passages: the parched corn from 1 Samuel 17: 17, which David brought to his brothers while they were fighting the Philistines; the figs probably to Jeremiah 24: 5, and the pomegranates possibly to the Song of Songs 4: 3. As with the images of Jacob's ladder and Abraham's sacrifice, the pilgrims are passing through a biblical landscape at this stage of the journey.

60. *a Gold Angel*: A coin, worth between a third and half a sovereign (£1).

61. *Let thy garments . . . no Ointment*: An allusion to Ecclesiastes 9: 8.

62. *Through all my Life . . . from Age to Age endure*: Once again Bunyan is quoting from the Sternhold metrical version of the Psalms, 23: 6 in the first stanza, 100: 5 in the second.

63. *fat Ground*: Compare 1 Chronicles 4: 40, 'fat pasture and good'.

64. *Hearts-ease*: The wild pansy, believed to be an emollient; but also literally meaning peace of mind.

65. *Resist the Devil, and he will flee from you*: James 4: 7.

66. *a great mist and a darkness fell upon them*: In Acts 13: 10–11, Paul causes Elymas the sorcerer to be temporarily blind, and this is described as 'there fell on him a mist and a darkness'.

67. *The heart knows . . . with its Joy*: Proverbs 14: 10, slightly reworded.

68. *This is like doing business in great Waters . . . the Bottoms of the Mountains*: A reworking of Psalm 107: 23–6.

69. *the Earth with its bars . . . for ever*: Jonah 2: 6; the image of prison bars is significant.

70. *let them that walk in darkness . . . their God*: Isaiah 50: 10, slightly reworded.

71. *Snares*: Probably an echo of Psalm 141: 9.

72. *Maul*: Literally, a heavy hammer (hence the club); and associated with Satan's arguments in Bunyan's *Good News for the Vilest of Men* (1688; *MW* 11.76). The charge of sophistry has led commentators, notably Charles Firth, to associate Maul with Catholicism. See his *John Bunyan* (London: English Association, 1911).

73. *from darkness to light*: Acts 26: 18, the words of St Paul to King Agrippa.

74. *under the fifth rib*: From Abner's slaying of Asahel in 2 Samuel 2: 23. Many of the aspects of the fight, however, including Greatheart's fairness, echo chivalric romance.

75. *Cock of the right kind*: This sounds proverbial; but may be connected to *OED* sense II.8, where there are examples of ministers of religion as 'Christ's cocks', waking people up from their sins.

76. *Kiss of Charity*: See 1 Peter 5: 14.

77. *James the Just ... James the Brother of our Lord*: As Owens points out, these two are generally agreed to be the same; James the Just was stoned to death in 62, and Bunyan would have read of this in Foxe.

78. *the Root of the Matter*: Job 19: 28, in the context of suffering and persecution.

79. *wet-shod*: With wet feet.

80. *Mr. Great-heart began*: In the early editions Bunyan seems to have forgotten that Great-heart is telling the story.

81. *some must Pipe, and some must Weep*: There are allusions here to Matthew 11: 17 and possibly Ecclesiastes 3: 4, and more generally to a key issue in Puritan pastoral psychology, addressed by Bunyan in the posthumously published *Desires of the Righteous Granted* and Thomas Goodwin's *The Child of Light Walking in Darkness*.

82. *as the Proverb is ... had it stood in his Way*: There seems to be no other record of this proverb.

83. *the fear of God is the beginning of Wisdom*: Proverbs 9: 10. Bunyan wrote about this extensively in his *Treatise of the Fear of God* (1679; MW 4).

84. *To have to do with other men's Wives ... and therefore he could do so too*: In each case Selfwill does describe biblical events correctly, though he omits parts of those stories where there is repentance for such actions.

85. *died as they in the Wilderness ... the promised Land*: Several disobedient Israelites did not get to the Promised Land (Numbers 14: 22–3); Moses at least got a sight of it.

86. *Gaius*: Paul's host (Romans 16: 23, and cf. 3 John).

87. *Ignatius ... to be drowned*: Bunyan's account of the early Church martyrs is from Foxe, except for those from the New Testament. 'He that was hanged up in a Basket' was Marcus, the fourth-century bishop of Arethusa, tortured and left to die during the reign of Julian the Apostate.

88. *a Posterity in the Earth*: Said by Joseph in Genesis 43: 7.

89. *highly favoured*: The angel's words to Mary in Luke 1: 28.

90. *Ordinances*: Technically, in Reformed theology, ceremonies such as baptism and communion; Bunyan calls them 'holy duties' in *The Doctrine of the Law and Grace Unfolded* (MW 2.73 ff.) and expands the term to include prayer and almsgiving.

91. *a Heave-shoulder and a wave-Breast*: Forms of animal sacrifice in Leviticus 7: 20. The identification with the later figure of David is Bunyan's.

92. *sick of Love*: A direct quotation from the Song of Songs 2: 5. The apple is, by tradition, the forbidden fruit of Genesis, though it is not identified as such in the Bible.

93. *Hard Texts*: Of the Bible, of course; difficult to understand. The metaphor recalls the discussion of Bunyan's method in the verse Apology for the first part.

94. *rub up*: Revive yourself (usually transitive).

95. *I conceited*: I thought.

96. *Robbed*: Feeble-Mind is referring to the Calvinist doctrine of the perseverance of the saints, that no one who is chosen by God will be damned; a doctrine reiterated by Bunyan in several works throughout his career. Lapses are still possible, though, an issue that Bunyan had dealt with at some length in *The Holy War*, published two years earlier.

97. *Complexion*: Habit of mind, nature.

98. *Hands Cross'd*: A reference to Genesis 48: 14, where Israel unexpectedly blesses Joseph's younger son in preference to the older.

99. *faces like Flint*: An image from Isaiah 50: 7.

100. *Mnason*: From Acts 21: 16, 'an old disciple' who gave lodging to Paul.

101. *a good Stitch*: A good distance on foot; this is the first example cited by *OED*.

102. *cumbered*: Constricted, burdened – again, this is the first source in *OED* for this shade of meaning.

103. *A good Man must suffer Trouble*: Perhaps an echo of Job 5: 7, but a persistent theme of Bunyan's writing. He had recently published *Seasonable Counsel, or, Advice to Sufferers* (1684; *MW 10*).

104. *The Monster . . . had seven Heads and ten Horns*: The Monster is clearly based on the beast ridden by a scarlet woman in Revelation 17. The beast was often associated with Catholicism by Protestants; the Catholic King James II was to come to the throne the year after this part was published. The beast's attacks on the children may mean Catholic proselytizing, which Bunyan may have been more aware of in his visits to London, although he shared Bedford jail with a number of recusants in the 1660s.

105. *Nature . . . has an attracting Virtue upon the foolish Eye*: Bunyan is referring to human nature before conversion and regeneration, which is not able to respond to spiritual danger if it has 'Virtue' (i.e. strength) enough to attract it.

106. *Leaves . . . against Surfeits*: A remedy against indigestion. The emphasis here balances Bunyan's earlier adaptation of another

metaphor from Psalm 23, the Valley of the Shadow of Death (and see ch. 5 of Hamlin, *Psalm Culture*).

107. *This man*: One of the incognitos of Christ in the book, like the King in the next paragraph.

108. *Lesson*: A musical composition. Although Bunyan laments in *Grace Abounding* that it took him a year to give up dancing during his conversion, he retained an interest in music; the John Bunyan Museum has his flute and violin, and *A Book for Boys and Girls* includes tunes which appear to be original compositions.

109. *the Wain*: The seven bright stars in the Great Bear, used for navigation.

110. *tumbled the Hills about with Words*: A free paraphrase of the verses from Mark cited in the margin; the sense is that mountains can be moved by the prayer of faith.

111. *And the Cake . . . in her Barrel*: The story of the prophet Elijah's residence with the widow, 1 Kings 17: 10–16.

112. *washing an Ethiopian*: A common saying in the period. See e.g. Whitney, *A Choice of Emblems*, p. 57, though the verse draws a different lesson; and Richard Crashaw, 'On the Baptized Ethiopian'. For a history of the saying, see Jean Michael Massing, 'From Greek Proverb to Soap Advert: Washing the Ethiopian', *Journal of the Warburg & Courtauld Institutes*, 58 (1995), pp. 180–201.

113. *the Glass was one of a thousand*: Bunyan compares a mirror to the word of God in 'Upon a Looking Glass', in *A Book for Boys and Girls*.

114. *a Bracelet . . . Jewels on their Fore-heads*: The adornments come from Ezekiel 16: 11–12.

115. *resisted unto Blood*: A phrase from Hebrews 12: 4.

116. *green-headed*: Young, inexperienced, foolish.

117. *wag along*: Move along (colloquial).

118. *Slabbiness*: Muddiness.

119. *Book or Map*: Probably the Bible, but it might also refer to Bunyan's own *A Mapp Shewing the Order and Causes of Salvation & Damnation* (possibly 1664; MW 12).

120. *as poor as an Owlet*: This is a compressed version of a saying, 'No more money than an owl loves light', quoted in George Offor's 1854 edition of the text. Owls are generally associated with ruins or deserts in the Bible (e.g. Psalm 102: 6, Isaiah 34: 11, 13).

121. *Madam Bubble*: An emblem of the vanity or emptiness of the world; possibly from Quarles, *Emblemes* (Sharrock).

122. *Limner*: Painter of portraits.

123. *Absalom . . . Jeroboam . . . Judas . . . Demas*: Biblical characters, all led astray by ambition or money: see 2 Samuel 15, 1 Kings 12: 21 ff., John 18: 2, Acts 1: 16 ff. and 2 Timothy 4: 10, respectively.

124. *when you have done all, stand*: From Ephesians 6: 13.

125. *Camphire . . . all chief Spices*: From the Song of Songs 4: 13–14; the beloved, whose orchard is described here, is often taken as an allegorical representation of Jesus. In the imagery of the ensuing paragraphs Bunyan develops a parallel between Christiana and the figure of the woman longing for her beloved in the Song of Songs, usually interpreted by Christian commentators as the Church.

126. *Behold . . . no Guile*: The words that Jesus uses of Nathaniel in John 1: 47.

127. *a Token*: This and the following tokens all come from Ecclesiastes 12, where together they can be read as images of the decay and death of the body.

128. *Welcome Life*: The last words of the martyr Laurence Sanders in the illustration in Foxe, *Acts and Monuments*, 2.140; as Owens notes, the description of Sanders as apparently 'fearful and feeble spirited' indicates that he might be the source for the character of Ready-to-halt.

129. *Ghosts*: Spirits.

130. *Death . . . Victory*: From 1 Corinthians 15: 55.

131. *his strong men*: The final quotation from Ecclesiastes 12; the 1599 Geneva Bible identifies them as the legs.

132. *to go that way again*: There was a third part, published in 1692, but it is clearly not by Bunyan.

Index

THE STORY OF PENGUIN CLASSICS

Before 1946 ... 'Classics' are mainly the domain of academics and students; readable editions for everyone else are almost unheard of. This all changes when a little-known classicist, E. V. Rieu, presents Penguin founder Allen Lane with the translation of Homer's *Odyssey* that he has been working on in his spare time.

1946 Penguin Classics debuts with *The Odyssey*, which promptly sells three million copies. Suddenly, classics are no longer for the privileged few.

1950s Rieu, now series editor, turns to professional writers for the best modern, readable translations, including Dorothy L. Sayers's *Inferno* and Robert Graves's unexpurgated *Twelve Caesars*.

1960s The Classics are given the distinctive black covers that have remained a constant throughout the life of the series. Rieu retires in 1964, hailing the Penguin Classics list as 'the greatest educative force of the twentieth century.'

1970s A new generation of translators swells the Penguin Classics ranks, introducing readers of English to classics of world literature from more than twenty languages. The list grows to encompass more history, philosophy, science, religion and politics.

1980s The Penguin American Library launches with titles such as *Uncle Tom's Cabin*, and joins forces with Penguin Classics to provide the most comprehensive library of world literature available from any paperback publisher.

1990s The launch of Penguin Audiobooks brings the classics to a listening audience for the first time, and in 1999 the worldwide launch of the Penguin Classics website extends their reach to the global online community.

The 21st Century Penguin Classics are completely redesigned for the first time in nearly twenty years. This world-famous series now consists of more than 1300 titles, making the widest range of the best books ever written available to millions – and constantly redefining what makes a 'classic'.

The Odyssey continues ...

The best books ever written

PENGUIN CLASSICS

SINCE 1946

Find out more at www.penguinclassics.com